ONCE IN A NEW MOON, PART 2

THIRTEEN STONES

An historical novel by
Nancy Warren

 FriesenPress

Suite 300 - 990 Fort St
Victoria, BC, V8V 3K2
Canada

www.friesenpress.com

ISBN
978-1-5255-4021-9 (Hardcover)
978-1-5255-4022-6 (Paperback)
978-1-5255-4023-3 (eBook)

1. *FICTION, HISTORICAL*

Distributed to the trade by The Ingram Book Company

Centrewood Cycle, 1.2

ONCE IN A NEW MOON, PART 2

THIRTEEN STONES

An historical novel by Nancy Warren

October 13 - October 31; November 2, 15, 1957
Epilogue, 1959

This is a fictional plot based on events occurring in Canada in 1957.

Major themes include the rise and demise of the Avro Arrow, the outstanding land claim of the Mississauga Indians, the covert activities of the RCMP's Secret Service in 1957, the ripple effect of the wartime internment of Japanese Canadians, and the impact of the Hungarian Revolution on the postwar Canadian-Hungarian diaspora.

These events are seen through the eyes of a precocious fourteen-year-old girl living in a cutting-edge suburban development north of Toronto in 1957.

Thirteen Stones

Once in a New Moon, Part Two

Centrewood Cycle, 1.2 (1957, 1959)

An historical novel by
Nancy Warren

Disclaimer

This is a work of fiction. Any resemblance to actual persons or families is entirely coincidental or pure fantasy.

Acknowledgements

Personal

Many thanks to Keiran Paquette at Western University Technology Services, London, Ontario, for the ongoing benefit of his computer expertise; to my good-hearted, long-time friend Joanne Rennie of St. Jacobs for her cheerful, ever-ready contributions of her artistic skills; to the staff at Friesen Press for their excellent service, and to those close friends and family, who so whole-heartedly offered their support, respect, and encouragement.

Literary Nods and Winks

The author wishes to acknowledge the following writers for passages paraphrased from their established works:

Yann Martel. Life of Pi
"If you stumble about believability, what are you living for? Love is hard to believe, ask any lover. Life is hard to believe, ask any scientist. God is hard to believe, ask any believer. What is your problem with hard to believe?"

T.S. Eliot. The love song of J. Alfred Prufock.
The yellow fog that rubs its back upon the window-panes,
The yellow smoke that rubs its muzzle on the window-panes

Michael Andaatje. The English patient.
Almasy: "Maddox, that place at the base of a woman's throat. Does it have a name?"
Maddox: "In case you're still wondering, [that place] is called the suprasternal notch."

E.J. Pratt. Erosion
It took the sea an hour one night / An hour of storm to place
The sculpture of these granite seams / Upon a woman's face

Dedication

To Genet and Marilyn

Whose friendship helped make London my home

Table of Contents

After a bit more doodling, he proclaims:
"Et voilà— Centrewood!"
Father seems to have finished.
He stretches out his arms so that his long, artistic
hands and fingers expand way out from his wrists.
"There you go, Kiddo! There is everything here!
It's perfect. Every need has been met. It's beautiful,
is it not? An Ideal City! What more could a person want?"
He folds his hands over his flat belly with a sigh of satisfaction.

— Graham Michelsen, Once in a New Moon v. 1 pt. 1, p. 62

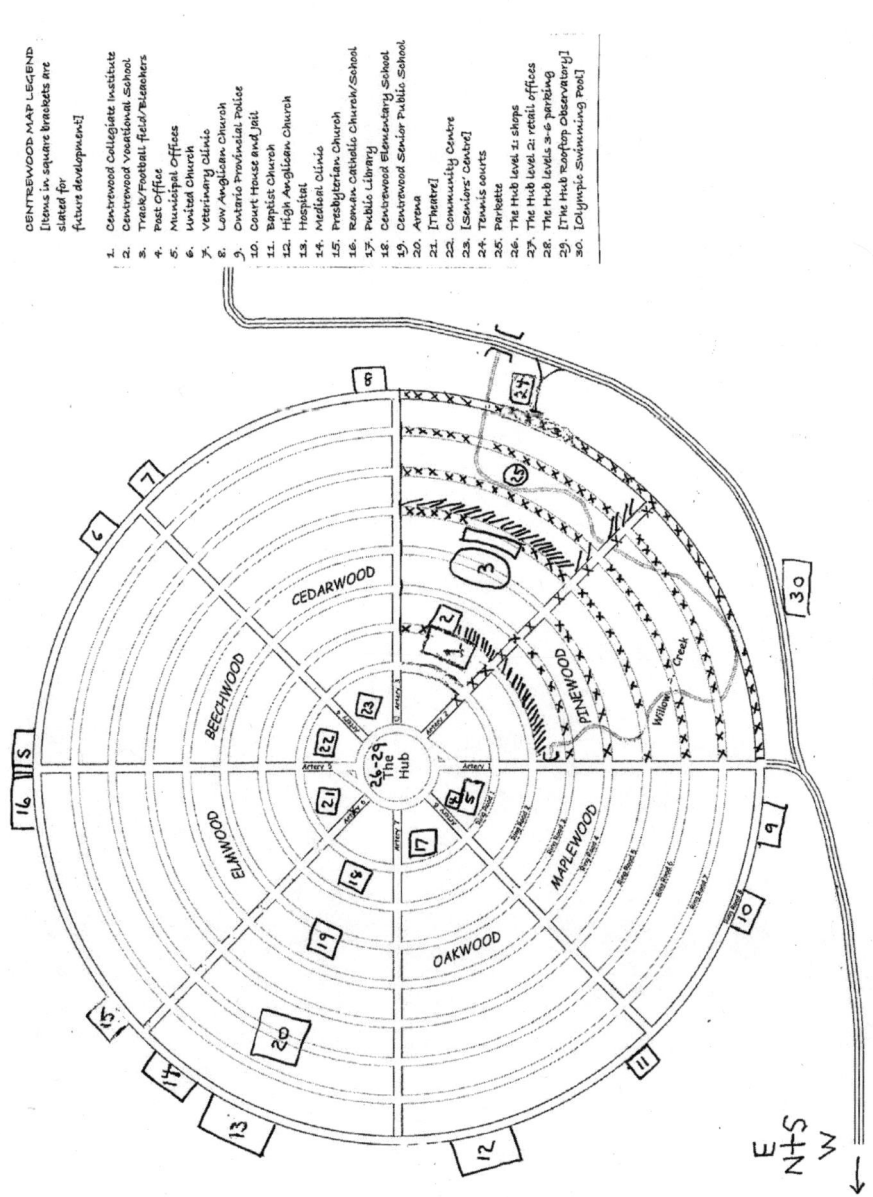

Centrewood Plan

CHAPTER ONE
Thanksgiving Saturday

Teiaiagon
1-1

October 12, 1957

9:30 a.m.

Through the rear window, I see the last wisps of the rising mists from Niagara Falls receding from view behind the interfolding buildings of the skyline.

From the right back passenger-seat window, the steep shoulders of the narrow Gorge, glimpsed from the road only moments ago, had flattened out into a low shoreline. The torrent seen coursing through the confines of the Gorge had burst out into the broad expanse of rushing water that has now become the Niagara River.

Flotillas of foaming whitecaps dot the entire length and breadth of the river. It is a fact that eons ago some act of nature caused evenly-spaced rocks to be spread out so that they protrude in

perfect rhythm from under the water's surface. The whitecaps themselves seem to be racing headlong down the channel, lifting their
elbows in unison like swimmers doing the crawl in an open water
marathon. Scrambling and scudding, having already survived the
treacherous tumble over the Falls, and having just run the gauntlet
of the Whirlpool Rapids in the Gorge, they are crashing their way
downriver toward the wide open waters of Lake Ontario, desperate
to escape any more surprise assaults.

Father and Mother and I are driving back home to Centrewood
north of Toronto. We are leaving Niagara Falls after an overnight
stay at the Brock Hotel.

The view from our hotel window overlooked the Falls. There
below us, laid out in a perfect "U" symmetry, were the Canadian
Horseshoe Falls. To their left, on the other side of a precariously-
tilted sliver of land called Goat Island, are the American Falls, equal
in height and force, but carved in a straight line and totally anticli-
mactic in comparison.

Father bet he knew what the battle of Queenston Heights in 1812
was really all about. The Americans wanted to claim the Horseshoe
Falls for themselves. There is something in the Yankee's nature, he
said, where they'd be damned if they didn't have the best of everything. In this instance, the international border between the U.S. and
Canada was drawn on this side of Goat Island, and they lost.

This is the first Thanksgiving long weekend in Canadian history.
In addition to the statutory holiday on Monday, Father decided to
take the Friday off and make it a four-day break.

We had travelled here to Niagara after an impromptu visit yesterday to the New Credit First Nation Reserve of the Mississaugas
located near Brantford. We had never visited a Reserve before, and
I for one had never met an Indian, so taking this journey, to quote
Mother, "Was all very out-of-character for the likes of us folk."

Father was compelled to investigate the cause of my waking
vision of an Indian chief—along with ten dancing warriors—that

had appeared to me on the tarmac during the Rollout ceremony of the Avro Arrow in Malton. That was when the top-secret Arrow was unveiled. Unbelievably, it is already two weeks ago, on Friday October 4, since that aircraft was hauled out of the hangar onto the tarmac and put on public display.

Father was Avro's chief aeronautical engineer, in charge of designing the Arrow, an innovative interceptor jet fighter. It was his crowning achievement. However, on the same day that his pride and joy made its first presentation, the Russians had the audacity to launch the Sputnik. That was a blow to his spirits. Therefore, upon hearing about my sightings, he was not prepared to tolerate any further detraction from his triumph, and resolved to "investigate this unmitigated balderdash to the hilt" in order to put an end to it all.

At the Reserve, we had met Chief Fred King and an honoured elder of the tribe. She was a tiny, wizened-up, old wise woman, who I ended up calling "Aunt Ani" due to cross-wired miscommunication when she told me she was Anishinabe—sounding out the word ever so slowly—which I misconstrued as her attempt to tell me her name. She was the one who solved the problem by telling me to just call her "Aunt".

During our visit, she confirmed that the Indian chief I saw was Chief Peter Jones of the Mississauga. She even brought along a photograph with identifying features to prove it. She listened closely to my waking visions, and insomuch as said that I hadn't gone loony, which Father had feared. Instead, I was gifted.

Together, Father and Chief Fred surmised that Peter Jones' appearance had something to do with the Mississauga Treaty Land Claim of 1805. A great swath of land covering most of the territory around Toronto both east and west above Lake Ontario had been purchased for the paltry sum of ten shillings. Consequently, the two men spent the duration of yesterday afternoon pouring over old treaties and maps, until it was too late for the three-hour drive home.

In the kitchen of the poet Pauline Johnson's former home, I listened to their animated conversation while working on my burr project, which was due that very day, but had been given an extension till the following Tuesday. I had tried to finish it, but had run into a major stumbling block, and it turned out that Aunt Ani had the solution! That cemented our friendship.

"Like the burr, from now on we stick together, hm?" she had grinned at me. When we parted, she slipped me a piece of paper with her telephone number, and told me to tuck it away in my binder, "If you ever need help," she said, "This is how you can reach me, and I will come to you!"

After all our fretting about getting back home by suppertime (so I wouldn't miss another Friday night episode of "Beaver"), Mother and I found out that Father had already booked the suite overlooking the Falls at the ritzy Brock Hotel before we had even left Centrewood. It was a treat never before experienced. I think it was Father's way of celebrating his own triumph with the Arrow.

This morning, after a light brunch at "The Nook", having loaded up the car in the hotel parking lot, we took the time to walk across the lane to see the Falls, as Father said, "up close and personal".

The three of us stood at the railing side by side, with Father holding us tight around the waist. The draw of the water was magnetic, he said, and he didn't want either of us to be lured into the vortex by its power.

I leaned over the railing and watched the clear, dark-blue water surge round the bend from upriver and sweep by us directly underneath at a fearsome, forceful rush. In tandem with the sheer drop-off, the colour of the water split into two bars, the first a sparkling turquoise blue, and the second, a strong brackish yellow. At the brink, the water poured over the edge in a lucid-green sluice, only to turn into a thundering, foaming frenzy when it hit the rocks immediately below.

Past the churning foam at the base of the Falls, the tour boat, the Maid of the Mist, chugged about nonchalantly on the slick, black, swirling waters. Long strands of braided foam broke way from the pummelled rocks below and formed chains of froth leading round the bend into the Gorge.

Springing off the face of the cliff to our left, on the Canadian side of the Gorge, the arc of a perfect rainbow plunged vertically into the basin below. Oddly enough, I had seen an identical photograph of that very rainbow, which I recognized had been taken from the same vantage point as where I now stood. The image was featured in one of the coloured glossy postcards on the rack at the tourist booth in the hotel lobby.

This led me to wonder if the rainbow was permanent, and if so, it might be one of those rare instances when the elusive pot of gold could be found at the end of a rainbow!

My imagination set to task immediately. Retrieval would be a precarious task, since diving off the cliff would be the only means of achieving that goal. The first step would be to pinpoint the exact point of entry. Would the rainbow still be visible when standing on the ridge behind it?— Surely not, if a transient phenomenon. Conversely, according to laws of refraction, if it were permanent, the rainbow's bars of colour should theoretically remain clearly visible, shimmering and taunting. The second step would involve plotting the descent down the face of the cliff, which looks treacherous, made of slippery, wet shale. The third step would be the actual physical approach. This would require teetering backward on the very edge of the cliff's precipice, then clambering down one foot at a time until reaching the lowest protruding ledge. Once having arrived there, one would need to turn and face the water. Then would come the jump itself. After drawing in two full lung-loads of air and taking a final bead on the target, there would be the grand leap in tight cannonball position, followed by the icy plunge into the choppy waters below. After sinking like a stone, and enduring a painful, eternal, lung-bursting trial of uncontrolled toss and tumble, the aspiring victor would hit rock bottom, where he would begin dragging both hands hither and yon, searching doggedly for the pot of gold, and, once successful, elatedly grasping it, then holding the prize in both hands, with lungs threatening to collapse for lack of oxygen, there would be the frantic, frog-kick fight to return to the surface, where he would break through, and emerge triumphant, holding the pot of gold in both hands above his head.

I asked Father, "What if someone decided to leap into the Gorge because he believed there was a pot of gold at the end of that rainbow? What kind of person would do that?"

Father took some time to mull over my question.

"He would have to be a daredevil, to be sure."

"What would that entail?"

"Why, any definition would include a willingness to risk life and limb. Mind you, there are two types. A top-notch daredevil cannot be in the least bit impetuous, he must be level-headed and have nerves of steel, he has to have high powers of reasoning and observation, be fully cognizant of all the odds pro and cons, must be one hundred per cent confident that he has mastered all the requisite skills, and has applied all laws of both physics and probability—by which I mean, he has reckoned on how to deal with every variable and possibility before taking the leap." He paused, and then added, "The other type is an idiot."

Father turned his head to include Mother. "You will recall we talked about the daredevil Maria Spelterini yesterday while I was reading from the hotel brochure. To celebrate the American Centennial in 1876, she tight-roped across the Gorge with a bag on her head and with peach baskets strapped to her feet. Another time, she crossed blindfolded."

Maria Spelterini, tight wire walker across Niagara Gorge, 1876

"If you ask me, that girl was a *first class* idiot," Mother said.

"Did I also read to you about the young man called Sam Patch?" Father asked, "It was in 1829, as I recall, that he built a platform on Goat Island and dove headfirst over the Falls. He survived!"

"All in one piece? Or did they have to 'patch' him back together again?"

That was earlier in the day. We have since done a quick detour to view the Whirlpool Rapids. Now we are heading home.

The river so evenly dotted with whitecaps rushes along next to us, its silken surface at eye level, its swollen surge barely contained by its banks.

The paved road is whooshing by underneath as we barrel along the new Queen Elizabeth Way, the first divided freeway in Ontario, if not all of Canada.

Father's foot on the gas pedal keeps the speedometer needle stuck on "50 mph"—that being the speed limit on each highway signpost we pass.

Father has been yammering away at full tilt. He had so much as promised Chief Fred King that he would try to rectify the injustice

7

of the First Purchase Land Claim. But how—and where—could he even begin? Would he have to take on the challenge all by himself? He wouldn't dare be so presumptuous as to act in his capacity as an Avro employee, so he would have to present himself as an independent citizen, and if so, what kind of sway would his appeal have with the authorities? With no personal interest vested in the land, he would be asked what business of his could it be? Also, since up till yesterday, he had had no contact with Indians whatsoever, how could he account for his sudden concern for their rights? It was becoming patently obvious that he needed help. But where could he turn for advice? Who could he trust?

"Why don't you call the Bigwigs and the Brass?" I offer from the back seat.

Father mutters under his breath, "Is that little Nancy Big Ears I hear, piping up out of turn?"

I see Mother jab him in his side with her elbow.

He changes his tune, and asks politely, "What's that, Lois?"

"You remember, Father, when we were driving to Malton for the Rollout? Isn't that what the security traffic guard called those with reserved parking—the "Bigwigs and the Brass"?"

"Father could hardly call the Brass, Lois," Mother comments, dourly, "Those are the top guns in the Armed Forces."

But Father latches right on to the idea, saying, "Quite right. That would be reaching too high. But the Bigwigs—You mean, call Admin?"

He falls silent.

Mother twigs onto the idea immediately, and says, "Why on earth not, Graham? You're on Admin, you're in a squeeze, you have nothing to apologize for, and you need to talk to someone who can help!"

"But won't they question why I am suddenly so concerned, let alone what this has to do with Avro?"

"It is my impression that the Mississauga Treaty Land Claim has a lot to do with the land that Avro occupies, if not only a good portion of Malton. I say, call your fellow Avro CEO's for advice!"

"Oh sure! I go to Admin and what will they do when I tell them that my daughter saw a phantom Indian chief during the Rollout ceremony, along with a bunch of Indian braves dancing some kind of pow-wow, and then shooting off a stream of arrows at the podium. I'll be the laughing stock!"

"What's the worst they could they do?" Mother replies.

"They could call in the men in the little white coats and cart me off to the loony bin, that's what they could do!"

"But you're one of their equals, are you not? The other men on Admin, they know you, you're a CEO on their team!"

Father reflects.

"True. I've just never thought of myself in that light. In my role as chief aeronautical engineer, I rank as high as the others, and so I guess I am on Admin. I've earned their respect, and I've established an excellent reputation, in every regard. But what if I were to approach my colleagues to ask for their advice? None of us has ever treated each other as confidants. What would I do if they shunned me, or laughed me out of the room?"

"You're afraid of being ridiculed, but what are the consequences if you don't give it a try? You seriously want to be sitting on this egg trying to hatch it all on your own? If you can overcome your fears and doubts, I say this would be the wisest way to turn." Mother folds her hands in her lap. "And the sooner this is all settled, the better." There is an ominous element in her tone.

Father mulls. In the rear view mirror, I see how the cloud over his face seems to clear with some new resolve. He says, "I don't have to tell how I found out about all this. And I don't have to tell all of them. I'll start by taking just one of them into my confidence."

Father drives straight past the turnoff north up Highway 27 toward home, puts on his indicator for Lakeshore Road East, and takes the exit ramp.

10:00 a.m.

A few blocks along, Father spots a public phone booth outside a smoke shop. He pulls in and parks, but there are some strange-looking men hanging about. Not wanting to leave us alone in the car, he makes us get out with him, and hurries us along.

All three of us end up jammed into the one phone booth like a human totem pole, with our heads stacked on top of each other, and all three of us tucked into each other's armpits.

Our difference in height makes it possible. Father is the tallest, at 6'3 ½", I am well past 5'8", and Mother is 5'2". I suppose it helps that Father and I are slim as Alberta lodge-pole pine trees.

"Crawford, it's Graham Michelsen here! Yes, quite the surprise! Yes, likewise—Happy Thanksgiving to you! Pardon me? Where am I? I'm just pulling into Toronto from taking the wife and daughter to Niagara Falls. You were what? Sorry, the line is crackling. Listen, I'm calling from a phone booth—on Lakeshore Road just past the QEW turnoff. Do you have time for you and me to talk in confidence—Pardon me?"

Father nests the receiver in the other crook of his neck.

"Yes. Now. That's my thinking! You're just up the South Kingsway from here, right, not too far away. Exactly!"

"Tell him we're not coming for tea," Mother interjects, pressing her face into Father's jawbone.

"Would you mind if we just dropped by for a few moments? No no no, thanks though, very kind of you! We won't come in. The wife and daughter want to eat at the Pancake House. Yes, the one just north from here at Jane and Bloor. I'll need directions to your place. Yes, Yes, Okay. Yes. All right then! Yes, yes, m-hm, fine! We'll be there in a jiffy. Thanks, Crawford!"

We turn north off the Lakeshore, cross under the brand new, four-lane Queen Elizabeth Way bridge, take a normal-sized two-lane bridge over the Queensway, and then up the South Kingsway we head, until we whip past a sign that says "Baby Point" with an arrow pointing up the hill.

Father slams on the brakes, pulls an abrupt U-turn and doubles back to a road that snakes upwards following the soft curve of the Humber River.

"What gives with that 'Baby Point' sign?" I muse out loud, more for my own entertainment than for my parents, "Is there some historical landmark up top? I don't remember learning anything in school about a heroic baby. But if so, why didn't they make the sign a cutout-shaped baby pointing its finger? Hey! Do you think this is where Laura Secord warned the people that the Americans were coming? Did she take her baby with her?"

"Lo-is!" Mother says, "That's quite enough of that nonsense!"

Father interrupts, "Nonsense indeed! Laura Secord carried neither a weapon nor a child, all she had was her cow."

"Lamentably, not even chocolates," Mother adds.

"She had nothing to do with chocolates! Really, Emily! How can we teach the girl anything about Canadian history if you mislead the girl? Although now you mention it, I could go for a box of Laura Secord assorted swirls and clusters right now!"

He rubs his tummy.

Father decides to impart some local history. His voice takes on an authoritative, nasal tone when he speaks, "The whole area up top is named after a man named Baby, pronounced *Babby,* who purchased this entire tract of land back in the early 1800s.

"The tract was called a 'point' because it lies on a promontory jutting out over the Humber River."

Okey-dokey.

We travel upward along a narrow tarred road that is built into the face of a steep clay cliff, thankfully relegated to the inside lane which is just far enough for my liking from the sheer drop-off into the river. Quietly, I am sincerely hoping that we don't have to come back this way.

"Amazing topography. Sharp cliff. High elevation. Indians favoured it, used it as a lookout, could see for miles."

"Did they send smoke signals from up top?" I ask.

"No doubt."

"How? I'd like to have seen that!"

"Built huge bonfires and waved blankets over the flames to control the smoke. Sent messages in gigantic huffs and puffs," Father contributes, "They didn't have flags or the alphabet, so the delivery was probably similar to Morse code!"

"The more adept of the elders used whole hieroglyphs. They looked like pictographs in the sky!" Mother offers, drolly.

"I like it! It's quite possible, you know. They had a highly evolved style of drawing so why not draw in smoke?" Father makes this remark with a straight face.

And they tell me not to be silly!

Mother swivels around and looks past me through the rear window: "Look how far you can see!"

I gaze over my shoulder at the flat blue vista of glistening water that filled the entire breadth of the horizon.

"If you follow the course of the river down below, Lois, you will see the mouth of the Humber emptying out into Lake Ontario," Father says, "This is where the coureur-de-bois Etienne Brulé came to be the first European to see Lake Ontario!"

"Ah yes," I comment, "Etienne the Barbecued."

Mother neck stiffens. She says, "What?"

"He betrayed the Hurons. For his disloyalty, he was dismembered, cooked, and eaten."

"Chief Fred King said the Indians were not cannibals. Now you tell me this? Where did you learn that drivel?"

"At school."

Mother is not amused, and swiftly changes the topic.

"Look at the horizon line!" Mother exclaims, "Only the steady hand of God could paint such a long thin blue line so straight, so true! See how he selected a slightly darker hue from his palette to finalize the separation between water and sky."

"No horizon line is final, Darling!"

"That's not what I meant," Mother replies, "I was only imagining God as artist. What gets me is, as real as the horizon line seems, it is an illusion!"

"It is as much as an illusion as it is real. It is an enigma," Father says, "For as we climb, the horizon line ascends. When we descend, it will descend with us."

"Why is that, Father?"

"Its level alters according to our own particular vantage point!"

"You mean that the horizon line is parallel to our own line of vision?"

"Yes, if you want to put it that way," Father huffs.

Father shifts his attention and shares something he learned this past week from reading the files given him during his visit to the Victoria University archives at the University of Toronto.

He says: "From what I recall from the past week's cram session, the Humber River harbour was a major 'Carrying Place', so translated from the French by the British, who have never been that adept at languages other than their own."

This is a dig at Mother, who was born in England and would still be there, if not for the War and meeting Father while they both worked "for the effort".

"Easy, Charlie-Boy," Mother ribs back, "Parlezz-vooz yourself good franssezz?"

Father grins and resumes where he left off.

"It was a poor translation of 'portage' derived from the French verb 'porter' meaning 'to carry'. The Indians would meet here to load their canoes and begin their annual trek north, back to their original homeland along the north coast of Lake Huron as far as Sault Ste. Marie. They would follow the Humber River, then portage to linking waterways along the ancient trail that extended all the way to Lake Simcoe then Georgian Bay."

"That's a lot of portaging! Would have tuckered the likes of me right out!"

"As a woman, you'd have to being doing your 10BX exercises in earnest leading up to the trek, because you would be the one bearing all the food and camping gear. The men carried the canoes!"

"No wonder they made the canoes of the lightest wood available—out of birch bark! Smart move! The men got the best part of the deal, I'd say!"

"Yes, but with their heads inside their inverted canoes, they wouldn't exactly be able to enjoy the scenery!"

"You'd have to pay me to be a mule!"

"You would have had to be one. There was no human rights court of appeal in those days! But think how delicious the meals would be whenever the party stopped to fish. Think of all the fresh salmon on the way!"

"M-m-m! I love wild salmon!"

"Father, if this land belonged to the Mississaugas, it was their home, right? So why did they return to their homeland farther north once a year?"

"They refer to their homeland the same way as we refer to the 'old country'. Mine, was Norway," Father replies.

"Mine still is England," Mother says, wistfully, "We Brits call it 'over 'ome' or 'across the pond'."

"So they just go back to visit relatives?"

"Exactly."

Directly below to our left as we climb, I can see the wide open mouth of the Humber River with several canoeists lazily pitting themselves against the soft current, and some local fishermen in wooden motorboats with anchors dropped, lolling about closer to shore in an eddy on the gentle waters.

Farther off upstream, there is a marsh with its tall, luscious, deep-green grasses soaking in the sun. The red epaulet of a redwing blackbird flashes from its perch on the bull rushes.

The road continues to climb at a steep angle until at the crest, the land abruptly flattens out into a wide clearing. It is filled with tall weeds and wild grasses, and is bordered all round with trees—stands of birch and larch, maples, some red oak, and an occasional lone elm. There is an ancient apple tree holding up craggy arms to the sky. Otherwise, the clearing itself is empty of any vestiges of life, as though meticulously cleared of anything that might have formerly been there.

The car bears left to drive around the clearing along a narrow road. There are tire tracks showing that it is well used.

What I see at the far end of the clearing makes me gasp out loud. "Oh, look!"

Mother whirls her head around to look at me.

Father glances over at me from the driver's side, looking concerned.

Mother turns completely around and asks: "What's the matter, Lois?"

"Look, Mother, don't you see?" I point. *"There are Indians camping at the far side of the field. They are dressed like those little figures in the model village that we saw at the Royal Ontario Museum."*

Mother gives Father a quick glance and says, "Graham, stop the car."

"How many?" she asks.

Father applies the brakes. He shrugs, turns rigid, and stares straight ahead, like a carved wooden statue.

Since neither Mother nor Father can see them, it starts to dawn on me that I must be experiencing another waking vision.

"Several. Mostly women. They're milling around next to a long oval structure. It is clad all over with shingles made of birch. Looks like a stretched-out

wigwam. See the dog in harness? It's pulling a huge bundle of sticks stacked on a strange triangular-shaped contraption that drags on the ground behind it. A woman with long black braids is leading it on a leash toward the gathering. She is wearing a shift with a cloth bundled around her waist as a long skirt."

I feel breathless.

"What is happening now?"

I take in some air, wet my lips, and then I speak. My voice is hoarse.

"All at once, they are lifting their heads and stiffening, looking alarmed. What's that?"

"What, darling?"

"Look! Over there to the right, bursting through the trees, there are Indians on horseback! They are bearing rifles high in the air and calling out to them, rushing toward them, warning them about something!"

"What are they wearing?" Father asks.

"Head bands. Armbands. Buckskin vests with fringes. Breech cloths with leggings. Moccasins."

"Breech cloths?" Father croaks, "What do you know about breechcloths?"

"Those are the men's pants. They learn all that in school, Graham. Ease up!" Mother snaps, "What now, Lois? What is happening?" she asks.

I continue to watch, incredulous, till I find my voice again.

"That was so weird! *In a flash, almost like a sped-up film, all the women tucked themselves away into the long oval wigwam. Then it lifted up on wheels and like a horseless covered wagon, rolled off at full tilt along the edge of the clearing toward—through the gap in the bush over there!"*

"Oh, for the love of Mike!" Father moans, leaning the back of his head against the car seat.

I am feeling dizzy, as though about to faint, both from the unnerving experience as well as from Father's biting remark.

Mother turns to look at me and says, "Graham, the girl is white as a ghost!" She jumps out of the car, comes to the back door, opens it, and reaches in to hold me. "There, there, Lois dear," she coos.

Father remains seated in the front. "Oh brother," he groans, "What next!"

***

Father studies the scribbles he had jotted down after leaving the phone booth near the Kingsway. Accordingly, on the other side of the clearing, we take the first left fork in the road, and look for a driveway leading through a stand of red oaks.

Mr. Gordon's house comes into view. It is a three-storey house, which Father is immediately able to describe from the university course he had taken in domestic architecture as a "Tudor revival, black-timber-framed mansion with white wattle and daub".

It is tucked into the woods as though it has existed there forever. It has a steeply pitched roof with three, large, A-shaped gables that run down the face of the entire structure to ground level. The middle A is the largest, and forms the overhang for the front porch.

There is smoke wafting from the stacks of several tall narrow chimneys on the roof, indicating fireplaces in key rooms such as drawing room and bedrooms. A larger chimney poking up out of the middle of the roof is bilging blacker smoke which tells of a coal-burning furnace with octopus arms pushing its heat up from the basement along an enormous network of huge ducts and out vents throughout a drafty old house in the wintertime, just like Grandpa's big mansion in St. Thomas.

Parked at the carriage house off to the left is Mr. Gordon's big, fat, black and shiny 1957 Eldorado SeVille Cadillac. He had backed the car into place as though on the ready for a speedy takeoff.

"Mr. Gordon likes to throw his weight around, and has a penchant for small-busted women," Mother surmises.

Father jerks his head and eyeballs her, "What makes you say that?"

"Look at the bulging bulk of his car and the comparatively teeny size of its 'Dagmars'!"

Father's jaw drops. "Emily!" he says, sternly, "What a thing to say, and in front of Lois?"

Mother shrugs. "Don't look at me like that! You were the first to mention them. Remember? At the Rollout while we were all standing under the Arrow looking up at its undercarriage?"

"Yes, but as a man, I'm entitled to say crude things. Besides, I would never have mentioned it at the time, but I just wanted to tell you what that minx Mitsy said that morning while I was detailing the car in the driveway," adding with a droll expression on his face, "I must say, it sounds even more vulgar coming from you, a proper lady!"

"Oh, get off, will you!"

Mother gives his arm a playful tug.

I groan at the thought of Mitsy, obligatory school companion, and the bane of my existence. Even when she's miles away, she still manages to invade our lives and cause trouble.

When we pull in slowly over the crunching, white, crushed stones into the circular drive, the front door is already open. Mr. Gordon has been peering out, watching for us.

"There's Crawford!" Father almost shouts.

The man is wearing a Stetson cowboy hat, a white denim jacket and embroidered shirt with matching wesket and trousers, and calf-brown, tooled cowboy boots. His jacket lapel is wider than normal, scalloped along its edges and traced with pale brown-embroidered lariat loops. Instead of the standard businessman's tie, he is wearing a black string bowtie.

"Is Mr. Gordon a cowboy?"

"You'll have to ask him!"

Mr. Gordon steps out from under the shelter of his large A-shaped porch, bounds down the steps, and shuffles through ankle-deep, freshly fallen, shiny auburn-red oak leaves to the car. He is a big man with a large, pink, square face, snow-white hair and a matching snowy-white push-broom moustache somewhat discoloured by tobacco stains.

I recognized Mr. Gordon as one of the men who had been on the VIP platform at the Rollout, but he was dressed in an ordinary business suit back then.

Seated in the front visitor's row with Mother, to entertain myself while waiting for the proceedings to begin, I began scrutinizing the names of the VIPs listed in the programme, imagining how each of them would look. I had pictured Crawford Gordon as stiff and hard, like the shell of a crayfish. He would be wearing a lustrous mother-of-pearl suit with a pinkish polished sheen. In my imagination, he would have a shrunken little face, beady little eyes and oversized claw-like hands. He would walk sideways, slowly and deliberately, like a crab. He would carry a cane in one claw, which he would use to whack his prey to crack them open. I nicknamed him Cracker Jack.

Turns out he is not at all the way I had imagined him.

As he approaches, Father winds down his window.

"Howdy! How are you-all? Welcome to Teiaiagon!" Mr. Gordon booms out with a hearty voice.

"That what you call your place?"

"Not the house alone, but it's what this whole plateau used to be called when it was the site of an early Iroquoian Indian village shared by the Mohawk and the Seneca, that is, until the Mississauga took over at the end of the 1600s. La Salle and Hennepin reported that it was inhabited by as many as 5000 people."

Father rubbernecks wide-eyed at Mother, while the two men shake hands through the car window.

"That so? I knew it was a key lookout for the Indians, nothing more."

Father introduces us, and then he hops out.

Mr. Gordon reaches out to grab his hand firmly and shake it ardently.

"Michelsen, where the heck have you been? We've been trying to get in touch with you."

"What's the problem?"

"Smye is calling a snap executive meeting for this afternoon. Seems we have a bit of a bother on our hands."

Mother leans across and calls through Father's car window: "On a Thanksgiving weekend? What is so urgent it can't wait?"

"Emily!" Father blurts. It is apparent that Mother too can speak out of turn. He turns back to Mr. Gordon: "What's going on?"

"Seems there is some skulduggery afoot," Mr. Gordon responds, "What's worse, we're not quite sure who or what is behind it."

"How so?"

"We're thinking it might be dirty tricks by the new government in Ottawa."

He hesitates.

"To be frank, I'm not comfortable with 'Devious Dief', if you don't mind me calling him that."

"I don't mind one bit," Father says.

"I'll vouch for that," Mother intercedes, still opting to weigh in by talking through the driver's side window, "Graham makes no bones about disliking that man!"

"It's not so much dislike as distrust," Father sighs.

Mr. Gordon switches the tone.

"So! You are just getting back from a road trip, are you? Took the family to Niagara Falls, did you?"

"Yesterday, stayed overnight."

"Hope you-all stayed at the Brock, has the best view of the Falls!"

"Yes, yes indeed! Lovely, we had a beautiful view!"

Father doesn't want to talk about our trip to Niagara. He wastes no time trying to get to the crux of the matter.

He takes Mr. Gordon by the elbow.

"Here's the situation, Crawford. I need to talk to you about something that happened at the Rollout. It has led me on a crazy chase searching for an explanation, but now I have found it, I'm in a quandary as to what to do about it. I need your advice."

"What the heck happened?"

They take a few paces away from the car, and then walk toward the back of the house.

Father casts a worried look over his shoulder at Mother and myself.

I hear him say, "You see, we didn't drive directly to Niagara Falls. We went first to the New Credit Indian reserve down near Brantford."

"God's sakes! What for the price of all the tea in China took you there?"

"Believe me, it was the last place on earth I ever expected to be."

I lift the handle of the back passenger door quietly. Without latching it shut, I slip out and follow close behind, walking along the grassy middle part of the cinder laneway to tamp down my footfall, dodging any chance backward glances by hanging in behind a string of saplings, benefiting from being skinny by taking them one at a time as I make my way along the path.

I can follow the gist of their exchange without hearing each word clearly.

Father apologizes in advance for sounding crazy, but asks to be heard out. "Without getting into the specifics", he tells Mr. Gordon that a "certain event" had occurred during the Rollout proceedings. This had led him to visit the New Credit First Nations Reserve located adjacent to the Six Nations reserve. During a meeting with the Mississauga Chief and an elder, he was told about an outstanding Mississauga Land Claim that includes the land where the Avro plant now stands.

"There are land claims in abundance all over the province, Graham!"

"Ah, but the evidence pertaining to the Malton lands, as provided by the Chief, clearly proved to me that the terms of the treaty in question are spurious and the signing was fraudulent."

Most worrisome, he confessed that he had been moved so far as to promise the current Chief Fred King that he would try to take action.

"Good grief, Graham! Why on earth did you do that?"

"The Chief was very persuasive. Since all of the Mississauga protests over the years have fallen on deaf ears, he looked to me as a 'white man' to use my influence. I didn't for one moment try to pretend that I was any more than I really am, I mean, even though to gain his help, it was necessary to reveal that I worked at Avro, and as a CEO I was on the dais and in fact, gave one of the key speeches, I didn't try to look like some big shot—But Crawford, have you ever found yourself cornered by Truth?"

Father must have started to tremble or look faint, because Mr. Gordon takes Father by the elbow and turns him about. I dive behind a tool shed.

"Take it easy, Graham. I'm still in the dark about the evidence you gained, or the purpose. To my mind, however, you never know what might be involved here. You'd best step back a pace, and take the time to assess the situation before you do anything rash."

"That's where I need your help."

Mr. Gordon takes Father by the elbow.

Walking slowly, Father accompanies Mr. Gordon to his car.

Mr. Gordon is talking low. I hear him say, "I have an idea. Tell you what I suggest we should do."

"What do you have in mind?"

"First of all, I think that Smye will be interested in hearing about this. He has put the word out to Admin that any and all unusual developments should be brought to his attention. I say we have a preliminary confab with him before this afternoon's Admin meeting. It might warrant adding this issue to the main agenda."

"'We'?" Father croaks, "I was hoping to discuss this in private with you, Crawford!"

They stand facing each other at the front of the Cadillac, which faces out on the driveway.

"But it's not a private matter, is it?"

"I suppose not."

"I think Floyd should join us as well."

"Really?" Father squeaks.

"Each of them lives only a hop, skip and a jump away from the Pancake House. Smye's just up near the Old Mill, and Floyd lives further north apiece off Burnhamthorpe. I'm going to radio them now, and have them meet us at the Pancake House to 'parlay'!"

He takes out a little spiral notebook from one pocket.

I scurry from the shed to the back of the Cadillac, squat down low, and take a peek over the trunk. Father looks ghastly.

"Crawford, you seem willing to humour me. But I'm concerned that you and the others might all think I've gone over the deep end when I reveal how I learned about all this!"

"I've got their call numbers in my book here. I'm contacting them now. Meanwhile, I suggest you head off and enjoy brunch at the Pancake House with your wife and daughter! We'll meet up with you there!"

Mr. Gordon turns around suddenly, and cocks a big bushy white eyebrow at me, where I am crouching next to his car's back bumper. I am startled and leap back, almost falling over.

"Who is this pretty little blond, blue-eyed girl playin' Hiawatha, makin' like she's stalkin' us?"

I blush as red as a radish.

"A-ha! Cain't fool me, I had mah built-in radar turned on full blast, I knowed you were there!" he smiles.

I hang my head with embarrassment, and then I bolt straight-backed and stiff-legged, as ladylike as possible, back to Father's car.

Mr. Gordon hops to the driver's side of his car, and jumps in.

I see him reach for a handset attached by a long curly cord to somewhere under the dashboard. It was the same kind of radio used by that policeman who stopped me on my bike on the highway because of an APB released by the Neighbourhood Watch. Mother was anxious because I hadn't come home yet. I arrived home later than usual, with my carrier filled with burrs that Bert had culled for me on the other side of the highway for my botany project.

Mr. Gordon punches some buttons.

A great racket of high-pitched hissing and coughing of electronic noises comes out through the speakers set in the dashboard. Mr. Gordon barks a series of commands and code numbers into his mouthpiece, makes contact, relays his messages requesting callbacks, and signs off.

This man is not at all like the Crawford Gordon I had imagined from reading his name on the Rollout programme. He doesn't move sideways or slowly like a crab. No-sirree-bob, this man listens, and in a blink, he takes action.

I was right about one thing. He doesn't waste any time in the Decision-Making Department, he really is a Cracker Jack!

Father gets back in the car and turns on the engine.

I get back in, and lean with folded elbows on the back of Father's seat. I look over his shoulder at his reflection in the rear view mirror.

Father's face is ashen grey, with bright, red spots in his cheeks. He puts the car in gear, and sets the car in motion. While slowly following the curve of the circular driveway, he seems to regain his composure, the colour returns to his face.

He reaches back with his hand, cups me toward him by the back of my neck, and plants a kiss on the top of my head.

"You did well, honey," he says.

"What did I do?" I ask.

"You suggested that I call the 'Bigwigs and Brass' for help!"

"Which is Mr. Gordon?"

"A Bigwig."

This is the first time, I think, that he realizes that he, too, is a Bigwig.

The car wends its way back out through the stand of blaring-red oaks to the road around the "plateau". It makes its nerve-wracking descent down the narrow river road, this time with Father having to drive precariously on the right side of the pavement along the very edge of the embankment. One glance straight down into the river valley with nothing to impede my view but the car window ledge gives me vertigo. I sit on my hands and hang on tight with elbows and fingertips, praying we will not slide sideways over the edge into the valley far below.

When we finally reach The Kingsway, I can exhale.

***

I have a question to ask.

"What does 'Nancy Big Ears' mean? I've never understood why you call me that at times. Am I not supposed to know you are refer-ring to me because you're using another girl's name?"

"In Australia, the common term is 'Suzy Stickybeak,'" Mother says, "I believe there's an expression for one in every culture."

"I'd just call her Betty the Buttinski. That's for someone who butts into other people's conversations with unsolicited opinions. It's a euphemism for someone who eavesdrops, only to meddle."

"But how can I help not overhearing your conversation when I am right here in the back seat?"

"Your Mother and I have the right to discuss matters despite the fact that you are present," Father says, tersely, "Sometimes we have no alternative, as there is nowhere else to go. At such junctures, it's preferred that you keep your opinions to yourself."

"It is used to be kind to the offending party rather than cruel, as a broad hint at such times when they should mind their own busi-ness," Mother adds.

"Yes, I can see that it would be exceedingly rude if you told me to 'butt out' or 'mind my own beeswax'. But how am I supposed to know when I am part of this threesome and when I am not?"

"She has a good point, Graham," Mother says.

"All these adages have a purpose," Father muses, "I suppose it is a companion piece for the saying 'Little girls should be seen and not heard'.

"I feel just about as stung hearing that saying, as I do when I'm called 'Nancy Big Ears'," is my rejoinder, "Since when have I never been allowed to express my opinion?"

"When you were little, your outbursts were cute. Now you are almost fourteen, your precociousness isn't always welcome."

"Nonetheless, you liked my idea that you should consult with the Bigwigs."

"For Pete's sake, Lois, let it go," Mother sighs.

The Pancake House
1-2

Saturday, October 12, 1957
11:30 a.m.

Father, Mother and I are sitting in the curved, padded, brown vinyl booth around a large oval table in the front bay window of the Pancake House. We are seated facing the parking lot, keeping a close eye out for the expected arrivals, while devouring our stacks of blueberry pancakes smothered with butter and maple syrup. We must have burned off any goodness there might have been in our light breakfast at the Brock's "Nook" in Niagara Falls early this morning, because we are eating like fiends—at least, I am.

I am the first to spot Mr. Gordon's shiny black Eldorado SeVille Cadillac pull in off Bloor Street. It is followed shortly by the same blue Pierce Arrow convertible that we had seen in the VIP parking lot at the Arrow Rollout in Malton. Close behind comes a snazzy, glossy-red '56 Thunderbird sports car. I point out to Mother and Father that it is "the two-seater model" with "white-wall tires" and the spare tire tacked "continental-style" to its back bumper. I had picked up all these terms while listening to the guys at school.

"How did you get to know so much about cars, dear?" Mother comments, "It's such an unusual interest for a girl!"

"Is it?" I reply, feeling defensive. I automatically look blank. That is my reflex shield against criticism. The constant insinuation that there are subjects that normally fall outside a girl's realm of interest niggles me.

"You showed an interest in Mr. Gordon's car, Mother," I say.

"Yes, I did. But that's different! Women are more interested in the personalities of the men who choose to drive certain cars, not so much in the features of the makes and models themselves."

Over the roofs of other parked cars, I follow where the three vehicles park. Car doors swing open and three men huddle together for a brief exchange. From afar, their expressions look serious, if not grim. I track the tops of their three hats—a white Stetson, a black felt fedora and an English hounds-tooth deerstalker—as they bob in and out of the other parked cars toward the main entranceway.

Into the restaurant bustle three men, who glance around, spot us, and then come over to our table.

They hang their hats on the wooden pegs of the nearby rack.

Father leaps to his feet to shake their hands.

"Gents!" Father greets them.

"Look who the cat dragged in!" Mr. Gordon proclaims, pointing to his companions.

"Blame Colonel Sanders himself here!" the tall, thin man says, indicating Mr. Gordon with his thumb, "Geez, Crawford, you look like you stepped right off a Chicken Villa billboard! Either that, or you escaped from the Calgary Stampede! Thank the Lord you never wear that god-awful outfit to work!" he joshes.

I am all agog from these surprise antics. Father had warned me that a meeting with CEOs was a serious business, and here's the tall man ribbing Mr. Gordon on his likeness to Colonel Sanders, presumably because of his shock of white hair and white bushy moustache, and next he takes a jab at how he's dressed—like a Westerner—with the Stetson and all. I've already learned in the Manners Department that one doesn't make fun of others' appearance, at least not to their face, so I'm baffled and watch closely.

Mr. Gordon sticks his thumbs in his wesket pockets and puts on a thick drawl, "Cain't do! In these-here parts of T.O. known to us all as the Big Fog, it's strictly my cas-u-al weekend gah-rb."

"Do men wear that kind of 'garb' to work in Calgary?" one of the men asks.

"Darn tootin', they do, and they ride their horses to work as well, right downtown where there's hitchin' posts for parking right on the Main Street!"

I stare at him in disbelief.

"Do you ride your horse to work, Mr. Gordon?"

"Why yes I do, Miss Michelsen, and ah park it in my special VIP double parkin' spot with the sign posted 'Reserved for Buster'."

"Do you leave him out there all day?"

"Ye-e-p! But I see where you're goin' with that question. Just so he don't get the sun-burn, he's hitched up under a custom-made bur-lap awning. Jes' in case he gets thirsty or hungry, there's a bucket of water and a bale of hay set out each day just for him, courtesy of the City of Calgary Parking Officers!"

He bends over, looks me straight in the eye, and winks.

The men are all still standing, crowded around Father's chair. Father turns to introduce Mother and myself to the men, gesturing in turn, "You have already met each other at the Rollout—Fred Smye, President, Jim Floyd, VP Engineering, and of course, Crawford Gordon, General Manager, whom you met earlier today. Gents, my wife Emily, and daughter Lois. Please, gentlemen, be seated!"

"Move over, Lois!" he says, shunting Mother and myself toward the far end of the table and around the curve, so that our backs are now to the window.

The men seat themselves around the curve closest to Father.

Mr. Smye assumes command.

"Good!" he says, signalling the waitress with a beckoning hand, "Let's order beverages—coffee or tea or—?" He places his briefcase on the floor next to him.

I recognized Mr. Smye when he first entered. He is the man with smooth, sandy-coloured hair, and a slightly receding hairline who had delivered the first speech at the Avro Rollout.

While waiting in the audience for the dignitaries to arrive on the platform, I had nicknamed him "Sly Smye". From his name alone, I imagined him to be tall and slim with a black handle bar moustache. He would be wearing a little black fedora clapped to the top of his head. He would look like Fearless Fosdick in a one-button, single-lapel black suit. His body would be riddled with bullet holes. One eye would be half shut in an expression of suspicion.

I was way off the mark. Except for his height and slender build, he lacked bullet holes, and looked neither shifty nor sly.

Instead, just as he does now, he was wearing an ordinary business suit with a matching diagonally- striped tie and an Avro service pin in his lapel.

He stands straight and tall, and has a boyish aspect to him. He doesn't look old enough to be president of such a big company as Avro. However, the way he takes command, I can sense why he is in charge. He has an air of authority.

The men settle into their places while Mr. Smye opens his briefcase and sorts his papers.

I turn my attention to the other man with the deerstalker, 'Lloyd the Boid', as I'd dubbed him sight unseen at the Rollout. Mr. Jim Floyd does not look at all like the seagull I had imagined. Arms not pinned behind his back while strutting along the beach with yellow pointed beak holding a half-swallowed sardine. No webbed feet slipped into yellow Wellingtons. He isn't the one wearing the white suit either. Instead, he is the one who is wearing the hounds-tooth deerstalker hat, a matching brown hounds-tooth jacket with dark brown leather elbow patches, and a brown corduroy bowtie. He has a kind, gentle face, twinkly blue eyes, and a calm, quiet nature. When he first approached Father, he had warm greetings for him, first of all throwing an arm across his shoulders, exclaiming, "Ah, there's the man who helped me 'unfunk the Clunk'!" followed by wrapping his arms around him with a warm hug. Father looked pleased but embarrassed. "You know this is the man who helped rescue the CF-100 by solving the cause of ominous noises coming from the plane when landing? It was Graham here who saved the day!" He turned to me. "The grinding metal sound was all caused by the landing gear!"

Father looked sheepishly flattered.

"Your family ordered?" Mr. Floyd asks Father.

"Yes, we've just eaten. Just waiting for beverages."

Mr. Floyd looks at my polished plate and then at me. He widens his blue eyes. "Well, I must say, you knew I was on my way and you didn't save even one wee bite for me?"

"No-o-o!" I say, feeling shy, and shrinking back.

He pretend-wails, "Boo hoo hoo!" Then he smiles.

"It's okay. I'm only teasing you. I've already had a huge breakfast and my wife would kill me if I had one more nibble before dinner!"

I think he is catering to the child in me, trying to make light conversation. Like Mr. Gordon, I can tell that he is just trying to ease the tension that hangs so heavy in the air.

"Attention all! For your amusement, I am going to prove that I have psychic powers. I am going to tell you what kind of pancakes this young lady had! She shall now stick out her tongue!"

I glance at Mother for permission, and then I comply, shyly and reluctantly, as normally that would be very rude.

"A-ha! Blue tongue! So you had the blueberry pancakes!!" He thumps his fist on the table like a judge with his gavel. I try to look down over my nose to see if my tongue is blue.

The men all laugh obligingly, but not Father. They all look at him. He is noticeably pale, his face drawn.

"Not feeling up to par, Michelsen?"

Father hesitates.

"To tell the truth, I booked off this past week as a vacation, but fell dreadfully ill over the weekend after the Rollout. Ended up midweek in Toronto General for tests. Results so far have been inconclusive."

"Think you blew your bolt after all that pressure leading up to the Rollout?" Mr. Smye asks, "You worked 24/7 that last stretch leading up to the deadline."

"Yes, he did!" Mother interjects, "He worked night and day. If he wasn't at the office, he was flogging away downstairs in his den. It totally wore him out."

"Deserves a lot of credit," Mr. Floyd says.

"Sure does," Mr. Smye and Mr. Gordon agree.

"That cursed Sputnik going up the same day as the Rollout last Friday mustn't have helped your spirits any. That was a crusher," Mr. Floyd says.

"I'll tell you straight out, men, it damn near did me in," Father sighed, "I wager it knocked the stuffing out of me so hard, there was no resistance left to ward off any new bug that might opt to come along," Father responds.

"It was a cruel blow, to be sure. Affected everyone," Mr. Smye says, "Just a skeleton staff on the floor at the plant. That was a good name for them, they were already so worn out, gaunt and almost lifeless, and really down. Good thing we'd planned a shutdown on the floor for the week. Because it shut us all down, one way or the other, at work or not!"

"On top of that, something else happened that knocked me for a loop—"

Mr. Smye cuts him off. "If you don't mind, Graham, before we get into that, other matters need to be discussed. I can assure you that you will have the floor as soon as some other items on the agenda have been addressed?"

"First off, Graham, you need to know it was yesterday morning that I called a snap Admin emergency meeting for today for 1:30. We tried to contact you. Sanderson lives around the corner, so he went over to check on you and the house was battened down, your car not in the driveway or garage. By last evening at our last attempt, to be honest, we were getting worried!"

"Why didn't you call my school?" my voice sounds out, "Both the secretary AND my science teacher knew where we were!"

I suppose that sounded too disrespectful because Father glares at me and Mother kicks me in the ankle.

I splay my hands. "What—? It's so obvious!"

Mr. Smye's voice wavers for a moment, but then continues to float right over top of me.

"Fortune smiled this morning, Graham, when you dropped in on Crawford here. When Crawford called me with the news, I decided that it would be best to meet with you beforehand, to fill you in on recent developments."

"What's so urgent?"

"The thing is, Graham, based on extenuating circumstances, our meeting will be convening in Centrewood, at your house." His eyes turn to Mother, "I concede that this is highly irregular. Would that be an inconvenience, Mrs. Michelsen?"

"Well now, that's all fine and dandy, but the three of us have plans to be somewhere at 3:30! You'd better be finished by 3:15 at the latest!" Mother's tone is peremptory. Father frowns.

"Hope you don't mind!" Mr. Smye smiles.

"We left in such a flurry, the house is probably a mess!" Mother flutters her hands, and sighs under her breath while attempting to put on her best gracious smile.

"But what is this all about?" Father asks, "And if it's so urgent, why not meet sooner?"

"We need seven members to make a quorum. Thanks to your timely resurfacing, we've got four here, and we'll have three more. We can't meet earlier than 1:30. Sanderfield has to pick his son Bert up from his chess club tournament anytime after 1:00. Pesando will be delayed till 1:30 due to a family birthday event. Jack Frost lives a bit further away up in Woodbridge and can't leave home till after 1:00. I'd ask Zurakowski for backup, but he is out of town visiting relatives and is unable to make it. It is Thanksgiving weekend, after all!"

"Are we establishing a precedent?" Father asks, looking truly baffled, "I don't recall any of us ever meeting at someone's home before now, let alone on Thanksgiving weekend!"

Meanwhile, my attention has been snared. I ask Mr. Smye: "Is there really a man named Jack Frost?"

"Sure is!"

I stare back skeptically. "I saw his name on the Rollout list of dignitaries but I didn't believe it! I thought he was a 'typo'!"

Three of the men burst out laughing. "He's no 'typo', believe me! He's an invaluable member of our team!"

"Say, young lady," Mr Floyd says, "You'll like this. Guess what Mr. Frost is perfecting right now! A flying saucer! It's called the Avrocar!! Really!! It's the prototype for a VTOL, a 'Vertical Take off Or Landing' craft!! Commissioned by the U.S. Air Force, it is right now being tested in beta stage. He has already personally patented his 'air cushion effect and propulsion control'!"

"Holy Moly! First you tell me there's a Jack Frost? And now you're saying there's a real flying saucer? I don't believe you!"

"You'll be meeting him today and you can ask him yourself! He's quite the brilliant inventor—as are we all, of course!" Mr. Floyd exclaims, straightening his shoulders, then beating his chest with his fists.

"Hear, hear!" the men cheer in unison, including Father, who is fidgety and manages to emit an "aye, aye", his effort not so hearty. He tries to keep up with the other men, so he smiles wanly.

"Hey, if we don't beat our own chests, who will, eh, pahdners?" Mr. Gordon says, putting on his Western accent again.

"If not our new lacklustre Prime Minister, maybe the Canadian public at large," Mr. Floyd says, drily.

The comment casts a sombre note on the gathering.

"Indeed," Mr. Smye concurs.

Ottawa Delegation
1-2A

Avro Arrow in flight

11:45 a.m.

Mr. Smye raises his hand to call the meeting to attention, saying, "This brings us to our interim agenda here at the Pancake House. We have three urgent matters to discuss, with very little time to do so."

He slips a spiral memo pad out from among the sheaf of papers in his briefcase.

"Floyd," he says, handing him his pen, "Could you take the minutes, please. Note that we do not have a full quorum. List those present, be sure to add Mrs. Michelsen and daughter Lois as honorary auditors, with our apologies for barnstorming their Thanksgiving getaway.

"Right then. First item on the agenda concerns the looming threat to the ultimate fate of our Arrow due to two causes. First, the surprise launch of the Sputnik by Russia—most cruelly, on the same day as the Rollout of our beloved Arrow."

"Second, America's recent proven success of its BoMarc intercontinental missile. With its capability to intercept enemy fighter planes—along with its potential to bear nuclear warheads, questions are being raised about the need for such a long-range supersonic jet fighter as the Arrow, its principal raison d'être being to intercept any Russian fighters coming from over the Arctic Circle before reaching Canada. In short, with this new stage in the Cold War, the future of the Arrow is in jeopardy."

"What?" Mother exclaims, "After all the time and money that has been poured into the Arrow? I hardly think so!"

Father reaches over and places a cautionary hand on her forearm.

Mr. Gordon says, "Think of the number of jobs on the line! Cancellation would mean not only the dashing of our dreams, and a blow to our national pride, but at least 15,000 workers will be flung out of work."

Smye nods, and then picks up where he left off. "Skepticism about the financial viability of the Arrow project has been no classified secret, by any means. Even during the election campaign this Fall, our new Prime Minister, the Honourable John Diefenbaker, expressed his reservations about the costs involved in launching the Arrow, and seriously advocated for the BoMarc instead. We need not be reminded how stung we all felt when our Yankee-pandering

P.M. failed to turn up on October 4 to celebrate the Rollout of the Arrow. Another indication of his wavering support was his delay of the contract renewal, which was withheld right up to the day of the Rollout."

"Is there any chance to stop him from cancelling the project?" Father asks.

Mr. Smye continues, "Let us be cognizant of the fact that he is in a key position to cancel the project, despite the acclaimed aeronautical superiority of our product."

Mr. Gordon says, "He's made no bones about favouring American aviation products over our own. It's a pity that the leader of our very own country lacks faith in Canadian enterprise."

"We have created a supersonic jet that has earned international respect," Mr. Floyd says.

"At any rate, Graham, just to fill you in, during your absence, Admin agreed that it's time for us to make a bold move, before Diefenbaker makes any attempt to shut us down entirely. Consequently, this past week I have set the wheels in motion for sending an Avro Admin delegation to Ottawa. Meetings in Ottawa are being slated for October 21 to 24. "

"Since the Prime Minister calls the shots, where would we go to lobby on behalf of the Arrow? Who in Ottawa can stand in his way?" Father muses.

"Precisely. I have been putting feelers out in an attempt to understand the power structure in order to identify the hidden links, if any, to block him. Unlike the American system with its built-in set of checks and balances, our parliamentary system has very few institutional checks, any or all of which come to an abrupt halt at the Prime Minister's Office. Indeed, as you intimated, there is no authority above the P.M. that is empowered to check him—unless there's a minority government. Which there is not, in this instance.."

"The Crown would have been the last resort for appeal, but the Statute of Westminster quashed that in 1931 when we gained our independence from Great Britain. Now the Governor General is just a figurehead," Mr. Floyd offers.

"When it comes down to it, isn't there something intrinsically flawed about calling a political system a democracy when a citizen has only one vote at election time, but no more say over major decisions throughout the P.M.'s term? After an election, the leader has absolute power to do whatever he wants throughout his term," Father says.

"You're right. Nonetheless, this is no time for philosophy. Or insurrection. It is a given fact that Diefenbaker has all the power for the five coming years he is Prime Minister," Mr. Smye asserts, "Theoretically, there's nothing to stop him, once he gets a bug in his ear about anything!"

"The only deterrent would be a P.M. who fears negative repercussions from his base in the future, and is tossed out on that ear in the following election," Mr. Gordon says, "But obviously, by then it would be too late."

"When you look at the whole framework in the light of day, any astute P.M. could be so Machiavellian that he would know how to destabilize the government, and knock out its underpinnings. By what narrow margin does our system come to a dictatorship?" Mr. Floyd ponders.

"Come, come, it almost smacks treasonous to be thinking along those lines," Mr. Smye rejoins, "But it's true, that if one opposes an action by the party in power, there is very little that a citizen can do, other than write your M.P., vote for the opponent, cross your fingers and hope for the best."

Mr. Gordon tries to bring the conversation around to the main topic. "Perhaps the only prospect for support with the Arrow might have to come from the Conservative caucus itself. By which I mean, if there were a revolt from within the caucus, which is highly unlikely, that might be the most we can hope for!" he says.

"That's a novel idea. Hit the enemy from within!" Father smiles.

Mr. Smye says: "There is also the former Prime Minister, St. Laurent, who didn't lose his seat in the last election, and is currently the leader of the Opposition."

"Of course!" Mr. Gordon interjects, "Surely, with St. Laurent's widespread influence in the course of his two terms in office as P.M., he would be the one most cognizant of which levers to push. Or pull."

Mr. Smye continues, "Staff from Louis St. Laurent's liberal office have already led me to the names of former key government leaders such as Howe, Dobson, Simonds, and Slemon plus key figures on the civil service side. Queries to various other leads have as well produced names among the military apparati who were responsible for authorizing the Arrow in the first place. As a result, I have been besieged by acronyms: the CSA, CDC, CGS, ADC, SSEA!"—waving sheafs of papers about in the air— "and consortia of organizations such as the All-Weather Interceptor Requirements Team, which consists of the Defence Research Board (DRB), the National Research Council (NRC), and the National Aeronautical Establishment (NAE), which was formed way back in January 1952 and note this! was issued an operational requirement for an *advanced two-seat, twin-engined, all-weather supersonic interceptor.* Sound familiar? This was the genesis for the Arrow!"

"I know about that team, because I served on it," Mr. Floyd says.

"With that in mind, you will be the one to lead that particular sortie," Mr. Smye responds, "And the rest of Admin will assist me in establishing contact with all those other leads."

A wave of exhaustion flows across Mr. Smye's face. He says, "I must say that the exercise of trying to track down persons of influence from both the current and the former Parliament, along with attempting to pin down key links in the chain of command, all with launching any appeal in mind, has felt like nothing more than a wild goose chase!"

"Would that be a wild CANADA goose chase, Sir?" I chime in.

The men burst out laughing.

Father is livid. "Lois, do be quiet. Did you not hear Mr. Smye refer to you earlier as an *auditor?* That means *listener only.* I'll thank you to keep your comments to yourself!"

"There there, Michelsen, with all our burdens, surely there's room for some levity!"

"Don't encourage her," Father replies, folding his arms and scowling.

"When our Ottawa plans are finalized," Mr. Smye resumes, "I will be sending out the itinerary by internal delivery to all Admin members and will require confirmation by return mail.

"Just an addendum: As is customary for out-of-town conferences, wives are welcome to accompany the contingent so as to partake in evening and other after-hour events. Confirmations will require a signature for statement of intent to that effect.

"Now let's get on with it, we have two more items on our agenda, and our time is limited as we must meet the others at 1:30."

"I still don't understand what can be so important that there must be a meeting on a Saturday," Father repeats, to no avail.

Land Claim Issue
1-2B

12:00 noon

"This brings us to the second item on the agenda," Mr. Smye says, "It was raised by Michelsen and vetted by Crawford, who briefed me this morning. I must warn you, however, that we have to make short shrift of this, due to the pressing issue that is third on the agenda. Over to you, Michelsen!"

Father clears his throat: "Thank you for providing the opportunity, Fred, to present my concern.

"Gents, the day after the Rollout, I was made aware through a very unusual set of circumstances that there is a disputed land claim with the Mississauga Indians which includes the land in Malton now owned by Avro. Last week, I took advantage of the time spent convalescing at home from that dreadful case of the flu, and phoned around to investigate the matter.

"The Malton Public Library gave me a lead to the Victoria College Archives at the University of Toronto. With the assistance of the archivist, some pieces of the puzzle started to fall into place.

"These clues were further substantiated by a visit to the Mississauga New Credit First Nation Reserve where I drove yesterday with my wife and daughter, en route to Niagara Falls. I must state categorically that the facts have been corroborated, my sources verified, and the basis for the unresolved land claim substantiated. As a result," he looks around anxiously, and then blurts nervously, "I found myself making a pact with the Chief Fred King of the Mississaugas to take whatever action I could to redress the situation."

The men look startled, and sit rigid as carved, wooden statues.

Father's whole demeanour is downcast. He doesn't want to look anyone in the eye and stares straight ahead.

"Far be it from me to presume to make such a promise," Father sighs, "But it was incumbent on me to do so. It was not so much a matter of false pride, as a matter of deep shame. With fully documented research in my hands that showed how the Mississauga Indians had been cheated, betrayed, and duped over the years, I was sorely embarrassed about our colonial forefathers' less than honourable conduct. It was excruciatingly painful while sitting directly across from the man representing those most offended."

Father looks so vulnerable, I could never have imagined seeing him like this. I had never thought of him as anyone other than the strong man who ruled our household with an iron fist, and had presumed he was as unquestionably in charge of the outside world as well.

Mr. Smye asks, "This land claim, Graham, how far back does it go?"

"It goes far back to the 'Gun Shot Treaty' in the late 1700s that took away a huge stretch of land north of Lake Ontario from the Bay of Quinty as far as Toronto. The Crown maintained that the Mississaugas had surrendered that land in exchange for gifts. That was what was called the 'First Toronto Purchase'. But from the outset, the Indians disagreed! They regarded those gifts as expressions of gratitude for their support during the War of Independence against the Americans, and for donating some of their own land to Loyalist Iroquois. Further along, there was a 'Second Toronto Purchase' that virtually nailed the so-called surrender of all lands to the west and north of Toronto, including Niagara as well as Malton and its adjacent townships. As for gifts, from the very first deal, the Mississaugas were promised annual gifts that would continue 'as long as the sun shone and the grass grew'. However, the Crown failed to honour the promise and the annual payments dried up!"

Mr. Floyd says, "Well, you've got to admit the Indians were pretty gullible, expecting to be paid forever!"

Mr. Smye asks, "Was it gullibility on the Indians' behalf or sheer chicanery on the Crown's behalf?"

Mr. Gordon offers his opinion, saying, "Listen here, the way I see it is: if those 'gifts' were seen as expressions of gratitude, they could also have been regarded by the Indians the same way as we view 'rent', or 'right to access'. The Indians knew that the British were far away from home, and needed somewhere to live. Since the Crown had valuable items which made a big difference to their comfort level, the Indians accepted gifts for letting them 'stay' or 'camp' on their land."

Mr. Floyd insists, "Yes, but to be paid in perpetuity! Wasn't that a bit much to expect?"

Mr. Gordon turns to him, "Since when does the average tenant rent to own? Surely asking a tenant for rent from one year to the next isn't too much to expect."

Mr. Floyd exclaims, "Oh, I see it now. What irony! What a reversal of fortunes! They thought they were the lessors and suddenly found they were the lessees!"

Mr. Gordon replies, "Exactly!"

There is a long pause as the men mull.

Then Mr. Smye offers, "In this day and age I, for one, am starting to understand how the Indians feel!"

"What do you mean?" Father's expression brightens, as he swivels his full attention toward him.

"The War has amply demonstrated how our own basic rights can be stripped away without any recourse to appeal. Likewise, we too have witnessed losing access to public places that have always been considered common to all. That's what happened to the Indians, just as easily as it could happen to us. Let's face it: what we own today is only that which the powers-that-be don't yet want until possibly tomorrow. Our own properties can be expropriated for a whole range of reasons, properties that we consider as valuable as the Indians viewed their rivers and their forests. Look how hectares upon hectares of fertile agricultural soil and fruit farms are being stripped away for the sake of highways, like the Queen Elizabeth Way, not to mention that atrocious 401 expressway, which have ruined farms, chopped up communities, and destroyed the viability of local villages."

"Hold on," Father interjects, "I moved house and home to be adjacent to the 401! It is saving me hours of commuting time."

Mr. Gordon replies, "Point taken, but point made! One man's gain is another man's loss. We are also witnessing other ironic reversals, such as the measures taken for the conservation of nature through the creation of provincial parks. This is all well and good, and should please us. However, it has ended up that the lands might be theoretically owned by the public, but public access has ended up restricted on the government's terms. One minute, nature's amenities are available to all. Next minute, a chain link fence is thrown up around its periphery, and there is an entrance fee along with opening/closing times."

"Well, you know," Mr. Gordon comments, wiping his bushy white moustache with his napkin, "I never gave a sweet flying—uh, lump of cow dung about the Indians before I moved from Calgary to Toronto." Leaning back on his chair legs, he continues, "But since moving to Baby Point, I've learned more about the Indians who lived in this very area. I have often found myself wondering how the Indians who populated this territory felt, thinking they had been granted perpetual free run of the place, suddenly having all their rights of access systematically removed, unable to fish or hunt when they were given guarantees by the Crown that they could do so, turned off land they didn't believe they had given away without so much of a how-de-do, in the course of which forced to endure so many broken promises! They were deprived of their livelihood, left without a pot to piss in, if you'll excuse the expression, ladies. If anyone were so inclined to follow their story, he'd learn from the time any major treaties were signed, persecution of the Indians has continued to go on and on to this very day."

Mr. Floyd wonders, "If their treaties were violated, why didn't they sue for breach of contract?"

Father is quick to reply, "Having just had a crash course on aboriginal legal rights, I'll ask if you knew that the 1927 amendment of the Indian Act prohibited solicitation of funds for legal claims without special licence from the Superintendent General of Indian Affairs, which—get this! just happened to be a cabinet position since 1876. Talk about being hog-tied! This pretty much put an end to any appeals and sewed up government control, quashing any aboriginal grievances, including land claims! It has meant that dismissal of their claims has gone on unimpeded as always, ever since. Nothing much changed in this regard with the recent 1952 Act."

"What does living on Baby Point have to do with Indian rights?" Mr. Floyd asks.

Mr. Gordon explains, "My wife and I fell in love with our house up on the plateau. We loved its proximity to the city yet its seclusion. We had no idea about that area's previous history. Turns out that it is one of the last parcels of land still 'claimed' by the Indians in the Toronto area, aside from landmarks in Toronto proper such as the Queen Street asylum grounds which were their sacred council grounds, Centre Island which was their place of healing, and a wide strip along the Queensway up and around the Humber River. The area now called Baby Point was part of that parcel.

"Up top, the site where we live used to be an Indian village called Teiaiagon. It was a strategic position located high up on the only plateau in the region where you can see forever, giving out over the mouth of the Humber River. That was a major travel route for the Indians on their annual migrations north to their spiritual homelands near Sault St. Marie, and later for the French fur trade. Brulé, de la Salle, the Franciscan Recollet missionary Hennepin all visited this village, which was huge! Hennepin recorded more than 5,000 inhabitants. To give you some idea, Teiaiagon had over 50 longhouses!"

My ears perk up. "Longhouses?" I interrupt.

"Yes, they lived together in long, oval-shaped structures. They were built much the same way as wigwams, with bent interlocking willow branches for the frame, and the whole works covered with birch bark for protection from wind and rain. An extended family would share it. It had several openings in the roof for fires."

My mind spins. I hear my voice ask: "Did the 'long, oval-shaped structures' have wheels?" to which Mr. Gordon replies, "Ha ha! Good one! Wouldn't they have loved to have dwellings like Airstream house trailers built on wheels for their annual migrations!! No no, my dear, these longhouses were permanent, and with neither aluminum roof or siding. Unlike their wigwams, which they dismantled and took with them, they left the longhouses standing for their return. Although come to think of it, curiously enough, they called those buildings waginogans!"

I look meaningfully at Mother, and then at Father.

"Not now, Lois!" Father commands.

"At any rate," Mr. Gordon resumes, "that whole plateau had a long and flourishing history until the French arrived, and then the British. By that time, the Mississauga had driven out the invading Iroquois, but their own occupation was destined to be short-lived in comparison with the centuries their aboriginal predecessors had lived there."

Mr. Smye breaks through, asking, "I trust that we are still addressing the land claim issue on hand?"

Mr. Gordon nods, "Leading up to the purchase by James Baby in the early 1800s, there were outstanding claims against the entire tract of land, which had been left relatively undisturbed.

"When Baby bought it, he grew apple orchards there—"

"That's true! I saw one remaining apple tree in the clearing!" I exclaimed, with a discouraging glare from Father.

"Despite his own and Mississauga objections, the government bought the entire tract for a fortress and army barracks. Afterward, with the American threat settled, there was no more need for that and those structures were torn down."

"It was sold one century later in 1912 to a Robert Home Smith who selected the choice property and built what is now my house. There were still the Mississauga land claims. However, true to form, local officials supported by the Crown opted to disregard them.

"It was only after we moved in that I learned how the Indians were cheated out of their rights to Baby Point. The fact that there is a land claim right where my own house now stands has continued to rest heavily on my conscience. I have done nothing about it. What to do? Do I give my house and property to the Mississaugas, or hand over just the assessed value in cash? Either way, the former or the latter, I cannot afford because I would end up with nothing. It's a tough one to equivocate."

Father opens his mouth, and then shuts it again.

I look at him, expectantly.

He feels me eyeing him.

"It's rare to hear folks speak in defence of the Indians and their land claims," Father says, tentatively.

"That's for darn sure!" Mr. Floyd says, to my surprise, "You wouldn't hear the likes of this conversation where I come from. I grew up in Napanee near the Bay of Quinte, a small southeastern Ontario town not too far from the Tyendinaga Indian reserve. All I heard about the Indians while growing up there was from people badmouthing them. The natives hung around the liquor store, mooching for nickels. The townsfolk lambasted them for being drunken louts, troublemakers and useless bums. There were constant complaints about them getting everything for free from the government and not having to pay taxes, not having to work. Why don't they 'getta job', so forth and so on!! For a stretch, the townsfolk almost succeeded in running them out of town. There were laws passed that banned them from leaving the Reserve. If they did and caused a row, they were jailed for disorderly conduct, fined for possessing liquor and packed off back to the Reserve.

"My Mother says that the downtown is still teeming with drunken Indians, pestering the shoppers for handouts! She complains about how uncouth they are, and unkempt! She says, 'I understand they're poor, but can't they at least have a shower and wash their hair?!' "

"With due respect to your mother, doesn't she realize the townsfolk are victimizing the victims?" Mr. Gordon cautions.

Mr. Floyd counters: "The prevalent attitude to this day is that the Indians have it good, much better than anyone else, and they'd live better if they didn't 'piss' all their government money away on alcohol. They say the Church takes care of them where the Government leaves off, that between the food and clothing drives and government money, they have more safety nets than the average Joe!"

There is tension in the air.

I sense that the conversation had taken a turn, and the men were all working silently on how to retrieve it. In a way, I can see that they had covered both sides of the argument, and either way both sides were just about as right as they were wrong.

"The way I see it," Mr. Smye says, "Nothing can be done to resolve the situation unless something major changes."

Again, Father says nothing.

Mr. Gordon dares to upset the balance, by saying, "Right. And that means change of attitude. What strikes me profoundly is that the Indian has had nothing but an uphill battle against compounded public ignorance, which is the result of indoctrination handed down from the government via our biased public education system. The government's so-called 'assimilation' policy is nothing more than an attempt to wipe them out."

"Whoa! Those are harsh words!" Mr. Floyd objects.

"Not really!" Mr. Gordon rejoins, "Sugarcoat it if you will, there is a fine line between relentless persecution and outright annihilation. First, tell them to act more like white man and adopt his ways. Then if they succeed, strip them of their achievements and pack the whole lot of them back to a reserve."

I say: "That's what happened to Chief Peter Jones of the Mississaugas. He took the advice of the white man to heart, and did his best to assimilate. He built up a fine, flourishing business community at Port Credit, only to have his businesses confiscated and his properties expropriated, then his people were moved away to land further north that could not be farmed."

The men pause and look at me.

I wish Father had said that.

Mr. Gordon carries on. "Exactly. Punish them if they succeed. Strip them of any achievement. Force them to live communally on designated land. Make sure it's land that's not arable. Don't let them own their own property. Don't let them run their own businesses. Remove their livelihoods. Make them live on dole. Interfere with every element of their culture by foisting white man's religion on them. Punish them for speaking their own native language, for observing their ancient traditions. Find ways to ridicule them, and tear away their self-respect in every way you can. Hey, control their upbringing, let the church take away their children, send them to residential schools! These poor souls have been badgered, beaten, and beleaguered, and we consider ourselves civilized!"

"No, I'm afraid we just consider ourselves superior," Mr. Smye says.

"What they have left is a stalwart pride in their own survival," Mr. Gordon asserts, "I doubt that any of us could withstand such ruthless attempts at outright exterminatiaon."

"I'm hearing 'reluctant admiration' in your words," Mr. Smye says.

"Indeed," Mr. Gordon replies, ruefully, "Growing up out west in Calgary, we were taught very little about the Indians, let alone much about their history, or their status after they were supposedly 'conquered' ".

He makes air commas with his fingertips.

"It turns out, I learned later, that the Indians in Canada weren't conquered after all! After the War of Independence, the Americans declared their own Indians 'conquered' but not the British, who continued to honour King George III's Royal Proclamation of 1763. It granted them full rights. The Indians regard that pact as their own Magna Carta."

"That is what Chief Fred King told us!" I cry, "But that's not what we are taught in school!"

Father has been listening on in disbelief. His eyes are the size of golf balls. I wait for him to say something. But he remains resolutely silent.

I am compelled once again to dip in my oar. "Can anything be done to appeal the Mississauga land claim?"

Mother kicks me under the table and looks meaningfully at Father.

Father glares at me, and continues to say nothing.

"Not a snowball's chance in hell," Mr. Gordon replies, "To our great and everlasting shame, those poor suckers are screwed. Let's hope our own rights and freedoms don't meet the same fate!!"

Father shifts in his seat and looks immensely uncomfortable. I could sense he is trying to summon up courage from somewhere inside of himself to say something but his tongue seems to be tied.

Mother looks at him, anxiously waiting for him to speak, and getting more annoyed by the minute.

To my surprise, I hear my own voice pipe up again, despite tattooed ankles, and Father glowering at me.

I cry out, "The Indians trusted the white man! Those men who represented the Crown and deceived the Indians were shysters—and—and charlatans! They knowingly and deliberately abused the Royal Proclamation and cheated the Mississaugas out of their land! They are not the honourable men we have learned about at school. They were nothing but thieves—robber barons! We are taught to respect our country's forefathers but how can we, if it turns out they were nothing but scoundrels whose accumulated wealth was based on theft, duplicity and outright larceny?"

I feel the entire room rock violently. My cheeks turn hot and red. I shudder with dread that I had overstepped my bounds and I am about to be punished severely in a way I do not yet know how. I feel my Self swimming hard, trying to maintain my balance. Battling against a force that is threatening to subsume me, that sets my head to spinning inside a giant whirlpool, I struggle to hold my own.

I find more courage building up inside me.

I hear myself speaking again, "It's disgraceful how the Mississaugas were rooked by the British for the land that is now Toronto! Do you know how much the Mississaugas were paid in 1805 for that entire tract?"

Mr. Smye responds, "How much?"

"Ten shillings."

"Get away with you!" Mr. Smye exclaims.

"No way!" Mr. Floyd cries.

"How do you know that?" Mr. Gordon prods.

Dumbfounded silence.

But I haven't finished, it seems, "On top of that travesty, Mr. Gordon, do you know how the Mississaugas were cheated only just recently of the remaining parcel west of Toronto, close to Baby Point?"

"How?"

"A treaty dealing with that area was signed in 1923 with seven other bands. But guess what? Because the Credit River Mississauga Nation people had already been removed through trickery to the New Credit reservation near Six Nations in Brantford, they were excluded in the 1923 agreement and duped out of their share in that settlement!"

Mr. Gordon looks at me seriously, "This is rather arcane knowledge for a girl your age! What grade are you in again?"

"Grade nine!"

Mr. Floyd interjects, "You are one smart cookie! Graham, you've got a right young whippersnapper on your hands!"

Father says grimly, "Getting too smart for her own good."

I glance at him, see him frowning his disapproval and I hear Mother say, "Since when?"

"Lois, you might just be the next generation that the Ojibway have been waiting for!" Mr. Gordon asserts. "They call it the Seventh Fire, when the Light Coloured Race comes to terms with native values and people learn to live honourably with one another. That's a prediction according to their legend in their Book of Mishomis!"

I sense Mr. Smye rising up, leaning across the table toward me. He asks me, "How, pray tell, young lady, did you become so involved in this issue?"

His question flows across the gulf beween us, and slams into me like a tidal wave.

Now I understand why Father wants to shut me down.

How should I answer that question? Where would I begin? Was I supposed to say that an Eagle had protected me from the Red Eft in the woods (which Father himself didn't even know about), and he befriended me by the gift of his feather? That the Mississauga turned out to belong to the Eagle clan? That it was through Eagle's influence that I saw Chief Peter Jones at the Rollout? Is that where it all began? Is that how it all happened? Not even I know that for sure.

Father remains silent.

I can see Father's chin quivering. He is afraid on two counts, afraid to tell the truth himself, and afraid I'll beat him to it.

Mr. Smye looks at Father for a long time as though apprising him.

He has landed the one bomb shell in Father's lap that he has been trying to avoid. "Michelsen, want to fill us in on how you yourself got involved in all this?"

Father swallows hard.

"I knew this was coming. I have honestly been reluctant to say, as it all sounds so preposterous! I must ask that you all keep this confidential until such time, if ever, it might be appropriate to share any further."

"Try us!"

"You have ten minutes before we absolutely must move on to the next item on the agenda," Mr. Smye warns.

"Well, here goes. The day after the Rollout, my daughter Lois told me she saw Indian braves dancing in a circle in front of the Arrow hangar just before the ceremony began. Suddenly, they stopped and in unison shot arrows in the air over the presentation platform. At that, they vanished. To her, they seemed very real at the time, but later on, she came to agree that they were phantoms.

"While I was delivering my speech, she told me she saw an Indian Chief standing in the same location where the Indian braves had been dancing, facing the presentation platform. She was able to describe every detail of the man, his dress, his unusual headdress, the objects he held in his hands, his medallion. Again, the apparition seemed real to her. Now she knows that it was an illusion, what she has learned is a 'waking vision'.

"I will admit that all this upset me terribly. My daughter seeing phantoms? Her report, along with the decimating disappointment with the Sputnik the day before, seemed like the last straw. It almost put me under. But something drove me to pursue the matter further. Was there any substance behind what Lois had seen? As soon as I could, I took action. Thinking perhaps that she had a residual memory from having seen this Chief somewhere before, I endeavoured to ascertain that possibility. She had not. His image does not appear in any source, either museum or textbook, that she might have seen. It turned out that her descriptions of the Chief's dress and some of his appurtenances jibed with photographs provided by the archivist at the Victoria College at the University of Toronto, but they were not conclusive. At the New Credit First Nation Reserve, there was a photograph shown us by an elder, that very Chief Peter Jones' own great granddaughter, Paula Jones, who encouraged my daughter Lois to call her Aunt Ani. The photograph clinched it for us all. In it, the Chief was wearing a unique headdress that Lois had described. Likewise, he was carrying a unique object that only he would possess. Who Lois saw was real and not sheer fantasy!"

Mother is compelled to dip in her oar. She says, "Mrs. Jones is an elder of the Mississauga clan who defended Lois, explaining to us that Lois has a gift. 'There is nothing wrong with 'waking visions',' she said, 'Many people have them but in white man's culture, they are suppressed and denied, since it is taboo, as is seeing ghosts. Acknowledging their substance would mean accepting that there are more planes of existence than formal religion permits, a fact I have found very difficult to swallow as I am religious, and follow the dictates of the Church. "

"Your daughter Lois here saw the ghost of a deceased Mississauga Chief," Mr. Smye comments.

"Yes," Father says, "He was Chief Peter Jones, born 1802, died 1856. He rescued the Mississaugas from assimilation, and established a home for them on the Credit River, later New Credit. He fought his whole life to redress the injustices of the Toronto Purchases."

The men take a moment to pause and reflect.

Perhaps Mr. Floyd senses Father's discomfort, for he decides to be first to speak.

"Well, I for one," Mr. Floyd says, looking around at his fellows, "would not be ashamed or embarrassed about seeing ghosts. I myself have seen one, and others have also told me about such occurrences."

"Really?" Father reacts, his shoulders slackening, his head wobbling, as though he might pass out with a combination of relief and disbelief. I notice how his eyes are half-closed and seem bruised, with large creased bags under each of them. He looks as though he has aged about twenty years.

"Same here," Mr. Smye contributes, "In all confidence, the ghost of my Grandfather appeared at the foot of my bed, shortly after his death. No mistaking who he was. He drew near. He was so close to me, I reached out and passed my hand through him. It shook me to the roots of my boots!"

Mr. Gordon says, "Normally the sighting of a ghost is connected with a family member—Or it is a vestige of some local murder. But to experience a visitation from the beyond by an historical figure is extraordinary. Nonetheless, I buy Graham's story. Why else not?"

"It wasn't a story, Mr. Gordon," I say, "It was the truth."

Father lifts his hand to silence me, "I can't tell you how reassuring it is to hear this. I have been terrified of being mocked, knowing that to be a real possibility but not knowing what to do or where to turn. I only know that I can't handle this alone. Please tell me you're not just humouring me. I don't want to be the laughing stock of Avro after everything I've done till now to establish a creditable reputation, let alone serve to bring a superb aircraft like the Arrow into fruition!"

Mr. Smye asks, "You have discovered the purpose behind these apparitions?"

"Yes," Father replies.

"Which would be?"

"A direct appeal from Chief Peter Jones to redress the injustice of the 1805 Treaty!"

"But the Treaty has already been signed, sealed and delivered!"

"So claimed, but as I said, it was obtained through duplicity and there is an outstanding land claim!"

There is a prolonged silence.

Mr. Smye speaks again, "Several factors are puzzling me. Why did the Chief appear at the Rollout? Why Lois? Why Malton? And what did you, Graham, have to do with him?"

"I learned that it was Chief Peter Jones' predecessors of the Eagle clan, who signed the Toronto Purchase at Malton. In their tradition, each ensuing Chief assumes responsibility for what their forefathers did before. So the mantle of responsibility fell on his shoulders. You ask: why me? How to account for the connection with myself? The only possible explanation must be due to Lois's gift for 'waking visions' combined with the blood tie due to the fact I'm her father, and there is my job at Avro and my work on the Arrow. It was all either entirely coincidental, or, because, as Chief Fred King proposed, I was the one extolling the Arrow—our own Avro Arrow of course—which Chief Peter Jones might have construed as the 'arrow' itself, which of course is the traditional weapon used by the Indians. Even to me, it is a bit of a long shot, if you'll excuse the pun. Along a similar vein, however, Chief Fred King proposed that I might have unwittingly summoned Chief Jones when I extolled the Orenda engine. That, too, seemed far-fetched until he informed me that the word 'Orenda' means 'soul' or 'spirit' in the native tongue. There was another rather ironic twist: the way I pronounce 'engine' might have been misinterpreted. To Chief Peter Jones, I might have been exhorting the appearance of an 'Injun' when I was extolling the imminent supersonic jetfighter called the Arrow with its Orenda *Engine*."

Father looks sheepish.

I speak out, "There is also the matter of what Chief Peter Jones held outstretched in his open hand the second time I saw him!"

"What was that, Lois?" Mr. Smye asks.

"Ten silver coins."

All the men's eyes open wide.

For a moment, time is suspended until Mr. Smye says, "It is time to make a decision about how to proceed. As curious and confounding as this is, there is no denying there is considerable substance to Michelsen's petition. Admittedly, the first reflex is to reject the entire issue as preposterous, to say that it can be easily sloughed off as irrelevant, and to regard the present land claim that has stood the test of time as permanently settled."

My body starts to quake.

"On the other hand," Mr. Smye continues, "what would be the consequences if it were ever determined that Avro does not hold full title to Avro land? Considering the capital that has already been poured into its operations, would it not be propitious to be proactive and initiate action to settle the matter now, thereby offsetting any lengthy lawsuits in the future? My question is: what would the basis for any appeal lodged by Avro? The action would have to be purely economic in its motivation, but there are also compelling ethical reasons for pursuing this injustice. Has an appeal ever been lodged for ethical reasons?"

Mr. Gordon asks: "Theoretically, if a party has been wronged, it is the wronged party that takes action, most likely through a class action suit."

"Exactly," Mr. Smye replies, "Suppose that Avro takes the initiative by seeking resolution of the land claim by opening it up with the Government for review. What would be the legal role we would assume? As much as our ulterior motive would be to correct the injustices committed to the Mississauga, we would have no recourse but to make our role appear as though we wanted to take action out of self-interest and not in defense of the Mississauga interests!"

Mr. Floyd says, "It's true. It would have to be handled carefully to avoid setting a legal precedent wherein the pot ends up calling its own kettle black."

Mr. Smye's retort: "You grasped my point but I'm not sure if that's an accurate analogy."

After a pause, Mr. Smye asks: "Anyone want to move for further action?"

Mr. Floyd raises his hand. What he says surprises me, since he had given the impression he didn't care much about Indians, "I move that this Mississauga land claim issue, on the premise that it has the potential to adversely affect the security of Avro properties, be added to the roster as a matter that warrants further action."

This motion is seconded by Mr. Gordon.

Mr. Floyd hurriedly jots down what he said, hesitating at times to recall the wording, as it was rather a lengthy and tortuous sentence.

I pipe up.

"What does 'further action' mean? Does it mean that it will be addressed some time in the future, or will action will be taken immediately?"

"We'll see, we'll see. All in good time," Mr. Gordon responds.

I feel as though he is patting me on the head, either to placate me or worse, to shut me down. This infuriates me.

I say, "What about your own house, Mr. Gordon? Are you hoping this whole land claim issue will slide by until enough time has passed so far into the future, you won't have to cede your Baby Point property to the Mississaugas?"

The men lean back and look at me with arched eyebrows.

Father is aghast, his face a white sheet.

Mother yelps, reaches out and places a reprimanding hand on mine. She would have covered my mouth if she could. "She's over-tired, Gentlemen, do forgive her outburst. It's been a very stressful time for us all."

It is Mr. Gordon who recuperates first. He lets out a bellow that can be heard throughout the restaurant. "Ha ha ha!!" he shouts, "Touché! Good one, Lois!"

Rogue Agents
1-2C

12:40 p.m.

Mr. Smye looks at his watch. "It's now 12:45, we're due in Centrewood at 1:30. Allowing fifteen minutes for travel to Centrewood, we have thirty minutes on the outside for the third and last item on our agenda. May I emphasize that this matter is of paramount importance and requires our undivided attention."

He looks very serious, very grim.

"Graham, I want you to know that Crawford, Floyd and I together agreed from the outset that you must be informed immediately about the following development. As unusual as it is to have your wife and daughter attend an Admin meeting, it is imperative that you be enlightened, for reasons that will soon become evident."

Mr. Smye's eyes focus on Father.

"We have a crisis on our hands, Graham. Certain events have taken place about which you need to be informed. This is the time to bring you up to date."

"This past Monday, October 7, the weekend after the Rollout, Pesando was accosted by uniforms on his doorstep when leaving his home. He was wheeled about on his heel, and taken back inside his house, where he was interrogated by two agents who claimed to be with the RCMP. He baulked when they refused to supply any identification. With some strong-arming—he claims he was roughed up somewhat—they forced him to retrieve vital pieces of identification from private files he kept locked up in his home office. Afterward, he had to fill out a questionnaire that demanded detailed personal information about his past."

Father opens his mouth to speak. Mr. Smye lifts his finger.

"The following morning, on Tuesday October 8, after parking his car in the Avro lot, Zurakowski was escorted—or 'frog-marched' in his words—to an unmarked car, where he was stuffed into the back seat, and driven off the Avro grounds to the shoulder of Malton Road. There he was interrogated by what sounds to be the same two men. Before gaining his release, he had to complete the same kind of questionnaire as described by Pesando."

"What was going on? What authority did these agents have?" Father asks.

"Exactly what I have been trying to find out. These two interrogations led me to wonder if this was the end of it. If not, who else might be on their hit list?"

"If it were me, I'd be asking what Pesando and Zurakowski have in common," Father contributes.

Mr. Smye nods.

"There is a third incident to report. On Thursday, the day before yesterday, Sanderfield was pulled over on the Centrewood Main Artery by what sounds like the same outfit—"

"Sanderfield?" Father interrupts.

"Yes, they ordered him to turn around and return home. He complied, closely followed by their unmarked car. Once inside his house, he was subjected to a battery of questions, while they rigorously filled out the same sort of questionnaire as the others, before letting him go."

"Sanderfield picked up three very important bits of information during their visit. First, on Sanderfield's insistence, they finally provided him with formal identification, their badges identifying themselves as RCMP intelligence agents under the Criminal Investigation Branch.

"Second, one of the agents let slip that the questionnaire was called a 'C-215' form."

Impatient, Father interrupts again: "What did they want from him?"

"Proof of some sort that he is not and has never been a Communist sympathizer."

"Sanderfield? He is a true-blue Canadian, born and educated in Ontario, same as myself."

"As if that would preclude his ideology? He was questioned why he didn't serve in the War. He explained that although he was not in the military, nonetheless, he had still been part of the war effort, as he had worked on the Canadian team in close collaboration with the Brits and the Yanks on a top-secret radar project at the Rad Lab at MIT. When he supplied them with proof of same, they let him go."

Mr. Smye looked around at everyone: "Each of these interventions constitutes an unconscionable breach of authority, invasion of privacy, appalling ignorance and colossal disrespect.

"Sanderfield, as you well know, is our radar expert in charge of the advanced radar dishes and tracking system for the Arrow. He comes from a long and auspicious line of physicists starting with the inventor, Watson-Watt at Bawdsey Manor in Suffolk back in '36, whose Chain Home system helped the Royal Air Force to win the

Battle of Britain. His top-notch performance is everything to laud, with absolutely nothing required to justify."

"Hear, hear!" the men say in chorus.

Father demands: "But why were Pesando and Zurakowski detained and questioned? What possible reason would there be?"

"Well, as you know, Pesando came here recently from Argentina. As a civilian aeronautical engineer, he worked throughout the Peron regime at the nation's Aerospace Centre. That is where Latin America's first fighter jet interceptor, the 'Pusqui II' (coincidentally, Spanish for 'Arrow') was being developed. In the late '40s, the much-touted engineer and designer Kurt Tank joined the team. He was a post-War emigré from Germany, and was the creator of several jetfighters in the German Luftwaffe.

"Two years ago, there was the coup d'état that threw Juan Peron out of office. Eduardo Lonardi, the junta leader, saw fit to immediately lay off all employees at the Aerospace Centre. All staff was dispersed. Tank was enticed to India. We enticed Pesando to come here. Because of his expertise, we were more than eager to sponsor him when he applied for Canadian citizenship."

"So why would he be cross-examined now? Wouldn't his eligibility for citizenship have been vetted at point of entry?" Father asks.

"Exactly the question I posed to him. It seems that there is a political cloud that still hangs heavy over his head, with little likelihood of its ever being expunged. Even though he was not politically active in Argentina, he was labelled a loyalist under the Peron regime and therefore at odds with the new military government. Peron himself had already been under an international cloud of suspicion, not because of any questionable actions internally, but because he refused to comply with U.S. aspirations for a Pan-Latin American League. He declared Argentina as a 'Third Position' country, that is, not a member among the Allies, but no friend of the Axis either; in other words, neutral. But America suspected him as a Fascist. You know Americans: if you're not This, you've gotta be That. Add to this stance his close collaboration with Tank, who of course, coming from Germany, was automatically labelled as a Nazi sympathizer. These negative credentials found their way into Canadian national security files. Pesando figures he could be hung on both pegs and left swinging on either, if anyone wished to nail him."

"What were the RCMP charges?"

"There were none. He was detained, but not arrested. He was not charged, but cautioned."

"Meaning?"

"His political activities will be tracked from now on. Also, he must report in to RCMP headquarters, if any of his particulars happen to change."

"Well now, isn't that a fine how-de-do!" Father remarked, in disbelief, "And Zurakowski?"

"Before the War, Zurakowski was born on a border in Poland that switched hands between the Russian Empire and Poland, then Soviet Russia and the Polish Republic. Growing up in that muddle would be enough to addle anyone's brains. However, his parents were adamantly Polish. He fought in the Polish Airforce against Germany. When Poland was defeated by the Germans and suffered under the Occupation, he made his way to France where he fought with his compatriots in the Battle of France. Afterward, he found his way to England where he flew Spitfires, shooting down German Messerschmidts. After the war, he stayed in England as a fighter trainer and an experimental test pilot, famous for his 'Zurabatic Cartwheel' with the Gloser Meteor."

"What was that, Mr. Smye?" I ask, hoping politeness will spare any more tattooing on my ankle.

"It was a famous aerobatic manoeuvre created by Zurakowski himself. It starts with a vertical climb to 4,000 feet, at which point the Meteor is slowed to 80 mph. The power of one engine is cut. Then the aircraft pivots until the nose is pointing downwards. When the second engine is throttled back, the aircraft will continue to rotate through a further 360 degrees on momentum alone until losing nearly all velocity. At this point, the pilot must carry out the cartwheel and recover from it without entering into an inverted spin, which the Meteor itself lacks the controls to avert."

"You mean the plane must pull out of the cartwheel right-side up or crash?" I ask.

"You've got it!"

"He invented the aerial loop-the-loop!" I exclaim, my eyes wide open, as I imagine flying straight up into the air, then cutting an engine to soar momentarily upside down.

I turn to Father and say, "He would be classified as a 'Top Notch' type of daredevil. He wouldn't be the 'Idiot' type, would he, Father!"

"By no means," Father coughs.

"Zurakowski invented more than that. After he came to Avro in 1952, he was the first to break the sound barrier. He flew the CF-100 in an aerobatic display called the 'falling leaf', which I will leave to your imagination. He has proven himself to be daring and fearless! At this crucial moment, he is our highly esteemed, designated test pilot for the Arrow, which with our much-heralded, new Orenda Iroquois engine installed, will be taking its maiden flight next March. We are proud to have Janusz as one of our own."

Mr. Smye's eyes start to look watery.

"Why was he detained?" Father asks.

"He has been informed that, because of his life as a youth under Russian rule, he is under surveillance as a Communist sympathizer. Also, because he was in Poland during the German Occupation before he fled, it is thought he could have been tainted by Nazism."

"What happened in the end?"

"The end result was pretty much the same as Pesando's. After rigorous cross-examination, he was given permission to proceed as normal, but with a caution that he remains under suspicion, and henceforth his activities will be tracked."

"How's that for an oxymoron?" Mr. Gordon asks, bushy white eyebrows raised.

"A world-renowned pilot! An acclaimed war hero! How do you like dem apples?" Mr. Floyd asks, splaying his hands.

"But how can this be?" Father exhales, "The man risked life and limb for the Allies!"

Mr. Gordon states, "The remaining question is: Who are these ruffians? Are they really with the RCMP? Are they legitimate officers? Or, are they rogue agents, functioning beyond the arm of the law?"

"Any idea why these three men in particular have been targeted?" Father asks, "Is that the end of it, or, who else might be on their hit list? Any idea?"

"Exactly the question I have been working on," Mr. Smye replies.

Father is impatient. "What have you come up with?"

Mr. Smye says, "I mentioned that there were three bits of information I picked up, thanks to Sanderfield. I've told you about two. The third still seems like a slender lead. All I have to go on is something one of the agents said to Sanderfield when they were at his house. He had given the agents a rough time during the course of his interview, refusing to cooperate, challenging their right to invade his privacy, defending his civil rights. As the agents became more forceful and the altercation escalated to fisticuffs, fearing he might be carted off, he managed to break away, and made a dash to his car, hoping to get to his mobile phone to call out, and to lock himself in until help arrived. I'll remind you that it was Sanderfield who was the third CEO designate on rotation to mind the mobile phone network along with Crawford and myself over the shutdown. He didn't make it. Sanderfield was hauled back into the house kicking and shouting. In a rage, one of the agents warned him not to try any other tricks or they might give you, Michelsen, an even worse time on Saturday afternoon when they were planning to come and pay a visit on you. The other agent chewed him out royally for leaking that information."

"Me?" Father cries out.

"Yes."

"So that explains the urgency," Father mutters.

"And why the meeting is at our house," Mother adds.

There is a stunned moment while this last bomb drops. This is not news to Mr. Gordon or Mr. Floyd. I watch them wait for Father and Mother to grasp the significance.

"Why these four, I have kept asking myself," Mr. Smye says. "They are all CEOs. Was it merely coincidental that they were among the dignitaries attending the Arrow Rollout? Could it be that these renegades are using the dignitaries' names on the programme as their prospective hit list? I began investigating the status of others on the list that might be eligible as potential targets, and determined that the majority of the remainder were Brass, all of whom could be readily eliminated, as they were all military and served in the War. Surely, I reasoned, these men must have had rigorous security clearance and if tracked, would prove to have impeccable attendance records with no opportunity for any monkey business with foreign operators.

"In the end, it came down to four men on Admin who had not served in the Armed Forces during the War. They are Pesando, Zurakowski, Sanderfield and yourself. Only you, Michelsen, as far as these agents are concerned, remain as a potential question mark."

Mother gasps. Father lets out a croak.

"But he served his country!" Mother cries. "He was seconded from Downsview by DeHavilland England to work as aircraft engineer at Hatfield. I can testify to that because I too was seconded from my job in London to work as an aircraft interior designer. That's how we met! He worked 24/7. He never left the base except when we dated. He was no spy, for Pete's sake!"

"All of this is based on sheer conjecture. None of this absolves anyone else at the moment, as we are still in the dark as to what it is, precisely, that they are looking for, let alone who is their command-ing officer. Nonetheless, at a top secret Admin meeting yesterday, it was agreed, on the basis you are among the four who did not serve in the Armed Forces, that you might also be targeted as a Communist sympathizer. Also, due to that leak by the agent, you might be lined up as their next target. If so, we shall attempt to intercept them this afternoon."

"We'll cut them off at the pass!" Mr. Gordon roars.

"What's the plan, Fred?" Father asks.

"We formed a network to keep tabs on everyone else on Admin over this Thanksgiving weekend. Everyone has been put on standby. Crawford, Sanderfield and I have maintained constant direct contact through both our home and mobile phones. But no one was able to contact you, Michelsen. As I said, Sanderfield went round to your house several times yesterday, and telephoned this morning. You were not there. Our greatest hopes were that you had taken your family away for a Thanksgiving break. Our worst fears were that you, and possibly your family had been 'intercepted' if not worse, 'disappeared', as we do not know the extent of their powers.

"Needless to say, your absence exacerbated the situation. I was uneasy. If the agents did not find you at home, how urgent was their mission? What were the chances they might break in to get whatever they were after?"

"Break in?" Father yelps.

Mr. Smye reaches out and places one hand on Father's arm. "Rest assured, your house remains intact as of this date. You see, just in case the agent meant what he said, I commandeered two of our Avro security guards to stake out your house over the long weekend, since last evening until today, at least until you turned up, if not longer. They have been connected up with our mobile phone network.

Father looks at the three men present in alarm. "What do they want from me? From all of us? What is this C-215 form all about?"

Mr. Smye looks about the restaurant and lowers his voice. "I'm not sure. At first, I thought it was an attempt by the P.M. to undermine or disparage or tarnish us in some way."

"You mean 'dirty tricks'? Is he capable of that?"

Mr Smye lifts his hands. "Initially I thought, if Diefenbaker is the cause of this harassment, and if it has to do with discrediting the Arrow, it's time for us to make a move, before he succeeds in shutting us down entirely! But after the panic subsided, I asked myself: what would be his motive? What would he achieve? There would be no need to hassle or intimidate us. If he wants to see Avro canned, he has the power to cancel the whole operation. So why undermine us by hitting us below the belt, one by one? My thoughts therefore moved on to the RCMP. At first, I suspected that there were only these two rogue agents, but I set that notion aside, mainly because of the existence of this peculiar C-215 form, which is indicative of some sort of central documentation file. There was also the way that the agent I.D.'ed himself to Sanderfield as an agent from the 'Criminal Investigation Branch'. I have since verified its existence, and have concluded that these activities really might have something to do with the RCMP itself.

"Was it possible, was the next question I asked myself, that the RCMP was exceeding their authority by attempting to weed out Communists and/or Communist sympathizers by screening all Canadian citizens at large? Had they expanded their powers to include domestic surveillance?"

Father says, "Are you saying that we now have our own Secret Police?"

Mr. Smye says, "I phoned around and talked in confidence with several personal contacts inside the RCMP apparatus. I heard, on the q.t., you understand, that there is indeed a top secret RCMP operation, spawned within the Criminal Investigation Branch, named the 'Special Branch', the purpose of which is to identify and track suspected Communist sympathizers in our midst, in the event that there is a war with the Soviet Union."

"Good Lord, Fred! You tapped a mole inside the RCMP?" Father exclaims.

"All due to a mouthy agent who said too much for his own good!" Mr. Floyd adds.

"Would you call that a leak inside a leak?" Mr. Gordon quips.

"Has the public been informed of this 'Special Branch'? I've never heard of it!" Father asks.

"No one has," Mr. Smye replied, "To boot, no Canadian citizens have an inkling if they are on the black list of suspects due for roundup on M-Day."

"What the hell is M-Day?"

"Mobilization Day. When the Russians attack."

"And then?"

"According to my source, everyone on the list will be gathered up, deposited in holding centres, and held without bail until the war ends. The sweep will include whole families. Men will be separated from their wives and children. None can be traced. They will, in effect, be 'disappeared'."

"Tell me you're joking," Father says.

"I'm not."

Father opens his mouth to speak: "So if any one of us disappears, is that a sign that the Russians have attacked? Is that why you all wondered where I was?"

Mr. Smye cuts Father short, indicating he has more to say.

"I did my best to find authorization for creation of this Special Branch. In order to pursue this line, I was able to determine the chain of command above the RCMP. Turns out that the head of the RCMP is the Commissioner, Stuart Wood, who is directly responsible to the Solicitor General of Canada, Leon Balcer. I reached the Commissioner directly, who maintained that any word about a 'Special Branch' was all rumours, nothing but stuff and nonsense.

Next, I had the privilege of a private consultation with the Solicitor General, who categorically denied it all as utter rubbish.

"It was only afterwards that I learned that the Solicitor General is on the Privy Council and is also a member of Cabinet.

"Initially, when Canada was formed, he was not. Surely, in principle, the Solicitor General of Canada should be an independent pillar of government. As it was, upon construction or our system, the Solicitor General was to play a vital role in the fragile system of checks and balances. As it is now, I have been forced to wonder: What is the Soliticitor General's mandate? Does he function on his own recognizance, or if he is a member of Cabinet, to what extent is he under the P.M.'s thumb?

"This brought me to ask: Has the P.M. been fully informed of this 'Special Branch' of the RCMP, or is he as unaware of its existence as the rest of us? Which brought me round full circle to ask: are our men on Avro Admin being blacklisted by a secret police operation under the aegis of the RCMP's 'Special Branch', or, reverting to earlier conjecture, are they being harassed by the P.M. in order to tarnish the Arrow's credit? You can see how I've been going round in circles, never sure if I'm on the right track!"

"Whew-ee!" I offer, grinning around at the men, "Mr. Smye, Sir, it sounds to me like you've gone through a real Kurabatic, loop-the-loop, wild Canada goose chase!"

None of the men thinks this clever or funny.

"Indeed," Mr. Smye sighs.

Father rolls his eyes at the ceiling in exasperation. He chooses to ignore me.

"It's wondrous strange to me that Canada would have a Secret Service that is so top secret, we Canadians don't even know it exists!" Father exclaims.

"All the better to trap the unsuspecting?" Mr. Floyd asks.

"Well now, pay heed!" Mr. Gordon intervenes, "During the War, we knew Canada had a Secret Service. We were all quite aware that we had spies and we were damn proud that we had our own counter-spy agency—heck! Espionage agents were being trained with the MI5 in our own backyard! You know they were! We were all more than aware of the 'top secret' training ground just north of Toronto near Buttonville!"

"Yes, but that was for entrapping known German Nazi sympathizers. After the war, when they were rounded up and interned, we figured that was the end of it."

"But listen here," Mr. Gordon interrupts, "We were all aware that the role of the Secret Service was to perform counterintelligence against *foreign* spies infiltrating Canada and Allied countries! So how could they trace these spies if they were not here, in Canada, among us, on our own terra firma?"

"Indeed," Mr. Smye says, "But tell me what you think of this: Now the War is over, what if there has been some 'spillage', so to speak, from foreign intelligence into the domestic realm? Would you put it past the workings of a highly efficient and overzealous bureaucrat high up in the RCMP organization to want to find something else to be done with the 'war surplus' talent? Who's to say that those postwar efforts once focused on foreign intelligence haven't been transmuted into domestic surveillance?"

"You're saying, with all those trained agents milling around after Armistice, someone higher up thought it expedient to make use of them somehow?" Father asks.

"Yes," Mr. Smye replies, "I'm positing—that there might have been a paradigm shift from protecting our nation from foreign Communist takeover to weeding out potential Canadian Communists in our midst!"

"But if this is so, it is becoming patently clear that this is being done quite arbitrarily, with concerted method, and is clearly abusing our civil rights in the process. I hope there isn't a quota system!" Mr. Floyd says.

Mr. Gordon says: "That leaves it wide open to any one of us."

Father muses: "So that's what Pogo meant when he said: 'We have met the enemy and he is us!'"

"Apparently!" Mr. Smye remarks, "It's quite possible that in the eyes of the Secret Service, everyone of us poses a potential threat to national security and is eligible for domestic surveillance!"

"When did the 'Secret Service' become the 'Secret Police?'"

"Don't expanded police powers have to be approved by Parliament?"

"Theoretically, but so much of our system runs on the honour system! As it is, the RCMP is at the pinnacle of trustworthiness and honour. All annual reports from the RCMP are submitted to Parliament for review. But I would wager that not one Member of Parliament or Cabinet Minister examines it closely because it doesn't fall within anyone's portfolio to do so, and consequently, has never warranted close perusal. Any review is perfunctory. Not even the Minister of Justice scrutinizes the reports! The RCMP has never given anyone due cause for concern. Everyone trusts that the RCMP is doing the job we expect of it. On top of that, there is no set format for the report, so the full range of categories is not set in stone. It is ludicrous but with very few legal impediments, it is quite feasible that the top intelligence agency in Canada has taken it upon itself to decide on its own recognizance just what is its role in light of ongoing fear of Communism, by identifying Canadians with Communist tendencies and which of us ordinary citizens meet those criteria!"

Father protests: "Is this some sick brand of Canadian McCarthyism?"

Mr. Smye grimaces: "From what I have discovered so far, it is lamentable but possible and therefore: yes."

Mother says: "But the War is over!"

"But the Red Scare is not."

"My Good Lord in heaven," Mother says, placing a hand on her bosom, "Graham was just saying this only a few weeks ago and I refused to believe him."

While Mr. Smye was conveying this information, Mr. Gordon had excused himself, clapped on his Stetson, and headed out to his car.

He returned a few minutes later.

He reported that he'd gone out to use his mobile phone.

"Security guards are still holding the fort. Good thing, too. Fred, the RCMP agents are there! They arrived a few minutes ago, pulled into Michelsen's driveway. Avro Security was watching for them and pounced, pulled in behind them. Caught them by surprise. Shortly after, Sanderson, Pesando and Frost arrived. They've converged and blocked the driveway, so there's no egress. All together, they've got them critters corralled, and are holding them at bay until we get there."

"Let them sweat a few moments till we have our game plan ready. The agents, I mean," Mr. Smye growls.

"Goddam right," Mr. Floyd says, "We've done our share of sweating, wondering if, when, and where they'd turn up. Suspicions have been confirmed."

"Pikers," Father mumbles, "First the Russians, and now our own country, betraying us."

Mr. Smye creases his forehead and looks at Father: "Their arrival pretty much clinches it. They have you in their sights now. The most critical question at the moment is: How do you suppose you got caught up and entangled in their web?"

"I haven't a clue. Tell me, how can I defend myself? What are my rights? Anyone know?" Father asks, beseeching the other men's faces with tired, worried eyes.

"Haven't the foggiest," Mr. Gordon says.

"I thought we had our rights pretty much secured in this country. It's a mystery to me," Mr. Floyd says.

"Should I call my lawyer?" Father wonders.

Mr. Smye turns to Mr. Floyd: "Hey, Jim, can you see about ordering two pieces of blueberry pie as take-out along with a couple of cold Pepsi's for our security chappies? Include plastic forks and some serviettes as well. Put that and the whole works for this entire table on the Avro tab!"

"Done!"

Everyone stands and the men start reaching for their hats.

Mr. Smye grabs his briefcase.

He asks Father:

"Might you consider dropping your wife and daughter off somewhere en route, Graham?"

"No. All of us have to go back to the house. My daughter has to fetch her flute and her music. She's in a concert mid-November. Arrangements were made before we left town for her to practice with her friend this afternoon—and to stay there overnight."

"I'll have to pack an overnight bag for her as well," Mother says. Meaning, fresh underwear and a nicer nightie than the one Father had fished out of my dresser drawer. It's still so hot out, I hope she packs my baby dolls.

"I suggest you think about going with her, Mrs. Michelsen. Can you stay at her friend's overnight?"

Mother shakes her head. "There's shopping for Thanksgiving dinner tomorrow. We're having company. Besides, I'll not leave my husband's side," Mother says.

Mr. Smye says: "I'm thinking the four of us should all arrive at Michelsen's house at the same time. What do you say that we meet on the Main Artery at the Centrewood gates and drive in together? When we pull in, let's all converge around the driveway apron, so there's no way out for them unless we budge."

Father's voice cries out: "What do they want? Do you think they would have broken in, if they got there before the guards? If they want in when we get there, can they seize anything they want? What about my family heirlooms? Is there no protection of personal possessions, if they turn out to have a warrant?"

The men shrug.

I hear myself shout, "What about the Mississauga land claim?"

Hat already in hand, Mr. Smye says, "It's just not the right time and place, Lois. If what your Father learned is true, it's a given that action should be taken on that score, for sure. However, we have to deal with this other hot potato first!"

I look at Father. He says nothing.

"So you're going to put the Mississaugas on the back burner?" I ask Mr. Smye.

"No, we're just not going to deal with it today."

"That's just another way of stalling," I shoot back.

His shoulders stiffen.

I glower at him and say, "If nothing is going to be done about this injustice NOW, then I swear, when I grow up," I announce, "I will find my own way to appeal the wrongs committed against Canada's Indians, especially the Mississaugas!"

"Will you now?" Mr. Smye asks, lifting an eyebrow, not knowing whether to give me a patronizing smile and discount what I said because I was only fourteen, or if he should take my words seriously.

"Yes, I will!"

Mr. Floyd is looking at Father with envy and admiration.

"I could only wish that my son would have the perspicacity to speak up for himself the way your Lois does! She's a real firecracker!"

"Lately, Jim, my daughter scares the hell out of me!" Father replies, shaking his head.

The men break out into nervous laughter.

I continue to fume.

Father turns to Mother as though I was her fault: "That girl has more nerve than a canal horse!"

The men burst into another round of spontaneous laughter.

The look on Father's face says he has no idea why that was funny.

Mr. Gordon turns to Mr. Smye: "May I suggest that another clause be added to the resolution passed at this meeting?"

"Of course. What is it?"

"That the Mississauga land claim issue should be addressed immediately, and consultations should be opened as soon as possible with Indian Affairs."

Mr. Floyd is scratching this down frenetically.

I'm not going to let Mr. Smye off the hook.

"Mr. Smye, I hope this means that Father can take the Mississauga issue to Ottawa this month when you go!"

"Of course, of course! Enter the following in the minutes, will you, Floyd?" He waits for Mr. Floyd's pen to be poised, "That Michelsen will assume responsibility for same when Admin goes to Ottawa at end of October."

Mr. Smye looks at his watch.

"It's going on 1:10. Who moves to adjourn?"

Mr. Gordon responds, "Moved." Reaching for his Stetson, he claps it on his head, and heads for the main door, roaring, "C'mon, Cowboys, let's get this posse on the road!"

Ride in the Blue Pierce Arrow
1-3

1:15 p.m.

Pancake House parking lot.

I am walking alongside Mother and Father, heading for our car.

Mother is making the most of some snatched time with Father by saying, "We've arranged to be at Becky's by 3:30. What if this meeting goes past that time? Don't think for a moment you can stay back at the house and leave me dropping off Lois, then doing the grocery shopping all on my own! I'm not lugging a twenty-pound turkey and a ten-pound bag of potatoes home alone, along with all the extra fixings we'll need for the dinner!"

I can see from his wrinkled brow that Father had this in mind, and has been cut off at the pass.

This is when Mr. Floyd approaches, and touches the tip of his deerstalker hat, "Lois might enjoy a ride in the convertible. What do you say, Lois?"

"Oh, Yes!" I beam, delighted, "May I, Father—? Mother—? Please?"

During the drive, the hair on the back of my head is blowing all over creation in short, pale, straw spikes, despite the fact that it is bound back gypsy-style in one of Mrs. Floyd's freshly ironed kerchiefs that had issued forth from the glove compartment.

Mr. Floyd has lowered the flaps on his deerstalker hat, and tied them together under his chin with the straps. "Now I know why you wear that deerstalker!" I laugh. He tosses his head back, and laughs, too.

When we pull out of the parking lot from the Pancake House, Mr. Floyd conveys that he has a confidence he wishes to share with me. While stopped at a red light, when there is no more noise from gunning the engine and when there is no more roar of the passing wind in my ears, he says: "Lois, back there in the restaurant, I regret that I lacked the opportunity to make it clear where I stand on the Indian question. I want you to know that as much as I respect my Mother's right to have her own opinion, I disagree with her and my townsfolk! I believe that treatment of our Indians has been a national disgrace and something should be done to rectify their situation!

"It's a pity, I think, that the Indians have all been tarred with the same brush. Not all of them are laggards and ne'er-do-wells. Since I left home, when both at university and in business, I've met some real standup Indians, intelligent, educated, civil, well-spoken, and self-respecting men who conducted themselves with dignity and integrity!"

Just as the light turns green, I have time to respond.

I stare back at him. His blue eyes are watery, so I know his words are heart-felt. I believe him. "That's a relief, Sir!" I say, "Sounds like you met men like Chief Fred."

All too soon, we are standing beside the blue Pierce Arrow. The ride is over. He is looking at me with serious, deliberating eyes. He cups his hand around his match and lights a cigarette. I can tell he is choosing his words carefully:

"Good luck with your future studies! You will need a law degree, and a solid grounding in constitutional law, if you truly want to help the Mississauga Indians. That will require post-doctorate work. You have the intelligence, of which there is no doubt, so all you need are the skills to do it. Once you have the tools, may you get out there and clobber whatever stands in your way. May you get the government to make amends with that land claim," he smiles, the smoke billowing out his nostrils like a bull in frost.

"You bet!" I reply.

"You want a piece of advice where to start, there's no point going to Indian Affairs. There is no point in appealing to the civil servants or the Minister either, as the only purpose of anyone in that Ministry is to enforce the Indian Act. Nor is it worth appealing to the Governor General, Vincent Massey. He may very well be the Queen's representative here in Canada, but he is just a rubber stamp for whatever government policy may be at the time. I suggest your best bet would be to aim directly for the Supreme Court."

I say: "Perhaps you can suggest that to Father, Mr. Floyd, as he will be delivering the Avro appeal to Ottawa, only a week and a half from now!"

●

Possé

CHAPTER TWO
Centrewood

The Possé
2-1

Saturday, October 12, 1957
1:30 p.m.

Parked in the driveway with its front bumper almost touching the garage door, there is a sleek, black, Crown Vic cruiser. I ask Mr. Floyd why it doesn't look like the black and white squad cars with the big flashing red light on top of its roof that the kids at school back in Unionville called 'bubble gum machines'. Mr. Floyd explains that it is an 'unmarked' police car, otherwise it too would have the 'red cherry' on the roof, it would be called a 'black and white', and there would be an RCMP crest emblazoned on the wide white bar on both sides of the two front doors.

Two Avro security guards in their beige serge, wearing their peaked caps with Avro badges, stand resolute, with folded arms, at the front door. Their Avro Security car is parked directly behind the cruiser. Because their beige-painted vehicle is clearly marked on each door with the Avro insignia, Mr. Floyd figures that the security guards must have parked on the curb up the street a house or two, facing the Main Artery during their stake-out, and by doing so rendered their own car unremarked, to the rogue agents' eyes at least, while lying in wait for the Crown Vic cruiser to arrive, before they pulled in behind.

Drawn up behind the Avro security car are the first three cars that had arrived earlier, now parked side-by-side, blocking the apron of the driveway: those belonging to CEOs Mr. Sanderfield, Mr. Pesando and Mr. Frost, accordingly. Four more cars now converge on the apron, those belonging to Mr. Smye and Mr. Gordon, Father and Mr. Floyd. Two each pull up on either side of the first three and fan out, lapping well over onto the lawn, rear bumpers hanging over the curb. All seven of the cars together are in a V-formation, bearing the Avro VIP parking sticker on the licence plates.

As soon as we arrive, two big, surly men get out of the cruiser. They are not dressed like RCMP officers. Rather than wearing the standard red tunic with navy jodhpurs and yellow pinstripe, brown riding boots and brown stetson-like hats, these men are wearing black suits with black shirts and black ties. Their stride is cumbersome the way they lumber, pushing their heavy, thick thighs forward. They move with their elbows out, indicating either beefed-up biceps, or they have hams taped to their underarms. It crosses my mind that they might have holstered guns strapped in their armpits. However, not ever having seen an armed officer, I put their act down to intimidation, the way tough guys flex their muscles. With black felt fedoras pulled down over their foreheads, and tinted sunglasses set on the bridge of their noses, they take up their positions at the rear bumper of their car with arms akimbo, in an attitude of hostility.

Seven Avro men and one Avro youth step out of their cars, close ranks, and stand side by side, facing them. The Avro youth is directed by his father to go over and stand beside Mother and myself on the lawn.

"Hi Lois."

"Hi, Bert."

"Hello, Mrs. Michelsen. I've been assigned to look out over you and Lois."

"Hello, Bert. Thanks for helping out," Mother replies, stiffly.

Next to the agents, the Avro men look like pipsqueaks. Mr. Smye is tall, and slim, but his desk job hardly makes him fit enough for a fistfight. Father is the tallest, he towers over all the other men, and has always seemed like a Norse god to me, but picturing his long, slender, artists' fingers clenched in a battle pitted against these two agents, a Viking warrior he is not. In fact, facing these sturdily built men in black, the Avro men, standing properly at attention in a row, look like wooden peg dolls that with a solid sidelong swing of an arm could be knocked over one by one with one hefty clobber.

They could all topple over with one blow.

Mr. Gordon's reference to a "posse" comes to mind. Mr. Gordon is the only one dressed like a cowboy, what with his Stetson and all. I want the Avro men to stand there glowering fiercely, thumbs hooked behind large, engraved belt buckles, their jaws plugged on "chewin' tabacca" as they face the two officers—or rogue agents? in black. They don't. They just stand like gentlemen in a formal banquet reception line with their suit jackets buttoned, their polished shoes close together, arms hanging at their sides.

Except for Mr. Gordon and one man with a light Panama hat, the rest of the men are wearing business suits, jackets and ties, all with fedoras.

So here we have it. The Showdown. High Noon. But no Gary Cooper. No gun-twirlin' cowpokes. Only seven men and no horse named Buster.

Onlookers: one gangly youth, a nervous mother, and a tall girl with flaxen blonde hair poking out all over the place in wind-blown spikes.

Cue the music: *Oh don't forsake me oh my darlin'*

Mr. Smye is the first to make a move. He steps forward a pace. "Help you, gentlemen?" he asks. "I believe you've already met

81

three of us, due to your unsolicited interventions this past week. However, allow me to introduce ourselves, all of us Avro CEOs, with our respective titles."

He holds out his hand. "My name is Fred Smye, President of Avro," then he escorts the agents from one man to the next, "Meet Crawford Gordon, Vice-President and General Manager. Jim Floyd, VP Engineering. Graham Michelsen, VP Aeronautical Engineering. Bert Sanderfield, VP, Radar Innovations and Doppler Tracking. Mario Pesando, Chief of Flight Testing. Jack Frost, Advanced Aircraft Designer."

As he moves across the row, each Avro man removes his hat, steps forward and holds out his hand. The agents are obliged to shake hands, but do not remove their own fedoras or sunglasses.

I know who Mr. Sanderfield is, from meeting him at the Rollout. Bert is an exact younger replica of his father with his tall, angular body, short-cropped auburn brushcut and large square face. We are in some of the same classes at school, have had some unsavoury dealings outside of school with the lewd and brash 'Jezebel' Mitsy, and most recently found ourselves at the highway together, collecting specimens for our botany class. Correction: I watched, while Bert stepped with his feet sidewise down the embankment, and waded into the tall weeds to collect milkweed for himself, and burrs for me.

Mr. Pesando has to be the one with the Spanish-sounding name because of his tropical tan and Panama hat. He is very dashing and mysterious-looking. At the Pancake House, I recall Mr. Smye mentioning the Admin man from Argentina who had been intercepted by the RCMP agents. This must be him.

The remaining man, Mr. Jack Frost, is not as I had imagined him at all. He is not covered in ice and snow. Nor does he have long icicle tentacles for fingernails. Instead, he has a sun-blotched face and a craggy nose, which is severely sunburnt. Rather than snow-white hair, what is most striking about him is his shiny black hair slicked straight back off his forehead with more than a little dab of Brylcreem.

> *Brylcreem, a 'little dab 'll do ya'*
> *Brylcreem, you look so debonair ...*

The Showdown
2-2

1:40 p.m.

Mr. Smye resumes addressing the agents:

"Take note, and take note well. Standing here, numbering seven out of ten on the Avro Admin team, we constitute a forum. Let it be known, that whatever we decide, whatever action we take today, will be considered an Avro company decision and will be registered as company policy.

"I don't know what you're after. However, let me be clear. Each one of us standing here today has worked our tails off to design, build and complete the Arrow, the most advanced supersonic aircraft of its kind. We have dedicated hours of our lives toward realizing its completion, and toward witnessing with great national pride, its timely Rollout last Friday, October the Fourth.

"I know that I speak on behalf of all men present, and for the entire company that we will not abide having our accomplishment tarnished through any skulduggery or tomfoolery— by you two men specifically, by the RCMP itself, or any other party who might be playing dirty tricks on us. Nor will we abide having any of us—I repeat any of us—hassled, harassed, intimidated or bullied!"

"Hear, hear!" and "Well said!" declare the Posse.

Mr. Smye clasps his hands behind his back, and starts pacing back and forth in front of them, addressing them, nose to nose.

"What exactly are you after? Why are you here? Who are you, really? You are driving an RCMP vehicle. Was it poached? Or is it safe for us to believe that you are both RCMP officers? As far as I am aware, the RCMP is responsible for national security. Does any one of us—or do all of us constitute a threat to national security? I doubt that very much. Every man on Avro Admin was subjected to rigorous security clearance before joining Avro. Since then, every one of us is subjected to routine security checks each and every day going both in and out of the Avro plant."

Mr. Smye is a vital being. His eyes glare and his lips snap when he speaks. Heaven help his kids, if he has any. I'd hate to cross him!

He steps back a pace.

"Allow me to forward a message to your superior, to whomever it is that issues your orders. When you look at members of the Admin team, you are looking at national treasures. Each man here today constitutes the cream of the crop in aeronautical engineering and research. Each man has a brilliant, scientific mind. Each man is as trustworthy and patriotic, loyal to Canada and the Crown, as the day he was born."

He walks right up to the agents and eyeballs them.

"What do you want from Mr. Michelsen?"

All of us are taken aback when one of the agents opens his mouth, and replies:

"We are here with three counts. First, on the grounds that Mr. Michelsen is under investigation as a Communist sympathizer, we have orders to charge Mr. Michelsen with illegal possession of Avro Arrow aeronautical plans."

"Communist sympathizer!" Father howls, "What utter poppycock!"

Mr. Floyd curses from his position in front of his blue Pierce Arrow, "Of course he has copies of the plans, you jackasses! He drafted them!"

"Nonetheless, according to our orders, he has no right to have them in his possession. Those plans are top secret and belong to the state."

Mr. Gordon steps forward from where he stands in front of his black Eldorado Seville, and barks: "You're right on one score, the plans are indeed top secret! But here's the scene, pahdners. They do not belong to the state. The plans are the property of Avro, not yours—whoever you are—or the RCMP's—whatever their claim—or the government's. As for Mr. Michelsen, he has company clearance to have them in his possession."

Mr. Smye reinforces the point. "Mr. Michelsen is authorized to have the Arrow plans at home with him because he is the very man who has worked on them and created them."

"We intend to seize them."

Mr. Smye intervenes, "Not a chance!"

He steps back and summons all seven of them into a huddle. When he returns, he says, "It is agreed, to avoid any physical confrontation, that this is what will happen. With the consensus of the Admin team present, the plans will be returned to Avro today—not by yourselves, however, but by our own Avro security guards. There the plans will be safely stored away in Avro's vault, away from the likes of you! Okay with you, Michelsen?"

"Absolutely!"

"Not without us as escort," one of the agents retorts.

Mr. Sanderfield steps forward, "Wait! How do we know that you two are legit? How do we know you won't hijack the cargo on the way? Show us your identification papers!"

"Yeah, maybe you're the ones who are the Commies!" Bert calls out, unbidden. Then his face turns beet red.

The agents oblige. They open their jackets and flash their RCMP badges that are pinned to their shirt pockets. From inside their jackets, they slip out their RCMP I.D.'s, with their names and mug shots, all of which Mr. Smye examines carefully.

"No dispute about their credentials, men! Now let's see your orders!"

One of the men produces an envelope that holds a legal-looking document. It is folded length-wise so it fits into a deep inner pocket of his jacket. "This is the warrant to seize and retrieve the Arrow plans."

He hands the paper to Mr. Smye who scrutinizes the paper closely.

Mr. Smye says, "This warrant is in accord with the charge delivered. However, I question its authenticity. It has been typed on stationery with an RCMP letterhead. But no department or branch is named. There is a signature, but it is blurred, virtually illegible. Under it, there is no name in plain, legible typeface that should correspond with same. On that basis, I reject this order!"

"At your peril!" one of the agents snarls.

Mr. Smye whirls around:

"How so? Is that a threat?"

"You keep this up, you might find yourself added to the Black List, along with the rest of you," the other agent sneers.

"So it's true, you really are putting ordinary Canadians on some Black List? On whose authority?" Mr. Smye asks.

Mr. Smye slips a sleek, Papermate fountain pen out of his suit pocket and unscrews the top. He takes the document, turns it over, and lays it on the roof of the agents' car.

While writing, he says, "On this very document, I am stating that Mr. Michelsen is authorized to have possession of the Avro plans. Also, that full proprietorship resides with Avro, not with the RCMP or any government body. To that effect, the plans will be transported back to Malton by our very own Avro security guards where they will be stored safely, and legally, where they belong.

"Furthermore, under no circumstances will the RCMP agents take it upon themselves to escort our security detail, as all seven of us will do so.

"You will report back to your superior to this effect. Unlike your superior, my signature will be legible. If this warrant is indeed authentic, I will expect to receive a return response in short order, with the name of the superior officer clearly printed alongside his signature."

One of the agents speaks, "The warrant includes permission to search Mr. Michelsen's home office, to ensure that all Arrow plans have been identified and removed."

Another huddle.

Mr. Smye returns to face the men:

"You, Sirs, may gain entry to the house and bear witness to the transfer of the plans from Mr. Michelsen's home. However, as they are indeed top secret, you will neither touch nor examine them!"

Mr. Smye turns to Father:

"Michelsen, unlock the front door, please. With your permission, Gordon and Floyd will escort you into the house along with these two agents while you fetch the plans."

He turns to me:

"Lois, where are your flute and music?"

"On the hallway stand, Sir."

"Please, I must ask that you go in, fetch them, then go back outside directly, and stand by your father's car.

"Mrs. Michelsen, if you can put together some overnight things for your daughter and get back outside to your car as quickly as possible, I'd appreciate it!"

Four remaining Avro men stand next to the security guards by the front door as reinforcements.

As I enter the house, I realize that Mr. Smye is no longer standing near the cruiser. I look over my shoulder and see that he has returned to his red Thunderbird.

Father leads Mr. Gordon and Mr. Floyd downstairs to the den, followed by the two agents, then by Mother and myself. Mother whispers to me, "We'll do what Mr. Smye requested but not immediately. Now it is imperative that we keep an eye on Father!"

Once downstairs, Mr. Gordon and Mr. Floyd stand guard at the entranceway to Father's den to prevent the agents from entering first.

Using the combination that only he knows, Father unlocks the door, enters and flicks on the overhead fluorescent bars.

Mr. Gordon steps in first and looks around.

"Finally, a visit to your inner sanctum, Graham!"

"Father calls it his 'den of iniquity'!" I say.

Father's shoulder twitches as he turns to frown at me.

Mother quickly offers, "I have always preferred to call it his lion's den!"

"Nevertheless," Mr. Gordon waxes eloquently, "Despite the horrid circumstances in which we find ourselves, we have the rare privilege of seeing where all your impeccable and perfectly-rendered aeronautical plans were drafted. This is comparable to visiting the studios of great artists such as Picasso, or Matisse! Mark my words, this will be an historic site as well as a tourist attraction in the future, I'm sure."

I have my private doubts. "*Yeah, right!*" I think, "*An historical attraction in the basement of a house in suburbia. Hardly the picturesque streets of Paris!*"

Father mutters: "Soak it in, it's the rare man who has ever stepped foot in here!"

"Not even Mother or I have been allowed in here without Father's permission!" I add.

"It remains locked whenever my husband is not home," Mother adds, nervously.

We have all entered now, watching as Father bends over and uses another secret combination to unlock the long, low built-in safe. The heavy metal door is swung open. There, tightly scrolled, top-secret Arrow plans lie stacked on their sides.

Meanwhile, the agents have inspected the bars on the windows, and once the safe is empty, have inspected the construction to confirm that the back metal wall was solidly embedded in the foundation.

When Mr. Gordon questions him, one of the agents replies, "No possible escape hatch."

The plans are transferred into Mr. Gordon's and Mr. Floyd's cradling arms, the safe is locked up, and then the door to the den as well. Fore and aft, the agents escort Mr. Gordon and Mr. Floyd upstairs. Father, Mother and I follow. We meet outside. We watch as the plans are entrusted to the two security guards, who go directly to the Avro car, get in, and lock themselves in, securing all doors and rolling up all windows to just a crack for air.

Father comes over to Mother, "Rest assured the plans are in good hands. The worst travesty of all has been the invasion of my private space, my inner sanctuary."

"The worst travesty to me would be if they had barged in on us in our bedroom," Mother replies.

The showdown is not yet over.

It seems that there is more work to be done.

A formal questionnaire materializes from the agents' car and Father is obliged to answer a gazillion questions. This must be the C-215 form that Mr. Smye was talking about.

Father is sent inside to fetch his birth certificate, driver's licence and any other type of identification, especially if they include photographs. He hands over his outdated passport, which he used during the war only, all stamped with places in England proper.

They ask him to go back inside and fetch the same particulars for Mother, claiming that they are obliged to fill out a C-215 form for her as well. He objects, and is told it is merely a matter of routine.

Once that procedure is complete, Father speaks:

"Are you quite finished? Why have you trampled on my civil rights and freedoms by having me go through this rigamarole? I have always held the RCMP in the highest regard. It is our national pride, our very own world-renowned 'top notch police force' that serves to protect us from criminal activity at home, and from foreign threats abroad. Can it be that you are now harassing innocent Canadians such as ourselves, wantonly apprehending us and abusing our civil rights? If so, then I fail to regard you so highly. If you are willingly and knowingly doing this kind of work for the RCMP, you must realize that you are doing so without legal or public permission, acting without principle or conscience, sorely lacking in pride and self-respect. You are the ones who are the real threat to our democracy and can hardly consider yourselves patriots. Suddenly you have made me fear that we are now living in a fascist state. God help us! Do you realize that what you are doing is paramount to treason?"

"Bravo!" the Avro men cheer.

A man calls out, "I suppose you'd do anything for a pay cheque, eh?"

Another man says, "Have you no scruples?"

One of them says, "You're top notch numbskulls."

Another says, "If not downright thugs."

I suppose all that venting made Father and the other men feel better.

Mother goes off to pack an overnight bag for me. I grab my flute and music from the hallstand. Once she's finished, she takes the car keys from Father and plants my overnight bag, flute and music in the back seat of Father's car. We stand by the car, on the lawn.

Eventually, all the Avro men are hanging together around Mr. Smye's red Thunderbird, two of them smoking cigarettes, one of them biting the end off a Cuban cigar.

I sidle up next to Mr. Floyd who is smoking a cigarette. Not sure if everyone was about to part ways, I took the opportunity to approach him and say: "Thanks for the ride in your convertible, Mr. Floyd! That was a totally new experience for me! It was super!"

"You are most welcome, my dear!"

I seek out Mr. Frost who is leaning against Mr. Smye's car.

"Excuse me, Sir," I say, "I am Lois Michelsen."

"I gathered that, young lady. Easy to tell. Tall, blonde hair. You've got your father's Nordic blood in you, for sure!"

I look at him. "Are you Mr. Jack Frost?"

"Yes, I am!"

"Earlier, I was told you would be here. I just couldn't believe I was going to meet a man whose name is really Jack Frost."

"Well, it is!"

"I'm told that you are inventing a flying saucer!! Is that true?"

"Indeed it is!"

"Well, Sir, I had my first ride ever in a convertible today with Mr. Floyd. Do you think some day I could have my first ride ever in your flying saucer with you?"

"I'll put you right at the top of my list, my dear!"

I thank him.

Avro Canada VZ-9 Avrocar

Mr. Gordon wanders over.

"Lois, young lady, I have never met anyone in my whole life who has 'waking visions'! Do you think you could share some of them with me? Or is your supply strictly classified?"

"I can share one with you right now, Sir! Today on our drive to your place, up on the plateau I saw a longhouse that suddenly lifted up on wheels and rolled off through the bush."

"No!"

"Yes, indeed. It was what you described as a "waginogan" on the move!"

"Get out with you!"

He thinks I'm kidding.

I ask him, "Do you think there is any linguistic connection between the native word 'waginogan' and the English word for 'wagon'?"

Mr. Gordon looks at me, flabbergasted, then turns away.

***

Out of nowhere, minxy Mitsy appears at my side, short legs slung over the crossbars of her bicycle, draping her ample bosom over the handlebars. Ever since I started at Centrewood High, she has plagued me, mostly because she lives just around the corner from me, and mainly because Mother has persisted in flinging us at each other. Because we had moved and I was going to a new school, she wanted me to have a new 'little friend', who from Day One has been a complete and utter pest. She has bewitched Mother, and she's given me a life of living hell.

"Hey, Lois, what's up? What's with all the swish cars?" Mitsy asks, pressing her green eyes into my face, while flicking a gob of frizzy red hair out of her eyes.

Father's voice resounds over my shoulder. He had spotted her and had taken long strides across the lawn, scolding, "What on earth are you doing here? Get on home, Mitsy. Shoo! I mean it—Now!"

Fortunately, Father is not as entranced by her as Mother.

He looks at me: "Lois, you will say not one word to her!"

"Not the first time I've been told to 'shoo'," Mitsy says to me, drolly, as she turns away.

Her remark flips me back to that time when the construction foreman rushed out and told her to 'Shoo'. The freshly organized "Neighbourhood Watch" in the form of my Mother and another lady had heard about some construction worker consorting off-hours with one of the girl students, and had dropped by the site to put an end to it.

While walking to school, she got an earful from the foreman, and was driven away down the muddy gravel road of the construction site, while the rest of the workmen hid behind churning cement mixers and half-built layers of brick walls.

Mitsy was enraged. She didn't know that it was Mother who initiated the action.

The RCMP agents had not yet left.

It didn't seem that they were ready to leave.

They couldn't leave anyway, as the Avro Security vehicle and some of the Avro cars blocked them.

They stood with folded arms, leaning against their car.

One of them stepped forward.

"Mr. Michelsen, you will recall when we arrived that we had more than one count."

All the men cluster around them.

Mr. Smye hops out of his car and joins them.

"What now?" Father asks.

"We have two counts against your wife, Mrs. Emily Michelsen, who is also under suspicion as a communist operative. We have a warrant to search all her correspondence and papers."

Father rushes forward and grabs the man by his collar. He growls, "You leave my wife out of this, you bastard!"

Mr. Sanderfield holds him back by the elbows.

Mr. Floyd intercedes, "Can you substantiate those accusations?"

Mr. Gordon comments, "This smacks to me of a trumped-up charge, if ever there was one. Can you show us your search warrant for these charges?"

"We don't require a search warrant. The only authorization we need is this citation." The agent pulls yet another legal envelope from inside his suit jacket.

He reads, "Before emigrating from England, Mrs. Michelsen infiltrated DeHavilland Aircraft at Hatfield. Authorities have reason to believe that she was a mole for the Communist Party. She was known to have contacts in Coventry and was traced placing a telephone call there just prior to its bombing."

Mother lets loose. Her voice goes up two octaves. She shrieks, "That's ridiculous! My parents, my sister, my aunts and uncles, cousins, they all lived in Coventry! How dare you insinuate such a thing? I lost my entire family in that bombing! Whenever I phoned there, it was to talk to them! You think I knew what was about to happen that day and was trying to warn them?"

She takes in a breath.

"Me, a 'mole?', an infiltrator into DeHavilland? You're daft! I was requisitioned by the government from a London interior design company to work at Hatfield. I didn't apply! I was content at that job in London. But I went willingly to serve my country. Let me be clear: I was seconded there upon request from the British authorities!"

One of the agents holds up a hand and with a condescending air, and says, "This is neither the time or place to lodge a plea, Mrs. Michelsen. The judge will be the one to listen to your objections at the hearing. Not us!"

"Hearing? What hearing?"

The other agent continues to scan the citation and states,

"We have a second count against Mrs. Michelsen. Our files on her activities in Unionville are somewhat sparse. However, once she moved to Centrewood, pursuant to a citizen complaint forwarded from the local police, it has been verified by a reliable source that

Mrs. Michelsen was directly instrumental in the formation of a secret vigilante ring called 'Neighbourhood Watch'."

Mother cuts him off.

"'Vigilante ring'? Hardly! The Neighbourhood Watch is comprised of a group of mothers from Centrewood, trying to keep a protective eye out for our children when they are away from home. It's no secret operation! In fact, it is a chapter of the local ratepayer's association!"

"It is under the guise of such innocent organizations that Communist activities find fertile soil to flourish. It is how Communism gains a foothold and assumes control, first through local politics, then expanding outward and upward through all branches of government."

"Bull shit!" I hear Mr. Sanderfield say, "What are you, a robot? You're yawping along as though you've been brainwashed!"

The lead agent tries to take Mother by her arm.

Father blocks him.

"You will stand back, Sir, and let us gain re-entry to your house so we can conduct a search, or we will have to use force. You, M'am, will have to accompany us."

"A search of what?" Mother asks.

"All your papers and minutes pertaining to Neighbourhood Watch, in the course of which, you will also hand over your full list of Neighbourhood Watch operatives."

"Operatives, you say!" Mother sniffs, "Piffle! The members on that list are women—mothers, just like me!"

Father grabs one of the agents by the elbow, "You already had me fill out your C-215 form for her. You said it was just a 'matter of routine'?"

"Watch that you won't have to fill out one for your daughter as well, Sir. And I'll warn you now, if you press us, we'll demand full plans for your house with delineated details about all means of access and egress, including all windows that are not barred."

"What! Why? Just in case you might plan a raid on us some day?" Father starts cavilling, "Just in case we might try to escape via the vault in the den? This is preposterous!"

Mother bursts into tears. She has her hands over her face.

We are standing side by side.

I reach out to put my arm around her.

At the same time, I quietly take the car keys from her hand.

Father looks at his cohorts with disbelief. His face is wracked with consternation, confusion and embarrassment.

There is not only fear registered, but hurt pride.

His worst fear is public humiliation.

This public performance in our front yard is compounded by the sudden appearance of a straggling group of curious neighbours who are one-by-one stepping out of their houses as though the timing has been orchestrated, and are approaching cautiously down the sidewalk like light-stricken insects crawling out of the woodwork. Other people from elsewhere are collecting down the middle of the street, ogling the swank VIP cars with their Avro licence plates, gawping at the Avro Security car with its two uniformed occupants, whispering out loud about the two slick 'men in black' with their black fedoras and sunglasses and their sleek black car.

These are people I have never seen before.

During his visit on Father's birthday, Cousin Gordon might have been right about the suburban streets of Centrewood being deader than a doornail. But clearly, there is more than meets the eye. It seems there are all kinds of people behind those closed curtains after all.

Father steps inside. Mother follows.

The agents stop at the threshold before entering the house.

In a loud voice one of them turns and bellows to the crowd,

"Mr. and Mrs. Michelsen are suspected of leaking company secrets to the Russians! It is quite feasible that they are a sleeper cell!"

This is their parting shot at the onlookers who all start to whisper among themselves, getting increasingly agitated, as though a kettle had been set close to boiling.

Father forces his way back out. He stands on the concrete landing.

"What is this—some kind of FARCE?" he yells, lower lip trembling.

The Avro men are outraged.

"Bull shit!" Mr. Pesando shouts.

"What a crock!" Mr. Sanderfield joins in.

"Get stuffed, you jerks!" I hear Mr. Floyd yell.

The Avro Admin contingent shout to the crowd on the street that these are flagrant lies, and that they shouldn't buy them for a minute.

They shake their fists at the front door, which is now closed.

"You'd better think twice!" "Look at who you're targeting for this seamy exercise!" "Look at who you're picking on!" "You are WAY off base, gentlemen! You're singling out the Michelsens? Graham? Emily? They are two of the most honest, decent, hard-working and patriotic citizens you could ever ask for!"

One of the agents sticks his head back out the door.

"That's why they make good material for espionage. Get it? By the way, while we're inside, don't even consider damaging our car!"

"Don't give us any ideas!"

"We have connections, you know, we have a hot line straight to the Minister of Justice!"

"I know the Governor General personally. Wait till you hear from him!"

"I don't care if you know the King and Queen of Sheba, you touch our car, you will all be charged with damage to government property, as well as obstruction of justice!"

All the Avro men continue to protest loudly, calling out encouraging words to Graham and Emily, vowing to stay until they come back out and to stand by them until these unfounded charges are put to rest.

I open the car trunk, draw out Father's manilla envelope as well as my zipperbinder. I walk over next to Mr. Smye, who is still sitting in his red car. His window is rolled down.

"Mr. Smye, Sir, will you please take these research papers for the time being, just in case they decide to search Father's car?" Crossing my fingers, I add, "After all the hard work piecing together the history of the Mississauga, it would be a pity if they were confiscated!"

"Of course!" he complies.

I hand over Father's manilla envelope containing all his precious notes, the Peter Jones photographs, copies of Mississauga treaties and historical maps. Mr. Smye transfers the bundle into his back seat.

I smile, gratefully.

He hands me a paper bag through his car window.

"Lois, be a dear, and take these two pieces of blueberry pie and the cold drinks over to the security guards. I hope the pop is still cold. Otherwise, it won't be much of a treat."

I go over, stand next to Father's car and wait, clutching my zipperbinder to my chest. In it is the sum-total of my burr project, not yet complete, due for school upon return on Tuesday, and the precious eagle feather that I always carry with me, A school binder is unlikely to arouse attention, but I don't want to risk not having them in my clutches. Let those two dreadful rogue agents search Father's trunk now, they'll find nothing of interest.

At this point, I'm not worried about Mother.

I know she hasn't done anything wrong.

I'm sure she'll be out in a jiffy.

I am prepared to wait.

Only thing is, time is getting on, it's well into afternoon and Becky will be wondering about me if I'm late.

Bert materializes and stands next to me.

When Mother emerges, she is in handcuffs!

Father bursts out the door after her.

"She's innocent! They're just trying to intimidate us!" Father shouts, as much for the crowd of onlookers as for his colleagues.

"Shame on them! Show my colleagues what you've taken from the house, you fools!"

Father lifts his voice and call out to the pool of onlookers,

"Listen, everyone, these two men posing as RCMP officers have charged my wife with operating a vigilante ring. What have they taken as their evidence? They have seized the membership list for Neighbourhood Watch! All of you surely know it is an organization formed by concerned Centrewood mothers in order to keep an eye on their children in a new neighbourhood. Is that a crime? Is it? Is it?"

Father is going berserk.

One agent holds him back, will not let him accompany Mother.

The other man stuffs Mother in the back seat of the long, black, shiny, Crown Vic cruiser, slams the door, and locks it.

Father stands up to them and points at them, "How can you hold your heads up high? You call yourself Royal Canadian Mounted Police? You are a Royal Canadian embarrassment! You are supposed to defend us, not persecute us!! Law-abiding police do not abuse their power!"

Mr. Sanderfield calls out to the growing crowd. "Do you understand who these men in the black suits are? They claim to be RCMP Secret Service agents, but they are behaving like Secret Police, you know? Like the Gestapo! They are interrogating the Michelsens, threatening them with cockamamy charges! They did this to me, too! Plus two other CEOs from Avro. Take a good look at these two men! Remember their faces! Either they are impostors, or we Canadians are in the process of losing our precious civil rights— Invasion of privacy, seizing personal possessions, adding our names to some kind of Black List! Can these be true RCMP officers? Or are they rogue agents, acting illegally, fabricating charges, counterfeiting the signatures of their superiors, functioning out of bounds! Did you know they are empowered to search and arrest without just cause? What are you all going to do about it? Think hard! You might be next!"

Obviously, the people intend to do nothing, certainly not immediately, for they all hang back and huddle together like a herd of cattle behind a wire fence— All except for one scruffy-looking man who steps out from among the crowd. He is wearing a faded plaid suit under a short tan trench coat with deep bulging pockets. Next to him on a leash stands a tall, elegant dog with red-and-white markings bearing a curious contraption with two saddlebags slung on its back. I could see pencil-scrubbed pages in a spiral notebook protruding from one of the open flaps.

"Run that past me again?" asks the man, drawing Mr. Sanderfield closer to him.

Behind me, I hear Mr. Frost's voice. "Crack open the car window, for the love of mike," he is urging, "The poor woman is suffocating in that hot car!"

The image of Mother's tear-streamed face is starting to blur through the fogged-up windows.

One of the agents sees the sense of it, strides over to the car, unlocks the door, reaches to roll down the window. But Mother beats him to the draw. Despite her shackled wrists, she has managed to grab the handle and roll down the window a few inches all on her own. She is sobbing, and holding up her cuffed hands in a plea to be released.

"Can you tell me again what's going on?" the man asks, his dog following close by on its leash.

The man in the trench coat listens to Mr. Sanderfield intently, while behind his back his hand slips into one of the dog's saddlebags, and draws out a camera, the kind like you see in the movies, with the big lens stuck to the front of an accordion— big and professional, not like my Brownie Hawkeye or Father's Polaroid. I watch the man take two, three, four long strides, and then lickety-split, he photographs Mother in her handcuffs through the half-open car window.

"What the hell?" Father shouts. "Get him out of here!"

"We're finished now! Get your vehicle out of our way!" one of the agents says to the security car, "We want to get going!"

"You two men aren't going anywhere until we hear from a higher authority!" I hear Mr. Smye shout from his car.

I can see him talking on his mobile car phone.

"Who are you calling—God?" one of the agents sneers.

This time, it isn't a showdown, it's a standoff. The Avro men are standing between the security car and the agent's Crown Vic, facing the agents grimly. The atmosphere is strained and silent, the tension stiff and about to snap, if prolonged.

Bert is standing by my side again. He had disappeared for a bit. I don't know where he had gone but here he is again.

"What's in your bindercase, Lois?" he asks.

"Just notes, and my burr assignment. Why?"

"Can I see?"

I unzip the case across the top. He peers into it, looking interested in the contents.

He says: "Is anyone looking this way?"

I glance around us. "No."

He says: "Do me a favour, will you? Can you leave your case unzipped like this for awhile?"

I do as requested. Then he evaporates.

Suddenly, Mitsy is at my side again.

I stare at her.

"What's up now?" she poses.

Suddenly she spots Mother in the Crown Vic.

Her voice caterwauls over everyone's head, "Hey, Mrs. Michelsen! What are you doing in there? Whoa, are those handcuffs?"

Mitsy turns to me and asks: "What's she doing in there?"

I say: "Mother's being arrested by the RCMP for running a so-called 'vigilante operation' called Neighbourhood Watch."

Mitsy's face fell. "Oh God! Really? Oh no! Oh my God—No!"

Something has crossed her mind.

Inside my mind, something twigs.

I face her. "You complained to the police that day, didn't you! You ratted on the Neighbourhood Watch, just because it stopped you from flirting with those construction workers on the way to school!! You said they were Fascist, and called them the Gestapo, and other ridiculous names. It was you, wasn't it? Who else would do such a dreadful thing?"

"I didn't know your Mother was responsible. Besides, I complained to the police—I didn't complain to the RCMP!" she declares, as though that exonerates her.

Father marches across the lawn. "Didn't I tell you to go home, young lady? I mean it. Go away. Scram. Go home, Mitsy, now!"

He points to the man in the trench coat. Father growls: "You! Likewise. Beat it!!"

The man has a smile of triumph on his face. He is leading his dog away by its leash. The speckled red-and-white Irish setter responds eagerly, wearing a happy smile and proudly prancing alongside his master. "Come on, Finn!" I hear him say, "Back to the typewriter—and darkroom—we go!"

"Who's he?" I ask Mitsy.

"Oh, that's the reporter from the Centrewood Weekly. His name is Jason 'Bud' Longford. It was because of him that I ended up here. I was just tooling around the neighbourhood riding my bike Tonto, and I spotted his old crate parked around the corner. I figured something was up. I had no idea it was as big a deal as this!" she exclaims, spreading out her hands dramatically.

By then, Father has wheeled around and has walked back over to the car to stand next to Mother.

Mitsy hasn't budged.

"Those guys in black look like dicks!" she says.

Bert's voice behind me says: "They aren't dicks!"

"What's a dick?" I ask.

"There's more than one definition. In this instance, a dick is a detective!" Mitsy smirks, eyeing Bert coquettishly.

"These aren't detectives, they're RCMP agents," Bert says, "They've laid false charges against Mr. and Mrs. Michelsen."

"Well, they say the RCMP always get their man. In this case, they also got their woman!"

"Have you no conscience, Mitsy Gardiner? We're talking about Lois's Father and Mother here!"

"Serves the stupid Neighbourhood Watch right!"

"What a Dennis the Menace you are," Bert says, "Don't you realize that Mrs. Michelsen was the prime organizer?"

Something dawns on her face. Mitsy looks contrite.

"Oh well then, I am sorry about your Mother, Lois! I really didn't know that!"

"You know what, Mitsy?" I croak, my throat dry with rage, "You're not welcome here. Do what Father says and go home! And by the way, don't call your bike Tonto anymore, it's disrespectful of the Indians."

"Ho ho hoo ha! sez who? Okay, so, what do YOU suggest I call it?"

"Name it after yourself—Bad Penny!"

I turn my shoulder to her, and she begins to push off. But she stops, and turns her head.

"Say," she says coyly, "Are you two a number now?"

Bert looks at me, "I wish!" he says. Then he blushes. "But I'm here to support my dad."

Mitsy looks around and quickly matches father with son, same as I had done.

"Oh yeah, your father, he works at Avro as well. Remember when you told me about the top secret interceptor jetfighter he was working on?"

"To my everlasting regret," Bert mumbles, casting an ashamed eye at me.

"So you were the source of that leak!" I exclaim.

He knows that he should never have told our teacher about Avro and the project our fathers were working on. I had caught royal hell when I got home and Father caught word of it through the local newspaper.

Bert hangs his head, nodding. "Mitsy's the one who would make a good spy, Lois. She can squeeze blood out of a stone!"

1952 Willys M38A1 Jeep

Out of the blue, an army-green Jeep comes roaring pell-mell up the street, hops the curb, lumbers diagonally across the front lawn to where I am standing, grazes by my knees, and comes to an abrupt halt at the driveway's edge, its front fender almost touching the driver's side of the cruiser. Almost run over, I call out, "Hey, what gives you the right to drive on people's lawns?"

The driver replies, "Why not? That's why they call this Jeep an 'Overland'." He grins.

Two military officers in uniform, the tall one wearing a peaked cap, a jacket with three gold bars on his sleeves and many decorations on his chest, and the other slightly shorter, less ornately-dressed officer, swing out of the Jeep and confront the agents, ordering them to get out of their car.

Next to the tall officer, with his height and broad shoulders, it's time for the two agents to look like runts.

Meanwhile, Mr. Smye has hopped out of his car and is approaching the two officers.

He greets them warmly, shakes hands. "Welcome! Fred Smye, President, Avro," he says.

The officer with more regalia than the other offers a full salute and introduces himself: "Lieutenant-Colonel Arthur Kemp, Commander of Lorne Scots Regiment, Peel-Dufferin-and Halton, at your service! This is my adjutant, Sergeant Christopher Banks."

I sidle up next to the passenger side of the Jeep, and listen in. This seems to be my métier today, hunkering next to cars, eavesdropping on conversations.

The Commander relays that he is already fully informed about the situation and is prepared to act. Mr. Smye gives a nod. He calls the rest of Admin to join them.

I take the opportunity to step out and ask another question, "Excuse me, but why is there a white star on the hood of this Jeep, and another two on each front fender?"

"These have been used on Jeeps ever since the War in Normandy. They are air recognition signs. They signal that we are allies, not the enemy."

I pause for a moment and say: "But wouldn't they also alert the enemy of the opposite?"

The Commander smiles, "Oh dear, I hope that's not why some of our Jeeps went missing in action!"

I smile back, not sure if my point had been acknowledged favourably, or not.

What ensues is totally amazing. First, I overhear the Commander explain to the agents who they are and why they are here, that they have been summoned from the local army base. Notified of the agents' odd, if not spurious activities, he has come to intervene.

The agents object, and demand under which authority is he acting. With rules that sound as obscure to me as paper-rock-scissors, it seems that a Commander from National Defence is empowered to stop any agents who claim to be functioning under the auspices of the RCMP from completing their mission, based on his own judgment of the circumstances.

I see the agents' jaws drop.

Commander Kemp asks Mr. Smye to delineate the details of the situation, so that both sides are clear about the issues at hand.

Mr. Smye relates the false charge laid against Father, that he was supposedly unlawfully holding top secret Avro Arrow aeronautical plans in his home, which, he explains, are now lodged in the Avro security vehicle. The intention is that the Avro security agents will be entrusted to take them to the Avro plant. There is a problem, however, since the RCMP agents want to be the escort but due to dubious identification, Mr. Smye doesn't trust them. This problem is resolved when the Commander offers to serve as escort all the way to Malton, instead of the RCMP agents.

Next, the Commander turns to deal with Mother's situation, as she is still in the cruiser, handcuffed, pale and desperately hoping she has not been overlooked, or forgotten.

After an intense verbal altercation that involved considerable arm waving, expressions of objection, disbelief, and some shrugs of acquiescence, the RCMP agents relent.

They unlock the cruiser door, and allow Mother to get out of their car.

They unshackle her.

Father splits from the Avro phalanx to meet her.

She rushes to his side and they embrace.

The standoff is over.

Three Possé cars back out from the driveway apron, to make a break in the phalanx for the Avro security car to back out. It waits for the military Jeep to get back on the street, and lines up behind it.

I have been watching for an opportunity to ask if the green canvas roof on the Jeep was meant to double as a tent when fighting in the field, but time has run out.

Off those two vehicles trundle, in tandem, moving bumper to bumper, like a sombre little motorcade.

Next, it is the RCMP cruiser's turn to back out into the street. Once facing the Main Artery, the cruiser pulls away slowly.

After that, it is time for the Avro Admin team to depart. The men form a tight circle and shake hands with each other vigorously, clapping their hands on Father's back. In turn, they go to Mother, reach out to hold her hand respectfully as though she were the Queen herself while praising her for her courage, and pledge undying fealty to both Father and Mother. As they walk back to their respective cars, I stand and wave them off as they get in, toot horns triumphantly, and one by one drive off.

Further down the road, I see that the black cruiser has slowed down and is pulling over to the curb.

The Sanderfield car is the last to leave.

Bert's door flies open and he hops up the front lawn to me.

"Your zipperbinder still open?" he asks.

I nod.

"You mind?"

Politely, he reaches into the bottom of the case, fishes around, plucks out his jackknife and deftly slips it into his pants pocket.

"How did *that* get in there?" I ask.

No answer.

Up the road on the other side of the Main Artery, I see the two RCMP agents jump out and start walking around their car, looking at all four tires, which from this distance appeared to be distinctly oval.

Bert looks at me with wideopen, innocent eyes.

"There is more than one kind of leak!" he winks.

He bounds back to his father's car.

Shortly after the Sanderfield car leaves, Mr. Smye reappears. His red Thunderbird pulls into the drive. While turning off the engine, I see him reaching into the back passenger seat before getting out of the car.

"Fred! What's up? Forget something??"

Mr. Smye is holding the manilla envelope, extending it out to me through his window.

"Oh thank you, Mr. Smye!"

Father recognizes the envelope, looks bemused, but doesn't ask.

"What happened, Fred? What persuaded those hooligans to fold their tent and run away? They sure capsized quickly once the military had a talking-to with them!"

"You see me talking in my car on my own 'horn' during the fracas?" Mr. Smye asks.

I nod.

So does Father, who says: "I did—and I wondered what was cooking. When that Jeep pulled up, initially I thought you might have had something to do with a rescue. But it seemed to me to be a futile hope, because the RCMP have the higher authority, the highest in fact over all other forces in the country."

"Not quite. As far as police forces go, yes, it's true. RCMP agents sit close to the very top of the policing hierarchy. However, from my close familiarity with the principles that lie behind the structure of our government, I know that there is more than one way to counteract abuse of power."

"I won't push you any further, Fred, if you don't want me to! You pulled rank on those fools, but do I dare ask you how?"

"There will always be the tendency of those who are on the top rung of their organization to think they are superior and untouchable. However, in our system with three pillars of government: executive, legislative, and judicial, there are some standalone agencies that do not fall under the umbrella of any of these. One is the Armed Forces."

"What do you mean?"

"Graham, it's like this. I've said before that in my opinion, the Avro Admin team is a National Treasure. It follows naturally, that since it deserves National Respect, it follows that it deserves *National Defence!* Shall I just say from contacts established during the Rollout, we have our own 'Perks', so to speak!?"

"What? You mean Defence Minister George Pearkes?"

Mr. Smye winks.

"He was the man who pulled the rope at the Rollout ceremony to draw back the big curtains," I say, "It reminded me of Owl using Eeyore's tail as a bell pull!"

"Yes, good analogy, Lois! I was the one who arranged that honour, on his request may I say, so theoretically he owed me one— ha ha! In return, I had no compunction about pulling *his* chain!"

All these double entendres.

"But as Minister of Defence, he is in Diefenbaker's Cabinet," Father says, "Doesn't it follow that he serves under Diefenbaker's command?"

"Ah yes, but when I contacted the PMO to explore the strange raids being taken by what seemed to be agents acting like Secret Police, I was told that the Prime Minister knows nothing about it. Which told me that the P.M. is either totally innocent about these agents' activity, or if he is in collusion, the operation might be so top secret that he is not empowered to control, or interfere with, or divulge what is going on.

"My next idea was to contact Mr. Pearkes who before going into politics and running as a Conservative, served for many years with the Armed Forces. I informed him about what was going on, he concurred with my suspicions, and offered to help. It was too far away for him to arrange for a contingent from his own home base in Alberta to come to our rescue. But as a former General, he has connections across the country. All he had to do was tap the help of a fellow Commander nearby, in this instance, the Lorne Scots Regiment. We established contact. He was the one who set the whole caper up, so that one brief call from my mobile was all that was required for help to be on its way."

"But how does he know our suspicions about these 'rogue agents' are legit?"

"From all the phoning I did over the past week or so, I learned that the head of the RCMP is Commissioner Stuart Wood. When I contacted him, he maintained that there is only one division under the RCMP, and that is the RCMP Special Branch, established to conduct counterintelligence operations and oversee national security. He denied any knowledge of domestic intelligence involving random surveillance of Canadian citizens.

"I felt obliged to go higher. Responsible for the administration of the RCMP is the Solicitor General of Canada. You can't go any higher than that. His name is Léon Balcer."

"What did he say?"

"He knows nothing about a C-215 form or any such authority under the RCMP to intercept, cross-examine, scrutinize the credentials of any Canadian, demand identification, or detain.

"With this in hand, I contacted Mr. Pearkes. In total confidence, I revealed to him what had happened this week to Zurakowski, Pesando and Sanderfield, and that you, Michelsen, due to that inadvertent leak by the agent at Sanderfield's, might be next on the agent's hit list.

"So he took your word for it!"

"Why shouldn't he? He contacted Lieutenant Colonel Arthur Kemp, one of his old battle buddies and filled him in, and then referred him to me. He offered to be on stand-by, and if-or-when the agents should turn up, I was to call him." We agreed that my first call was to be when I learned that the agents had appeared. Whereupon, the base was immediately alerted, and the Jeep was on its way, equipped with mobile phone. My second call relayed the fact that they were charging you with theft of top secret Avro Arrow plans, which was preposterous enough in and of itself, let alone that you were being charged with operating a sleeper cell with your wife. With my third call, I reported the warrant issued against your wife for espionage, etc., and arresting her as a Communist sympathizer. General Pearkes was kept posted at every juncture point. The latter charge was the last straw."

"He had no qualms about possibly overstepping the will of the P. M. or the Commissioner?"

"Would it make any sense for a man with his commonsense and wisdom to support the actions of overzealous, possibly rogue agents in discrediting the architect of Canada's most advanced supersonic jet, let alone in embarrassing an innocent woman by sending her off in handcuffs, to jail?

"True, he is an MP now, and as Defence Minister is in the P.M.'s Cabinet. But he opted to step outside that role, and used his influence from his time with the Army to pull rank."

He winks again.

It dawns on me: Father had called in the Bigwigs, and Mr. Smye had called in the Brass.

After Mr. Smye drives off, the three of us stand on the front lawn like mute statues.

"I thought I was caught in a perpetual nightmare," Father says, "The kind when it's impossible to wake oneself up."

"It all struck me more like the Keystone Cops," Mother says, attempting a wan smile.

"You can laugh now that it's all over," Father replies, gruffly.

"True. Whenever I think of it all, I'll be sure to laugh until I cry."

He puts his arm around her and wheels her about. "Let's go inside," he says, "I'm thirsty. I need to wet my whistle."

Mother says, "I have to visit the loo." She looks at her watch, "We have just enough time to drive Lois over to Becky's."

She turns around to talk to me where I am standing behind them, "Lois, phone Becky and say we're on our way!" she says.

I follow them as they walk inside the house.

After I phone Becky, I walk down the hallway and into my bedroom.

At the threshold, my heart stops.

My turtle Beetlebomb is floating upside down in the tank.

This is my precious, wild, baby turtle Beetlebomb, who I rescued from being trampled by his own sisters and brothers in their rush from the woods to the waters of Willow Creek in Pinewood. That was the day I climbed up the sandy embankment into the woods to see if more baby turtles might be coming down to the water, and when I reached for the poisonous red salamander, I was stopped by Eagle, who rewarded me for saving Beetlebomb with his gift of a feather. Since that time, I have been protected by Eagle, and I carry the feather in my zipperbinder.

That, at any rate, is how I see it.

When I brought Beetlebomb home, paddling about in my gob hat in water dipped from the Creek, Father got involved. He bought Beetlebomb an aquarium, and other supplies, which we set up in my bedroom.

Beetlebomb kept me company while I did my homework. In the spring, I had hoped to find more wild food for him from Willow Creek. I learned that turtles like crickets, and slugs.

Now he is dead.

Pause by the Pasture
2-3

Saturday, Oct. 12, 1957

3:10 p.m.

The 'snap' Admin meeting at the house is over. The driveway is empty of vehicles. Except for ruts left in the grass by the Jeep, Father's sun-stricken front lawn remains sparse, as pristine as ever.

Odd that there is no vestige left in the front yard of the chaos that so recently took place there. The meeting at the Pancake House with its intense, compact, four-item agenda was pressing enough for one day. But what happened on our front lawn was like a three-ring CNE Grandstand show, starting off with a Wild Western replete with a posse of seven CEOs hitching up their gleaming upscale executive steeds to the Centrewood Corral, a solid rendition of High Noon when Mr. Smye confronted the two renegade RCMP agents, and a Showdown between public and private policing services culminating in a World War Two military operation rolling into the theatre on a one-star Jeep, all this interspersed with stray ingredients including a Greek chorus of curious neighbours gathered in the street, a scruffy reporter appearing with a professional accordion-type camera and a red-and-white Irish setter with saddle bags on a leash, a brazen bird-brain with big boobs on a bike, a tear-stained soap opera starring my own mother, a valiant boy soldier carrying only one small weapon—so many acts playing out, some on parallel planes, others trotted out one at a time.

Father's car pulls out from our side street onto the Main Artery. We are finally on our way toward dropping me off at Becky's.

We pass the RCMP cruiser and the agents, who look up from tending to their flat tires and start making angry finger signs at us. "Not very professional at all," Father says. He still has no idea what caused the flats.

I am feeling hot, strained and overtired, not really ready to be somebody's company, even if it is at Becky's and Mrs. Molnar's. I'd rather take a nap.

To my great relief, Father turns to Mother and says: "Let's just pull over for a moment, shall we, and take a breather?" He draws up close to the edge of the pasture at Pinewood, and stops, puts the gear in P for Park, rolls down his window, and takes in a long breath of fresh air. From his profile, I can see that his normally long face is even longer, and ashen grey.

"What a day this has been!" he moans, "I'm done in."

"Not until after you help me at the supermarket with the groceries, you aren't. You're coming in with me, to push the cart. I'm beat, too!"

"Do we have to bicker?"

There is a long pause.

Mother decides to shift her own gears:

"Look at the field in all its fall adornment! It's like a pioneer's rough-hewn patchwork quilt!" Mother exclaims, clasping her hands, "Isn't it beautiful!"

I had been thinking the very same thing.

In the late afternoon sun, the pastureland is draped in that extraordinarily soft apricot glow unique to afternoon autumn light. There is not a hint of a wind. The fields are quiet and still. Perhaps the delicatessen display case at the restaurant left its imprint on me, for what I see is a patchwork quilt of overlapping wedges of fresh pie. Spread across the fields are interlocking slices the colours of pumpkin, raspberry, lemon, raisin, blueberry and gooseberry, some of the patches separated by thin crusts of light pastry, others resting on shades of brown, like graham wafer crust and mocha crumble. The dark red massed clusters are mulberry; the dried blood-red clumps, the last of the densely packed sumac. The bands of white milkweed tufts are like meringue floating above the fading yellow of the goldenrod. The dark layer of earth above the riverbank smacks of chocolate pudding. The scene is exquisite, and leaves me breath-less. A latch in my heart slides open and love for Pinewood flows outward over the field.

Curiously now, although the remaining leaves on the solitary dutch elms and the needles on the slender bows of the pine stand remain motionless, it seems as though a breeze has picked up, shuffling low and sidelong across the grasses, gently tossing them to and fro, like a brush through short, tangled hair.

It was then that the quilt starts to breathe, so to speak, for without a sound or rumble, the land itself turns into a softly undulating cloth, wave upon wave coursing across the whole expanse, as though being lightly ruffled by a low current flowing across from underneath the surface toward the far end of the field. There is a similarity to a light earthquake, which I have never experienced in real life. I take note and pay close attention, as I have only recently learned that whether it is just a fertile imagination or a 'waking vision', what comes to me in this way is not a generally shared experience, and can have import only to myself.

"Looks more like a dog's breakfast," Father says, drily.

I try to let his remark slide. But his lack of appreciation for the beauty of the pasture in its present state slices its way into my heart.

"Well, I also happen to think it's quite beautiful!" I say.

"You mind your tongue, young lady, you've aired quite enough of your opinions lately!"

Whiplash.

"Whatever are you saying, Graham?" Mother asks.

Father wheels his head around and drapes his arm over the pas-senger seat so he can look at me. His eyes flash dark.

"I want to make something perfectly clear. I did not appreciate your outbursts at the Pancake House. You were entirely out of line. When we want to hear from you, we will ask. Otherwise, you should know your place and button up!"

"Graham, I have to disagree!" Mother exclaims, "I was proud of her, speaking up as she did for the Mississauga Indians! After all, we'd spent a whole day on an Indian reserve learning about their abysmal treatment and their plight! It was certainly an eye-opener for me! I was impressed with how much had stuck with her while all along I thought she was working with 'Aunt Ani' on her burr project. As I recall, when you were with Chief Fred, you too were completely engrossed, you were right in there with early maps and treaties, sopping up as much as you could about the Mississaugas and their ongoing appeals to the Government!"

Father is glowering at her. "You hold your own peace, too, Emily!"

"I shall not! I say that Lois should be commended for absorbing as much as she did, and for stating her case so lucidly! Opportunity knocked, and she leapt to discuss the issue with your Avro men! She's becoming an adult, Graham, she is no longer a child, and she deserves our encouragement in finding her own voice!"

"Well, she needn't speak out of order!" Father barks, "Or be downright saucy. What she said to Crawford about yielding his own property to the Indians was impertinent and rude—It was unconscionable!"

I blush. My cheeks are burning hot.

"I don't see what I did wrong, Father. All I wanted was to see something done about the Mississaugas land claim, and to speak up for Chief Peter Jones which you promised Chief Fred you would do!"

I hear my voice blurt out those words at the same time as my ears start ringing. I find myself leaning askew against the back seat, holding onto my head with both hands.

Father had clobbered me.

The silence that ensues is appalling.

I can see Father's shoulders freeze.

I can see Mother's head turn away.

I start to bawl my eyes out.

Father forbids Mother to move, "Don't you budge!" he yells at her.

Then he barks, "Hand her over some kleenex."

Several fistfuls of tissues are handed to me from the front seat.

He speaks, "I told you to mind your tongue and I meant it, Lois. You are getting too big for your britches!"

I mop my eyes, which are now totally sore and swollen.

My thoughts spin in my head like metallic mirrors churning in a kaleidoscope.

Father has never ever hit me before. I am stunned. If his remarks could cut, now my heart feels slashed, and bruised.

I am shocked.

Why doesn't Mother reprimand Father? Why has she stopped defending me?

These thoughts are intertwined with other practicalities, such as what a mess I now must be, with bloodshot eyes and crimson face.

I want to go home. But we are expected at Becky's. They are just dropping me off. After that, they will get off scot-free. Becky and her Mother are bound to notice. How can I go in?

Eventually, after a long silence, it is Father who speaks first.

"No need to shop for a Thanksgiving turkey, Emily. Grab your BB gun and take a pot shot at that turkey vulture up there!"

What is he on about? Mother doesn't own a BB gun! Which would hardly kill a large bird anyway. Besides, what turkey vulture?

I prop myself up with one elbow on the arm rest and look out with blurred eyes.

A bird of prey is wheeling about high in the sky above the fields.

"You see its forked wings? It even brings its own utensils!" Father quips.

Mother says: "Ha. Ha." Woodenly.

Now I understand. Father is trying to introduce some levity.

The closer the bird comes, the more I know what kind of bird it is.

I ignore Father's warning not to speak.

"A turkey vulture does not have a white head and a white tail," I half-snarl, biting my lip.

The bird wheels closer and closer into view.

"What is it?"

"A bald-headed eagle."

Father is craning his neck in all four directions, but it seems Eagle has flown out of view and is wheeling somewhere overhead behind the car.

A dark shadow falls over us and comes gliding from overtop the roof, hovering above the windshield then over the hood. To my astonishment, his wingspan is broader than the width of the car.

All I can see under his broad flapping wings are his mighty muscular legs and his claws outstretched beneath him like grappling hooks.

Eagle hanging mid-air, landing

With a horrific screech, he lands on the hood ornament, teeters to find his balance, and then turns carefully to face us.

"Oh my God!" Father yells, cranking the lever, "Wind up your window!"

"Mine is already up," Mother says, her eyes like glazed marbles, "Now what?"

The great bird lifts his wings, and shakes them. He dangles on his perch carefully, as though knowing enough not to scratch the finish. He leans out, stretches his neck as far as he can, and screeches directly at Father through the glass.

He reassembles himself on the hood ornament. He cocks his massive head from one side to the other, peering through the glass.

He is looking for me.

I hang over the back seat between Father and Mother as far as I can. I wave at him through the windshield.

He spots me.

"KAW-K-K-K-K!" he screams in recognition, ruffling his feathers, spreading then folding his wings.

I want to call out: *It's okay, Eagle, here I am!* But it is as though there is a cork in my throat. I am silenced. He leans toward me, cocks his head this way and that. With another "KAW-K-K-K-K!" almost as rebuke, he lifts off and flies away.

"Well, I'll be,"Father remarks, "Did you see that!!??"

"I think he knew you hit her," Mother whispers.

"You think?" Father stammers, "If so, I promise I shall never do that again!"

"You bet you won't!" Mother murmurs.

Through blurred eyes, I see that the pasture no longer looks like wedges of pie. The cast of light has changed. Now there are patches that are soft and fuzzy and the pasture looks flat, smoothed out, like a huge bedspread of soft rose and pale mustard and mossy green chenille.

It took only five minutes for us to drive over to Becky's place.

When we pull up, I spot Becky looking out the front window for us.

As she opens the front door eagerly, Father turns to me and orders:

"Mind you tell Becky nothing about anything we did this weekend. That includes our visit to the New Credit Reserve, the CEO meeting at the Pancake House, and the whole shemozzle that happened on our front lawn."

"Becky and Lois are close friends. Why can't she share, as long as they both agree to keep it to themselves?"

"You can tell Becky about the Brock Hotel and Niagara Falls, also what you ate at the Pancake House. Otherwise, keep mum about anything else."

I get out of the car with my overnight bag, my flute and my music. I don't say a word. I just shut the car door behind me. I can't wait to get away from both of them.

●

CHAPTER THREE
Thanksgiving Sunday

Battle of Wills
3-1

Sunday, October 13, 1957

3:30 p.m.

"What's going on in the kitchen?" Father asks.

"Mother and Mrs. Molnar are squabbling," I say.

"What about?"

"Food."

When we arrived back home from Becky's, Mrs. Molnar got out of the car first, went round back and opened the trunk. She was dressed to the nines in a smart scoop-necked sheath dress made of an elasticized, gold knobbly material, with pale ochre nylon stockings and strappy gold lamé high heels.

She was wearing a heavy gold necklace with clear shiny golden stones that clung high around her throat like a Queen Mary's choker.

The stones were large and flat, highly polished, transparent, a colour warm as honey, each one gripped by firm claws embedded in an ornate continuous braid of thick strands of gold. She wore a matching bracelet and earrings. A complete set.

Becky and I piled out of the car.

Summoning us to help, Mrs. Molnar unloaded a stuffed, oversized cloth-carrying bag which she passed to Becky. After instructing me to close the trunk behind her, she approached the front door lugging a large, covered, wicker basket.

Her jewellery glinted, sent off amber flashes in the afternoon light.

She rang the doorbell with her elbow.

Mother answered the door wearing "The Apron"—the one that Mitsy had borrowed from her under false pretenses, allegedly for her class cooking demonstration and not as a prop for her 'Teaserama' performance at the Big Culvert—over her Reitman's gingham housedress. She was holding her flour-smudged hands and forearms upwards toward herself.

"Ezster, you are early! Why are you here at 3:30 when I specifically said 5:30? I even wrote it down for you on the note I gave you."

"No, no, you wrote 15:30 which is now. We are exactly on time," Mrs. Molnar replied, pointing to her watch.

When Mother clapped her eyes on all the chattel being lugged in, she exclaimed, "What's all this?"

"I bring contribution to dinner!" said Mrs. Molnar.

"No, no, no—You were not to bring anything!" said Mother.

"Oh yes, yes, that's what we do, it is our custom in Hungary, we bring food when invited for dinner!"

She swept past Mother, stepped in and sailed up the short flight of stairs to the next landing, then through to the kitchen.

"Not when you come here, you don't! There is plenty of food to go around!"

"But I bring you my special goulash with nokedli, chicken papri-kash and pedahey—they are like perogies, you know? also borscht with sour cream, and my grandmother's traditional cucumber salad. For dessert, apple strudel!"

With each pronouncement, she unwrapped and set each con-tainer on the counter, lifted lids, peeled off saran wrap, revealed to Mother in succession the contents of each vessel.

"That is enough food for an army, Eszter! You will put it all back in your car and take it home this instant!"

"No, no, no! Em-i-ly, you listen to me. You don't take my food, you insult me!"

"Eszter, you listen to me! If you bring food to *my* house when I have invited you to dinner, you insult *me*!!"

What ensued was a forward then reverse tug-o-war.

While Mrs Molnar unwrapped and unloaded, Mother rewrapped and reloaded. Whatever Mrs. Molnar managed to place on the dining room table, Mother briskly followed after and whisked it back into the kitchen.

"Sit down, please, Eszter."

It was as though Mrs. Molnar's feet were on little rubber casters, she scooted so quickly back and forth, to and from the table.

"Eszter! This is not acceptable! I am asking you to sit—down!" Mother took her by the elbow, escorted her into the kitchen, backed her up and plopped her on a chair.

Mrs. Molnar made attempts to rise but Mother shoved her right back into place.

"Are you afraid you won't like my cooking?" Mother asks.

"No! No! Of course not!"

"Did I ask you to bring something with you?"

"No!"

Mother opened the fridge door.

"Look how stuffed the fridge is! That is what I've prepared for our main course! And this—" pointing to the flour-smudged kitchen counter where she had been interrupted rolling out the pastry, "Is dessert! I'm just making the pie!"

Mrs. Molnar grunted, folded her arms.

"There is more than enough here for us all. I will be serving maple-syrup glazed ham with baked pineapple, home made scalloped potatoes, corn on the cob with butter, steamed green beans, and freshly boiled beet with red vinegar. For dessert, there will be pumpkin pie with whipped cream. Tell me, does that sound to you as though there is not enough food here for all of us? Is there anything here that is not to your liking?"

"No! I mean, Yes! But—"

"Well now, you listen here. It just isn't done, bringing enough food to feed everyone when you are invited to dinner!"

"But that is what we do back home in the old country! When we go somewhere to eat we also take food, so I bring. And that's that!"

Up she popped from her seat, reaching for her bowls, determined once more to lay out her dishes on the table.

"No, Eszter, that isn't that. And that's final! You know the saying: When in Rome, do as the Romans do?"

"Ah, we have some similar way to say, in Hungary we say—"

"Never mind what you say! I think you get the drift, Eszter. My point is, 'When in Canada, do as Canadians do, you hear? You have upset me, bringing all this food!"

"Well, so, so, still it is something I must do. I have been raised to do so. It is custom in Hungary!"

"Well, you can go right ahead and follow your custom with any other of your Hungarian friends. But here with Canada-born friends, you only bring food if you are asked to do so, and only then if it's a prearranged event specifically designated as 'potluck'. Even then, you would contribute only one dish. As it is, I have gone to great lengths to prepare a traditional Canadian Thanksgiving dinner for us all."

"Yes, yes, what I brought with, will add to what you have! I want your family to taste all my special national dishes!"

She got up and started to push Mother aside.

Mother took her by both shoulders and pressed her back down on the chair.

"Allow me to make myself clear. Are you listening? When I serve dinner, I don't want anyone else's cooking on my table other than my own!"

At this point, I swear I heard a growl in Mother's voice.

My last glimpse of Becky—Caught between the two of them bickering, she is shrinking backwards into the kitchen corner, trying to find some way to slither out and disappear.

I do better. I am standing at the kitchen door during this round, so it is easy for me to escape. I slip out to the living room.

As I evaporate, I hear Mother pull out the all-powerful Husband Card, "Besides, Eszter, Mr. Michelsen would not approve. He is a very particular about which foods are to be served for certain occasions. On Thanksgiving, he expects glazed ham. Scalloped potatoes are a must. So is the corn on the cob. It wouldn't do to have foreign food on the table. You could have brought a roasted wild boar with truffles and he would still disapprove!"

"Truffles, what are they, truffles?" Mrs. Molnar huffs

"Don't bother getting into the definitions word game, Eszter, you just do it to control the conversation!"

"What you mean by 'definitions word game'? —Control? Who does the control?"

***

Father is sitting in his easy chair in the living room.

"Come in here, and sit down," he says, lowering the newspaper, "You have a good flute practice?" Father asks.

"Not really."

"Why? What went wrong?"

I stare at him, look away—I don't even bother to shrug.

There are several contributing factors to my mood.

For one, I was already overloaded with food. I was so stuffed after last night's supper at Becky's that I had barely been able to concentrate when it was time to practice. Mrs. Molnar had prepared so much food and ladled into me so many second helpings of each dish, I thought I was going to be sick from trying to please her, trying to eat it all. Beef goulash loaded with sour cream soaked in a bed of little grated bits of noodle called 'spaetzle', chicken 'paprikash' with perogies which Hungarians call 'pedahey' stuffed with mashed potato, minced onion and ground pork, and then her very own grandmother's cucumber salad called 'uborkasalata' which was loaded with salt and dill and a new substance to me, something strong-tasting called fresh garlic. Mrs. Molnar told me it was a species in the allium family, and was related to onions, shallots, leeks and chives. That was informative, but I'd never heard of the other members. Except for spring onions used in salads, I have only known the white cooking onions in Mother's cuisine, and doubted she would ever introduce any new ingredient that had such a repugnant taste and pungent odour.

Father had smelled it before we'd barely opened the front door, before we'd even begun to climb the stairs, before we had even gained the landing.

"Phew!" he'd called from the living room: "What stinks?"

Second, I have developed a headache. The thing is, I hadn't felt like learning new words from a foreign language while eating supper, but every time I was served a different dish, I had Mrs. Molnar's suddenly-turned-all-rubbery mouth pressed into my face as she exaggerated the pronunciation of every word, enunciating each syllable loudly in an effort to make a dent in my linguistic "deaf ear." She would put her face up real close to mine and say: "'peh—da—heh' no no! Heh, not hey!" She would make me repeat the word. She had a notepad at her elbow where she wrote each word down in an elaborate and foreign-looking, lacy cursive script to demonstrate how it was spelled, and she repeated it over and over while I ate so I could barely taste the food. "U—borkah—sala—ta! Yes? Yes? Now 'spaytz—ell—ah! Spaytz—ell—ah! You say now!! Gooood, gooood!"

I wanted to please her but it was all too intense. Much as I adored her, she was forceful, her voice was shrill and I was getting a dull throbbing in my temples.

Consequently, after supper when we were sent upstairs to practice, I was already tired from my too-full day—was it only that morning that I woke up at the Brock Hotel in Niagara, and after that drove to Mr. Gordon's, then the Pancake House before arriving back home for the floor show on the lawn—? My stomach was so loaded after that gargantuan supper that my eyelids were heavy. I felt really dopey. I could hardly play the flute at all. I flubbed almost every note, fumbled every passage, missed the bridge to every repeat. My fingers were no longer supple. They were disobedient, little, fat sausages. Later, just when I was almost able to focus, and my stomach was calming down, Mrs. Molnar came upstairs with a tray and served us apple strudel ("Al—mas—re—tes!") with European ice cream and Belgian chocolates.

Worse, when I was finally tucked in, I couldn't get to sleep. My breath kept overpowering me despite the fact I'd brushed my teeth. I guess it was the garlic. My head was pounding from the futility of my language lessons and the humiliation of not being able to play one note decently on the flute. Worse, it was so stuffy in the guest-room, I don't think it had been aired all summer. I didn't dare open the window in case there wasn't a screen and I'd let bugs or bats in. Becky had already gone to bed in her own bedroom with her door shut, before I discovered I couldn't breathe. Besides, it was pitch dark in the room and I didn't know where the light switch was, should I risk finding her door and knocking to wake her up.

Also, I was upset. I couldn't get it out of my mind that Father had struck me. Or how he carried on afterward so blasé as though nothing had happened. His limp attempts at humour irritated me, by making light of Eagle, calling it 'dinner', pretending it was a turkey vulture, making that remark to Mother about hauling out her imaginary BB gun. Acting jovial as though everything was back to normal. Was that his right? To carry on as though hitting me was a mere blip that could be forgotten, given a blink or two and a bit of time? Now can he really be serious, wanting a little light chitchat about flute practice?

I am scowling.

"I hit you yesterday, in the car," he says.

I nod.

"Mother says I should apologize to you."

This strikes me as an odd way to apologize, deflecting the onus back onto Mother.

I say nothing.

"I hope you didn't mention it to anyone."

To which I shake my head slightly and study the floor.

On top of all this, I have a big sob in my throat, like a solid, unburst bubble. I can't swallow. I am heartsick over the loss of Beetlebomb.

This afternoon when I got inside the house, I carved a beeline straight to my room.

Beetlebomb was gone.

The aquarium had been emptied, the glass gleaming clean and immaculate, the little coloured pebbles and the limestone ledges rinsed clean, no longer tinted green with algae. The pump with its tube, all the equipment and food had been neatly stacked on the floor.

Sadness is seeping in, numbing my arms. It is trickling up from a jab in my heart into my throat. I was very fond of Beetlebomb. My eyes brim with tears. He died all alone. Did he panic? Did he think

I'd abandoned him when I went away? Poor little fellow. What had Father done with him? Why didn't he wait till I got home? Was he trying to spare me? I mean, I saw him floating upside down, I knew he was dead. I hope Father buried him outside in the back garden. I wish I'd had a chance to say good-bye.

"So what did you do with him?" I hear my voice say.

"Who?"

"Beetlebomb!"

"Why, I flushed him away."

"Down the TOILET?"

"Yes!"

Father's matter-of-fact attitude scorches me. I am filled with disgust. I glare at him.

"Come on, Lois, when it all comes out in the wash, it was just a turtle."

"But he was my mine—and he was my pet!" I protest, "I was the one who found him, so why shouldn't I have a say what to do with him?"

"Yes, all fine and dandy, and yet he might very well have been what made me sick. Your 'Aunt Ani' at the Reserve said so, remember? Do you think we want his carcass sticking around? He could have poisoned you, all of us. What I did was best."

Mrs. Molnar's shrill voice is still nattering away in the kitchen, alternating with Mother's firm responses.

Oblivious to my mood, Father cocks his head toward the kitchen.

He asks, "Is that the fifth Geneva Convention in the making, or is World War III about to erupt?"

He adds, "If that woman thinks she will hold sway over Mother, she's got a surprise coming! When it comes down to sheer iron will, your Mother is strong enough to sink the Bismarck!" and wiggles his eyebrows at me.

From what I recall about differences of opinion between him and Mother, I doubt that very much. Father usually won any spats hands down.

There seems to be a truce when I hear Mother call out, "Lois, Becky, can you help, please?" followed by the sound of aluminum foil being unfurled from its box, and serrated teeth tearing off chunks in various lengths.

"Mrs. Molnar has kindly offered her food to us for tomorrow night's supper. We will have to wrap it securely. Take it all downstairs, please, and store it in the back-up fridge in the laundry room."

While Becky and I help pack up Mrs. Molnar's food, Mother finishes up in the kitchen.

We see her slapping the pumpkin pie fixings together, laying out the crust in the pie plate and carving off then neatly pinching the edges all round, sliding the works into the oven, and setting the timer for 40 minutes. She had removed the corning ware dish with the scalloped potatoes along with the roasting pan with the cooked ham, and placed them on the sideboard to await warm-up after the pie was done.

Mother leads Mrs. Molnar and Becky into the living room.

"Supper won't be ready until *5:30*—as planned," Mother says, eyeing Mrs. Molnar meaningfully, "Mind if we join you?"

Father puts down his newspaper reluctantly. Cornered on a holiday weekend with no excuses either real or imaginary to fabricate, he has no choice but comply. "By all mean!" he says, evenly.

"Would anyone care for a glass of wine?" Mother asks, brightly. This is a daring move since any form of liquor is a rare sight in our home. At Christmas, we put out sherry for Santa Claus. Liquor is imbibed at New Year's, and only beer by Father and my Uncle during hot summer months.

The Grandfathers
3-2

4 p.m.

"So you are from Hungary, Mrs. Molnar?"

"Yes, yes. Of course!"

I've noticed this habit at other times, the way she says "Of course!" as though she knows the truth of any matter, so why shouldn't we?

I can tell this instantly annoys Father, the way he blinks hard and pulls in his breath.

"Your country is in the throes of a revolution. Canada has been receiving many refugees as a result."

"Yes, yes. Hungary has had three revolutions—big one in 1849, next in 1918, and now this one since last year, 1956. All of them blood baths."

Glum silence.

"Are you a refugee, Eszter?" Mother questions hesitantly, "I've been meaning to ask but I didn't want to pry—"

Mrs. Molnar shakes her head, cuts Mother off and replies, "Almost, but not quite so, as I left just in time. I have landed immigrant visa. It is important that you ask, for I want to tell you now how we come to be in Canada, Bo and I. I also need to tell the truth of why I am here today. There is more to say now than just visit."

"Oh, surely we can leave that till another day, Mrs. Molnar," Father says, shifting pleading eyes to Mother.

"No. I say to you it is imperative that I tell you *now* our story! Soon you will understand why is important I do so! Okay?"

Father looks puzzled. "I was unaware of an agenda for today's get-together. Were you, Dear?"

Mother brushes that off quickly by saying: "Only to enjoy a traditional Canadian Thanksgiving turkey dinner," and with hostess vigour, inquires: "Did you live in Budapest, Eszter? I hear it is a beautiful old city! It is on the Danube, is it not?"

"Yes, I lived in Budapest. Very ancient city, so much history! But as a child, mostly I lived at the Zemplen estate, in north-eastern Hungary, which had been passed down from my Great-Grandfather."

"So your family were landowners?" Father asks.

"Yes, yes."

"Was it a country estate? Or was it a mansion, with enough surrounding grounds for extensive lawns and gardens?"

"No no, my family owned big estate, with barns and stables, livestock and horses, it was a large working farm with many parcels of land held by tenants—"

"Oh!" I clap my hands together eagerly, "Was your Great-Grandfather a feudal lord, Mrs. Molnar? Were the tenants his serfs?"

She looks back at me balefully.

Nonetheless, I am transported.

"In grade seven, I learned about the manorial system. Were the large estate owners of Hungary as rich and powerful as the lords and ladies of England?"

"What you wonder is: was my family part of the nobility, do I have royal blood? The answer to both questions is no."

"You look very regal, all dressed in gold!"

She was even sitting in the gold satin-brocade armchair.

"Why now, thank you, Lo-iss!" Mrs. Molnar simpers.

"You said your family owned an estate, and horses." Then my mind goes sailing unchecked on its own whimsical tack. I ask, "Did you have your own horse?"

"When I was a child, I had my own pony. But first, to be exact, I had a miniature horse. So did my childhood friend, later to be my husband Bence! Do you know about miniature horses? Ours came down from the line bred in the 17th century by the Habsburg nobility. They used them as ornamental pets. Ours were named Ici and Pici. In English I think is meaning Itsy and Bitsy."

Inwardly I wince, remembering what the guys at school call Mitsy and me: 'Titsy and Bitsy'. Ouch. I realize how distant Mitsy had become in my consciousness, how free I felt in this short time away from her terrorizing antics. Was it only yesterday when she turned up at the Showdown? Today, it is a shock to even think of her, she seems so inconsequential. Then I am drawn back into Mrs. Molnar's tale:

"We were free to ride all over his Papa's and my Papa's adjoining estates, through the woods, across streams, over grass-blown fields—so much true enjoyment—with the komondors Samson and Delilah galloping along parallel with us, happy too to be running full tilt, breathing in the fresh air and fun!"

"What are komondors?"

"Those were our sheep dogs—You not know that breed? Perhaps they are only in Hungary. Their coats have long white tight curlilocks that make them look like factory floor mops! They would spot us heading out on a ride and would come barrelling out of the herd to come along with us, delirious at prospect of every outing, panting alongside us happily! They served as our guardians as much as they also protected the sheep. I tell you, sometimes they would dive into a flock, and only we knew where they were because of the V in the parting of the animals, otherwise, they blended in so well!"

"Did you ride your horses bareback?" I press.

"No no, they had their own tack—is right word? By which I mean little saddles, bits for in mouths, with reins, very, very cute. But Bence and I grew, Ici and Pici did not. By time we became six and eight years old, our feet almost dragged on ground! So our fathers bought us ponies. They were imported Dartmoor shetlands. One was pinto and other one dappled grey. We named them Hinta and Palinta after children's Hungarian swinging song.

"Come, Bo, sing the song along with me!
Hinta, Palinta
Regi dunna

Kis katona
Ugorj a Tiszaba!
Zsupsz!"

"What does it mean?" I ask.

"I cannot translate exactly. Only to say that that one child pushes the other one on swing so hard that 'Whoops!' the child flies off swing and lands in Tisza River!"

"That sounds as harsh as our Rockabye Baby lullaby," Mother contributes, "Do you know it?" Mother starts singing, emphasizing "bough breaks" and "cradle will fall" ending with:

"Down will come cradle
Baby and all!"

"Oh—ah! how strange is that?" Mrs. Molnar exclaims, clasping her hands, "In folk songs of both cultures, such a buried death wish for the children!"

"It's a wonder that they manage to survive at all with such menacing thoughts!" Mother laughs.

Meanwhile, I am obsessed with Mrs. Molnar's estate.

"Did you live year round at your estate?"

"No. When we reached school age, we children were moved to the city and only went to Zemplen estate during vacation breaks."

"Quickly, I shall explain about the estates because it is important!

"Our Great-Grandfathers were in mining industry in Zemplen Mountains which is how how they came to know each other. They became business partners and close friends, so they each bought expired estates side by side out in Zemplen County.

"In Hungary, there was the upper nobility, called the 'magnates', who in the parliament occupied the House of Magnates, comparable to the British House of Lords, whose wealth was mostly based on the vast estates they owned. Well into the early nineteen hundreds, magnates continued to have tenants and lived from the rent.

"Our families were what one calls 'new gentry'. New gentry wealth was acquired in commerce or industry. In essence, we were the 'bourgeoisie', in cities called 'nouveau riche'. Along with purchase of those estates came tenants whose rents supplemented the income.

"So there both industrial magnates and royal magnates!" Father grins, slapping his thigh, feeling his oats for being so witty.

Mrs. Molnar stares at him, not comprehending. Neither did Mother, or myself, for that matter. It was an inside joke that Father is enjoying with himself.

"Our estates endured many changes. With impending takeover of Communist leader Béla Kun in 1919, the Grandfathers were forewarned that all landholdings of more than a certain size—more than 400,000 square metres—would be seized by the Government, taken over in name of agricultural reform, chopped up, distributed among farmers who would work the land. But clever Grandfathers were one jump ahead! They broke up their two estates beforehand, in such a way that divided lands would be suited as much to locals' liking as to their own, and would still satisfy new rules coming in soon.

"They transferred title to long-time tenants?" Father attempts to clarify.

"Yes. The tenants continued to lease, not pay rent. But they were not like what you say? serfs, for they had status, were vital to the community. By their action, the Grandfathers honoured and protected their heritage before new rules could disperse them elsewhere, or break up their farms into tinier impractical bundles. The Grandfathers still retained enough of estates for their own farming and pasture-land.

"Close to the village proper, there was some common open space that was used as public fairgrounds. But mostly the common lands were the woods, the forests, the little waterfalls and natural streams. This is where for centuries everyone had access to enjoy hunting, fishing, foraging for wood, mushrooms or berries, could go picnicking, enjoying the beauty of nature! To protect the forests and wild areas, the Grandfathers retained the common lands inside the entire estate boundaries. This way it could not be wrested away by Government and was reserved for general use in perpetuum by the local people. "

"Sounds like our provincial parks, which are to be preserved in their natural state for posterity," Father said with a tone of national pride.

"Yes, yes, but those provincial parks of yours are too far away from day-to-day life of the people. And they are not left in natural state. There is still logging, the woods are pruned, and much of the grasses are mown! You even have to pay an entrance fee!" Mrs. Molnar sniffs in reproof. "Grandfathers' common land was left wide open, unfenced, untouched, growing wild as always, and in the forest everything was left as is, as was, always had been!"

Clasping my hands, I exclaim: "This is what Pinewood is going to be!"

"Really?" Mrs. Molnar asks, with a tone of doubt in her voice.

"Yes! As you know from your participation as a Ratepayer, Pinewood will be left natural, similar to the common land that you have described, Mrs. Molnar! It is my dream that the fields and the woods and Willow Creek of Pinewood will be preserved just as is! That way, no matter how built-up the land around and beyond Centrewood becomes, people will have a place to go where they can appreciate nature, and the natural way of life for turtles and butterflies and birds, and all wild things can go on undisturbed! Right, Father?"

Father's face turns still. Mother's hand slips out toward him, as though to calm—or caution? him.

"Mrs. Molnar," I ask, "If the Great-Grandfathers had not claimed the commons land as part of their own property, could the Communist Party have seized it, and would they have ended up building anything they wanted? Except for putting Pinewood aside as a park, are the Centrewood developers free to destroy every morsel of pastureland, just because they own it? I mean, do they have the right to reshape the original lay of the land itself into huge mounds and berms, as if it isn't good enough the way it is?"

Each query is interspersed with: "Probably. Most likely. Yes." She said: "Communists very much are like modern developers in that regard. Whatever was not in use was for the taking!"

I don't let it go at that. I pursue my line of thought:

"That's what our forefathers did to the Indians during colonial times. White man arrived, they presumed they owned everything, and they started dividing up all the land without any respect for treaties where the Crown had promised to honour land that the Indians claimed they owned. The newcomers felt free to use the land any way they wanted. They had no respect for the Indians' fishing or hunting rights, either!"

"Lois, button up," Father snaps.

"White man continues to do it even up to this day!" I object, "For example, over on Mississauga Road, developers have built a golf course on top of a Mississauga Indian graveyard without even saving the markers."

"How do you know that?" Becky asks.

Because of Father's restrictions, I can't tell her how I know it is true.

Chief Fred King told us this when we visited the New Credit reserve.

Just in the nick of time, I remembered that Father forbade me to talk about our visit.

***

Father does not rebuke me for saying as much as I did. Instead, he wilfully ignores Becky's query, and marvels, "What an eidetic memory that girl has!"

Mother clings to Mrs. Molnar's words, "I can't help thinking how generous it was of the Grandfathers—to grant the tenants deeds!" she says.

"Although let's face it, it was pragmatic, Dear!" Father comments.

"It must have been painful to give up owning so much land."

"Yes and No," Mrs. Molnar says, "Yes, because it meant irreversible change. No, because their title-transfers earned the Grandfathers valuable bonus."

"What was that?"

"Later, when it really counted, it earned our families a whole wealth of good will."

***

"How did the magnates fare who did not break up their own estates?" Father asks.

"With Communist nationalization, our two estates were still able to function, although greatly reduced in size and income, because the remaining land on our estates continued to be worked, also because we had livestock.

"What about Government approval?"

"Our operation met the requirements of agrarian reform."

"Did the Government seize much of your produce?"

"Yes, increasingly so. Times became very tough for most farms."

"But your Grandfathers were involved in mining as well?"

"Of course!"

See Father flinch.

"That was our main business. However, opportunity knocked for us. Mining and estate became not the only source of income. It turned out that new gentry and magnates who owned estates but did not work the land, who had no livestock, no additional income, no other income but rent from their tenants, those were the ones who knew that once their landholdings were dispersed that they would have nothing. They would have to flee or face ruin.

"This is how else our Grandfathers had vision! In such instances, before the Government could expropriate over-large estates and confiscate the contents, before there was no longer enough time for those to sell off possessions themselves before fleeing, our Grandfathers established a new business. They persuaded those facing bankruptcy to entrust their estate chattel to Molnar-Nemeth Antiques. With agreement signed with Grandfathers, the émigré magnates were able to plan their own departure independent from sale of estate possessions. Before confiscation of their estate property by Government, they commissioned Grandfathers to proceed with liquidation of all assets, that is, for their homes to be stripped holy-boly—"

"You mean 'holus bolus'?"

"Yes, yes! Of art and valuables, including all furnishings, all contents. Whereupon, their belongings were immediately removed by the Grandfathers, leaving the mansions—some residences almost as large as castles, empty."

"All the furnishings? Carpets and tapestries and everything?"

"Yes."

"They virtually—er, stripped the mansions of those old estates, licked them clean?"

Mrs. Molner nods vigorously, and proudly.

"Anything 'with legs', our Grandfathers would say, was spirited away."

"What about all the history that was dismantled? Surely this was one step away from grave-robbing!"

"They did not feel the least bit guilty, if that is what you imply. They had learned to their horror what the Bolsheviks during the Revolution, the ignorant 'proletariat', did to the mansions in Moscow—they used everything that would burn, to warm themselves, yes, for fire during bitter cold months, but still—no respect for historical artefacts, so the Magnates had no qualms about estate treasures being rescued for other people who would appreciate them."

"And not see the furniture burned for firewood, or elegantly etched brass spittoons for pisspots."

"Graham!"

"They divided the chattel into two categories. Large furniture pieces like armoires—that is called in Europe wardrobes used in bed chambers as clothing closets, yes? Also, large sideboards and buffets from dining halls, deep storage cupboards and bookcases, any large items were stored in 'secure' barns, sheds, attics, village basements in the immediate area of wherever the dismantled estate was located."

"What happened to the rest of it?"

"Molnar-Nemeth Antiques dealership was established in downtown Budapest. Smaller to medium-sized items such as urns, settees, lamps, mirrors, paintings, dressing tables, writing desks, were sent directly to the Molnar-Nemeth warehouse. In due course, these items were restored and refinished to immaculate perfection by expert craftsmen—woodworkers, cabinetmakers and such."

"What happened to these articles?"

"On street side of warehouse, they established a storefront."

"But who in Budapest would buy estate sale furnishings?" Mother asks.

"It took no time at all to build a regular clientele, because what we had to sell met the interests of the 'new wealth' growing in the city who were building big new mansions and townhouses, and wanting to make big impression as members of establishment, no?"

"What happened to all the larger pieces? Are they still stored somewhere in the country?"

"Many of these pieces ended up being shipped out of country. Later. At advent of War." At which point, Mrs. Molnar drifts off for a while in thought.

She snaps to abruptly. "Where was I?"

"Didn't the government object?"

"By the time they realized what was happening, it had all become 'above-board'. The Government could not charge Molnar-Nemeth Antiques with theft since every item was recorded and the signature of its original owner available on command. Meticulous books were kept which showed date of acquisition and amount of compensation at time of sale once business had taken its commission."

Father strokes his chin.

"Why didn't your Grandfathers leave in 1919 with the other estate émigrés?"

"We were in similar pickle as others in that there was not enough cash flow. The Grandfathers saw opportunity to capitalize on others' situations. As for time of departure, our Grandfathers opted to stay till they saw best moment. They had a plan to get out of Hungary, to get away from totalitarianism without arriving elsewhere without a single pengo to pinch!"

"What's a pengo?" I ask.

"It is a coin—like your penny."

Mother said: "Over here, the expression is 'without two pennies to rub together.'"

"So—so—interesting how close are some expressions, no?!"

"At first, they thought they had very little time. But as it turned out, they had twenty years—Yes! Over the next two decades they built strong business inside Hungary while continuing to expand. They created additional new business named Molnar-Nemeth Import-Exports.

"During that time Hungary still had close economic ties with Germany, so stops along the Rhine as well as ports such as Hamburg and Bremerhaven were used until around 1935. Alternate routes were forged west into Switzerland and France. Cities in Russia and Italy were altogether avoided. The chains led away from totalitarian countries to Scandinavia and Great Britain as far west as Canada.

"Over the course of twenty years, our Fathers ran a reputable company which was recognized everywhere along the way by officials and customs houses."

"Who would have guessed there would be so much estate chattel to sell," Father comments.

"Oh yes. With entire belongings, so much activity, emptying the old, filling the new."

"Sounds like musical chairs!"

At various points in the conversation, Mother excuses herself, first to take the pie out of the oven and to put the ham and potatoes in again for a 'wee warmup', and then to check the cooking pots simmering on low on the elements.

Finally, she rises, hops into the kitchen, and puts out the call for us to start laying out the dinner on the dining room table.

"Supper's ready—at last!"

"Lois, fill the pickle dish, dear!"

"Becky, take the pickled beet dish from the fridge, remove the saran wrap, and put it out, please!"

"Eszter, follow after me, please, take these hot plate pads, put them under the scalloped potatoes and the corn and other hot dishes before I set them down!"

"Graham, please get in here and slice the ham!"

Thanksgiving Dinner
3-3

5:30 p.m.

With her troops under full command, Mother manages to get the dinner out onto the table and have us all seated.

Mrs. Molnar delivers a lengthy grace in Hungarian filled with plenty of rolled r's and long extended vowels. This makes Father fidget about the foreign intrusion to one of his traditional customs, also about the food getting cold. To his relief, the platters are finally passed clockwise until everyone has filled their plates.

We all dive in. For a brief spate of time, there is only the blissful sound of silverware clanking against Mother's treasured porcelain china dinner plates.

I can hardly say I am starved but I love maple syrup on ham with glazed pineapple, and I could eat the entire pan of scalloped potatoes on my own. Fresh corn on the cob rolled in a patty of butter is divine. I could ruin my appetite just gorging on that.

"You people," Mrs. Molnar says, breaking the blissful silence, "You people have to learn to use spices, your food is so bland!"

" 'You people'?" exclaims Father, "Is that what we're called now here in Canada?" at the same time as Mother looks up and says: "You mean this food is tasteless?"

"We-ll-l-l—" Mrs. Molnar begins.

"With all due respect, Mrs. Molnar," Father says, "May I posit that perhaps 'you people' have become accustomed to overloading your own tastebuds with spices to such a degree that you now drown the real taste of food!"

"Not at all, not at all! It is your tastebuds which need to be wakened up!"

Father rejoins, "I disagree. The less spiced up the food, the more the natural flavours can be savoured and appreciated. In comparison, look at it this way: there are only so many spices 'you people' can use, so the end result is that everything 'you people' cook ends up tasting the same—not like the original food at all, but just like the limited range of available spices themselves!"

"Ah, you are wrong! And that you will find out tomorrow, Mr. Michelsen, when you compare your English-style boiled beets and cider vinegar with my Hungarian beet borscht served on top with a spoonful of sour cream, then you will see there is no comparison! Have you ever heard of goulash?"

"Yes, I have! I wear two of them on my feet in wintertime when it's cold and wet out!"

"Graham!" Mother is forced to laugh, "He is referring to his galoshes!"

"What? No, no, not rubber boots! This is a Hungarian food dish about which I am talking!"

Mrs. Molnar's face has turned into a dark thundercloud.

Mother had laughed at Father's wit, but sees that Mrs. Molnar is not amused. Always the diplomat, she says, "It all just depends on what we have become accustomed, does it not? Everything comes down to custom. With food, it's either heavily spiced or lightly flavoured."

But then she turns wicked. "Same as with scents. Some prefer a light spray of eau de cologne behind the ears, whereas others douse themselves in perfume, splashing it on their wrists and behind their knees, wherever they please, like crazy people!"

I suspect that this is Mother's way of retaliating for serving 'bland' food.

"You are saying that my perfume is too strong?"

"Not necessarily!" Mother hedges, "I'm only saying that to me, there is always the full spectrum of possibility, each according to custom. From my perspective, it is probably the Englishwoman in me that prefers subtlety to anything overstated. That goes for all manner of tastes, be they cuisine, scents, even such embellishments as, well, say—jewellery!"

Mrs. Molnar was indeed drenched in some kind of heavy smelling perfume. Being next to her was like standing with your nose in a clump of lilacs in full bloom—like those left growing in Pinewood by the old farmhouse foundation. Before Mother mentioned it, I hadn't really noticed anything offensive about Mrs. Molnar's perfume. Or at least, I didn't find it off-putting at all, until the power of Mother's opinion began to seep into my awareness.

As for Mrs. Molnar's jewellery, during dinner I found myself staring at her bracelet and earrings, but mostly her choker necklace, the large polished yellow stones set in the solid ornate braid of gold. From this vantage point, I can discern more closely how deftly the stones were notched at the corners, and the sides beveled downward from a flat plane in two concentric rectangular steps. Compared with Mother's delicate little diamond studs and modest diamond chip on a thin silver chain, I have to admit to myself that Mrs. Molnar's chunky jewellery is overbearing, and almost overpowers her small frame. This is how Mother's opinion can so quickly hold sway with me.

But simultaneously, I let my imagination carry me away: It struck me that Mrs. Molnar, already in her gold dress and jewellery, should be crowned by a gold tiara heavily bedecked with even more matching yellow stones. Rather than our streamlined Scandinavian-style teak dining room chair in which she sat, the gold brocade armchair in the livingroom suited her better. In fact, I suddenly see Mrs. Molnar seated in a plush, gold, upholstered, royal throne, its solidly carved and fluted wooden frame gilded with real gold. Overhead, rather than the sleek wooden arms bearing the four glass-hooded bulbs in our dining room, I see an elaborate chandelier plugged solid with gobs of golden crystals made of the same stone.

Oddly, without ever having met a European lady, or any foreigner for that matter, I am struck how out of place she is, here in this room, if not in this country. A fish out of water. A queen outside her realm.

"You do not like my jewellery either?" Mrs. Molnar growls, her fork and knife hovering mid-air.

"Some of us prefer a modest sprinkling of jewellery rather than the Taj Mahal!" Mother retorts, stabbing at her peas. Her tone is turning even more cutting.

Father's fork and knife begins to hover, as though fearing a clash of utensils.

"Well you know what they say: 'Garish or Garnish!'" Father proclaims.

Luckily, his impromptu outburst falls on Mother's good side.

"Oh, Graham! You are too much!" Mother laughs.

But Mrs. Molnar doesn't get it. She just bends her head over her food and resumes eating, sawing at her slab of ham as though it is the culprit that had offended her, and that it is at fault in some way.

I find myself looking at Mother in a new light. I have never seen her quite so spunky, and certainly never so snippy. Her conduct was still lady-like, still civil, but verging on pugnacious. Mother has always been the paragon of politeness to me, my role model to whom I could turn for showing how to deal with touchy situations. Obviously, she is irritated. Mrs. Molnar has insulted her cooking. Her manner bothers me though. I feel my hackles rise. Am I feeling defensive on behalf of Mrs. Molnar, who I adore? Is it because she is a foreigner with a language barrier and cannot fight for herself?

I also find myself looking at Mrs. Molnar in a new light, unwillingly taken aback by a side of Mrs. Molnar that I had not seen before. I realize that I had only really known her when she was at home, not when she was out visiting. In her own home, she was very warm and attentive, almost gushing the way she fluttered about, wanted to be sure I was comfy and content and well tended.

I suppose that at home, she feels at ease, in control, can name her game. Here, today at least, she is all wound up, she seems to be on the attack or on edge—one or the other, or both—and I fight against disliking her for her sharpness, for being so critical, and argumentative. She is so tense, so unnecessarily aggressive! Why is she criticizing the meal, instead of being appreciative. That is not how I was raised. You ate what was placed in front of you, and you were grateful. Everything she has said has been provocative and taunting. I watch her speculatively and wonder why. Was she trying to make her conversation stimulating, was this her way to trying to be a witty conversationalist? Was that it? If so, she wasn't doing very well.

As soon as the plates were empty, she springs up from the table and moves into gear.

"Eszter, why don't you relax? The girls will clear the table. Lois knows what to do in the kitchen—Scrape them off and give them a quick rinse, Dear, we'll do the dishes tomorrow! Once that's done, I shall put the kettle on and serve up the dessert."

"No, no, I help!"

Mother puts out a restraining hand, "No, no, you sit!"

"Your wife is very bossy, Mr. Michelsen!"

"There's the pot calling the kettle black!" Mother interjects.

I start wending my way around the table to collect empty dishes.

"You bet she is! You'd better do what you're told!" Father laughs, reaching out to Mother as she passes by, to put his arm around her, "Take it from me! My wife may be bossy but she's the best boss— and the prettiest—and the greatest cook—a husband could ever have!" he says, squeezing Mother's waist. He reaches out to hug me as well, but I duck his other arm.

It is now that the reason for her obnoxiousness comes out. Mrs. Molnar reverts immediately to her old grudge. She pushes out her lower lip, "I brought Hungarian cooking with me, so you could taste but no! Emily says not!"

"I said 'not today', Eszter, I didn't say 'never'!"

"But all that food, so much time I spent, cooking and preparing," she says, pulling a long pout.

"Didn't we agree that we will enjoy your dinner here tomorrow? Isn't it all safely stored away downstairs in the cooler until then? It is not going to waste."

Mother looks at Father, knowing he has not yet been consulted about her solution for the double-dinner argument.

Father chooses to come to Mother's defence:

"Well now, look at it this way, Mrs. Molnar. I've not been to any restaurant in town that mixes two traditional foods at once, have you? Just think, you are seated in a French restaurant at a table with a white table cloth and elegant candles when the maître d' arrives, white cloth over arm, and he says: 'Madame, voulez-vous a grand heap of meatballs and spaghetti with your roast chi-cken and red wine, oui oui? or we haff a très très grande special tonight, we are also serving Chinese chop suey with our pheasant under glass from Provence, you like?"

Mrs. Molnar sits back for a moment.

There is a painfully long pause for reflection.

"I grasp your point, Mr. Michelsen!" She looks around at each of us in turn. "I must apologize!"

She slumps.

With elbows on the table, she holds her face in her hands.

Like a punctured tire, all the air seems to rush out of her, until she is completely deflated.

Even her face seems longer and thinner.

The contrast between an overbearing queen bee and a wee flea confounds us.

"All week I have been very—how you say? Biscomdobbalated?"

"Discombobulated? You have been upset?"

"Of course! Yes, yes! Er—very upset. I tell you now. I have had bad news from home. I have been so looking forward all week to meeting today, hoping to share with you, hoping to ask for your help, for your support!"

"I knew there must be something wrong, Eszter! If you would forgive me, I would say that you have not been yourself this evening! What is the bad news, Eszter?"

Mrs. Molnar's brow is so rumpled, she barely has a forehead. Her eyes are hollowed out and bloodshot. She looks old and haggard. Her whole demeanour has changed before our eyes.

Finally, she speaks:

"I see now the reason that I cooked and brought so much food. I think I hoped I could bribe you into wanting to pay attention to me and my troubles. Instead, I have insulted and annoyed you. I made it even worse with that bad comment about Canadian cooking, but it is wicked to compare national cuisines, as both are good in their own ways. It was not meant to be critical of your own cooking, Emily! What a clumsy oof—" "Oaf, Mama!" "Oaf, I have been! I hope I have not made you all so uncomfortable that you cannot forgive me?"

The relief is palpable.

"Not at all!!" Father and Mother exclaim together.

"Shall we talk in the living room?"

"Yes! We shall have our tea and dessert in there!"

Dessert is Served
3-4

7:00 p.m. Living room

While we dip our dessert forks into our fresh pumpkin pie topped with swirls of whipped cream, with our little porcelain-china dessert plates resting on our napkin-draped laps, very little is spoken. I'm sure Father is glad of that so he can enjoy his pumpkin pie without interruption. I too am glad of it. The best way to enjoy a real treat is to savour it in silence.

Mrs. Molnar in her gold sheath dress and golden jewellery is seated looking regal as ever, straight-backed, ankles crossed, in the upholstered gold satin brocade armchair.

Facing her across the way, Father is sitting in his easy chair, knees crossed, one foot flapping a brown leather dress slipper.

The kettle is whistling in the kitchen.

It is getting darker outside by the second.

I am delegated to collect the dessert dishes from the end tables.

Mother comes out with the teapot, and starts pouring and passing out the tea.

Mrs. Molnar draws the nearby side table up close to her knees.

She clears her throat and holds the fort once more.

Nesting her dainty teacup and saucer in her strong regal hands, she looks us all in the eye in turn, and then she speaks:

"You must wonder, no? how Bo and I can afford to live here in such a fine setting as Centrewood, a mother and daughter, just the two of us? You ask yourself about my income, yes? how I make a living?"

Father shifts uncomfortably in his easy chair. "No, not at all! It has never crossed our minds!"

I see him glance sideways at Mother for agreement.

"It's none of our business!" Mother cries, to no avail.

It is true. Even at my age I know enough that grownups never talk about how much they earn. They compare the cost of things, true. Women compare the price of clothing between Simpson and Eaton's, or the cost of food from one grocery store to another. When men talk about cars, the price is never mentioned, there is only an exchange of some competitive remarks about the value by the way they compare the size of the tires, the dimensions of the chassis, or whether the engine is a V-6 or a V-8, whatever that is. The year and the model of the car in itself is enough to convey the value, rather than stating it in actual dollar amounts. At home, not even husbands or wives discuss their finances, certainly not in front of children, and not even between close brothers like Father and Uncle Ronnie. It just isn't done.

I have to admit that Mrs. Molnar has a point about a woman living alone with her child, supporting herself on her own, as that is indeed very rare. All women are supposed to have husbands to take care of them, the way Father takes care of Mother and myself. Mind you, come to think of it, Mitsy's mother is also on her own, supporting herself and Mitsy, at least she appears to be the only one supporting that family unit of two. But that is because her pilot husband is away. So she isn't entirely on her own. She's just alone for now.

Mrs. Molnar reaches upward with her right hand toward the heavy gold-linked choker necklace, her fingers favouring that particular flat yellow stone that rests in that curious indentation at the base of the throat located just between the collarbones. She slips her thumb under the gem, places her index finger on the shiny topside and proceeds to rub the stone on both sides with both forefinger and thumb. This action seems to serve as a pacifier, for she calms down visibly, more or less instantly.

"Excuse me, Eszter, but I thought you were going to share some terrible event with us," Mother says.

"May I say outright that any discussion of your personal finances is off the table," Father intervenes.

With a grand flourish, Mrs. Molnar flicks her right wrist, lifts her right hand palm up, fingers pressed together and waggles them as one unit at Mother and Father to stop their clamour:

"You both shush now!"

Whoa! This is new as well! I have never heard one adult to tell another adult to be quiet! I can see that neither Father nor Mother appreciate it much. But they clam up, just as they would for a school marm.

In a slow and deliberate manner, Mrs. Molnar fishes around in her bulky handbag and pulls out a purple velvet string bag which she slowly opens, carefully removing a cloth scroll which she unfolds in a succession of stones which she lays out in a row on the little table at her knees.

"Here before me I have thirteen different stones laid out in a special order."

She points to each stone, naming each one in turn:

"Red Garnet. White Opal. Purple Amethyst. Green Emerald. Black Onyx. Yellow Citrine. Blue Sapphire. Sulphur. Coal. Bloodstone. Blue Sodalite. Green Malachite. Stone pebble. "

"You will note that ten of these are semi-precious stones which have already been cut and polished, three of which have already been set in silver as finished pieces of jewellery. The remaining three are not in any way regarded as precious in the world of gemology. In fact, you will recognize one of them is a simple water-tumbled pebble.

"The other two are rocks, the Sulphur and the Coal, and would never be polished or used as jewellery due to their uncouth nature."

"An uncouth rock! I never thought of rocks as having human attributes!" Father remarks.

"Granted, I have heard how 'crude' coal can be!" Mother is quick to comment.

"Good one, Emily! I suppose many minerals are so rude, they are known to be 'base'!!"

"As for rocks, I've heard wives often warn husbands not to take them 'for granite'!"

"Oh now, Em, be 'gneiss'!"

Father and Mother have lapsed into one of their familiar sparring routines.

Mrs. Molnar neither grasps nor appreciates their levity. It is obvious that she knows neither the purpose of a pun nor its valuation on a 'wit' scale, based on its originality and swiftness of delivery.

(Becky doesn't get puns either. I explained to her the "play on words" by reaching for "double entendres", usually by employing a humble homonym. "She told me there is no other language in the world other than English where this is practiced. "Not French?" I jibed. "Well, certainly not German. Not Russian. Definitely not Hungarian."— "Not even *Pun*-jabi?" I asked. She laughed. I think that is the first pun she ever got)

Mrs. Molnar mistakenly thinks Father and Mother are making fun of her.

She glowers with fierce disapproval.

"Each of these stones will help me tell my story. One by one, I shall work my way through them! When I reach the last, then my tale will be done."

"My, my!" Mother inserts, "You came prepared!"

Father, for one, is not enthralled: "For 'scrying' out loud!" he barks, "What is this, some exercise in crystal-ball gazing? Mrs. Molnar, please put these stones away, and get to the point. What happened to you this week?"

"Tch, tch," says Mrs. Molnar, shaking her head, "All in good time!"

"Now now, Graham, be patient!" says Mother, attempting to placate him.

"To tell our story, I must begin at end of Great War in 1918," Mrs. Molnar states.

Father pleads, "Surely not a blow by blow historical account, Mrs. Molnar! That's—" he did a rapid calculation in his head: "Forty years ago!"

Trying to be facetious but still make his point, he yelps: "Should I grab a pillow and a blanket? Will this be an all-nighter?" He turns to Mother:" Do we have enough bacon and eggs in the fridge to serve all of us breakfast, Dear?"

Mother's brow creases.

Mrs. Molnar ignores him.

"At end of Great War in 1918, there was great rejoicing! We had revolution, yes? Freedom! We had first democracy!"

"I never knew until this very day that Hungary had more than one revolution!" Mother says, and on second thought admits: "As if I know anything about Hungary!"

"We have had three revolutions—one in 1849, and two since end of Great War—one in 1918 and the other, it erupted in earnest just last year, 1956," Mrs. Molnar states, gruffly.

"Is that so?" Mother says, politely.

"With violent uprisings come bloodbaths. Budapest has seen three bloodbaths, one in 1919, another in 1944, and this one now."

"One would wonder with so much turmoil, how any country would have a chance to recuperate!"

"It had too much against it, to ever stabilize. Each time there was another enemy, first the Reds versus the Whites, then the Nazis with Arrow Cross, and then the Soviets.

"I thought Hungary was always a Communist country ever since the end of the Great War!" Father says.

"Not so—No! In 1918, the Austro-Hungarian Monarchy, it collapsed! What came then was first major revolution since 1867! You have heard of Aster Revolution?" Mrs. Molnar asks, panning around to all of us with questioning eyes.

We all shake our heads, including Becky.

"That was when troops and peoples together all rushed into streets wearing aster flower on hats or lapels to show they wanted democracy."

"Does this mean that Hungary was independent? I thought it was attached to Austria, you know, as part of the Austro-Hungarian Empire!" Father inquires.

"Yes, yes. You see, Hungary already had separate parliament from Austria won during Habsburg regime way back with 1867 Compromise! So existed already in Hungary the Diet, the Parliament.

"With 1918 revolution, Hungary was declared independent republic! Was election! You have heard of Count Mihaly Karolyi?" Again we are panned. Again we shake our heads. "He became President, leader of Hungarian Democratic Republic!!"

"One year later, 1919, Karolyi won only minority, and formed coalition with Social Democrats."

"Socialist AND Democrat—that's a combination I've never been able to grasp," Father interjects.

Mother is quick to enjoin: "Whyever not? I grew up in England! There was both a Socialist Democrat and a Communist party. A Socialist government can still be democratic. It only means that there would be a more just society, if some of the profits gained from capitalism went to serve needs held in common by the public at large. That is how I know the difference!"

"Ah, but at that time Karolyi was not knowing they had merged with the Communists."

"Democratic AND Communist, that's really a new one," Father muses aloud, possibly egging her on.

"It is not possible. Suddenly, Hungary is no longer Democratic or Socialist, it is Communist!" Mrs. Molnar snaps.

"So Hungary enjoyed a democracy for only one year?"

"Exactly! Is now clear?"

"Clear as mud," Father grumps.

CHAPTER FOUR
Thirteen Stones

Red Garnet (#1)
4-1

Maybe so about mud, but it is clear that Mrs. Molnar is annoyed with us. She does not like our attitude, which to her seems both frivolous and indifferent to her country's ordeal, and our unwillingness to settle down and listen to her story. One contributing factor to our resistance is that we were neither consulted or advised that we were in for a long history lesson, even though Father had tried to tell her how tired we are from our outing to Niagara Falls. I suppose she figures we had a jolly, carefree holiday and should be up to a lecture. She is baffled as well by our attitude, not knowing such facetious behaviour is typical of Anglo-Canadians with north country British blood in their genes, it being their way of confronting adversity, be it bitter cold or famine or war. The more dire the situation, the more likely the ribaldry, as though making light of a bad situation lessens the severity.

I know this from overhearing Uncle Ronnie discuss this very thing with Father, which he said was a Canadian national character-istic. It isn't that we don't have a conscience. We are prepared to go off to help fight other peoples' wars, and we hand out a welcome to refugees who have been forced to flee their own countries, but once we are snugly home and out of harm's way, we'll find anything and everyone to laugh at.

He explained how the vast distance between continents helps to reinforce a sense of security, which is the evil companion to inap-propriate zingers and off-the-wall wisecracks. Now I see it in action. Mrs. Molnar is going to have to drag us—her cornered audience—joking, spoofing, kicking and fighting for our irreverent right to do so, all the way to the end.

We wait for a moment while Mrs. Molnar leans her head back against the chair. She shuts her eyes tight, then with eyes still closed hard, starts fluttering her eyelids, as though, I could only presume, to help herself concentrate, also to command our full attention as well as our silence.

Suddenly, she addresses us, eyes partially closed.

Her voice is muted as though she is coming from far away. She sounds old and gruff, as though she has been crying and awake all night.

"With 1919 came to power Communist Béla Kun."

"Who's that? Some relative of Attila the Hun?" Father chuckles.

"Graham!"

"No, no, but just as cruel, just as ruthless!" she wags her finger, "Béla Kun. After Great War, he found his way to climb high fast, he made himself leader for Communist Party of Hungary. Kun took over coalition! What a fine pot of stew! Hungary one moment was Kingdom, then was Republic, then with Kun, in one breath, becomes Soviet Republic!"

"I'm already dizzy. Are you sure we can follow this?" Mother asks.

"Or must we?" Father intercepts, "Right now, I mean, it's all very fascinating, I'm sure. But!! You must understand that we are all tired, Mrs. Molnar, we ourselves have had have some—what should we say, Dear, turmoil? over this weekend! So I must caution you that we are quite exhausted and are not fit to be ideal listeners!"

Mrs. Molnar dismisses Father's plea, and plows ahead.

"It is difficult, all these facts, all this history, yes, but I shall move quickly, you will see, and then you will know why I must share all this with you!"

Father opens and closes his mouth. But he's had his say. What more can he do? He seems to acquiesce. My guess is that he has decided he might as well 'go with the flow' if but for any reason he has not been able to stem it.

Deciding to get into the fray, he makes his next move.

"So Russia didn't impose Communism in 1919. Instead, the Hungarians themselves voted for Communism?"

"Yes, that is correct."

"But this man Béla Kun, how could he gain so much favour when the entire nation was enjoying the new democracy?"

"That Kun, while canvassing he made big splosh—?" "Splash, Mama"—"Yes, big splash, as election approached. He made big promises to suffering people—so much hardship, the poverty in postwar times was so bad, people were starving to death in city, the food chain had been broken during war, crops and livestock had been destroyed in country—he said he could help them!

"Also, there were along borders where war was not really over yet, many skeermushes?"— "Skirmishes"— "Which Kun declared to end, and to push back borders taken earlier by Czechoslovakia and Romania.

"As soon as election was over, there came one big blow after another! First, he set about to restructure the economy according to Communist principles. This reform meant nationalization, meaning that everything seen to give value to national revenue was to be nationalized! agriculture! transportation! banks! communications! commerce, industry, and with this wide sweep included mining industry!

"On the whole, nationalization was bad for entire country already limping from war. Kun's Communism made worse the damage done. Instead of restructuring, which he thought he was doing, he ended up dismantling whatever was left that had made the country run! He disabled most production lines while declaring he was reviving them, he demoted or fired management, scaring away expertise. For first bout with Communism, Hungary learned hard that Communism not good for anybody, definitely not good for us!"

"Must we talk about politics and economics, Eszter?" Mother asks, "I mean, it's usually more a subject left up to the men. I really don't understand politics or economics, or how a country is run, for that matter!"

"Then you must learn, Emily! Did you women in Canada not just recently gain right to vote? Then you must exercise that right!"

"I do! I vote at every election!" Mother replies, hackles raised.

"But for whom, for what leader, for what party, if you do not follow politics year round? If you do not know how a country is run? I tell you from experience, Emily! If you want your Canada always to be successful democracy—and not pulled out from under you by slippery politicians with self-interests, or certain ideologies that could endanger your freedoms and your rights—you must pay attention! What you have now will not always be if all citizens, both men and women, are not constantly vigilant!"

Father jumps, and clears his throat loudly.

"Uh, vigilant is a touchy word at the moment, Mrs. Molnar!"

I know instantly that he is referring to the RCMP charge against Mother for being a vigilante.

Mother's face has started to twitch. Father says, protectively: "This talk about politics and the economy isn't going to last long, is it, Mrs. Molnar?"

Mrs. Molnar is focusing on the next stage of her story and is as equally focused on ignoring him as he is hoping the opposite.

"It was unbelievable hard time! The worst blow for Hungary was Béla Kun himself. He was dishonourable, and he was a violent man. He broke up many large land holdings, but he did not divide up land to peasants fairly as promised! He enraged them, and they rebelled. To retaliate, he organized gangs called Lenin Boys, which rampaged around countryside requisitioning food for the cities, and then set about executing anyone who opposed them. They were armed thugs who terrorized by burning and beating, who intimidated and murdered anyone who opposed Kun's policies, even the peasants who had trusted him with their votes. This regime came to be called the Red Terror. I see it not just as 'Red' for Communist but 'Red' for the blood that was spilt.

"Meanwhile, he made battle with neighbouring countries. He pushed back Czechoslovakia. But his taste for triumph got the best of him. All puffed up he was with power and victories. Had he not wrested magyar land back from Czech borders?

"Next, he declared war on Romania. It boomeranged. Romanian forces swept across Hungary, drove Kun and the Communists out. Pffft! That spelled beginning of end to him!"

"I guess Kun was not as 'kunning' as he thought!" Father says.

"In 1919, Hungarians were not happy with Romanian occupation but thought: Good riddance to Kun! But then rises up a Hungarian movement just as vicious in their—what is the word for 'get-back at others'?"

"Reprisals?"

"Yes, yes, a gang known for their blood-thirsty reprisals against those who had supported the Reds. These new cutthroats were known as the White Terror. They were a band of hooligans which had

161

broken away from the Whites themselves. In they came to Budapest unchecked, vicious. In Budapest, it was all blood and confusion!"

"Red Terror, White Terror!" muses Father. "Sounds like a battle of the blood cells! Which are the good guys in the blood stream, Em? the red corpuscles or the white corpuscles?"

Mother groans a reprimand at Father. Mrs. Molnar does not appreciate his facetiousness.

I contribute: "I think the red corpuscles produce hemoglobin to make the blood healthy, while white corpuscles protect the body against infectious disease."

"This analogy is not accurate. The White Terror was like ramptious?"—"Rampant"—"Rampant disease spreading like cancer all about us in the streets! Mother Cathalin, my sister Zsofia, myself, we were all housebound in Budapest for fear of attacks on street."

"Why didn't you all escape to your estate?"

"It was winter, cold, not good to travel to country estate to escape violence! Danger was everywhere en route. Could not be risked. The Grandfathers summoned workmen with hunting rifles from the estates to our mansion in Budapest to stay and protect us.

"I mentioned already the bloodbaths. In this century alone, blood has poured three times in my city.

"It was first time for me when only as a child, that I saw blood and gore spilling out of fallen bodies lying toppled over in the streets. I saw blood running red in long-fingered rivulets over the cobblestone lanes of Budapest, mutilated bodies in the city square, corpses heaped like cords of wood lying at the feet of the statues in Heroes Square.

"For that reason, I bring this stone, the Red Garnet.

"It symbolizes the red blood running in the streets of Budapest in 1919.

"Even now, when I think of it, I cannot breathe."

White Opal (#2)
4-2

"Throughout 1919, there were many street battles and executions. I was very young, but I do remember the soldiers and the gunfire, boots pounding up and down outside, the sight of slashed and mutilated bodies in the city streets.

"When it could not become worse, in 1920 came Big surprise! Big sweep! Out went the Reds. Out went Red Terror. Out went Romanians. Out went White Terror. House is cleaned. Country became Kingdom of Hungary!!"

"Hurrah!" Mother cheers.

"Bravo for that!" Father joins in.

I can see that both are hoping this to be the climax of her tale.

But it is not to be. Not with twelve more stones to go.

"Now there is no government. Everything is in disarray. Nobody knows what is on foot for us," Mrs Molnar moans.

"I ask you what it was that happened next? Can you guess who stepped up? Who took the helm? It was the much admired, highly revered man Admiral Horthy!"

"Who was he?" Father huffs, annoyed he might be expected to recognize the name.

"Picture this with me!" Mrs. Molnar exhorts us, "It is 1920. Admiral Horthy is mounted on his white horse, his battered greatcoat opened wide to reveal his medals pinned over the left breast pocket of his uniform.

*Admiral Horthy on his white horse arrives
at the Gellert Hotel in Budapest .*

"Followed by his adoring crowd, he enters Budapest triumphant, having driven the Bolsheviks out of the city. Flanking him are grimy, grim-faced, rifle-bearing soldiers, some on foot, some mounted on emaciated, mud-splattered brown horses.

"He rides directly to the Gellert Hotel where the city officials stand to receive him.

"Facing him are the city councillors and there stands the mayor wearing his chain of office.

"And look, do you see?

"In the gathering crowd, a little girl stands on the curb, shivering. Her little knuckle-chapped hands are inserted into her wolf-fur muff. Her mother is holding her tight by one arm. With any strong gust, she has to remove one hand from inside the warm muff to hang onto her hat which keeps lifting and sifting, threatening to blow off in the gusts of a raw, early winter wind."

Mrs. Molnar folds her hands in her lap.

"I was that little girl. I was five years old, it was early winter, and I remember even now wearing a long grey woollen coat with wolf fur-trimmed collar and cuffs. It was what you call 'double-breasted', yes? With—I remember so clearly—Large, round, shellacked wooden buttons. It must have been drizzling rain because I can still smell the dampness of the wool.

"We were standing, Mother and I, at the edge of the crowd that had gathered at the Gellert Hotel which is in the city square in Budapest.

"Surrounded by many soldiers on brown horses, there is a grand-looking man, very elegant, seated upon a white horse, who is addressing the crowd.

"He speaks with a strong voice of authority. He seems to be lash-tonguing?— "tongue-lashing"—you mean chastising?" "yes, chastising!— the people for letting Communists into our precious nation.

"He is praising the National Army that he led for the expulsion—correct? the driving out, yes? of Béla Kun and then retreat of Romanian army. He says he is going from village to village exhorting the people to follow him.

"Soon, Hungary had election! First, the good news: it was to be first secret ballot in history! Then the bad news: Not everyone could vote! Turned out not entirely democratic after all, as election was fixed. How? The leftists were not allowed to vote! Those were the Communists for whom Horthy held perpetual hatred and distrust. Everyone wanted Horthy, so election was held on his terms and to his pleasure.

"This began what was called a 'Regency' with Admiral Miklos Horthy. He ended up serving as Regent from 1920 to 1944!"

Mrs. Molnar picks up the polished White Opal set in silver, on a silver chain.

"This is Hungarian White Opal, mined at our own Zemplen quarry. This is my Bo's. She has granted me permission today to use for our story, as I lament I lack any more white opal ore on hand.

"This White Opal stands for the Regent Admiral Horthy, his integrity, and his white horse."

"Horthy on a horsey?" I whisper to Becky, elbowing her in the ribs. Becky jostles me back.

Mrs. Molnar eyes us both, knowing full well that a disrespectful remark has been made. "It is only if one is completely naïve, or thinks one is totally out of harm's way, that one can dare make light of very powerful men!"

Becky shrinks into her seat, drawing me back with her. Something tells me that I too have been soundly reprimanded.

"Wait a minute! Doesn't a Regent represent royalty?" Father asks.

"Yes. In 1920, Hungary was established by National Assembly as a 'constitutional monarchy' and named once again as: Kingdom of Hungary!"

"But who was the King?"

"Technically, the Habsburg King of Hungary Charles IV. We called him Karoly IV. He had been exiled."

"Was he brought back, or reinstalled after the War?"

"No. The post-war Entente would not allow it. And Regent Horthy, he liked it that way, he was not eager to share power, was just as keen to keep the King out of country!"

"So there was a Kingdom without a King!" Father exclaims.

"Yes, exactly!"

"Everywhere Horthy went with soldiers from his National Army, he rode his white horse which was deliberately intended to stir up nationalistic feelings of Arpad!"

"Arpad?"

"Yes, Arpad who was almost mythological figure known as Grand Prince of Magyars, founder of Kingdom of Hungary many centuries ago, some say eighth-ninth century when Hungarian people settled in Carpathian Basin."

"I wonder if all cultures have myths about great leaders with white horses!" Mother remarks, "In England, we have a myth about our patron Saint George, who also rode a white horse! And come to think of it, there is the Uffington White Horse that for mysterious reasons was incised in white chalk on the hills of Oxfordshire, some say as far back in time as the days of King Alfred, others attributing it to the Iron Age!"

"Yes, yes!" Mrs. Molnar mutters, not wanting to be interrupted by tales of any other country's mythological knights on white chargers.

"When Admiral Horthy was proclaimed as Regent, it was declared that he was that very man Arpad!"

"Sounds like a Secular Second Coming," Father mutters.

"Never in Britain's wildest dreams was Saint George expected to reincarnate," Mother utters.

"Admiral Horthy became Regent, settled everything down and the country began rolling again. Following installation of Horthy, it was no more so bloody a bath afterward, and aside from occasional persecutions of one ethnic group or another, Hungary 'enjoyed' twenty-four years of stableness—stability, Bo?"

Becky nods.

"Did any of Kun's influence remain?" asks Father.

"Not entirely. But nationalization stayed. In real light of day, the Regency itself was a dictatorship.

"Not much different from pre-war conditions under the Austrian Empire?" Father asks.

"Exactly. Horthy governed by the familiar. It disappointed and disturbed our Grandfathers. But they played safe, kept a low profile. They appreciated the peace. They had their own goals. Besides, Horthy displayed time and again that he was a man of honour, a man of integrity, upon whom the people could rely."

Mother says, with earnest hope in her voice, "I sense a lull in the storm. I presume that Horthy brought along some peace and order to the country?"

"On the whole, there was overall good news—But never mind!! Always there were setbacks!"

"What now?" exclaims Father. "This is starting to sound like the Perils of Pauline!"

"It's a cliff hanger, all right!" Mother remarks.

Mrs. Molnar refuses to be sidetracked.

"Barely had things started to settle down with Admiral Horthy when in same year 1920 came Treaty of Trianon and extremely damaging blow for Hungary: war repairs! no, restorations? no no, the word is—"

"Reparations?"

"Yes, yes, of course! war reparations! Hungary was forced by the Entente at Versailles to surrender to Czechoslovakia more than two-thirds of lands gained during the War.

"Admiral Horthy himself lost out. He had hoped to negotiate what-you-call a 'hallway'? no, no—What is word?—" She waves her hands about— "Ah yes, a 'corridor' to the Adriatic. However! After new borders had been drawn, Hungary no longer had access to a sea. Hungary was landlocked!"

"A Kingdom without a King and an Admiral without a Sea!" Father turns to Mother: "He was a man without a port to piss in!"

Mother slaps her thigh. "Oh dear! Graham, really!"

Mrs. Molnar, not understanding his witticism, says: "Of course!" and Father roars, "This has all the makings of a Gilbert and Sullivan musical!" He chortles.

"For business sector, revised borders brought disaster! Industry was cut off from necessary raw materials. Transportation was disrupted. But what was most crippling for us was that the Grandfathers' mines straddled Czech border!

"Mines and minerals were in Zemplen Mountain region, which is in northeast Hungary on border of Czechoslovakia. Many of our mines were cut off from shipping routes and established markets. It was Grandfathers' great negotiating skill that made mining business work again, not only cross border with Czechoslovakia but with Government itself which was no longer Communist but did not know what it was.

"Before the war, our Great-Grandfathers and Grandfathers owned several mines. The minerals from those mines supplied much industry in Hungary and Austria. These were such minerals as dolomite, feldspar, gypsum, hematite, kaolin, muscovite, rutile and so forth. All these had been nationalized.

"Necessarily, the family business shifted emphasis. Our Grandfathers did not challenge the nationalization—no point. Instead, they declared their business no longer had interest in industrial minerals, only raw gemstone ore. That critical move 'saved our bacon'—I recently learned that expression. Is that how you say?"

Father says: "Yes, but in Canada we say, 'Saved our peameal bacon'."

"Oh Graham!" Mother laughs, "No, we don't! Don't pay him any attention, Eszter!"

"I should think raw gemstone ore would be of great interest to the government," Father says.

"No! The state only saw value in raw *precious* gemstone ore, such as rubies and diamonds, and no value in *semi-precious* gemstone ores, with the result that family mining businesses such as ours were given permits to continue culling semiprecious gemstone ore which the authorities viewed as useless."

"Such as?"

"Many prospects! There was yellow citrine, also apatite, azurite, garnet, obsidian, and there was amethyst, carnelian, chalcedony, jasper—of no interest to industry at the time. Included was the white opal, which the state in its bureaucratic ignorance only disparaged, and yet it is rare and valued in its own right, as the Zemplen area is the only place in the world that it is found."

She holds up Becky's white opal: "Is this not a beautiful stone?"

"The Zemplen Mountains are in far northeast of Hungary whereas Budapest is far west, also outlets to other markets were far northwest. To ship the raw ore had always been a challenge.

Therefore, the same challenge remained as to how to transport raw ore all the way west to Budapest and beyond?

"Before the War, Hungary had built a major complex railroad system which served many towns from west to east. But War brought much damage to rail track. Then with nationalization, the entire system was thrown into disarray through neglect and sheer bureaucratic bungling."

Mrs. Molnar eyes us coolly, as though assessing us. Is she wondering how much longer she can hold our attention? Her expression takes on a strategic look, as though she is plotting her next moves in a long chess game.

Purple Amethyst (#3) and Green Emerald (#4) 4-3

Mrs. Molnar picks up the next two stones:

"Third stone. Purple Amethyst.

"Fourth stone. Green Emerald."

"Hurrah!" Father shouts, "Two at once? Does this mean that some stones come in pairs? Rejoice!"

Mrs. Molnar spreads the fingers on one hand and gazes into the distance:

"The Emerald is for the soft-rolling, luscious, deep-emerald-green foothills of Zemplen County where were our two estates. The Amethyst is for the mighty Zemplen Mountains in Northeast Hungary, the purple mountain range rising up as in a dream, like evenly-spaced static waves, and marching grandly from one end of horizon to the other."

Mrs. Molnar points to the emerald, then to the amethyst.

We are spellbound as she lapses into a poetic description of the land she loves.

"Now we get on to the Black Onyx, shall we?"

Father leans forward eagerly to watch the progress—or elimination, however one was inclined to look at it—of the stones.

"Hurray!" he smiles, almost in a taunting way, "That makes it number five! Four down, only nine to go!"

"Graham, you never lose your boyish enthusiasm!" Mother smiles, affectionately.

Becky says, "I'm enjoying how you use the stones to tell your story, Mama!"

"It's like having the agenda laid out for us, which is way better than having to follow a printed programme, like the agenda at the Rollout."

"True that!" Father laughs.

"The stones are quite unusual, Eszter, quite beautiful!"

Thus bolstered by both good will and compliments, Mrs. Molnar picks up the shiny black stone.

"What does this mean, the Black Onyx? You can tell me what it represents once I've completed the next part of my story. Is that fair enough?"

We all nod in unison.

She is about to resume her story but she is caught with her mouth open, interrupted by Father: "Mrs. Molnar, may we have a brief recess, as I think some of us might want to take a bathroom break?"

"Of course!"

We women-folk dive down the hallway to the bathroom on the main floor, and Father takes the basement stairs to his private bathroom adjoining his den.

Becky and myself "pay a visit" first. Mrs. Molnar follows next. While waiting, Mother tells us that it might take time for her to 'freshen up'. We are to go outside for a bit, and catch some fresh air. She whispers to me that Father most likely lodged his request for a bathroom break on the pretext of taking the opportunity to step out on the back patio to suck on his pipe for a bit, so we can best give him fifteen to twenty minutes at the least.

Night Sky
4-4

Sunday, October 13, 1957

10 p.m.

The front drapes have been left open, as are the screened side-windows at either side of the bay picture window. As these are the only windows that open in the living room, this design feature is a dismal failure for any cross-ventilation on a hot day. Even though it is now evening, it is still stifling. There is a small fan on the sill, sluggishly churning to help move the air along.

I step out onto the front lawn with Becky to catch a breath of fresh air.

The street is inked in velvety blackness. There are no street lamps on side streets here in suburbia. No other lights are on in the windows of neighbouring houses. It is pitch black, "Like stepping into the back of a giant's eyeball," Becky says, blinking.

Overhead, the early night-sky canopy is a deep cerulean blue. The strongest stars have begun to poke through. Yet another month has passed, for hovering southwest behind the house there was another waning gibbous moon—doomed from now on, surely, to be dubbed a 'Rico' moon in my personal realm of memories. The sight of him standing there in Mitsy's night garden with his fly open, his 'thing' exposed and erect beside grinning Mitsy, floods back into my memory.

Facing east, the large, irregular, diamond shape of the winged horse Pegasus is already clear as a bell. It strikes me as a child's drawing of a house on stilts that has been knocked off-kilter by some colossal blow.

'Pugilant' Mars, the Red Planet, with its 'left hook', is coasting in from the upper southeast corner on its downward diagonal toward the right.

Floating far mid-left, in right-side-up W-formation—so far with only a hint of a tilt—is my favourite constellation, Cassiopeia, so compact and so readily identified in the night sky.

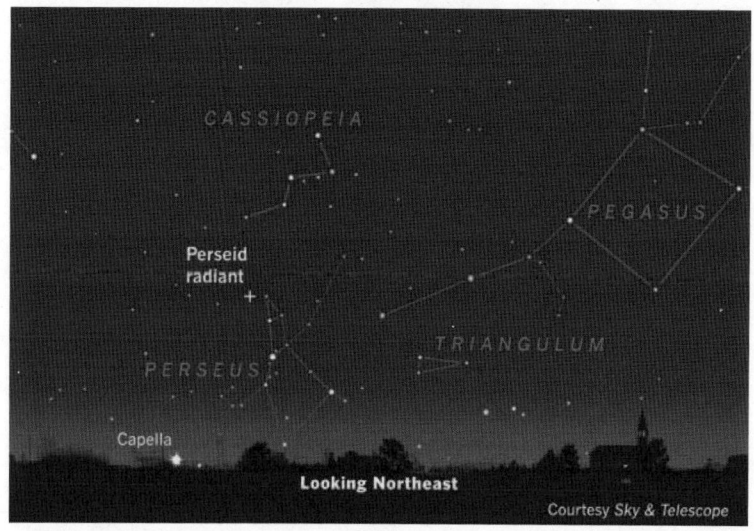

Cassiopeia and Perseus in northeast sky on October evening

"Between you and me," I confide to Becky, "As a Michelsen, I have always wished that my surname began with the initial W. I could look up into the heavens all summer long, and have my own existence affirmed with the blessings of the firmament! I don't like the approach of winter when Cassiopeia starts to tilt, and by mid-winter has turned completely ass-over-teakettle into an M—It makes me feel queasy!"

Becky laughs, nudging me, "I am happy to join you in your aspirations since as a Molnar with initial M, I am also only affirmed in summertime and fall, doomed as well to be dumped totally upside-down by winter!"

"Drats!" I reply, "You're right!" I had forgotten about her own surname. Slipping my arm into hers, I make a zigzag Charlie Brown face with my mouth. "Lucky us!"

Mother calls out and we go back inside where we gather in the living room, Father in his favourite easy chair, Mother next to Becky and myself on the chesterfield.

Black Onyx (#5)
4-5

10:30 p.m.

We have reconvened.

"Mrs. Molnar, it is getting late and we are only broaching stone Five. Can you pick up the pace a bit?"

"You must be patient! I go as quick as I can but all has a reason, believe me!"

"I'm trying, Mrs. Molnar," Father pleads, "But I fail to understand why we have to sit through almost the entire history of the first half of twentieth-century Hungary before we find out what upset you so much this week! Can't you just get to the point?"

"No, Mr. Michelsen, I cannot!" Mrs. Molner replies, sternly.

She draws in a deep breath, holds her hand to her midriff and resumes:

"I want to answer for you a question you must be asking:

"I mentioned disruptions in railroad after Béla Kun, also unsteady improvement in rail service during Horthy régime. I suppose you have been wondering how the ore was transported all the way from the Zemplen Mountains to Budapest, if not by railroad?"

Neither Father nor Mother look as though that question had crossed their minds. Becky and I look at each other. We shrug. It hadn't crossed our minds either! But that is all Mrs. Molnar needs.

"Back in early 1920s—"

"You see? You are back to 1920 again!" Father swivels to Mother with a plea, "We'll be stuck there forever, Emily!"

"Never you mind, Mr. Michelsen, allow me to resume. What did the Grandfathers do to transport the gemstone ore from the Zemplen mines?"

Team of Black Percheron horses

"We give up!"

"They used the Black Percherons!"

"The what?"

This makes Mrs. Molnar form her wide lips around her bared teeth the same way as she did on Saturday night trying to teach me words from Hungarian cuisine. She proceeds to pronounce the mystery word by emphasizing every consonant, vowel and syllable in an excruciatingly elongated manner: "PIAIR-CH-UH-RUNS!"

"What are Per-che-rons?" Father tenders, gingerly.

"The Percherons are great, proud, handsome, gleaming black giants of horses! It was my husband Bence's great-grandparents who were the first to bring them to Hungary and breed these world-famous horses on their estate. His Grandfather, then his Father himself, continued to breed and train them. Throughout Hungary, the Molnar family was known for their teams of heavy draft horses, the Percherons!"

Father is singularly unimpressed, "Never heard of them."

"These horses came long ago from Perche Province, Normandy, which explains the root name of the breed. Some say the Percherons date back to the Ice Age. It is also said that they were used by the Romans in the invasion of Brittany.

"They are very big horses. Black Percherons stand 16 to 17 hands high and weigh over 1130 kilograms, which for you would be around 2500 pounds."

"How high is a hand?" I ask.

"Ten centimetres plus a bit. For you: four inches," comes the answer.

"So 4 times 16 equals 64 inches divided by 12 equals 5 plus— between 5½ and 6 feet high?"

"Correct. That measure is to the withers, the shoulder."

"Now that's a very big horse, when you attach its neck and head to it," Mother says, trying to show Eszter her support, then bursts out laughing, hearing how comical it sounded.

"Our Percherons were strong, solidly built, magnificent beasts! Father-in-law Gyorgy swore that in better days, if he could take his prize team to competitions around Europe, the Percherons would win hands down against the Belgians and the Clydesdales."

"Oh, Clydesdales! Now you're talking!" Father nods. "Em, we've got the Budweiser Clydesdales right here in Ontario. You know? The ones that haul the big barrels of beer? They are brown with white foreheads and hooves the size of dinner platters—they are HUGE horses! We've seen them at the Ex!"

"Of course!"

"You mentioned a 'prize' team, Mrs. Molnar. How many other teams did you have?"

"That varied, but in general, from eight to ten, often more. Much depended on breeding time."

"Where were they sheltered?"

"In stables at both Zemplen barns and in Budapest, behind the Nemeth-Molnar warehouse."

"Why so many?"

"Primarily, the Percheron teams were used on our family estates as work horses, for clearing land for farming, for plowing and harvesting. They were also used for hauling cargo, the large wagons loaded with barrels of beer to the local taverns, or contracted to move other commodities such as lumber, building materials, machines for local factories.

"During the Great War, they were confiscated by Government, unfortunately, and used as war horses to pull artillery and haul materiel. Many of them expired from exhaustion.

"From 1920s on, from out of the Zemplen Mountains into the foothills and along the major roads, Percheron teams were used to haul semiprecious gemstone ore direct from the mines to the local railroad. Whenever rail was disrupted, they were needed for hauling all the way to Budapest and beyond, for processing.

"What was done with the leftover, you ask? It was crushed and sold to local towns and farms as gravel to make roads. Another side business, yes?"

"Your family was quite resourceful!" Mother says.

"Their motto must have been: 'Waste not, want not'," Father adds.

"But there was more! What else were the Black Percherons used for? Shall I give you time to guess? No? Okay, I give you answer: To transport estate chattel, yes? You forgot about that other business after nationalization?

"The Grandfathers had the signs on all the wagons relabelled 'Molnar-Nemeth Minerals and Antiques'. At first, this odd combination left many officials scratching their heads, when wagons passed them on the roads until they saw them often enough to let them pass.

"By late 1930s, these wagons were commonplace. Everyone had seen the wagons around for well over a decade so they were never questioned. I tell you this now: throughout the dismantling of estates and transport of chattel, fewer and fewer questions were asked at way stations along the route! The Grandfathers were rarely stopped for inspection. If they were, the Grandfathers with their shiny black top-hats and wearing their well-made business suits, always bearing the air of established gentry had only to show some transit papers with official-looking stamps and they would be let pass.

"But how could the wagons carry both?"

"The wagons were large, big and deep like huge, oversized storage bins. The bottoms were hinged so contents could be dumped, and dividers were slotted into place so that the wagons could carry different commodities, such as ore in one section and furniture in another! Or it could be all one load or the other.

"Increasingly from 1938 on, there was much concentration on the many larger pieces of furniture that had been held back in the outlying areas, those being stored by local estate tenants in barns, work sheds, attics.

"These larger furniture pieces were painstakingly refurbished by craftsmen expert in woodworking and cabinetmaking, and then they would be wrapped in heavy blankets to be transported to the warehouse in Budapest. It was there, in preparation for shipping out of country, that they would be custom packed in padded crates with very sturdy construction, with lids that lifted up on hinges or on sides for periodic inspections en route. With all this Molnar-Nemeth Antiques furniture traffic going here and there, back and forth, from the country to city, sometimes the reverse, very few were detained."

Until 1944, the pieces of furniture were delivered for export either direct out of Budapest via rail transport, or when rail was not in service, by Percheron team direct to Idar-Oberstein. All shipments were accompanied by the requisite meticulously-prepared waybills for highway transport, plus bills of lading and consist for railroad transport."

"You are very comfortably acquainted with shipping terminology, Mrs. Molnar. You even know what a consist is!"

"Of course, any shipment by rail must have a complete, detailed list enumerating contents of each car!"

"Amazing!" Father says.

"It does no good to patronize me, Mr. Michelsen!"

"No, that was not my intention! I am merely marvelling at your knowledge about shipping and your grasp of commercial shipping terminology in English!"

"Indeed!" Mrs. Molnar sniffs, lifting her head high, "I must learn such terminology to mind my business!"

"There you are then. You mind your business and I'll mind mine!"

"Agreed! Good!" They both laugh.

She leans her head back against her chair.

Once again, there is that mystical expression that passes across her face:

"I see a team of six magnificent Black Percheron horses galloping along the highways and byways of Hungary, stirring up dust and gravel! I hear them clip-clopping proudly through the cobblestoned narrow streets of villages and into Budapest itself.

"Driving their prize team of horses are two distinguished gentlemen. They are wearing their black tophats, their business suits, small black bow ties and freshly-starched white shirt collars, buttoned weskits where a loop of gold chain leads to the little pocket where a fob watch resides. See the gold flash in the sunlight! Who are the drivers? They are the Grandfathers!

"Shall I ask you to guess for what stands this Black Onyx?"

She picks up the black shiny stone.

"The Black Percherons!" we all cry out in unison.

"Correct!"

Yellow Citrine (#6) and Blue Sapphire (#7) 4-6

"We come to sixth and seventh stones: the Yellow Citrine and the Blue Sapphire."

"Hallelujah, another combo!" Father cheers.

"Our fathers' business in gemstone ore had two essential operations. One involved joint interest in the extraction and shipping of raw gemstone ore at Zemplen quarry. The other was cutting and polishing of shipments sent to Idar-Oberstein.

"Idar-Oberstein is major centre in Southwest Germany where is shipped gemstone ore to be processed. From there, finished product is distributed around Europe and overseas."

Mrs. Molnar gazes into her past:

"I see faceted, honey-yellow, polished gems glitter as they issue forth on a conveyor belt in Idar-Oberstein.

She picks up the shiny, transparent, polished "honey-yellow" stone and shows it around. Then she points to her own choker necklace, earrings, and bracelet.

"That is Yellow Citrine."

She rubs one of the larger flat stones in her necklace. "These very stones were extracted as raw ore from the quarry in the Zemplen Mountains."

"Is yellow citrine the same as topaz?" Father asks.

"No, no. By decree of Russian Czar, gold, red and pink topaz have only been available for Russian aristocracy. For that reason, the yellow citrine has for long time passed for topaz commercially."

"Did you charge as much for it as real topaz?" Father inquires, either his business acumen whetted, or his self-righteousness.

"General public does not know the real topaz, so they are prepared to pay our asking price, which falls within the higher range of most semi-precious stones."

"So you sell it as 'Topaz'?"

"In Europe, no. In North America, yes, we did, until real topaz was discovered in Brazil."

"So now how do you sell it? As Yellow Citrine?"

"Small chips used for popular birthstone in rings or pendants? No. Continues to be labelled as Topaz. Large pieces cut and polished for high end jewellery market? Yes and no. It sells as Citrine Topaz."

Father looks as though his mind has been put through a washing machine.

"Ah! The old village Idar! There is time stepped outside of time. So quaint, so pretty, where clear mountain waters of the Nahe River come rushing down the mountain side, plunging from great height over top of the giant flat-face cliff, pounding from such great height ledge to ledge, hitting jumble of rocks at bottom, splashing with joy. See the blue, icy cold, pristine waters rushing through the open sluice of the mill run at pell-mell speed! Ah, the fresh pure water! Such a colour blue, it can only being described as sapphire!"

Mrs. Molnar reaches for the stone, and holds it up for us to see: "This stone is for the Nahe River! It is the Blue Sapphire!"

"Holy mackerel, Sapphire!" Father cries jubilantly, placing his hands together in prayer like a gospel singer, and raising them in the air.

"What you mean?" Mrs. Molnar starts.

"It's just a saying from the Deep South, Eszter. Don't pay him any mind!" Mother laughs.

"Hallelujah, we've made it to Number Seven!" Father rejoices. But too soon.

Bitter Taste
4-7

"In 1940s come bad times that leave bitter taste in the mouth.

"1940s brought World War. Admiral Horthy tried for Hungary to stay neutral. But Hitler and Mussolini dangled grapes over his nose, lured him with promises, and he succumbed because they arranged, by two Vienna Awards, to return to Hungary those territories lost in 1920 with Treaty of Trianon! You understand what I say, how the longing for Magyar reunion caused my country Hungary's downfall? For it was in this way that Admiral Horthy was bribed, Hungary found itself forced into alliance with Axis powers, and Hungary could no longer remain neutral—It marked beginning of end of the line!"

"They knew his Achilles' heel. His national pride let him be sucked in."

"Yes."

"By succumbing, your Admiral Horthy must have known he would end up under Hitler's thumb," Father moans, "So that is how a whole country can be lost!"

"Just so. On large scale, it can happen to a country, just like to a person. One force squeezes while another force twists. Just like in wrestling. Then down you go!"

"Good analogy! Remaining upright can be difficult when pride contends with integrity."

"It was an unsavory alliance with Germany—How Hungarians hated it! Hitler used Hungary—he made Hungary do his dirty work! In 1940, Hitler made Hungary invade Yugoslavia!"

"I remember that! I couldn't figure out why!" Father says.

"What you mean, why?"

"That Hungary invaded Yugoslavia instead of Germany itself doing it!"

"Ah."

Mrs. Molnar heaves a sigh.

"Next year, in 1941, he made Hungary invade deep into Russia! On plus side, twenty Soviet divisions captured. But it went too far to sustain itself."

"Same story as how Napoleon met his Waterloo. He bit off more than he could chew."

"Exactly. Two years later? In 1943 came horrendous Fall of Stalingrad, with great suffering and staggering losses. Hungary defeated. Hungarian Second Army annihilated.

"Admiral Horthy saw that Germany will lose the war!

"He asked his faithful Prime Minister Kallay to put on a show for Hitler about Hungary supporting him against the Red Army, while secretly he negotiated with Western Allies. He wanted some way out of the vice in which Hungary was caught."

"Admiral Horthy tried to jump ship?"

"Yes. When Fathers Mihaly and Gyorgy heard of this, they knew how angry Hitler would be, how vindictive! They could smell German invasion in the air.

"Sure enough, Hitler caught wind of Admiral Horthy's betrayal. As predicted, along comes March 19, 1944, and the German Occupation called Operation Margarethe, yes?"

Mother, Becky and I look blank.

Father confesses: "It was too confusing to comprehend from so far away. Why the Occupation when Germany already had Hungary in its thrall?"

The expression on her face turns bleak.

It dawns on me how alone Mrs. Molnar must feel, to have lived through all this, and now has no one by to share it with, let alone understand.

"Kallay was dismissed and Dome Sztojay, a Nazi, became Prime Minister along with a Nazi military governor. Our nation Hungary became now virtually puppet state. Admiral Horthy remained Regent. But the noose was being drawn around Hungary's neck even tighter.

"In Germany, anti-Semitism was in upswing. From May to July, Horthy learned Eichmann had overseen deportation of over 437,000 German Jews to German death camps in Poland.

"Here is example of Horthy's integrity. He reminded Sztojay government that Jews were full-fledged Hungarian citizens. In August, he found a way to dismiss Sztojay and replace him with anti-fascist Lakatos."

"Hurrah for him!" Father cheered.

"This way, Hungarian gendarmes were forbidden to deport any Hungarian Jewish citizens.

"All along, Soviet Red Army was bristling at the border. They saw Hungary as weak and vulnerable.

"In September '44, the Soviet Red Army crossed border. In the October, Admiral Horthy announced an armistice with Soviet Union."

"Admiral Horthy tried to jump ship again?" Father asks.

"Yes. Second time he tried to wiggle out of Hitler's vice. Everyone was right that the Germans would not like it. It was only a matter of time.

"In October 1944, there comes the German coup d'état Occupation Panzerfaust, which literally means 'Tank Fist'. Admiral Horthy was forced, through very dishonourable, double-cross kidnapping by Germans of his son, to name Arrow Cross Party leader Szalasi"— at whose mention she shudders— "as Prime Minister."

"Were he and his son killed or jailed?"

"No, but Horthy had to step down."

I whisper to Becky: "Admiral Horthy got down off his high white horsey."

Becky leans into me, "Good thing Mama did not hear, or we will be sent to bed without hearing end of story!"

I see this as Becky's tactful way of shutting down my tomfoolery. After all, I was trying to make a lark out of a serious situation, also, she has the right to do so, for she is obliged to defend her mother. Her rebuff strikes me to the core, as in her gentle way, she is telling me to smarten up, that my remark was disrespectful, and well worth punishing. It sets me on my heels, makes me wonder what gives me the right to make fun of Mrs. Molnar's dilemma, and not even have the courage to say it to her face. I ask myself if being facetious in the face of someone else's anguish is based on sheer arrogance—done simply to exercise one's sharp wit at someone's expense? Or, on some sense of false superiority—looking down on the person, granting oneself permission to make comments from on high? If anything, it could be a form of bullying, which I abhor. And it is cowardly. I start to blush. Becky's reproof spells the end of my mockery.

I lean into Becky and say: "I'm sorry."

Mrs. Molnar's face registers the shock and the fear she was feeling at that time: "Horthy now abdicated meant collapse of Regency. It meant that none of us were protected anymore from the havoc and the horrors that might surely follow. And which surely did.

"Everyone held breath. Everyone prayed. We hoped help could come from Allies, hoping against hope for rescue from West! I remember this time of Not- Knowing-Next-What-Will-Come as living purgatory!"

Mother says, "It is impossible to live amid such chaos and uncertainty. How is a person to carry on with tending to the bare essentials in life, let alone try to live to the fullest? Purgatory? Surely, it was more like living hell!"

"That is why world history will be written next time by women," Father speaks, gently.

Mother takes this the wrong way. She huffs: "What do you mean, Graham? Was that just too 'typical' a thing for a mere woman to say?"

"Not at all. I only meant that in the future, if history were left to women to record, there would be many more relevant details about the real human struggle endured during an upheaval. Men think in a linear fashion. Most historians to date being male have a penchant for recording history by time lines where significant dates are annotated by political events, wars and battles, and heroes. But this framework only chronicles peak historical events. It has been men who have defined what those are. There is no room in their chart for the social or cultural ramifications. I hope that in the future, women historians will get more into the day-to-day nitty gritty of the human experience.

"I cannot describe 'nitty gritty' until I have provided you with the framework!"

Mrs. Molnar has also taken his comments personally.

"Of course!" Father replies, curtly. He bites his lip, annoyed that he has been infected by one of Mrs. Molnar's own expressions.

She resumes:

"From late March through April into mid-May, our two Fathers had continued to step up the shipping business, increase our exports. Often we had two-three full boxcar loads a week!

"Then all came to a halt. The Germans seized control of the railway, using it for war effort.

"All Molnar-Nemeth shipments were suspended, curtailed from May 15th to July 9th, 1944."

"How on earth do you remember all these dates, Eszter? It's a marvel."

Mrs. Molnar stares at Mother. She says, "I lived through them."

"In late July, Hitler who is getting more and more cash-strapped suddenly imposed a tariff on all 'value-added' exports destined for the West. This included finished gemstone products, both precious and semi-precious, intended for export market.

"Something else: With means of transportation in high demand, the Fathers caught wind of German intentions to confiscate Hungarian 'tangible assets' such as machinery, weapons, wagons, and so on. It was becoming apparent to our Fathers that the authorities were eyeing the Black Percherons. Father-in-law Gyorgy was afraid any day the horses might be seized. He sensed the Percherons' days were almost numbered for the family business. He dreaded that if used in war, they would be abused, their days would be numbered, and the breed would die out.

"In August 1944—that is a date I remember very well—Admiral Horthy somehow managed to take back control of railway from the Germans! You can see how this provided a window of opportunity! It freed up the trains for commercial shipments! But for how long? Father–in-law Gyorgy, he made a vital decision."

"Surely he didn't have the horses destroyed!" Mother cries.

"No, no! I tell you!" An admonishing finger is raised.

"We thought we had so little time in 1920 to complete plans for our exit and now, ironically, it is 1944. It seemed time had slipped through our fingers, that time had almost run out.

"The situation was too tight. Our fathers had been watching and waiting for a signal, they knew this quiet spell was it, might be the last. It was time to act.

"The family plan kicked into action.

"Ultimate plan was that all of us would find our way out of Hungary to Canada. Meanwhile, it was agreed long beforehand, that Father-in-law Gyorgy would be the one to go first to Canada. He was to go in forefront—Is that how you say?"

"In the vanguard?" Mother offers.

"Yes, yes. He would go in vanguard with Mother-in-law Borka, to make way for the rest of us in New World!"

"That was very brave of them!" Mother ventures to say.

"Yes! Very brave!!

"Gyorgy was the mineralogist. It made sense that he go first to Canada to prospect and find good mines. My Father Mihaly was the gemologist. It made sense that he stay behind in Budapest with Mama Cathalin at warehouse to receive and sort last shipments of ore from Zemplen, then go to Idar-Oderstein to wind down our family's gem processing there. With antiques business, he would complete brokership contracts with émigré gentry, also oversee legal transfer of estates management to designated third parties.

"Brother-in-law Tamas agreed to travel back and forth to Zemplen mines. His assignment was to oversee transfer of management of quarry operations, and to continue to organize transport of large furniture from country storage sheds to warehouse.

"Husband Bence already had teaching and research position in mineralogy faculty at the University. He was assigned to gradual downsizing of Budapest Molnar-Nemeth Antiques business. I was given responsibility as shipping agent. I did all the paperwork, prepared the ladings, and each *consist*."

She emphasizes the last word and looks at Father somewhat belligerently.

"My sister Zsofia maintained the shop front which continued to display lamps and chandeliers, ladies' dressing tables with mirrors, and other smaller artefacts gleaned from the expired estates. But in due time, it became nothing but a façade."

"What do you mean?"

"The shop front became just a *front*."

"A *front*? What was there to hide?" Father asks.

"Early August 1944, Father-in-law Gyorgy left with Mother-in-law Borka for Idar-Oberstein, driving his prized six-hitch Percheron team. He hauled upholstered furniture, mainly two large sofas and deep-seated armchairs, as much as one large wagonload could bear."

"Sofas and armchairs?"

"Yes. Indeed.. Now this fact I tell you: Over the course of previous years, all the finest specimens of raw citrine gemstone ore had been selected, shipped, and processed. This load was already waiting in the Idar-Oberstein warehouse. Father-in-law Gyorgy and wife Borka together spent two solid weeks hollowing out sofa stuffing and replacing by finished, polished yellow citrine, wrapping the precious cargo into muslin sleeves and slipping them burrowed deep into the sofas, all which were then crated and labelled Nemeth-Molnar Antiques, assigned a bill of lading for address in Toronto, and delivered by Black Percheron team from the Idar warehouse to the Idar train station.

"It was with that team, that Father-in-law Gyorgy and Borka with two small suitcases left for Canada."

"You smuggled the whole shipment of citrine out of Germany in the sofas?" I ask.

Mrs. Molnar nods.

I must be looking at her dubiously, for she says:

"Lo-iss, you yourself have sat in one of those sofas!"

"I have?"

"Yes, remember when all three of us together sat listening in livingroom to Bartok music?"

Yes, I remember the large, deeply-upholstered sofa with its high back and thickly padded raised arms. So that very sofa came stuffed with yellow citrine all the way from Hungary! I am mesmerized. It feels as though I am being told a fairy tale.

"Why was he not stopped by the authorities? Wouldn't such a wagon load weigh much more than the normal listed items?" Father is almost testy, as though he might catch her out in a bald-faced lie.

"Very easy. He had forged documents prepared beforehand, with false weight stated in bill of lading. With his reputation as well established import-export entrepreneur, all details about the shipment were accepted at face value.

"Did they really arrive in Canada with only two suitcases to their name?"

"No, no. Waiting for them in Toronto were forwarded belongings held in storage. The same way émigré gentry valuables were shipped, so were theirs, except not with their own names. Beforehand, here to Canada had come in shipments the balance of some of best antique family furniture and paintings, other artifacts, valuables, precious keepsakes, all as though part of the normal business, you understand, for export trade, but meant for us all, to get out of country as much as possible for us to start a comfortable life, enough to furnish a home, and fit it out properly."

The paintings on the walls, the old books, the elegantly carved furniture, the cut-glass vase in the foyer, all the furnishings in the Molnar home in Centrewood that had struck me as out of keeping with a modern suburban home come to me in a flash. The Molnar's home is filled with antique furniture and artefacts from their home in Budapest, and their Templen estate. How should I have known?

"What happened to the Black Percherons after they left Udarum-Uber-steen?" Mother asks.

"Ah, that was most exciting bonus. Father-in-law Gyorgy was able to ship unimpeded on same train in separate boxcar his prize six-hitch Percheron team, complete with harness and wagon and all gear, including food supply. Voyaging on same cargo ship that Gyorgy and Borka crossed the Atlantic, he was able to tend the horses. He was allowed down into the hold where were the horses' stalls—Shared, may I add, by some exotic zoo animals from Budapest Zoo!"

"Why on earth—?"

"Endangered species include not only human beings, Mr. Michelsen!"

"Upon arrival in Montreal, the Percherons were met as prearranged by contacts of new owners, and escorted further by train to Alberta. Gyorgy had arranged donation of his precious horses to a Mennonite farm north of Calgary in the Didbury area, near a place called Jackson Forks Ranch. Do you know it?"

"No. It is much too far away from Toronto for us to know it," Father replies, hoarsely. Turning to Mother, he asks, "Why does every Tom, Dick and Harry from overseas think that we know every place in Canada, let alone every other Canadian, just because we live here?"

Mother says: "I don't know about places. But, Dear, you do seem to know every Tom, Dick and Harry when we go out."

"She is right!" I say, "Father knows every policeman and parking lot attendant. So far, all their names are "Mack". He also knows the names of drivers up ahead when they are blocking him. He sticks his head out the car window and shouts, "Hey, Mr. Roadhog, get outa the way! You, Mr. Jack Benimble, move it! —Isn't that right?"

"True enough," he winks.

Mrs. Molnar is nonplussed, but goes on with her tale.

"Gyorgy knew that the Mennonite farmers of Alberta still worked the land with horse and plough. There he knew his Percherons would be respected and well treated! He gave the horses to them with that trust! It was his way of thumbing his nose at the Soviet Union. There was no way that hated Nazis, Fascists or Communists were ever going to take over his horses, his pride and joy!"

Mrs. Molnar holds up the transparent polished yellow stone.

"What did we smuggle out of Germany to be our nest egg in Canada?"

"Yellow Citrine!" we carol.

"Where was the citrine cut and polished—Becky?"

"Idar-Oberstein!"

"Very good!" she smiles.

"What is the name of the mountain stream with its brilliant blue sluice at the mill?"

Silence.

"The Nahe River!" calls out Becky.

"Which is represented by?"

"The Blue Sapphire!" I contribute.

"Very good!"

"Well, that takes care of numbers 1, 2, 3 and 4, 5, 6 and 7 — Bravo! Onward ho to number 8!" Father declares.

Sulphur (#8) and Coal (#9)
4-8

There are still six stones lined up on the little table in front of Mrs. Molnar, the seven already presented now ranged together in a separate row on the opposite side. I am hoping there will be two sets of twos coming next, if not two triads, for how long can this go on? At this late hour, my eyelids are getting heavy, I'm longing for my pillow and my light cotton babydolls. Mother's and Father's shoulders are also sagging. May Mrs. Molnar make short shrift of these last stones. Wishful thinking?

There is a long pause. Mother too thinks it is almost over, for she starts to rise from her place next to me, probably hoping to call it a day.

But Mrs. Molnar fools us all, and carries on:

"I bring you to very beginning of 1945 when poor Hungary teetered on brink of great collapse."

"1945? I was hoping we were well into the 1950s by now!"

Father starts shifting from one buttock to the other, crossing and re-crossing his legs. I can see he is pining again for his pipe. He is eyeing Mother, meaningfully.

Mrs. Molnar picks up the cloudy yellow rock from the row in front of her.

"This is sulphur!" she says, "It is not a precious stone. It is not a semi-precious stone. It is just a rock. See its ugly colour—putrid, like urine! It is a dense and cloudy rock! But it is here for a reason!"

She picks up the lump of coal. "This too is only a rock. Yes, this is coal. This represents whatever chars and turns to cinders."

She almost snarls at us: "I beg you now to pay attention, and tell me when I am finished why these two rocks are here!"

We all sit up at attention.

***

Her eyes move inward, and when she speaks, it is as though her voice is being prompted by an inner spirit:

"I see ravenous yellow flames leaping, reaching high, licking across the rooftops and at the sky, the shapes of buildings lost in a dense, dull-yellow noxious yellow smoke that rubs itself against the windowpanes, licks its tongue into doorways and alleyways, lingers among the columns of proud civic buildings and entwines around the statues of our heroes in the city square. My nostrils are filled with the stench of death mixed with gunpowder. The randomly exploding munitions at the armoury send up fireworks high into the floodlit sky.

"I see next the aftermath of the fire, the burnt-out, hollowed-out frames of what were once houses and shops and businesses of a beautiful city now reduced to blackened charcoal pillars leaning crazily against each other for support.

She swivels her attention and focuses solely on Father:

"Men like games, Mr. Michelsen? I give you sports analogy: Living in Hungary for people of Hungary at that time was like being stuck on open playing field with lines criss-crossing in every direction amid an ongoing, endless multi-sided, multi-team football match.

"Nazis from Germany, Communists from Russia, Fascists from within, all converged on same field, and clashed back and forth.

"Hungary caught in the middle of major players became a battlefield.

"Sounds like our front yard yesterday when we got home, doesn't it, Dear?" Father comments, "We had the full mix of least likely contenders blocking the driveway, and charging back and forth across the lawn, none of us knowing who was who or on whose side, or why."

Mother's face blanches.

Mrs. Molnar just glances at him, and then pushes on.

"What a terrible, terrible outcome! Most disgusting was that not all forces were external, one major force was internal. The Fascists were not from Mussolini or even Italy. They rose up from within Hungary itself!"

"After Panzerfaust, Germans installed Salazi as Hungary's Prime Minister—such a fiend—who unleashed his soldiers, with no restraints on members of the population—so much brutality, so much cruelty!"

A long pause. A long intake of breath.

"By December 1944, Soviets had formed alternate government outside Budapest, the Red Army circled Budapest, and Red Army started Siege of Budapest.

"January 18, 1945. When Germans retreated, all bridges across Danube were blown up, all rail and road and communications systems were demolished.

"February 1945, Soviets invade. Everything downtown was torched. Our beloved Budapest was left in ruins, including our Budapest mansion. Our Budapest warehouse, destroyed."

She mops her brow.

Her whole face has collapsed. She is the picture of grief.

"I already told you that there were three bloodbaths in Budapest.

"I witnessed two of them myself. In person. With these two eyes!

The First, way back in 1918-1919 was the battle between the Reds and the Whites before Admiral Horthy saved the day.

The Second was this horrific Siege of Budapest by Red Army from late 1944 to February 1945, where Communist Reds, German Nazis and Arrow Cross are in the mix.

"All of them, just as bad. Neither was worse than the other because all three were the worst you could ever imagine.

"The Germans, well, we already knew as enemy they were pigs. They proved it, as I just said, by blowing up all five bridges when they retreated, just like bad boys having temper tantrum when lose game. Caused terrible destruction and disruption! Final blow!! Buda and Pest with no bridges was separated—divided by fast-flowing River Danube.

"The Soviets, well, Hungarians had a taste of them at Stalingrad. Admiral Horthy hated them. Hungarians all hated them. They didn't feel any better about us! After the Germans retreated, the Reds stormed the city, destroyed it, soldiers being given permission to steal, plunder, pillage, destroy, burn!

"The Arrow Cross, they were very cruel. Painfully ruthless. Heartless. And they were many of them Hungarians, that is what hurt us most in the heart. They committed horrid atrocities!!

"Where were you during the Siege?" Father manages to ask.

"We were at the Uni, husband Bence and I. With baby Bo," she smiled at Becky, "Who by then was barely 3 years old.

"What happened to your family?"

"Szofia and husband Tamas had time to flee from Budapest mansion to our flat at the Uni. We all hid in catacombs under old buildings of the Uni with others who managed to retreat from downtown Budapest when it was being destroyed."

"Where were your parents?"

"My Mother Cathalin and my Father Mihaly died in the fire when both mansion and warehouse were destroyed."

I hear Mother gasp. "I'm so sorry."

We all hang our heads and look at our hands.

Both Mother and Father look ghastly.

This puts such a deadly hush on us all, it presses down on my chest so hard I can barely breathe. Becky puts her head on my shoulder. I place my hand on hers.

"What happened to your remaining Black Percheron teams?"

"Two teams burned in Budapest warehouse stables. Others gone. Taken. Escaped. Who knows?"

"Your Mother-in-law Borka, she went to Canada with your Father-in-law, right? Back in 1944?"

"Yes! Of course!"

"So she survived."

"So, yes! She died later. In 1951. Here. In Canada. Natural causes, doctors say. But what is that, 'natural causes'? She was already frail, wasting away, homesick for the old country Hungary that would never be again. So homesick to see her son Bence and daughter-in-law Eszter—and her granddaughter Boglarka, which is Becky's full Hungarian name. There was always sad news from home."

Mother speaks: "I lost my entire family, my Mother and Father, my sisters and brothers, aunts and uncles, cousins, everyone, in Coventry, during the blitz."

This seems out of place. As though the only way Mother can commiserate is to steal Mrs. Molnar's thunder.

But Mrs. Molnar does not take it that way. She stops mopping her cheeks.

"Who would know we would have so much in common, two women who have met virtually halfway around the globe, half a world away!"

"Yes," Mother says, "I don't talk about it much. It's so painful, and talking doesn't seem to help me any!"

"That's so British, I hear! To keep bad feelings all bottled up with stiff face!"

"What's that? You mean: to keep a stiff upper lip!"

"Ah yes, that is the expression? But Emily, believe me, I try to do same, but I must tell you my story now for good reason. Otherwise I wouldn't talk about it either!"

She throws her head back and sniffs, wrinkling her nose.

"What I remember most about the fire," Mrs. Molnar says, sniffing again, "There was a munitions warehouse downtown that exploded over and over. It seemed to hold no end of stores. The thick rotten-egg stench of gunsmoke and munitions will never leave my nostrils. The yellow blaze of flames and stinking billowing smoke licking high into the night sky is imprinted on my mind. When I close my eyes, I smell the gunsmoke, and I see those flames! I smell death!"

Mrs. Molnar holds up the piece of sulphur.

"What does this piece of sulphur stand for?"

None of us can speak.

"I say it to you. I say it for you. This sulphur represents the stink of death, the dull yellow glow of the ever-burning fires, the callous razing of a beautiful, gracious city by barbarians and brutes!"

She holds up the coal.

"I will not ask you. I will tell you. This ugly lump of black coal represents the charred ruins of my city, the decimation of my childhood home, the loss of my immediate family, the destroyed heart of my home town!

"Sulphur and coal: together they stand for hell and brimstone!!"

I glance around. Everyone's face is a frozen mask. Everyone's eyes are sunken. Everyone looks like they are reeling. The story has taken us beyond the point of exhaustion.

***

Eventually, Father rallies: "What happened after the Siege?" he asks, "Did Soviet Russia take over?"

"January 1945, Armistice was signed in Moscow.

"April 1945, all Germans expelled.

"War was over!"

"In November 1945, elections!! We rejoiced! At last, we were free! But no! It was a big sham. Soviet commander had remained behind, refused to allow democratic government. A Communist coalition was established.

"In 1947, elections again. But all to no end, again all a pretense of democracy, it was big disappointment.

"Power exchanged back and forth

"Each step, toward totalitarian government and police state.

"By 1949, is death knell. Is over. Name is changed to People's Republic of Hungary.

"Beloved Hungary: to go from puppet state to satellite state, a very sad state of affairs!

"Dashed every time, our new-born hopes for democracy! I look back now and see that it was but a dream, that these hopes were impossible to realize. But even if it was the illusion, there was the promise—We had so little tiny tastes of freedom. But Bah! Everything topple down, bad bad bad, so much hard work and all monies going to Russia where we sow and they reap. We struggle, we more and more poor, more and more of us go hungry."

She pauses and gives us a long, sly look:

"Yes! Hungry in Hungary!"

Mother smiles, "It's good that you are the one who said that, Eszter!"

Father says, "I'm tempted to ask if your parliament had to go on a forced Diet—?"

We all groan.

Mrs. Molnar speaks:

"Easy to make light when food is plenty!"

Father says, "I must apologize. Sincerely! All attempts at humour aside, the truth of the matter is that your story, what you have been through, how you express it with such calm and dignity, is very touching, and has touched me very deeply. You must forgive me, Mrs. Molnar. I have as weird a sense of humour as my wife."

"Hey, you. Don't shovel it on me!" Mother digs in, with good humour.

"Yes, I know. There are times when humour serves a good purpose."

"When you don't know whether to laugh or to cry?"

"Exactly!"

I know that Mother is just bursting to ask questions, but every time she has tried to speak, Mrs. Molnar has cut in. This time, she takes her chance. She asks, "Eszter, you mentioned Bence and your daughter Bo were with you during the fire. I gather you were married in the midst of all this chaos?"

Mrs. Molnar nods.

"I have told you that I knew my husband Bence and his family since we were very young children. We knew early that we would marry. Yes, in a way it was planned, our marriage, as our parents wanted it to be, but good luck! For we loved each other very much. Still do!"

"Where is your husband now, may I ask?"

"He is still in Hungary."

We wait. No one seems inclined to ask. Father looks apprehensive. Mother begins to fuss with her hands.

Finally, as it appears that there was nothing more forthcoming, Mother requests:

"Can this be the last stone for tonight, Eszter? There isn't much more, is there? It is getting quite late and we've had quite an exhausting weekend already!"

Father gives a grim nod of approval.

Bloodstone (#10)
4-9

12:00 midnight

Undeterred by the suggestion to call it quits for the night, Mrs. Molnar picks up the next stone in line and continues with her tale:

"I bring you closer to today. Everything was going smoothly compared to earlier days but ten years later in 1953 come signs of unrest in Hungary! Father-in-law Gyorgy, was well-established in antique business, and was increasingly successful in prospecting. He was making promising investments in industrial minerals while conducting ongoing testing for emerald, ruby and sapphire—none of which was ultimately successful, but good prospects in semi-precious gems. In Bancroft, he had good fortune in establishing controlling interest in a unique opaque blue stone with white streaks called sodalite.

"Father-in-law Gyorgy, based in Toronto, was part of the down-town Hungarian community, and had connected up with many other emigré Hungarians in Canada. They shared what they could of news from Hungary.

"In 1953, Father-in-law Gyorgy started writing to us still in Budapest, urging us to leave, pleading to Tamas and my sister Zsofia to go to him, telling Bence to drop everything at his work and leave for Canada at once, and when Bence refused, instructing him to send me and little Boglarka immediately."

Mother pours more tea, brings around the floral-patterned por-celain tray with its matching little milk pitcher, and sugar bowl with sugar cubes and little silver tongs.

"Sister Zsofia will not go without husband Tamas. Tamas cannot let her leave without him. My husband Bence refuses to leave, insists he must stay, as he must support the student protest. He appealed to me that I stay. I see in my heart I cannot part from my husband.

So I stay back in Budapest at the Uni with him, and we send little ten-year-old Bo with her Auntie and Uncle to Toronto."

"Wha-a-t?" gasps Mother, "I can't imagine ever being parted from my daughter!"

Mrs. Molnar tilts her head, "You do what you have to do, Emily, when you have no choice! In particular, when you do what you are told to do!"

"Nobody would get away with telling me to do that!" Mother protests.

"It was 1953 when Bence and I said good-bye to them. Then it was 1955, and my husband was getting more and more involved with the politics at the University. Even though there were purges and mock trials of leaders opposed to new rule, he was convinced that Hungary could get its democracy. By now he was on faculty, instructor in mineralogy. He joined with other faculty to support the students, he will not listen to me, my worries.

"Yes, there were promising signs in middle of unrest. In 1953, both Stalin and his ruthless henchman Beria died. Khrushchev— you know him? Was showing good indications, more progressive. In 1956, great excitement, when the Hungarian Workers Party came into control, and some of the former leaders convicted of treason were exonerated.

"Excuse expression, but suddenly it was all hell breaking loose.

"In early October of 1956, one year ago this month! I came back to apartment at the Uni, I found my husband Bence in our bedroom, and he was packing my things. He had heard rumblings, feared for my safety. My husband Bence, he handed me ticket, ordered me to go to Canada! He will not come, he will not leave, he is committed, he must stay.

"I arrived in Toronto and there are great tears of joy, to be rejoined with my little Bo, my sister Zsofia and her Tamas, and reunited once more with dear Father-in-law Gyorgy! It was three years since I had seen my Bo!"

She reaches out her arms, and Becky slips over into her embrace.

"Wasn't October 1956 the beginning of the Hungarian Revolution?" Father asks.

"Yes."

Tears begin to stream down Mrs. Molnar's face.

She apologizes. "Pardon me, pardon! I'm sorry, I'm sorry!" She roots out a lace-trimmed handkerchief from her sleeve.

"When you say 'Toronto', you mean here, in Centrewood?"

"No, no! We move here after!"

"After you arrived in Toronto?"

She nods.

"Very bad calamities happened in old country, one after the other. There was October 23 protest at the university in Budapest. Demonstration started out peaceful but then the police arrived, arresting students, using tear gas. The students started to riot to get back fellow students from paddy wagons—that is what you call them? and the police fired on them!! No reports how many shot. But many wounded. That night, officers and soldiers from our own Hungarian forces joined the protest, everyone marching and chanting through the streets 'Russians go home!', 'Long live Nagy!' who was our nation's admired new leader. That night by the news, we learned that Soviet tanks had entered Budapest. On October 25, the Soviet tanks mowed down protesters in Parliament Square! Over 12 dead and 170 wounded!

"We have radio, we have friends in Toronto, all our telephones are buzzing. My head is buzzing, too! Where is Bence? Where is my husband? I am tied up with fear—how you say?"

"Fit to be tied!"

"Yes, fit to be tied. Then brother-in-law Tamas decides he must go back to find Bence. If he goes, said Zsofia, then she goes too! I said to her, what are you, who you think you are, some modern-day version of Ruth? or was it Naomi, from the Bible, you know?"

"Yes, whither thou goeth, I shall go," Mother helps.

"Exactly. That was Zsofia. Whither Tamas goeth, she shall go! So off they go to Hungary. Here I am with Gyorgy and Bo. But another calamity!"

"What was that?"

"Gyorgy. He died! Yes! He had bad attack—in the heart, you know? He dropped down dead in the kitchen—on the floor."

"When? This week? Is that your bad news you came to share with us?"

"No."

"How long ago was that?" Father tenders.

"This past May. Year of our Lord 1957." She crosses herself. So does Bo. Mrs. Molnar is rubbing the yellow citrine at her throat again between thumb and forefinger.

"Good Lord!" Mother exclaims. "How did you manage?'

"I called Gyorgy's Hungarian contacts in downtown Toronto. The Canadian-Hungarian Association there. They came and helped right away. Called church with priest. Arranged funeral. Gyorgy gone—Mfft!"

"And your husband? your sister and brother-in-law? Have you heard from them at all?"

"Bo's Papa, my dear husband Bence, and Bo's Auntie, my dear sister Zsofia—no word! They have disappeared! So far, no trace! I thought so also, with Tamas, that he too had disappeared.

"But now, this very week, this is my bad news: it is that brother-in-law Tamas, is dead. He was shot. Source cannot say when. Through chain of communications, people have written us. Someone sent me his—what you call—personal belonging?"

"Personal effects?"

"Yes, yes, personal effects. His ring, neck chain, wallet, identity card. As proof. Yes, he is gone."

Bo sits stiffly at her mother's side, trying not to cry.

"You never said a word to me about this, Becky," I say.

"I was told not to say a word," she replies.

"Our poor Bence and Zsofia, they are either dead—or in hiding—or they have been taken away—maybe shot! Or in jail? Or sent to a camp in Siberia interior? Maybe do labour, maybe starve, maybe freezing, maybe mass grave! We do not know. Nobody knows!"

"We're so sorry," Mother says. Father and I nod soberly.

"Yes, yes, of course! Every day we remember, Bo and I, we pray for them. We think of Tamas, we shed a tear. Until we know where they are, or what has happened to them, we can do nothing more but wait. And cry. We will wait until they return, or so much time has passed that we cannot cry anymore, that there are no more tears."

She points weakly to Stone Number Ten.

"This stone is Heliotrope, commonly known as Bloodstone.

"Remember I said three bloodbaths in Budapest? First and second, I was there. Third, I was not."

She picked up the stone:

"Once more, there are dark pools of blood saturating the broad boulevards of my city, the bodies of brave citizens fighting against tyranny once more, crying out for freedom on the steps of monuments of great warriors who fought before them."

The Request
4-10

We sit in silence.

Father's mood is subdued. He is the first to speak: "I don't know if this is proper etiquette or not, but I'm thinking: would a shot of sherry be a good idea at the moment?"

Mrs. Molnar's face brightens.

"Oh Mr. Michelsen, I could very well do with a good shot of schnapps!"

"Schnapps? Is that sherry?"

"I do not think so, but I believe it is close enough!"

Father got up and went to the cabinet, withdrew five sherry glasses. Reached down below into the hutch and brought out the sherry. Poured sherry into three glasses.

"Got any apple juice for the girls, Dear?"

"Of course!" and Mother whips off into the kitchen.

Everyone seated once more, Mrs. Molnar says:

"Mr. Michelsen, I have something else to tell you and I have a request to make from you, if you not mind?"

"Certainly!" Father responds, stifling a sigh.

"I start before by wanting to tell you how I can afford to live here, yes?"

"Yes you did. But as I said, we do not pry into other peoples' affairs. It is of no importance to us."

"It is important to me that you know!"

Mrs. Molnar hand goes to her necklace. Her fingers found each large yellow-coloured faceted stone in turn and she rubbed them, thoughtfully, almost reverently.

"You will remember that our family investment was in mining, and that our fathers held controlling interest in Hungary-located Zemplen Mountain quarries for semi-precious stones such as white opal and yellow citrine.

"You also remember the furniture taken by my Father-in-law Mihaly with Percherons to Idar-Oberstein, the sofas and high-backed armchairs that were stuffed with yellow citrine. And of shipment taken to Canada with Black Percherons, yes?"

"Yes. How did that work out for you?" Father asks, rather stiffly. "It was a bit of a gamble on several counts, was it not? I mean, what if the shipment had been intercepted? Your in-laws would have been arrested for contraband, they would have been 'dead meat'!"

"Graham, that is hardly an appropriate expression, considering the blood baths Eszter has seen, and what could be going on right now in her homeland!"

Mrs. Molnar sips luxuriously from her glass, "As it turned out, the citrine could not have been a better investment! It was—what do you say, a 'long-shot'? Of so many semi-precious stones, we chose the yellow citrine! We were so fortunate in this respect, to be in such enviably good position! For of all semi-precious gemstones on which was chosen by our fathers to concentrate, the citrine decision turned out to be—how to say: providential!"

"How so?"

"It turned out that yellow citrine, so plentifully available to us and so close to topaz in quality of colour, came into sudden demand. We arrived in Canada with our stockpile just in time for the growing post-war market, the growing middle class. The growing interest in astrology was making itself felt by way of birthstones. Topaz was the stone for Sagittarius. For that reason alone, the topaz was wanted for rings and other jewellery. That aside, men and women alike wanted a yellow stone to colour-co-ordinate with their outfits. Women wanted yellow stones for their earrings and necklaces. Men as well wanted to decorate their cufflinks and tie pins with gems that complement the colour in their ties or their suits, yes? Well! The yellow citrine is the sole answer to a golden-yellow gem, and the yellow citrine is the only golden-yellow stone that come closest to topaz. I tell you there are many persons who think they own a real topaz, and would be stunned to learn it is not, it is yellow citrine! Citrine is a valuable semi-precious stone in its own right. But it is still not topaz!"

Mrs. Molnar held her necklace out from her throat with her thumb.

"You see this? Could be mistaken for topaz, yes?"

Mother leans forward to admire the necklace more closely. She murmured:

"I never knew there was such a business, mining and trading in semi-precious stones! But I suppose the stones used for rings and such that we see in jewellery shops, they must come from somewhere!"

"Of course!" exclaims Mrs. Molnar.

Father flinches, never failing to be annoyed by her expression.

"They are not all coloured glass. No! They come in raw form like any ore straight from the earth, from a mine, and then go for gem-cutting and polishing at centres like Idar-Oberstein, or my own gem processing plant established by Gyorgy in Fergus, right here in Ontario! Such centres themselves are quite rare, and therefore do good business!"

"Why Fergus of all places?"

"Clean, fast-flowing water on Grand River. Easy to build sluice next to existing dam."

"I tell you now: that entire shipment of citrine was our collective family nest egg for building a life for ourselves here in Canada. It is what Father-in-law Gyorgy used to establish and expand business here in Ontario, to invest in mines and other minerals and to build our gemstone trade."

"Well, I'm glad for you that you were not left here in Canada high and dry with no means for taking care of yourself and your daughter!" Father replies.

His voice takes on a nasal, business-like tone. He sounds a touch more reserved than before, less convivial.

"Yes! Indeed so! In so short a time that there was, Gyorgy had been teaching me the ropes since my arrival. I now run whole business myself from out of house. I have managers overseeing my quarries in Bancroft, and the gem-cutting and polishing centre in Fergus. I am taking care of myself and my daughter quite well, thank you!"

Mrs. Molnar seems satisfied.

Father draws in a deep breath.

We all take a breather.

Completion is finally in the air.

We think.

"As I said in the beginning, I had something to tell you. Which I have done. Now, as I indicated earlier, I have a request to make of you, Mr. Michelsen!"

Father shifts uneasily in his seat. His shoulders tense up. He places his hands palm down on the arms of his chair. "By all means, what might that be?"

"I have nobody here in Canada to take care of my affairs should anything happen to me. Why would anything happen to me? No reason that I can see, as I am still young, very fit and healthy!! Only danger might be if I go to Hungary—but no! no! That I guarantee I would not do!! Never!! Not with Bo here, and not without her! I would never endanger Bo's security and happiness! No, never!"

Mrs. Molnar becomes quite agitated, shifts forward to the edge of her seat toward Father.

Father pulls back with his hands gripping the arms of his chair, presses himself into the back of his seat.

"Mr. Michelsen, I run good, flourishing business, accounting is excellent, I keep all business books in order, always up to date. I have records of reported annual income tax. Inventory is registered. All is on up and up."

"And?"

"This is my request: For Bo's sake, if I assure you that I will always continue to keep good books, and if I sign an affadavit with surety that I will never leave Canada so long as husband Bence is away, I am requesting that you be my Power Of Attorney, and Executor of my estate—Only as stop-gap until husband Bence comes home. Would you do so, please, for me? And also agree to be guardian for Bo?"

Father looks dumbstruck. "Why, I—I—" he stammers.

Mrs. Molnar's fingers are pinching tight the stem of her half-filled "schnapps" glass, her watery eyes pouring a focused and determined plea into Father's eyes.

Father clears his throat.

"Mrs. Molnar," he asks, "Is there no one in your Hungarian community who could serve in this capacity?"

"No, there is not. There is only available the Toronto attorney who assisted with Father-in-law Gyorgy's death and settling his estate," she responds, "I do not like him. By which I mean, I would not entrust him with the welfare of either my estate or my Boglarka!"

Father sits back for a moment, thinking hard. I watch the blood drain from his face. His shoulder is twitching. It is obvious that this is the last thing in the world he wants to do.

"Then may we leave it this way for the moment? I promise that I shall give your request every consideration. However, I shall have to consult with my own lawyer and with my superiors at Avro before I can give you my consent."

"How peculiar!" she said, "You must obtain your employers' approval to be someone's P.O.A.?"

"Yes. Sounds to you rather reminiscent of a totalitarian regime, doesn't it? But no! It is merely that my work is classified, and there are some concerns at play at the moment. I will need clearance. It's a matter of security. National security."

"Of course! I see!" Mrs. Molnar replies. Even though it is clear that she does not.

Midnight Postmortem
4-11

October 13, 1957
2 a.m.

It is late. With three stones left to go, it is agreed that we should all call it a night, and that we will resume tomorrow evening after enjoying Mrs. Molnar's Hungarian dinner.

There is some of the usual "ditzy-doo" at the front door that women are compelled to do when saying farewell. Then we wave them off.

After Mrs. Molnar and Becky leave, the three of us migrate to the kitchen.

Father holds his head in his hands. "Whose life am I living?" he sighs, "First, caught up in the history of the Mississaugas. Then snagged by rogue RCMP agents—and the possibility of American McCarthyism brewing as a Canadian rendition of a Red Scare. Now I am immersed in the Hungarian revolutions—not just one, mind you, but three! I would swear that only two weeks ago, my main concern was with saving the Arrow. I feel as though I have been caught up in one vortex after another, fearing what might come next, and I'll be swept out to sea."

I think: *Yes, caught in the whirlpools then swept away like the whitecaps rushing down the Niagara River.*

I am sent to have a bath, with instructions from both Mother and Father that I am to go directly to bed. Look at the clock. It is well past 2 o'clock in the morning. There has been much too much excitement over the past three days and I need my rest. No argument there!

Mother is running hot, soapy water for the tea dishes.

Father is slumped in a kitchen chair.

Not even bothering to stifle a big yawn, I haul myself up out of my chair.

On my way down the hallway, I hear Father say: "My God, talk about a "Siege"! I thought her story would never end—and it's hasn't ended yet! With three more stones on the table, there's more to come, God spare us!—I swear I thought she'd never leave!"

"I thought her story was fascinating!" Mother's voice chimes.

"You did, did you? Lordy, lordy, it was like Ali Baba and the Thousand and One Knights! What was the need in that—would you call it a parable?— for so many knights, by the way? At any rate, every time I thought she was finished, there was more! No holds barred, she's worn me out!"

I can hear the rinsing of teacups and the placing of dishes in the rack.

"I believe it's 'Ali Baba and the Forty Thieves', Dear, from the Arabian Nights. You do know that's 'One thousand and one nights'—the nocturnal kind spelled without a 'k'!"

"Whatever! That woman should take Victor Borge's advice about Santa Claus!"

"What's that, Dear?"

"He said that Santa has the right idea. You should visit people only once a year!'"

***

When I step out from the bathroom, I hear them still talking in the kitchen.

"One thing for sure, I was relieved when she finally stated her 'request'. I was nervous as hell that she was lining up with a pitch to invest in her semi-precious gem company!"

"You thought she was about to hit you up for money?" Mother asks, sounding uncharacteristically like the mob boss, Al Capone.

"Yes!"

I can hear the rhythm of Mother's painted fingernails clacking on the kitchen tabletop.

"Quite frankly, Graham, when she finally lodged her request, I was surprised at you, that you didn't absolutely leap at the opportunity to assist that poor woman!"

"Emily, you know that I am under scrutiny by the RCMP!"

"So what? What does that have to do with helping Eszter?"

"It's better to err on the side of caution."

"Why are you cautious?"

"Well, it just doesn't feel right. Why can't she ask one of her own people, some other Hungarian in Toronto, to be her P.O.A.?"

"She already addressed that point: she doesn't want her father-in-law's lawyer to be responsible for Becky, should anything happen to her! She doesn't like him!"

There was a pause.

"What about her own credentials? Presuming that she came on a valid immigration visa, to my mind she's still a refugee until she's gained her full citizenship. Now with her husband and sister back in Hungary, what will the authorities say? I'd be asking: why the flip-flop? Where are their loyalties, to Canada or Hungary? Besides, aside from that, there are so many questions that remain! She's involved in the gem trade, the bulk of which she admitted was smuggled into this country! And her father-in-law, it sounds like he fled Hungary. Why did he leave? To elude Hitler? Or to avoid the Soviets? He left Hungary so abruptly, do you think he was escaping from the Nazis?"

"I can't remember. Was that during the German occupation?"

"Emily, do you think the Molnars are Jewish?"

"No, I do not! It hasn't even crossed my mind. Even if they were, what difference would that make?"

"Think about it: What kind of people trade in gems, other than coins—Jews, right? Or maybe they are gypsies?!"

"Graham, I had no idea you were such a bigot!"

"I'm not bigoted, I'm just calling it the way I see it!"

"Then the way you 'call it and see it' sounds like bigotry to me!"

"Well, I don't think so!"

"I firmly believe that we do not discriminate against Jews OR gypsies in this country. Or in this house! I won't tolerate it! Prejudice is totally unacceptable to me. Besides, your point is entirely invalid."

"Why's that?"

"How could two well-established families run estates in Hungary for more than three generations without already having been identified, let alone persecuted, as Jews?"

"Maybe they lived openly as Jews. Didn't she say all Hungarian Jews were full-fledged citizens?"

"Yes, until they were threatened by the Arrow Cross leader appointed when Horthy was forced to step down."

"I know for a fact that during the Arrow Cross, there was rampant anti-Semitism, and I believe very ruthless persecution!"

"Maybe it was the way it is here—or anywhere. We all live side by side and get along with each other. Everyone is a citizen, except when some Big Ignoramus Bully of a Bigot comes along to stir up hatred! Gr-r-r-r!"

"Well, consider her husband Bence then, where does he fit politically? How do we know if what he's been up to has also incriminated her? Who knows what his politics are? If he stayed behind to assist with the revolution, is he a Communist, a Socialist or a Fascist?"

"How about 'Lover of Democracy'?"

"More to the point, how does our own government view the 1956 revolutionaries?"

"They're letting Hungarian refugees into the country!"

"All of them? Carte blanche?"

"They must have some way to screen them!"

"Never mind! That's what I should find out before I decide one way or the other! I'm curious how our government determines who gets in and who doesn't? How does immigration distinguish between legitimate refugees and closet Communists? What if they find out this Bence is a Red? Here we have our government quaking from the 'Red Peril', and the RCMP hunting down innocent citizens like myself just in case! Yet at the same time, in praise of valour in the name of democracy, they could be letting in Hungarian Communists by the boatload!"

"From the news, I think they are flown in. It was the Italians that arrived by boatload," Mother states.

"At any rate, what I need to know is: have Mrs. Molnar's husband and sister disappeared because they've been arrested and imprisoned by the Soviets for being anti-communist or for being just common trouble-makers? Any government will arrest protesters that challenge the status quo. Look at the States and our own police, for God's sake, and how brutally they've handled the unions!"

"Where are you going with all this, Graham? You're starting to ramble!"

"No, no, I'm just wondering, that's all. Is there some way the Hungarian authorities decide whether a protester is an activist or an insurrectionist? Why does one get a slap on the wrist, and the other gets hanged or sent to Siberia? As for your friend Eszter, depending how her husband ends up over there, where does that leave her? He's still a Hungarian, probably doesn't even have his landing papers to come to Canada. Next major question: Where would that leave me in the eyes of the authorities if I obliged her request and became her P.O.A.?"

"Aren't you being a bit paranoeic? Look what she's been through! Does she sound like a Communist, Red or White? Or a Fascist? She sure doesn't sound like she enjoys either bloodshed or totalitarianism!"

Father takes one last leap, a desperate measure like a pacing lion in the circus ring trying to avoid the fiery hoop:

"I don't like your Mrs. Molnar. She is pushy, she's bossy! She has that East European uppity air about her, that air of superiority— noblesse oblige! entitlement! Call it what you will—it grates at my nerves, would surely grate at anybody's nerves!"

"How do you mean?"

"Her imperial manner, her pursed lips, the way she holds her chin elevated when she looks around— like this—" swivelling his head, "As though she is a Commander in command. She struts about like a Pomeranian, you know, the kind of dog with the big ruff?"

"And curled tail that hangs over its back like a feather duster?"

"Yes!"

"I love that dog! A next-door neighbour in England used to breed them! Orange? Black? Red? Wolf sable?"

Father barrels on.

"Orange. To go with her beloved Topaz Citrine. I dislike her presumption that others will do her bidding. I find her annoying, the way she monopolizes the conversation even when she's not the one talking—her constant running 'cluck-cluck-cluck' -ing inserted as commentary, her 'aha's' and her 'yes, yes'es and her throaty grunts, as though signalling she's on the verge of speaking again, always wanting to interrupt, if only the other person would button up!

"Most of all, I loathe the way she says 'of course!' every time she's asked a damn question, as though if she knows the answer so everyone else should know it, too!"

Then Father goes into a mock interview:

*Tell me, was the Archduke Ferdinand wearing a bow tie when he was shot? Of course!

* Is it always high tide when the ship comes in? Of course!

* Did Hitler's mistress really have six toes on each foot? Of course!

Father explodes: "All I have to say to this is 'Arrrrrgh!' "

"So basically, it comes down to the fact that you won't help her because you don't like her!"

"I suppose that's about the size of it, yes!"

"Oh Graham, must everyone be exactly like yourself?"

"The closer, the better!"

Another protracted silence.

"You know, Dear, Eszter is my friend, not yours. You don't have to like her if you don't want to! Yes, it's true she says 'Of course' too many times! And she does turn very imperialistic, I grant you that! However, I reserve the right to say that I like her! Despite her idiosyncrasies, my heart goes out to her!"

"Good for you!"

"Besides, whatever happened to tolerance? You're always going on about intolerance being the cause of all the world's woes! Do you only tolerate people you are not obliged to get along with?"

"Of my own free will? Probably!"

Mother's voice takes on a girlish tone.

"When it comes down to it, I can relate to Eszter even more now, because I'm an orphan, too! I don't have anyone left from my own family. What if something happened to you? Lois and I would be left all alone, just like Eszter!"

I could hear Father's aluminum kitchen chair legs scree and scraw as he torques about in his seat.

Finally, he mutters:

"Tomorrow's Thanksgiving Monday. I'll call my lawyer on Tuesday."

CHAPTER FIVE
Thanksgiving Monday

Bert
5-1

Monday, October 14, 1957

8 a.m.

I am up early.

All three of us are at the breakfast table, each of us planning our day. Father wants to get his nose into reviewing his notes on the Land Claim. I have only today left to complete my burr submission due tomorrow. Mother is stuck with doing all the dishes, unless she holds off till I am done with my homework.

Of course, tonight is slated for Mrs. Molnar's Hungarian supper. That is when her story will resume.

"It's a good thing that for the first time in our history the Government granted us a statutory holiday to celebrate Thanksgiving.

It gives Mrs. Molnar an extra day to wrap up her tale," Father says, not without a trace of sarcasm.

"And us the opportunity to taste Hungarian food!" Mother smiles brightly, hoping to both cheer him on, and remind him to mind his manners.

Around 9 a.m., I am downstairs in Father's den. Upon his extraordinarily generous suggestion, Father has granted me permission to use his drafting table to work on my project. I am completely caught up in the throes of drawing and naming burdock flower parts, when someone is ringing the front doorbell.

From up above, Father barks, "Lois, get that door, will you!"

I hop up the basement stairs and answer the door.

Bert is standing there.

"Good morning, Lois," he says, "I thought I'd drop by to see how you're doing. Is everything okay?"

"I suppose."

"What's up? Did I interrupt you?"

"I'm working on my burr assignment."

Bert says, "Haven't you done that yet? I handed my milkweed assignment in on Friday."

"I wasn't at school on Friday. I got an extension. It's due tomorrow—and I'm stuck!"

Bert says, "I don't know anything about burrs, but I'm happy to help!"

I say, "All contributions are welcome! I'm almost finished, but I'm having a really hard time dissecting the flower parts when all I have is a withered, half dried-up, semi-soggy dead flower head!"

Bert says, "I had problems with that part of the assignment as well, trying to dissect the milkweed flower.

Downstairs we tromp.

"Why is this burr soggy?"

"I was advised to soak the burrs, so the bracts don't damage the eyes!"

"Who would think?" Bert replies, "Sounds like a very knowledgeable source!"

"Well, here's my project, as it is," I say, pointing to the handwritten captions entered under the blank spaces reserved for each flower part, "All I have to do is find the seed, and I'll be finished!"

Bert smiles, "Well, lucky you! I bet you would never have guessed that the very person you need right now would turn up in the nick of time to help you!"

"Meaning you, I presume?" I smile back.

It turns out he is right.

"I have a sneaking suspicion where the seed is located!" he says, "I struggled with the same problem."

Bert takes the tweezers, tugs at one of the hooked burrs still buried in the ovary, and slowly reveals the seed attached to the other end.

"Et voilà!" he proclaims.

"Of course! Where else could it be?"

It is amazing. Within half an hour, I am able to use a dab of glue, mount each part, and affix a label for each part: Filament. Anther. Sepal. Calyx. Ovary. Ovules.

Bert helps me to arrange the separate pieces of the assignment into a folder, and then slip the whole works into a manila envelope.

"There you go, signed, sealed—and almost delivered!" Bert announces.

We tromp back upstairs.

"What a saga, getting this project done!" I exclaim, "I don't believe it!"

"Feels good to get that monkey off your back?" asks Bert.

I hesitate. "I'm not sure what that means, really, but yes, if it means a huge weight has been lifted off my shoulders, you're absolutely right! Thank you so much! You know, I would not even have been able to even start this project if you hadn't offered to fetch me burrs from that ditch on the other side of the highway!"

"Ah yes," Bert replies, looking directly into my eyes, "The day we—um, just 'happened' to 'bump into each other' at the Big Culvert!"

"As far as Mother is concerned—Exactly!" I respond, "She must never know the real reason we found ourselves over there—was Mitsy and her vulgar 'Teaserama'! Promise?"

"Mum's the word."

"Thank you. Since then, it seems like everything inconceivable contrived to keep me from getting this project done! There was the surprise trip on Friday to—to—er, visit Niagara Falls. I was able to get a bit done while visiting some folks en route. Then on Saturday afternoon—"

"There was the Avro Admin "Tournament of Champions" right here on your own front lawn."

"Ha ha! What kind of tournament would you say it was— Hockey? Football?"

"No, more Medieval, like Jousting Knights in Clashing Armour."

"Ha! I pictured it more as a Showdown in a Western movie. The fancy cars when they pulled in and faced the curb were the Posse!"

"Ha ha ha! I like it! And don't forget that Jeep!" Bert guffaws, "I suppose he was Marshall Dillon himself?"

"Or a One-Star General!"

"Don't forget the star of the show, Jack the Knife!" he laughs, pointing to himself.

"Ha! How could I? Yes, well, would you believe that immediately after that, it had already been planned for me to go over to Becky's for flute practice and an overnight stay. Yesterday was taken up here by Thanksgiving dinner and company—And we have more company tonight! At any rate, suddenly here I was this morning, waking up with only today to finish this thing off!"

"Yep," says Bert, "I was there at the beginning. Now it's come full circle, and here I am again!"

Ping! goes my brain. I stop dead in my tracks.

Father had said way back when, to watch out for geometric forms when making life decisions. He particularly cherished the Circle and advised me to be on the lookout for them. This is definitely an excellent instance, and points to someone I can trust. As I recall, he also had very firm reservations about the Square, namely because they are stodgy, and dull, and can be deadbeats at parties.

I look at Bert. He has a large, square face set on a tall, block-like body. If anything, he is a square. But a nice one.

Never mind what Father said. Bert is a regular kind of a guy. It feels comfortable being with him. The thought crosses my mind that he could be a friend. Then I think, *Look at me, here I am with a boy who might turn out to be a friend.* Ever since elementary school, I haven't had a friend who was a boy. It was odd how we all split off. Boys hung out together. Girls hung out together. In junior high, some of my girlfriends started 'going steady' with one boy or another. But I'd known all those guys in Unionville since childhood. I couldn't imagine holding hands with any of the boys I'd played baseball with, or cowboys and Indians, or tag football, let alone kissing them. Ugh! So while I look at Bert, I'm not thinking 'boyfriend' at all. I am just thinking: wow, a potential friend—Who happens to be a boy.

We climb back up the stairs to the front door.

On the landing, Bert leans in slightly toward me, and says quietly: "You wouldn't want to go to the Hallowe'en Dance with me, would you?"

It is nice, the way he asks. He seems so shy and uncertain when he says it. Not presumptuous. I am startled by the closeness of his face and by his sincerity, and without giving it any further thought, I hear myself say: "Yes, I'd like that!"

Lois's Completed Assignment
5-2

Field Work Assignment – Fall Weeds Teacher: Mr. Gladstone
NAME OF PLANT: BURDOCK By: Lois Michelsen
Due Date: Oct. 11, 1957
Submitted: Oct. 15, 1957 (Please see parent's note attached)

Taxa		Not fungi, protista, animalia
Plantae	Vascular	Not Broyophytes
	Angiosperm	Not seedless
	- dicot	- not monocot
	Leaf venation: palmata	
	Flower parts: 4s or 5s	
	Seed cotyledons: 2	
	Vascular bundle: herbaceous	
Kinds	Common or lesser	Arctium minus
	Great Burdock	Arctium lappa
	Woolly Burdock	Arctium tomantosum

Features	
Frequency	Bi-annual
Height	1-5'. Flower stalks: knee to shoulder height
Flowers	Heads: discoid and homogamous Outer bracts end in hooks

	Colour; pink, 1st season; purple, 2nd season
Shape	Bushy
Leaves	Heart-shaped, wavy on edges, underside whitish, texture felty with large distinctive veins like back of hand
Root	Deep tap root up to 1'
Habitat	Open fields, roadsides Sun or part shade
Growing conditions	Well drained soil where occasionally disturbed (see proliferation)
Proliferation	Seeds from dried flower heads spread via hooked burrs/bracts through hitch-hiking on passing birds, animals, humans. Can travel by bird gut.
Invasive	Not.
Disposal	Remove flower stalk only.
Hazards	Serious injury if dried burr caught in eye. To dissect, soak first, use tweezers
Human use	Medicinal - Topical (North American Indian) Leaves: for burns and wounds

* Not to be confused with cocklebur: leaves are poisonous

TEACHER'S COMMENTS: GRADE: B+

IT MIGHT HAVE MERITED AN A+ IF SUBMITTED ON TIME. BONUS FOR ADVICE ON DISSECTION PROCESS.

Centrewood Weekly

THANKSGIVING SPECIAL EDITION

MONDAY OCTOBER 14, 1957

AVRO AVATAR CHARGED WITH POSSESSION OF STOLEN PROPERTY. WIFE CHARGED AS VIGILANTE

by Jason "Bud" Longford

[Photograph caption]
Teary-eyed and handcuffed Mrs. Michelsen sits in
back seat of alleged Secret Police RCMP cruiser.
Photo credit: "Bud" Longford

On Saturday, October 12, charges were dropped about as quickly as they were laid against Centrewood's star Avro Arrow aeronautical engineer Graham Michelsen after an aborted attempt by the RCMP Secret Service to gain entry to his house. Brandishing a search warrant, the two agents' efforts were thwarted by two Avro security guards and a phalanx of seven members of Avro top management.

Allegations that Mr. Michelsen was in illegal possession of plans for the Avro Arrow were summarily quashed by testimonials from those members of the Avro team who had come in force to vouch for him.

"You think he stole plans that he drafted himself?" his fellows jeered, not without expletives.

Avro president CEO Fred Smye clarified the reason for possession being the tight timeline for production of the Arrow which entailed many hours for Mr. Michelsen, the lead aeronautical architect, working on the plans at home as well as on site at the Malton plant.

During the altercation, some Avro team members appealed to the gathering crowd of curious onlookers by tossing out accusations that the charges against Mr. Michelsen were completely fabricated. Another Avro CEO, Crawford Gordon, hailing from Calgary, wearing a Stetson and full cowboy gear, stated that the agents were acting under the authority of a covert branch of the RCMP which has allegedly turned its wartime foreign espionage activities into domestic surveillance and intimidation.

As though validation that these were outlandish charges, what occurred next was the preposterous sight of Mrs. Emily Michelsen being clapped in handcuffs and placed in the RCMP vehicle on allegations of founding an illegal vigilante organization called Neighbourhood Watch. This, of course, is known as an association comprised of mothers who recently formed an alliance to keep an eye out for their children's safety whilst going to and fro from school and attending extracurricular activities. She was charged by the agents as a communist operative who along with her husband was running a covert sleeper cell.

This brought a hush on the gathering crowd.

The baffling arrival of a 1952 Willys Jeep with Commander Lieutenant Colonel Arthur Kemp and Major Corporal Christopher Banks from the Lorne Scots Regiment brought the commotion to an abrupt stop. A truce was declared, when the Avro security guards were entrusted with the Avro Arrow plans from Mr. Michelsen's home office. They departed, escorted by the military Jeep.

Avro spokesman CEO Bert Sanderson said: "I am not permitted to discuss how the kerfuffle was resolved. All I can say is that after military intervention by the Commander with the RCMP agents, all charges have been dropped against both Mr. and Mrs. Michelsen."

Shortly thereafter, the Crown Vic cruiser with its suspect RCMP agents pulled away without their prey.

Blowback
5-4

Monday, October 14, 1957
10.30 a.m.

I had returned downstairs to tidy up from the completed burr project when I hear Father bellowing like a madman, and then I hear Mother cry out and start wailing.

I drop a fistful of coloured pencils, and run upstairs.

Father is pacing back and forth in the living room, clutching a crumpled newspaper in one hand. Mother is standing at the entranceway with her face in her hands.

"What's with all the ballyhoo?" I ask.

"We have been publicly shamed! It is unconscionable!" Father hollers.

"How can we ever show our faces?" Mother weeps.

I step past Mother.

"Why? What's happened?"

"Read THIS!" shouts Father. He stuffs a Centrewood Weekly newspaper into my hands. He is glaring at me as though it is all my fault. But after I smooth out the newsprint and absorb the newspaper article, I realize it has nothing to do with me, thank goodness, and everything to do with Avro, the Secret Police, and that newspaperman with the popout camera and the red-and-white speckled Irish setter.

I put my arms around Mother, our roles strangely reversed. Is this the first time I have ever comforted her? She puts her head in the nape of my neck and sobs, "This is so humiliating! What will Eszter say? Or Noreen? What will anyone in all of Centrewood say? Vigilante indeed! Oh I could just die from embarrassment!"

I read the article again.

"It's okay, Mother. It was all a mistake! Even the article says so! Nobody is going to think badly of you— Are they, Father?"

"Of course not! That part about you, Em, was patent nonsense! It's how others think of me—imagine, as a thief! that is bothering me most!"

"Why don't you call your Avro men. They would disagree, I should think!" I snap back. I'm thinking: *How could he be so self-centred?*

"Yes, Dear, they would! Why don't you go call them? How about that Bert fellow's father, Lois, what's his name?"

"Mr. Sanderfield."

"Go call him immediately, Graham! Get him over here. I can't handle this!"

At which point, Mother vanishes into the back bedroom and closes the door.

I can hear her weeping. Correction: bawling her eyes out.

There is a sudden rap on the front door. Then the doorbell is ringing.

"Who the heck is that?" Father asks, looks out the front window. "Oh no, for the love of mike, it's Mrs. Molnar—EMILY!"

I answer the door and Mrs. Molnar charges past me into the house, with Becky in tow. "Mr. Michelsen, where is Emily?" she demands.

He cocks his head toward the back room, reaches out to catch her by the elbow.

Undeterred, she marches down the hallway.

Knocking on the bedroom door, she calls out: "Emily, Emily! Open the door, or I come in. I need to see you right now!"

Mother obeys.

Taking her by the arm, Mrs. Molnar hauls her back out toward the living room, colliding with Father on the way.

Father was caught mid-stride, making to slip out down the stairs to his den.

"You too, Mr. Michelsen! You stay where you are!"

Into the living room she comes with Mother in tow.

"You sit down, Emily. You too, Mr. Michelsen! Now you come tell me what THIS is all about!"

She is brandishing her copy of the Centrewood Weekly, Thanksgiving Edition.

With Mother plopped down on the chesterfield and Father pacing about like a caged lion, they tell Mrs. Molnar an abridged, staccato version of the story, but only what transpired in our driveway on Saturday, not much more.

While they blurt out the situation in random tandem, Becky slips quietly from the entrance into the living room and hooks my elbow with her arm. "I saw the article. Are you okay?" she whispers.

"Who knows?" I say.

There is now someone else ringing the doorbell.

"Now what!" Father snarks, "Lois, get that door!"

I answer the door.

It is Mr. Sanderfield.

In response to "Your Dad home?" I nod, and in he comes without further ado.

Mr. Sanderfield has the Centrewood Weekly clenched in his fist. He strides right over to Father, grips his hand and puts an arm around his shoulders. "What a shocker for you, eh Graham? How are you doing with this? Listen, I've already called Smye. He's going to pull together the team to see what can be done about damage control!"

Then doesn't the phone ring. I go to the kitchen and answer it, and a man says: "Is that you, Lois? It's Fred Smye here. Can you put your Father on the line?"

I call Father into the kitchen, and rejoin the others, all of us hovering around, riveted to our positions, listening to the one-sided exchange despite ourselves. "Right! right then! I'll do that tomorrow, if he's available. You will? Yes, yes, that's a good idea. Okay then. Fine. Thanks, Fred!" None of which is very forthcoming in terms of content.

When Father hangs up, he looks a bit more settled, but still has bright red splotches in the centre of each of his chalk-white cheeks. Mother remains capsized on the chesterfield, with Mrs. Molnar holding her hand consolingly.

"Put the kettle on, will you please, dear?" Mother calls out to me.

To which, there's more knocking on the door, this time a solid banging—three loud raps.

We jump out of our skins.

Mrs. Molnar unleashes an ungodly gutteral scream. Mother would never scream out like that. Hers would be a high-pitched, feminine "Eeeeeee!"

Becky and I rush into the living room and there is Mrs. Molnar collapsed on the chesterfield, her hands on her face, moaning and shaking all over, bending forwards then backwards, with great streams of tears pouring down her cheeks.

Now it is Mother comforting her! "Shhh, shhh! There, there!! Whatever is the matter, Eszter?"

We all start, when Mrs. Williamson steps past us.

Mother looks up and calls out, "Noreen!"

"Mrs. Williamson!" Mrs. Molnar says gruffly, peering through spread fingers. I think she is embarrassed.

Looking overwhelmed by all the shrieking and crying, Father shouts crossly, "Why don't people use the doorbell around here?"

"The storm door was unlatched. The main door was ajar. I knocked loudly to announce myself!"

"Who are you, may I ask?" asks Father.

"Noreen Williamson. You must be Mr. Michelsen?"

"Yes indeed, and this is Bert Sanderfield, my colleague and friend." Father tacks that last part diffidently onto the end of the introduction. I see Mr. Sanderfield beam with pleasure, and sling his arm around Father's shoulder again. Father looks shy. It had never crossed my mind that grownup men might need friends.

Mrs. Williamson slides past us to stand before Mother and Mrs. Molnar.

"Anything we can do for you?" Father says, trying to regain his manners.

"I came over to make sure Emily was okay, after reading that ridiculous farce by that lickspittle muckraker in the local tabloid!"

"Bless you, Noreen, I thought you'd never talk to me again!" Mother sobs.

"Nonsense! If you're a 'vigilante', so am I!" Turning to Mrs. Molnar, she says, "We started the Neighbourhood Watch together! Really! All this malarkey with reporters and the RCMP." She turns her attention to Mrs. Molnar: "And I find you crying? What's going on with you, Mrs. Molnar?"

"I--I--am so sorry, Mrs. Williamson! It's just--well, you know I come recently from Hungary. Every time there iss a heavy knock on door, I think it might be 'Arrow Cross' and I think—how you say—'that 'jig is up'—that it is the end! for family! for Bo! for me!"

Becky dives into the bundle of entwining arms until she is spread-eagled onto Mrs. Molnar's lap. "Mama! You are in Canada, you are safe now!"

"Oh my Good Lord!" Mrs. Williamson sighs. She plunks herself down on the other side of Mrs. Molnar and embraces her, holds her tight, starts billing and cooing "There, there". She reaches out to Mother and draws her in, Becky is already caught up in the entanglement, so all four of them are rocking and crying together.

"What a wretchedly awful world we've ended up with!" Mrs. Williamson exhales, "We have all suffered, have all lost loved ones— How many of our men never came back? And the ones that did, that returned home, think of not just their dreadful wounds, but their emotional scars! They are not the same men who went to war! We must also remember those who lived through the horrors of persecution and terror, consider those such as yourself, Mrs. Molnar, who had the good fortune to escape the horrors of war in their homelands, and had to start a new life by travelling all the way here to Canada, free but nevertheless still end up carrying the scars in their hearts!"

Mother calls out: "Check the kettle, Lois. Is it boiling?"

The grownups manage to collect themselves in the living room. They sit there, genteelly sipping tea, reviewing the weekend events. The women discuss possible strategies for dealing with 'that cur' Bud Longford of the Centrewood Weekly, while Father and Mr. Sanderfield discuss their own strategies for dealing with these 'goons' who claimed to be with the RCMP 'Security Police', but behaved more like 'Secret Police', so secret not one Canadian having heard of their existence.

Father, Mother and Mr. Sanderfield to the best of their ability fill in Mrs. Molnar and Mrs. Williamson on what had transpired on the driveway, with speculation on the legitimacy of the officers. There were interjections by Mr. Sanderfield, such as: "If those two rude and uncouth men are examples now of RCMP crème de la crème, we're in big trouble!"

"But what's to be done about it?"

"Before this recent outrage, an Avro Admin delegation to Ottawa had already been slated to discuss the future of the Arrow with the Minister of Defence. Our Chief CEO Fred Smye thinks we might combine our mission with an appeal to the Attorney General, demandindg a full review of RCMP conduct," Father says.

"That is an excellent idea!" Mrs. Molnar contributes boisterously.

"Yes, a jolly good idea!" Mrs. Williamson cries.

Father says: "The entire Avro Admin team will go. We will need a strong and united front when we meet with the big guns in Ottawa! The more, the surlier!"

Everyone agrees, nodding vociferously.

It doesn't pass me by that no mention has been made of the Land Claim mission. It seems to have been overlooked. Or was it an issue that did not affect the present company?

CHAPTER SIX
Thanksgiving Monday Supper

Sufferin' Paprikash
6-1

5:30 p.m.

Over supper, without any complaints at all from Father about the Hungarian food, the conversation again pivots around Eszter.

Father opens it, "Why did your Father-in-law pick Canada—and Ontario, of all places?"

"Mr. Michelsen, if you were looking to vacate Hungary and to start another mining operation, where else but Bancroft, already proclaimed as the Mineral Capital of Canada? There would you find a large array of as yet untapped minerals and potential gemstone ore very closely alike to the Zemplen area. Where else, coincidentally, would you find a region with so many freshwater lakes and fast-flowing rivers? That too was essential—You will remember the Nahe River?"

She points to the Sapphire. We all nod.

"My father-in-law Gyorgy sat with my Father Mihaly for almost two decades at his desk in Budapest with Ontario mineral maps and charts in hand, and were excited by the prospects! From so afar, the Bancroft area had much promise. In '20s, it was still being opened up, the possibilities were limitless for new discoveries! Was not gold first discovered in a town called Madoc? Was not all the pink granite from that area being used to build your Parliament Buildings, the marble of finest quality to line the foyers—you say it 'fowyers' or 'fweye-ays?' " —"Both ways!"— "Of downtown Toronto banks? Remember although our current business interests lay in semi-precious stones, our Grandfathers had also dealt in minerals at large, so when Father Gyorgy learned about the uranium and cobalt discoveries, he was as much riveted on those reported prospecting finds as those of semi-precious gemstones: sodalite, agate, apatite, garnet, various forms of quartz. You may remember that there is more than just the ordinary white quartz, for rare occurrences of coloured quartz can include agate, amethyst, carnelian! and then there was the prospect of precious gems such as beryl—good green beryl means emerald, also corundum—good red corundum means ruby! good blue corundum means sapphire!! He came to this part of Canada for the industrial mineral potential, for the gemstone potential, and for gem-cutting operations combined."

"Can't argue with that!" Father concurs.

"They envisioned a place where they could conduct mining and not to have to contend with border disputes, fluctuating borders like Hungary and Czechoslovakia, Hungary and Romania, with fewer hassles, regulations, restrictions. They envisioned their own Idar-Oberstein gem-cutting operation that would be in their own control, at a location with no borders, not to have to ship raw ore across a border to the likes of Germany, so I ask you: where else in Canada would you look but Ontario, and primarily the Bancroft area!"

"But what's this bit about the Nahe and fast-flowing water?"

"At the Idar-Oberstein sluice, this is how gems have been cut for centuries: on water-powered stone-cutting wheels. Each gem-cutter lies face down on stomach in swiftly passing Nahe water and holds each stone with his bare hands against spinning wheel—Imagine!! This is how they cut, shape and polish individual stones into their perfect state!"

"No!" exclaims Mother, her eyes wide with disbelief.

Mrs. Molnar's eyes turn cloudy, "I dream now of a pretty little town with red-tiled roofs and cobbled lanes and fresh mountain waters rushing by.

"Father-in-Law Gyorgy and Father Mihaly surmised from Ontario to-po-graphical maps how many small lakes and rivers there were, and how many waterfalls there must be!

"Upon his arrival, Gyorgy explored the big dream: to build a gemstone processing plant at a waterfall at a central location leading direct from mines into Bancroft where there would be shops. It would make an ideal tourist attraction, such as that at Idar-Oberstein. It made such good sense from afar!"

"He must have found marvellous sites for his 'Udder-ublesteen'!" Father says.

"Indeed! But he soon discovered that waterways were already sewn up by logging! He was very excited about High Falls over Lake Baptiste. But that was in the path how logs were floated from further upstream at Sand Lake through Byers down the York River through Elephant Lake and Baptiste, across Crooked and Flat Rapids, finally reaching Bancroft itself. Once that door was shut, he went everywhere: Palmer Rapids, Egan Chute, Hastings, Crow River Valley, Smiths Falls, Fenelon Falls! He loved that place but it was a bit too far south and interfered with the Trent Canal system, as did Hastings. He went everywhere—you-name-it—he had his eye for a long time on the water-powered Austin Sawmill on Burnt River at Kinmount, which he thought would be ideal! No matter! Regardless, wherever he searched, you know what he found? He found flour mills, or lumber mills, or mills for other purposes where the owners had no interest in sharing their premises or in selling. By-laws had already been passed restricting further building on embankments! Other possible waterfalls were on protected Crown Land, or on tracts burdened with conflicting land claims—Yes, there are still Indians with claims, can you believe? that to this day have not yet been settled? There were sites where existing smaller falls or rapids flowing between lakes could not be sold, leased, drilled, built upon, tampered with due to water control management for uses downriver!"

"Mrs. Molnar sure knows that part of Ontario better than we do, right, Dear? How can you remember all the places he went?"

"Because he wrote us with every step of his way. Because we followed him on our own copy of Ontario maps he sent us. Because he kept detailed journals with his observations. Because he talked to Szofia and Tamas after they arrived! Because he took them with Bo, and then with Bo and myself out to show that whole area after I come here!"

"But surely there is a better way to cut and polish gemstones than lying on one's belly in cold water!" Father objects.

"That is where 'the necessary is what brings forth further invention', Sir!"

She doesn't have the saying quite right, but close enough.

"It is due to lack of suitable available waterfalls or water flow that Father-in-law Gyorgy was among first to develop motor-driven belts made of abrasives. The principles for polishing remain the same. The gem is either hand-held or is stuck to the end of what is called a dopstick. Debris is washed away underneath in a trough by water or different lubricants! Cold water is also necessary to reduce heat from friction. True, a water supply is still required but not from sluice. Such water pressure can as easily be obtained from a town supply water tower!"

"What would be the abrasives?"

"Would depend on the Mohs scale, or hardness, of the stone. For diamond, by way of example, the abrasive would have to be harder. For a quartz such as citrine for example, it could be an aggregate of finely ground diamond dust—a suitable use for an off-product, no? whereas, for softer stones, the belt could also be silicon carbide or corundum."

"Corundum or carborundum? Are they the same thing?"

"Um, No. Corundum is natural ore, aluminum oxide, but carborundum is silica carbide."

"Hm! Reminds me of that Latin phrase: *illegitimi non carborundum!*"

"And what might that mean, Mr. Michelsen? I studied Latin but I am not familiar with that phrase?"

"I believe it means: 'Don't let the bastards grind you down', Mrs. Molnar!"

"Oh, GRAHAM!" Mother squeals.

Mrs. Molnar says, "You must write that down for me. Perhaps it is your pronunciation that keeps me from understanding?"

Mother's face is suffused with red, and she is wiping tears from the corners of her eyes.

Siege Version Unabridged
6-2

Monday, October 14, 1957
7 p.m.

This time, we are sitting out on the back patio. It was Father's suggestion.

"We could sit out here until way past sundown without being eaten alive," Father had decided, "Surely the mosquitoes have all died off by now."

Nothing much had been done in the backyard since we moved here early summer. The patio stones had been laid near the sliding door. There is a huge clay flowerpot at the edge with some heat-badgered red geraniums, and a few valiant trailing vines, both of which are crying out for watering.

Early summer, long wide strips of grass sod had been laid out over the barren clay. "Green side up!' as the Newfies say!" This is one of Father's favourite quips). But the heat spell had checked their growth, and their frayed seams were still visible. A meager row of small cedars march in a line like a brigade from the Seven Dwarfs along the back chain-link fence. A few saplings in white ankle socks dot the yard. There isn't much else except for one major plus: a fresh 'Indian summer' breeze blowing toward us from the west. This makes all the difference for any heady conversation that might crop up, compared with the living room, which had turned into what Mother called a steam bath (Father's term: stink pot) by the time last evening's "siege" was over.

"I could have gone for that air-conditioner we had at the Brock in Niagara," Father had moaned, "Wasn't that a treat? Let's get one!"

"But in the living room? It was so ugly—it looked like a refrigerator!" Mother replies.

Father laughs at her: "That's because it was! Never mind I'll have it adorned with skirt ruffles! Anything you ask! Anything!"

We all lean back into our chaise lounges and breathe in some sweet silence with the wafts of fresh air.

Suddenly, Father adjusts the almost-prone position of his chaise lounge by lifting the arms and heaving his body weight forward. The back pops up, so now he is sitting upright.

"Mrs. Molnar, I spent some time while trying to go to sleep last night, thinking about your reference to the Arrow Cross during the Siege of Budapest."

"Oh yes?"

"The Arrow Cross," Father muses, stroking his chin, "Back then, I remember hearing about them on the news! Weren't they the bloodthirsty ones, even worse than the Nazis, for their cruelty against the Jews?"

"Yes! Very bad, very wicked!" Mrs. Molnar replies.

"The Arrow Cross?" Mother muses, "Why has the 'Arrow' appeared again, Dear? It's uncanny! Is it not, Dear?"

"Let's not misconstrue a coincidence of this kind with any semblance of divine significance, Emily," Father replies, annoyed to have his beloved Avro Arrow associated with this evil Arrow Cross.

Mrs. Molnar provides the answer:

"The Arrow Cross was Fascist Party which took over control of Hungary in October of 1944."

"According to my recollection," Father says gingerly, "The Arrow Cross brutalized the Jews in Hungary, and committed terrible atrocities."

"Yes, yes, their treatment of Jews was horrendous. Many of the gang members roaming the streets were just boys—in teen years! But the leaders of Fascist Party were full-grown men who encouraged, egged on, often supervised their actions!"

"Mrs. Molnar, did nobody try to stop the brutality happening in broad daylight in the streets?" Father asks.

"Not that I saw. Mostly, when brutal events happened, the streets were suddenly empty. Everyone was terrorized and rushed indoors."

"Was there no one who tried to help?"

"Oh, to be sure! But directly? In the street? Few. Those who did object would be beaten and killed immediately, and their families threatened. It wasn't daring to oppose on one's own, it was risking lives of loved ones. The Arrow Cross were ruthless to anyone that crossed them.

"Whenever I was on street and something started to happen, I would hide behind a wall, or I would knock on known non-Jewish neighbour's door, beg to be let in until the brutes passed. Yes, I heard shouts and screams. But I admit that I would hide. Cover my ears. Close my eyes. Yes I know! I saw none of actual brutality. I saw only the gory results."

"Well, it's appalling!" Mother contributes self-righteously, "I thought it then and I think it now. Isn't that when they showed photographs in the newspapers of Jews being rounded up in the village squares—while the townsfolk stood around and watched with their gobs open, doing nothing! It was appalling, to see them just stand there, letting those poor people be corralled, knowing that later—" she looks at Mrs. Molnar meaningfully, and then at Becky and myself, "They would have unspeakable things done to them!"

"Do you feel the same way, Mr. Michelsen?"

"Yes, I do. I've often thought about it. Speculated what I myself would do if I were there, witnessing the abuse! To be blunt, I see only my ambivalence, to act or not to act? Not knowing to this day what I'd do, it tears at my gut."

"In principle, there is no excuse. But in reality, life is never that simple, is it?" Mrs. Molnar's tone becomes compassionate: "Many did nothing because of fear."

"Or saw the futility of it."

"Exactly! If it were you, Mr. Michelsen, you might be asking yourself: what effect would a single act by one person have on such an occasion? You must agree that it was no good to step forward from a crowd of onlookers to protest, only to be dragged off and shot yourself!

"Many people stood there helpless, wishing they were brave, waiting for someone else to take the first step to intercede, more than willing to fall in line if it ever turned into a mob of protesters."

"There certainly appeared to be enough onlookers in the crowd to overwhelm any of the soldiers—Who it seemed from the photographs to be outnumbered ten to one!" Mother says.

"Then again, Emily, you might have more forgiveness in your heart, if you knew some of those brave souls in your news photographs might have been there to bear witness, might have been assigned to be there, to take back word about the atrocities and deportations to others, might have been helping behind the scenes, perhaps as part of the underground, as part of a team, to either rescue the poor souls, or to plan retaliation!"

"At any rate, for those who didn't care, who stood there just to see the spectacle, who had no pity, there must be many now who must live for the rest of their lives with the knowledge that they were too heartless or too cowardly to act," Mother says.

"It was mass psychology," Mrs. Molnar says, "To root everyone in fear. To make show at every opportunity that nothing could be done, that they were in charge.

"In truth, most citizens saw clearly how powerless they themselves were, and saw their only hope could be through foreign intervention!"

"I'm still confused," Father says, "Did you not say that the Jews in Hungary were full-fledged citizens?"

"Yes, these actions were a betrayal of civil law. In Hungary, the Jews had achieved formal Emancipation as full citizens back in 1867. The Jews of Hungary trusted, that of all Jews in Europe, they were protected! They were free—we all believed this to be so! They had become fully assimilated into the main stream of Hungarian society."

"Where were you and your family on this score?" Father queries, looking pained for having asked the question.

"We did our part."

An awkward silence ensues.

There is a sense in the air that something had broken, that a branch had snapped. Father looks nervous, as though he might have gone too far.

"Mrs. Molnar, there was something else you said last night that intrigued me. You were talking about the Black Percheron teams and the wagonloads which often bore both gemstone ore and furniture. As I recall you said something to the effect that 'very few questions were asked when on occasion wagons with the same piece of furniture could be seen going in one direction—then passing by in an other direction a few days later! Why would that be?" Father asks.

"Between you, me and the lantern, I tell you---" Mrs. Molnar leans forward conspiratorially, looks at Father with narrowed eyes and saya, quietly:

"It had to do with—Smuggling!"

Father's jaw drops.

Mother gasps.

I see their eyes flicking nervously back and forth at each other.

"More smuggling?! You told us about smuggling the yellow citrine in stuffed upholstery from Ibber-Obblesteen. What else did you smuggle?"

Mrs. Molnar shrinks back inside herself.

"Explain, please!" Father commands, with a self-righteous tone.

"Just between you, us and the *lamp post*, Eszter!" Mother conjures.

Mrs. Molnar a real live smuggler! I had heard of the rum-runners that ran contraband across Lake Ontario during Prohibition. Father and Mother are gawping at Mrs. Molnar as though she might be the offspring incarnate of a Hungarian version of Captain Morgan. Despite Hungary being landlocked, I see galleons in full sail, with pirates in the crow's-nests, black patches on one eye, the Skull and Cross-Bones hanging from the masts.

Mrs. Molnar bites her lip.

"Do you intend to tell us what else you smuggled?" Again, Father, sounding imperious.

"Yes, yes! I tell you now! We smuggled—Jews!"

Cat Out of Sack
6-3

The whole room rocks.

Father clutches the arms of his chair, looks as though he is going to pass out. His knuckles turn white.

Mother shrieks with alarm, throws her hand to her mouth.

Mrs. Molnar looks apprehensive, as though she has said too much.

"I hope I have not let cat out of sack too soon!" she says.

She takes in a long breath.

"The heavy furniture. The buffets, sideboards, dressers, tall wardrobes, as much as possible of it was given—what you say, modifications! You understand? Adaptations! Adjustments! Large pieces were given false backing, false flooring, secret latches, air holes through false vents. Once finished, moved from Zemplen area barns and sheds and stables by Percheron teams—and used to reach Jews, for helping them escape!"

"What? Escape where?"

"From various hiding places in the country, first they were carried to Budapest warehouse. Then once installed securely, shipped out in boxcars. By train. In crates. As Molnar-Nemeth Antiques cargo."

"Was your whole family involved?"

"Yes."

"You risked your lives! Why would you do such a thing?"

"It was a matter of conscience."

"How did you get involved?"

"I will tell you. But first of all, I want to point out to you how only moments ago, you were so pious against those in crowd who did nothing. Now you sound judgmental about my family for helping in rescue! I ask you: if one has a conscience, and the willingness of family who are also prepared to take the risk, as well as the means to act, how could one not get involved?"

"Why didn't you mention this last night?" Mother asks.

"I considered telling you but needed higher comfort level. I am very aware that Canada had no wish to help Jewish refugees, refused entry, and that your very own High Commissioner to Britain, Vincent Massey, said that one Jew was one too many. How do I know if all Canadians feel that way? I had to sound out first, how you yourselves feel about Jews. What you have said this evening has reassured me. You demonstrated ample compassion for those poor people."

"Well, yes, we did! We do!!"

"Besides, last night my first priority was necessity to concentrate on my own personal history and my own immediate concerns!"

"But you made not one mention of the Jews! Why not?"

"Yes, yes. That is true. Call my last night story the 'Molnar-Nemeth Sanitized Version' and now is my true story: 'Siege Unabridged Version'!"

Father looks puzzled and says, "How do you know that word?"

"Ah," Mrs. Molnar replies, "I learn my English many ways. One way is through reading. Since coming to Canada, I read 'Readers Digest Condensed Books'. On title page is subtitle: '*Abridged* Versions of Best-Selling Novels and Nonfiction books.' That way, I expand both my knowledge of current literature AND my vocabulary."

"I must say, Mrs. Molnar," Father says reluctantly, "I am singularly impressed!"

Meanwhile, Mother has been thrown into deep reflection. Waiting until some time has passed after Father has spoken, she broaches the forbidden, "Is anyone in your own family Jewish?" She glances sidelong at Father.

"No."

"But what did the Jews have to do with you, to make you risk your own lives?"

Mrs. Molnar flicks her shoulder.

"Life teaches us lessons. Through terrible times, I learned lesson and now I pass this lesson on to you. Before threats by Hitler and

Nazism, I did not think I had anything to do with anyone else's problems. It is common for us all in our little bubbles to think that others' problems have nothing to do with us! Until matters cut close to bone, come close to hand. Then they can have everything to do with what you cherish and value, but can be too late to act."

"But what did you have to do with the Jews?" Father presses.

"For us, living and growing up in '20s into '30s, nothing! Everything and nothing!! To me, to us, to our family, we regarded them as anyone else.

"It wasn't that no Jews existed where we grew up. On the contrary! They lived amongst us. That they were Jewish was irrelevant— to us it didn't matter! We associated with everyone.

"Over the '20s and '30s we would hear of occasional outbursts in other parts of Hungary against the Jews, but it was not extraordinarily unusual, for there were also outbursts against the Roma gypsies and always hostilities with the Czechs and the Serbs. I tell you from living there myself that Hungarians did not have pronounced prejudice against the Jews because the Jews were Hungarian themselves.

"I can assure you, I do not make up big lies when I tell you that there was very little discrimination against Jews before Hitler. True, as far back as 1920 the Prime Minister Teleki of the right wing government passed a law that limited admission of so-called 'insecure political elements' to universities. It turned out most of such elements were Jews. However, it was not until 1938 that Prime Minister Daranyi passed the First Jewish Law which limited to twenty percent the proportion of Jews allowed in the press, in theatre and film, in law, engineering and medicine. In 1939, there came the Second Jewish Law. Jews were defined by race, not religion. Only six percent were permitted in intellectual profession, and they were banned from state administration, justice, teaching, industrial and commercial professions, and any trade that required a licence.

"Living in Budapest, the passing of these restrictions registered on our awareness, but they did not directly affect us or anyone we knew. In day to day life, we never thought about who was a Jew. Even though we took our shoes to the shoemaker, our suits to the tailor, our dresses to the dressmaker, we never connected a trade with a certain 'race'. It never crossed our minds—my own mind, at least, that people who provided certain services were primarily Jewish.

"Before the Arrow Cross surfaced and before Molnar-Nemeth Antiques became deeply involved in rescuing Jews and helping them escape, I honestly did not realize just how many people I knew from daily course of living in the country, and also then in Budapest, were Jewish until suddenly their shops were boarded up, windows smashed, contents looted, nasty messages scrawled, and then they were not there anymore, overnight they were in ghettos, were murdered or disappeared.

"Living in Budapest as we were, and following closely the news, it became clear to us how their situation was increasingly hopeless. It was incremental, the laws that were being passed, so they could not get education, pursue certain careers, or participate in politics. They could not remain anonymous, as they were forced to declare themselves, and then tolerate racist signs on their doors, and their shops boycotted. Whatever they did to defend their rights, it didn't matter. However much nobly they conducted themselves as citizens, whatever they had done to demonstrate their goodness, their decency and integrity, it didn't matter! When the Fascists and the Nazis set their dogs on them, the Jewish people could not win!"

"But how did it get so bad, so quickly?" Mother asks.

"How could laws be passed against them without any formal protest? What happened to the parliament you had? Was there no political opposition? Did the people have no voice at all?" Father hammers.

"Back in the '30s, we heard of growing hostilities against the Jews in Germany, and of escalating persecutions. We had business in Germany, and when we went there, we did not see any signs of anti-Semitism. To tell the truth, I don't think even the German people felt so much that way against the Jews, until along came Hitler and the Nazis who stirred up the hatred, blamed the Jews for world's economic woes, then tried to make a point of punishing the Jews for it, deprived them of making living, demeaned them, made them poor and pathetic, put them in position to be ridiculed and then despised. It puzzled us younger ones, dismayed our Fathers. But understand that when any disruption in Hungary, we could count on our Regent Admiral Horthy to make short work of it. Frankly, with him at helm, we did not think there was anything worth worrying about!"

"What is a mystery to me is your Admiral Horthy. Where was he really in all of this? You give the impression how highly regarded he was—and how you depended on his protection! My own impression is that he was constantly dipping and dodging about! Was he always on his high white horse or did he prove himself to be a skunk?"

"Well now, Admiral Horthy, despite his often contrary actions, he had method behind his madness. There were whispers about his true sentiments about the Jews. Yes, yes, it was often said that Horthy was suspected of anti-Semitism! But many staunchly defended him, maintained that whatever he did, was to cater to the enemy just this side of capitulation, so he could protect the Jews. Proof is there, that he kept national Arrow Cross Fascists and German Nazi anti-Semites actions at bay as long as possible. After the war, he was arrested and charged as a Communist, then as a Nazi, then his actions were vindicated when proven he did everything in his power to protect the Jews, and he was released. He lives now in freedom in Hungary."

"Well, that's a consolation. At least his ship didn't sail without him," Father says.

I'm wondering whatever happened to his white horse, when Mrs. Molnar picks up the reins, "It is time to talk now about March 19, 1944 when Hitler marched in and occupied Hungary. 'Operation Margarethe' is what it was called.

"I did not tell you its significance to fate of Hungarian Jews.

"I did not tell you that Admiral Horthy was *obliged* to appoint Dome Sztojay as Prime Minister. He was a very avid Nazi.

"However, I did tell you it was in May 1944 when news arrived that Eichmann had been sent into Hungary. That is when we all shuddered. You know about Eichmann?"

Father says: "Not so much back then."

"We are just learning more of him now," Mother replies, "He has escaped from custody, and the international police are searching for him."

"He's called the 'Architect of the Holocaust," Father adds.

Mrs. Molnar says: "He was sent by Hitler to supervise deportation of Jews to death camps in Poland!" Mrs. Molnar voice goes up a register and she almost squeaks.

"They say he is hiding in Argentina, living under an assumed name," Father contributes. "The Jewish State of Israel has assigned a special force dedicated exclusively to hunting him down. A Holocaust survivor, Simon Wiesenthal, is also searching for him independently."

"May they find him and may justice be done," Mrs. Molnar says gruffly, "The Final Solution to this travesty will not be what he hoped would happen but will see him hanged!"

Mrs. Molnar slams her head against the chairback to express her anger.

"The evil man Prime Minister Sztojay cooperated with the Germans and Eichmann. Our very own Hungarian gendarmes were sent into the rural areas to corral the Jews. Many of them lived on and around the estates, in local villages, were as close to us as others, were part of our extended family. Out in the country places, that is where the persecutions began. Not in Budapest. Yet. In the end, they rounded up over 500,000 Hungarian Jews living outside Budapest!

"Sztojay had them enclosed in ghettos where they were made to live in crowded, wretched conditions, without food or proper sanitation or medical assistance, many of them exposed to elements without shelter. They would be shot if they tried to escape.

"Then came the time of Hungary's big shame.

"You will recall when I mentioned to you that span of time: from May 15 to July 9, 1944, when our shipments were suspended? When I told you the Germans had requisitioned the railroad?"

"Yes."

"Last night, I did not tell you the real reason why.

"I said it was for the 'war effort.' But in truth, it was the time when all those 400,000 Jews—" at which point Mrs. Molnar stopped, choked up, then resumed, "Were stuffed into crowded boxcars and sent on their way to the death camps. They travelled the same tracks as our shipments would normally travel.

"All other commerce was suspended during this time."

Mrs. Molnar hangs her head, silent, chewing her lower lip.

We too wait, heads hung, in silence.

"It was in August of '44 that through some miracle Admiral Horthy was able to replace that snake Sztojay and appoint a good man, anti-fascist Prime Minister Lakatos. Most likely because routine shipments had been halted, he managed to regain control over railway. At same time, he prohibited Hungarian gendarmes were from deporting any more Hungarian Jews because they were our citizens!

"This is when our family plan kicked into action. That was when Father-in-law Gyorgy and wife Borka left with Percheron team for Idar-Oberstein. It is when they left with citrine-stuffed sofas for Canada!

"It was also when smuggling of Jewish refugees by Molnar-Nemeth Antiques resumed.

"The smuggling began much earlier than that. It started from end of snows in winter of late February of 1944 and continued till May 1944. That was when first major phase took place for

Molnar-Nemeth Antiques to fetch large pieces of furniture from various locations in outlying regions.

"These were the large pieces of furniture that had been stored in the many barns and sheds to where they had been delivered over the course of time from the early 1920s when, as you will recall, bankrupt gentry émigré families abandoned their estates, entrusted contents to Molnar-Nemeth Brokers.

"From mid-30s on, when signs were there of upcoming persecutions, much work was being done on the chests, buffets, armoires and other such stately furniture by ingenious craftsmen who rebuilt and refinished the antique furniture so that it looked immaculately prepared for sale abroad. "We had much cooperation in the countryside from our tenants. Why did they comply? Because they trusted our Fathers Gyorgy and Mihaly. Because our family had proven themselves over and over in helping the less fortunate. Because there were tenants on our family estates who owed ownership of their land to our Grandfathers! Now all that good will paid off!

"They helped with local Jewish County Councils to arrange for many Jews, as well as Roma gypsies, to hide in buildings of abandoned estates—in stable lofts, mansion attics, storage cellars. From there, only a few at a time, matches based on their measurements, they were secretly transferred to the Nemeth-Molnar Antique Furniture barns and sheds, and transported to Budapest.

"Along would come a team of gleaming, well-groomed black Percherons driven by one of their immaculate gentleman masters. They would invariably be accompanied by village children as though out for a ride, or heading back to estate or school. After Father-in-law Gyorgy left for Canada, the drivers would be either Bence or Tamas, accompanied up front by either Zsofia or myself, out enjoying our husbands' companionship.

"The refugees would be strapped, taped, bound, bundled into the false backings, raised floor fascia, mock drawers of the 'restored' large pieces of furniture which awaited them. Some were roped standing up, spread-eagled or lying on one's side in tall wardrobes or in grand pianos with removed strings and legs. Wherever they were placed, whatever was requested of them, the frightened escapees cooperated fully with their instructions, drugged their babies, gagged their children, helped tie their hands and feet to inner support posts.

"The wagons had also been cleverly revamped. Fugitives were hidden in secret beds that slid out like trays from underneath the loading bins, were lashed to boards in the undercarriage.

"In this way, the escapees made it to the warehouse depot, to be extracted, tended and hidden in the back of the warehouse or in our house before being bound once more for next Molnar-Nemeth Antiques 'shipment' abroad.

"At Budapest Molnar-Nemeth Antiques business, Mother and Zsofia maintained the storefront and kept inventory of large furniture pieces which had been 'converted' for transport. They worked with Tamas in matching sizes and ages of intended escapees as much as possible keeping husband and wife, parents and children together—but with no promises. I too helped keep them hidden in far reaches of the warehouse, and in our house, behind false walls in basement, overhead behind false plaster ceilings in rafters and attic, outside on roof, even in false chimneys, and in tunnels which led behind warehouse to sheds in back lane. These tunnels had been dug and covered way back in late thirties under guise of reinforcing foundations and laying concrete sidewalks.

In the back of the warehouse, Tamas utilized all his carpentry and woodworking skills along with willing helpers, a couple of whom were Roma gypsies from Zemplen County who were expert illusionists, also magicians who knew contortionist arts—knew how small it was possible to bundle a human body—would you believe two infants were curled up and inserted into a matching set of thin-necked Grecian urns—the bases had been bored out and rubber flanges glued in to make invisible seal, like a big plug. They were happy to be working in exchange for escape of some of their own family members.

"But how did they survive the long train ride bound as they were inside the furniture??"

"This was another factor anticipated by the craftsmen. Once stock was rolling and the trip well underway, there was always at least one traveller who could release himself from hidden in his crate by lifting the lid from the inside. He knew which crates held covered jars of water, and chests which held bread. He was shown beforehand how to lift each crate's lid so carefully there could be no detection at next inspection point, how to reach in and provide to the shivering frightened souls some sips of water, small pieces of bread. There could be no splashing or signs of crumbs or they would all be dead. And so would we!"

"While a shipment was underway, you must have all been quaking in your boots until it reached its destination!"

"Oh yes. Very uncertain times. Much anxiety. Much fear."

Mrs. Molnar takes in a deep breath, and then folds her arms across her chest.

"As the shipments became fewer, the storefront gradually became just a shield for hiding remaining activities deeper inside the warehouse.

"But how were those activities hidden from view?"

"The horses were stabled inside directly behind the display floor. Back warehouse activities were separated by horse stalls and wagons, horse feed and hay. Some furniture looked like it was being stock-piled for refinishing—some of it was, while some pieces had papers tacked to them with fictitious names and destinations.

"Are you saying that you continued to ship throughout the Arrow Cross regime?"

"Our last shipment was in end of October."

"Early November, Budapest Jews enjoyed no longer freedom of any sort. All remaining Jews were ordered into a ghetto. It was very mean and cramped. Nearly 70,000 Jews were forced to survive in a space only one-tenths of a mile square."

"So no more shipments of any Jews?"

"None. Besides, it had begun to snow heavily. It turned bitterly cold that winter. We could not operate when there might be footprints left in snow. We could not ship human beings who might freeze to death in boxcars.

"Just in case there was a thaw, we planned a last shipment. But then the Germans blew up all five bridges on January 18."

"By the September, we had to curtail shipments from the countryside. It had become too dangerous. We had done our best. As far as we could tell, most of the country Jews had been expelled by then anyway.

"October came as fist in eye for both Admiral Horthy, and consequently for the Jews. You will remember that the Nazis kidnapped Admiral Horthy's son, in retaliation for Horthy's attempt to sign amnesty with the Soviets. This was the second time he tried to jump ship, Mr. Michelsen, if you recall! He was forced to abdicate and the Regency ended, remember?"

"Haven't you already covered this?" Mother asks, sounding weary, impatient, slightly annoyed. "We have an expression when someone repeats their story, we say 'they're chewing their cabbage twice!'"

"You think I am telling same story twice! Well, in some ways, yes I am. But I am telling truth now, as I knew it, about the Hungarian Jews!"

"Right!" Mother saya, trying not to aggravate Mrs. Molnar any more.

"Reason why this is important?" She wags her finger at us. "Condition for life of his son meant Horthy had to appoint Arrow Cross leader, the evil skunk Szalasi.

"This was a dark hour for Hungarian Jews now mostly remaining only in Budapest!

"Szalasi turned his attentions to Budapest.

"By mid-October, he had all Jewish buildings—shops, homes, businesses—marked with yellow stars. He established smaller ghettos, not like the ones in the country. At the time, we wondered why. Later, we realized this was a logistical move. The Jews were collateral. The Allies were less likely to bomb Budapest if so many Jews remained!

"For a while, Jews were even allowed out within a prescribed range, presumably to go to market, run small errands, attend their shops, keep small wheels of local businesses running. But then it started to escalate. Jews caught inside yellow starred buildings were not allowed to leave.

"On October 20th, the call-up notices began. Men between the ages of 16 and 60, women between 18 and 40 were organized into trench-digging defense lines around Budapest because the Soviets were closing in.

"Over the same duration, Szalasi unleashed his gangs to torture, mutilate, murder any Jews on sight, inside their shops or out on the street.

"Many terrible, unspeakable, brutal actions happened during that time. Shopkeepers that I knew were beaten, women and girls were dragged by hair, raped and tormented in front of their families. Women with their tops stripped off, their breasts then mutilated. Men with their pants pulled down and their private members chopped off. Faces bludgeoned, teeth bashed out, limbs severed. Infants swung in the air by their feet then slammed against brick walls, their brains smashing open like coconuts. The gangs ran amok, drunk with bloodthirsty, rampaging liberty to do anything they wanted. It was a terrifying time."

"Lordy, lordy," Mother sighs.

"The violence all began, it seemed, overnight. One day, Budapest felt safe. Quiet. One could go about one's business. But suddenly, next day, in a shake, it turned dreadful! Yes. Dread Full."

Mrs. Molnar is shaking all over. Becky slips over to wrap her arms around her. "Mama, Mama," she urges, "Be still, be still."

"You see how quickly this all happened? How stealthily, how methodically, how rapier sharp and swift was our government dismantled, taken over by thugs! How thin a veneer there really is between order and chaos, law and absolute barbarism!

"In November, thousands of Jews were rounded up from the marked buildings and sent off on forced death marches. No food. No clothing to protect from the cold winds. Stragglers were shot.

"In mid-November, the 17th to be exact, Szalasi presented his six steps to the "Entlösung", or his "Final Solution" to the "Jewish Question". This was their cloaked way of saying "Jewish Problem", meaning their existence on the face of this earth and how to get rid of them.

"Szalasi issued categories into which all Jews must fall, ranging from those eligible for leaving the country, those who could stay under stipulated conditions, and those who were to be sent to Germany, meaning, extermination camps."

Mrs. Molnar draws a wallet out of her purse and opens the photographs compartment. Out slides a picture of a stern youngish man in uniform smiling proudly at the camera with hands on shoulders of two little girls.

"This I show you, so that you too can wonder. This man is that Fascist Szalasi who oversaw the atrocities committed by Arrow Cross and the deaths of thousands of Hungarian Jews. And except for their mean little mouths, just like their Father's, these are his two lovely little innocent daughters."

"Eszter! You carry that picture in your wallet? Why torment yourself this way?"

"I carry his image with me to remind myself of the evil that lurks in all mankind. I carry this photo until I figure out how such a man—and father—can do what he did to other living beings."

She slides the photograph back into her wallet.

"Tell me, how did you decide which ones to help. Was there a personal connection when you became involved?" Mother asks.

"Our parents always had friends and business acquaintances all over the country as well as in Budapest, among them Jewish. Some of their friends were older, friends of our Grandparents. So their motivation to help them was clear.

"For our part, we had friends who were Jewish. Brilliant, intelligent, witty, loving, talented, precious friends whom we had known for long long time and with whom we often socialized. We cherished them. Suddenly they were in danger, their lives were in jeopardy, their day-to-day safety not secure. And Bence? He had a good, very close friend on the faculty at the University with whom he had studied, and who despite his brilliance had lost his job when persecutions had begun.

"That is when we got involved."

"How?"

"He and his wife and two small children were among the first we helped escape via the large furniture shipments of Molnar-Nemeth Antiques. They made it all the way up to Brussels and then to England! Later, one of our last shipments included a little four year old girl named Fifi, my dressmaker's daughter. That was in late October, 1944."

"You put your lives at risk!" Mother says.

"All our lives were at risk, every living day. The slaughter, the torture, the cruelties were increasing everywhere, vicious assaults, out of control, nothing but senseless, increasing lawlessness.

"We saw what the Arrow Cross—and Sjotjay, Szalasi, and Eichmann could do to innocent people. No, we had no regrets! We did not ask for it to be in our plans. However, we only lament that we could not help enough of them to escape. We did our utmost to rescue as many as we could!"

"How many, do you know?"

"At least four or five hundred, maybe more."

"How many Hungarian Jews died overall?"

"To our horror, our contribution toward saving the Jews was miniscule compared with the total carnage. Word is still coming, but it is said that of 800,000 Jews, only 200,000 survived. And all but 15,000 Roma went to Auschwitz-Birkenau."

We all sat quietly, the atmosphere almost funereal, as we mourned the loss of something so vital, something so precious.

"Thank goodness we live in Canada. Nothing like that could ever happen here!" Mother says.

Mrs. Molnar looks appalled, then incredulous.

"Believe me, Emily, it can happen anywhere. Do you think anyone could really imagine what happened to Hungary? to all the beautiful countries in Europe? Always, always you must be on watch for the slightest signs of moral decay and for attacks on civil liberties, beware all whittlings away at human rights! All bigotry, all persecutions of other races, all erosion of democracy—And fight against it!!"

"When did you know? that you must act? What was the ultimate sign?"

"It is difficult to pinpoint when exactly. But there comes a time when a line is crossed. It's when it finally dawns on you that what happens to others can just as easily happen to you! And if it's happening to them, it might just be you next. Soon!"

"You are telling us that you felt threatened as a Hungarian during the persecution of the Jews?"

"Yes."

"Not solely because you and your family were helping them."

"No. Because Hungarians generally thought it was possible we might be next. Look at how Hitler hated the Poles—he sent them to labour camps, treated them like slaves! And they were a blond race—they just didn't meet his stipulations. Not pure. Not Aryan. Hungarians are neither. To someone like Hitler, we are a dark and

Mediterranean race. We do not remotely qualify for the superior race, the 'Master Race.'"

"Was the Soviet Union hostile toward Hungarians?"

"Only if you stood in their way."

"And if no opposition?"

"Look at Stalin. What a beast he was to his very own people!"

"All I want is to live a simple life," Mother sighs.

Mrs. Molnar shakes her fist.

"Lead a simple life if you wish, but it is a moral imperative to fight against wrong and injustice wherever it occurs!"

Another long silence ensues.

Mother says: "Now I understand why you were so upset when Noreen knocked on the door."

Father says: "It wasn't that your family were all Jewish yourselves."

"No no, but authorities could find out at any moment that we were helping them. A loud knock on the door. Then we were as good as dead. Most likely shot as collaborators."

Blue Sodalite (#11)
6-4

Mrs. Molnar had brought the remaining stones with her to the patio where they are now laid out on the table beside her. They lie there, beckoning.

Father says quietly: "There are three stones left: the light blue one, the dark green one and the pebble."

"Yes."

"What do they represent?" he asks, with a new tone of respect in his voice.

Mrs. Molnar reaches for the light blue oval stone, which was finished and already set in silver with a chain.

"I see calm and powdery-blue skies, with wispy white clouds floating high over the ancient, overlapping hills around Bancroft, Ontario. Next time I am under its blue canopy, God be willing, I will share its serenity with my dear husband Bence.

"I tell you now about this stone. It is called blue sodalite. It is from our quarry here in Ontario near Bancroft. It has become our most widely-known gem that comes from our own blue sodalite mine. It is as rare among semi-precious stones as our Hungarian white opal. Now the blue sodalite is one of my favourites. You see it is opaque—not clear like citrine—and has medium blue colour with white streaks through It. The soapy softness to the touch speaks to me of Inner Peace found deep inside, when all fear is washed away. It is the kind of peace that can be felt under a light blue sky with just a few strands of white clouds in the air, the kind of high summer sky that has no trace of imminent thunderstorm on horizon."

"Sounds like you have fallen in love with our 'up north', which is what we Southern Ontarians call our lake district. It is not as far north to be truly Northern Ontario, but is a glorious escape from the city!" Father contributes.

"Torontonians' best kept secret, I'd say!" Mother adds.

"Yes, yes. Is so bee-oo-tee--full! We stayed at a lodge near Bancroft—Gyorgy, Tamas, Zsofia, Boglarka and I—where meals were cooked for us. Suppers— Fresh bass! Fresh strawberry pie! We went swimming in cool, clear, fresh water like sweet uncture for skin and spirit! Stretched out on the small-size wharf—a dock, is it called? Listened to the water lap its rhythm underneath us so gently. Lay on back and looked up at carefree blue sky. Ah, and the loons calling—So haunting, so reassuring! Extraordinary!"

Mrs. Molnar glances at Becky.

"We shall do that again, shall we, my little Buttercup?"

Becky is looking dozy but nods happily.

Mrs. Molnar holds out her hand.

"Bo and I wish to give you this sodalite stone for your birthday, Lois! This was mined in Bancroft, cut and polished by our own gem-cutting operation in Fergus, and set by our own local silversmith. Early gift, I know. But we want you to have it, so you can wear it to concert—and Bo will wear her opal necklace, yes?"

"Oh, Mrs. Molnar, I love it!"

The stone is set in a silver backing, with a loop through which the chain is passed.

"It goes with your fair hair and your pretty blue eyes! Blue sodalite becomes you, my dear girl! I like you to wear it now!" Mrs. Molnar comes over to me, lifts my hair, attaches the chain around my neck, and straightens the stone so it sits in the middle of my throat. "Ah," she says, "It fits just right. See the dip between the collarbones? That is the suprasternal notch. It covers the jugular."

She kisses my forehead and says, "Wear it in peace, Lo-iss! Always be happy!"

I feel a warm glow flood through my heart.

Green Malachite (#12)
6-5

"Twelfth Stone: Dark Green Malachite.

"I see a dark green-forested island, sleeping quietly on the Danube, resting equally between the two cities of Buda and Pest. The island is a stepping-stone that waited long time to wed the two cities into one Budapest.

"Margaret Island sits like a precious gem in river Danube. In fact, it is often called the jewel of Budapest.

"To me, especially from a distance—overlooking the river from high on Castle Hill, for instance, its shape always looked to me like an oval cabochon. For that reason, Bence gave me this malachite ring for our engagement. We chose it together, of course. He was happy when I told him I did not want a diamond ring, for that was too—how you say, ho-hum pedestrian for me. What I wanted was a stone symbolising our times together on Margaret Island."

She picks up the green ring, holds it up, and passes it around.

"See how softly polished the stone gleams, how warm and mysterious it is— a dark and deep luscious liquid-green with its lighter streaks that ripple through it like sunlight reflections on sandy shoals of the river!"

We all admired the ring before passing it back to her. It was quite large, and not at all what I pictured for an engagement ring. I didn't even know a fiancée had a choice! However, I liked the way the stone was mounted in a simple oval silver setting.

She slipped it onto her left ring finger, leaving her gold band on her right hand as usual.

"In the spring of 1939, Bence and I were married. We chose Margaret Island where we had spent many happy times in our younger years playing hide-and-seek, tag, 'cops and robbers', 'cowboys and Indians'—oh yes! Was already an American influence because of movies!

"The river had strong current, so a favourite pastime was to run imaginary regattas, releasing whole flotillas of tiny handmade bark boats, with sticks for masts impaled with dead leaves for sails, Bence and I chasing them along the shoreline to see how far they would float, before becoming snagged by rock or tipped over and sunk.

"The wedding ceremony took place at our favourite spot, the Water Tower. Built at turn of 1900s, it was one of first structures in all Europe to be made of poured reinforced concrete. It was eight-sided—octagonal shaped? Yes—with eight slender columns shooting up high to support first of two levels, dainty ornate railings around open second level and the lookout dome way up on very top. Painted entirely white, it was a fantasy we imagined was made of white chocolate and white icing. To us, it was a fairy tale tower.

"There as boy and girl, we played out Brothers Grimm story of Rapunzel, climbing up the various levels, Rapunzel pretending to toss her long ropes of hair over the railings, her Prince pretending to climb up to visit her! The imaginary Black Witch, the Enchantress, would appear, evil and dangerous, we would scream, and I would pretend to fall off and be banished to the ends of the earth. Bence would pretend to fall off and be blinded in a bed of thorns, doomed to wander lost and lonely, looking for me. Then we would play hide-and-seek with Bence pretending to be blind and me, ducking and squealing just beyond his outstretched hands, until I finally let me catch up with me, or he gave up and peeked!

"After the betrothal, we alone climbed the inner concrete spiral stairs then the iron stairs all the way to the top lookout to have our first kiss as man and wife—with our family and guests watching from below! What a joyful time!

"Such a beautiful panoramic view from on high did we have of our ancient and beloved city Budapest! And oh! What a beautiful man was my Prince, my new husband!! He was so handsome in his wedding suit. We hugged each other tight. I loved placing my hand around his waist. He was my 'Squeeze', is what I called him—and did so after that, as pet name.

Mrs. Molnar muses awhile. I see Mother gazing down pensively at her own diamond ring. Perhaps it never dawned on her that she too had a choice.

"I often think about the Rapunzel game we played there as children. I wonder if we unknowingly cursed ourselves. If marrying at that Tower doomed us to be flung apart, as we are now."

"But don't the Prince and Rapunzel come back together in the end?" Mother queries. "I think her tears of joy cure his blindness and they live happily ever after!"

"I can only hope."

Her eyes well up with tears.

Time passes. We sip our drinks. Enjoy the black softness of the night, and the caressing touches of the breeze.

Father asks, finally:

"And Stone # 13, the pebble?"

"Ah, that is a stone from the Danube."

Mrs. Molnar reaches for it, rubs it gently with her thumb, and then tucks it inside her palm.

"This tells how I experienced first-hand the terrible acts of Arrow Cross."

Stone Pebble (#13)
6-6

"Thirteenth Stone: The Pebble.

"I hold a smoothly rounded, soft, time-worn sandstone pebble that fits perfectly and snugly in the palm of my hand. It is from the Danube. It turns warm quickly, having soaked up aeons of sunshine in its core. It soothes me, whispers consolation to me. It reminds me always of what I saw and what I can never hope to forget.

"There is a poem by Hungarian poet Miklos Radnoti, which stays with me to this day. He was a much beloved Hungarian writer, a Jewish man who was torn from his wife and sent on work crews. When no more work, the Nazis raked all the men with bullets. He was hit but still alive, when a patrol came to make sure all were dead. He heard a voice saying, "That one is still moving". He hopes it is not himself who has been detected."

Mrs. Molnar lifts her finger to her lips. "Shhh!" she says.

'I whisper to myself:
'Lie still, do not budge.
Now patience flowers in death'.
Then I could hear 'That one is still moving', above, and
very near.

We wait for Mrs. Molnar to resume.

"One day, there was a frantic rapping on the front door. I had just put on my winter coat and scarf to go out, was standing in the foyer.

I reached for the handle and opened the door.

My dressmaker Fanni was standing there, shivering, pressing her little girl Fifi close to her side.

Fanni bent down, picked her child up by her armpits and threw her at me.

The child landed in my arms and clung to me, as light and lacking in substance as a desiccated moth.

"Take her, take her now, please. They have come, beaten up badly my husband Ferenc. I must go back to shop now and help him!"

She turned, but I caught her by the elbow.

"Who's come? What's happened?"

"They came to the shop, soldiers. Ferenc recognized their uniform through front window. Saw them coming. He said: 'Arrow Cross!' He took hold of me and Fifi, and shoved us under counter where we knew to hide behind a board. They slammed in, shouting bad words, calling Ferenc bad names. I held Fifi tight, covered her ears and mouth. I could hear what they do to him, their fists landing, his groans. They kept hitting and hitting him, asking where we were! They bashed in his face! When finally they left, I heard them threaten if all three of us did not all report to Seventh District Pest ghetto by midnight, we would be shot!"

"She tore herself out of my grip and scurried down the street, hunched over, heads and shoulders wrapped in a threadbare black shawl.

"As she fled, I saw the brilliants glittering on the tabs of her shoes.

"I closed the door quickly.

"I called out for Zsofia who came quickly down from upstairs on second floor. I told her what was happening.

"Come quickly, help me hide the girl, I must go now and meet Bence, or he will wonder if something also happened to me!"

"Zsofia and I pushed and released the hidden latch that opened the hatch under the stairwell which had built-in varnished tongue-and-groove oak paneling, same as rest of wainscoting in hallway. Out pinged the angle-cut door on its concealed hinges.

"There were already cushions and a blanket inside.

"You must stay in here, Fifi, lie down and do not make a peep! Do you understand?"

"The pale child nodded solemnly.

"Zsofia will bring you something to eat. I must run, you understand?"

"I said to my sister: 'I already planned to meet Bence at Margaret Island—so I must go!' I explained that if Bence was left standing alone on bridge it might draw attention, might look suspicious!"

I rapidly told Zsofia that the Arrow Cross were looking for Fanni and Fifi, she must lock the door behind me then run upstairs, and tell Mama to hide in special place with Bo. There was a long storage cupboard with concealed hinges behind built-in bookcase in Papa's study.

We were not Jewish, you understand. But the Arrow Cross were dangerous and unpredictable. We too needed places to hide, and where to hide Jews when necessary.

I said to Zsofia: 'Next, you must call over on extension to warehouse. Tell Tamas and Papa that it sounds like roundup of Jews has begun!' Then I told her, she will please take some food from kitchen and hide in closet foyer with Fifi until we get back!"

Then off I ran.

Husband Bence was lecturer of mineralogy at the Uni. After last class was let out midday on Fridays, he loved taking a long brisk walk along the river Danube. It helped clear his mind, blow away 'the spider webs', he claimed.

The Uni? That is what we call University of Budapest. It was across the river on the Pest side, near the Liberty Bridge.

Permit me to explain. Tying our city together, once Buda and Pest, now Budapest, are five bridges. From south to north across Danube, there is the Liberty, then the Chain, the Elizabeth, the Margaret and furthest north, the Arpad. Each bridge is about as far apart as say, distance from here to Centrewood Hub.

"Normally, to come directly home on his own, Bence would take Liberty Bridge then Metro subway. Yes, Budapest was one of first cities in Europe to have a subway!

"If he chose to walk all the way home, he would usually take riverside path on Pest side as far Chain Bridge, cross over, then weave his way up side streets. It was always a pleasure to stroll along the main promenade Andrassy with its stately buildings and large mansions along big tree-filled boulevard.

"If he called to say he was on his way via the Chain Bridge, I would meet him halfway, as our mansion was three blocks away west from Kodaly Korond, on Szondi Street, a deep property where warehouse behind gave out on Padmanovsky.

"I know that none of you have never been there, Emily, but I try to give full picture, okay?

"On that day, Bence and I had arranged to meet at Margaret Bridge on the little pedestrian bridge that links to Margaret Island, thinking we would take a walk around Margaret Island before crossing big Bridge to go home.

"His last lecture finished midday. He planned on making tea to eat with his packed lunch before setting off, so I knew how much time to give him for head start. I prepared to leave home at 13:30 hours."

Mother interrupts:

"Thirteen thirty hours? That's rather late for lunch, isn't it? What time would that be? Three thirty?"

"No, it would be half two!"

"You mean it would be—half past two?"

"No, no, half two is one hour minus a half!"

"You mean half two is thirty minutes after one? As in one thirty?"

"Yes! Of course!"

"That might explain something, I think! When I wrote you that note to come to dinner, I think I know why you came at 3:30 instead of 5:30!"

"Of course! I use standard *international way* to tell time. You must subtract the real time from 12 noon! 15:30 minus 12 would make it 3:30 p.m. Or 'half four'. Both ways, I am right."

"Wait! I didn't write 15:30, I wrote 5:30!"

"I still have your note as proof!" While Mrs. Molnar grabbles about in her handbag, Mother goes on a rant: "Eszter. You listen to the radio. You read the newspapers. You must know by now that in Canada, we don't tell time that way! Do you plan through sheer iron-will determination to convert all Canadians over to your way, one at a time?"

Mrs. Molnar surfaces from the innards of her handbag, flourishing a piece of paper. "Here, I have it now!"

Mother reads it out loud: "Please come at 5:30."

"There it is: 'a 15:30'." Mrs. Molnar folds her arms.

"There is no 'a' there, Eszter, are you French and think it means 'at'? AND: That is a not a 'one', Eszter, it is a 't'!"

"Is not."

"Emily, for heaven's sake, let it go for now and let's listen to Mrs. Molnar's story!"

Mother is livid. She says to Mrs. Molnar, "Why do you have to be so ornery?" She whirls round to Father, "She is the most stubborn person I have ever met," she pauses, "Next to you!"

Becky intervenes. She says, "Mama, our 't' looks like a 'one' to others. Our 'one' looks like a 'seven'. What looks like a 'one' is really Mrs. Michelsen's 't'."

She turns to Mother, "In our way of writing time, 5:30 p.m. would read as 17:30, but Mama," she ssys to Mrs. Molnar, "Here it does not."

"You see how hard it is for a foreigner to learn your ways, Emily? Must I spend hours learning the difference between a 't', a 'seven' and a 'one', just to learn how to tell time *your* way?"

"If it means arriving at a stated time and not three hours early? Yes!" Mother replies, practically hoarse to refrain from screaming.

"Please continue, Mrs. Molnar," Father flags her, with cupped hand, as though waving in a racing car.

"I arranged to meet husband Bence at half two, or thirty minutes after one, okay? okay?"

Mother nods, "In other words, in plain English: at 1:30!"

If she says "Of course" one more time, I think Father would be next in line to scream.

"Fanni was my dressmaker. She made my wedding outfit. Her husband Ferenc was a tailor. He made Bence's suit. They had shop along market street only short distance away.

"Fanni was so quick! so bright! so nimble with her fingers. I can still see her needle weave and flash as she worked the fabric with her tiny thimble.

"When I went to her and tried to explain to her what I wanted— not a big flouncy white wedding dress but a simple 'two-pieces' that was dressy but not so much I could never wear it again to a normal function, off-white not chalk white, a scoop neck but not plunging, to display nicely my Mother's double strands of pearls, the skirt flared so that I could climb stairs, Fanni interrupted me: 'There, there, I see exactly what you want, now you leave it to me!'

"She was right. I had conveyed so little, but just enough for her to envision exactly what I wanted. All I had to do was order the material and some special buttons that she could cover with the same fabric to make a pretty row in the light jacket bodice, and she did the rest!

"Fanni and Ferenc came with baby girl Fifi to the wedding. Invite such guests as shopkeeper tailor and seamstress? Yes! Of course!! We embraced everyone we knew, we opened our arms to them because we wanted to thank them! We wanted them to party with us, dance, to have some fun!

"Fanni was so proud of my outfit, she was beaming.

"She loved my shoes!

"I had found a pair of black leather sling-backs, in fashion at the time, so very comfortable with low wedge heels. I did not like what-you-call same word for tall driving nails? spiked? ah yes, spike heels—no high heels for me!—so painful to wear! Besides, I wanted shoes in which I could dance all night!

The design of shoe included a tab on the front, a slight bit of extra rounded leather, like now you have with your so-called 'penny' loafers. But these did not have slot for a penny! Just plain and smooth leather tab. What I found by sheer accident at hairdressing salon was on sale sets of hair clips, the kind that you pinch and both sides open on hinge like a claw, then close to grip supposedly hair. But these clips fit perfectly over the tabs on the shoes! Yes! One side claw was smooth so did not dig into top of foot—or scalp, I suppose! Other side was decorated with a cluster of clear little diadems—tiny rhinestones, you understand? These dressed up the shoes perfectly!

"I bought another pair of same clips with which to pin back my hair, you know, which I wore with middle part, sides swept back and up in a swirl like so? With the back rolled all round like a long sausage from behind one ear to the other! Very much in fashion and very much war-time hair-do, I learned later, as an army cap or nurse's cap, whatever kind of cap could fit over top without too much disarray!

"So now I tell you that afterwards, whenever I saw Fanni, in the street by chance or at times visiting her shop with my mother or sister, I noticed how rundown were her shoes. She spent so much time on her feet. Without good support, how her feet must ache!

"As time passed, I knew how poor she and her husband Ferenc were becoming. They had less and less business. Although Budapest seemed to be left out of the roundups and deportations, the citizens had begun to feel terrible pressure against taking business to any Jews in town. Signs were being posted to shop doors, saying: You just bought something at a Jew shop! Graffiti were painted on walls, such as: Jews are filth! Oh yes, terrible awful signs! Tear them down, only more would appear. Paint them over, there would be more.

"When Boglarka was born, in 1943, I took her round to Fanni's to show her off—and I took her my wedding shoes!

"No, no, you cannot!" she exclaimed, holding her hands together almost in a reluctant prayer.

"Oh yes I can!" I replied, "Fanni, you made my wedding so special, I never really knew how to thank you."

"But you paid me, Eszter! And you invited us to your wedding party!"

"Yes, but still I had to find a special way to thank you. My only regret is that it has taken me this long to think of one! And guess what? I want you to have these shoes. They are almost brand new. Except on my wedding day, I've hardly ever worn them!"

"Fanni tried them on and they fit her as though made for her.

"Eyeing me for permission, she said: 'I give you big hug, okay?'

"I nodded.

"Then she flung herself around my neck.

"When leaving, I felt how there was almost nothing to her, I realized how thin she had become and thought that food might have been a better gift.

***

"At Margaret Island, I saw Bence was there by the time I arrived.

"We embraced while I, out-of-breath, told him what had happened back at home.

"He drew me off across the linking bridge onto Margaret Island and we walked north a-piece along the east side toward our favourite bench under a bower of bare branches overlooking the river.

"The evening before had been pouring down solid heavy rain. By midnight, it had turned into icy rain combined with sleet that came down in long drools and drilled into the pavement. The wind came up, battering angrily against the window-panes.

"This explained how patches of ice still remained in shaded parts of the path and how ice-laden was the wrought-iron bench.

"Bence proclaimed: 'The Ice Witch reigneth!' while he took a fallen branch and banged away at the coating ice, chipping it off in spots where we could sit for just a bit of rest before pushing off for home.

"The sky was a dark slate grey.

"There were only patches of snow.

"Black water was running hard with huge chunks of ice drifting by.

"On the river's edge, encrusted rocks stood knee-deep in the crushed ice.

"It was freezing cold.

"My teeth, they were chuddering— no? juddering? yes, yes, much more descriptive than chattering,

"How clear is the memory how cold it was.

"The cold was caught in the small of my back. I remember how reddened hard was my face and how frozen hard felt my hands, how they were needing a good vigorous rub to warm them up, thanks to Bence.

"That winter of 1944 had come early, was unusually frigid. It was only toward end of October but already the Danube had been frozen over in parts upstream. The previous night's heavy icy rain must have broken it up, and sent these icebergs flowing by like an armada.

"Bence and I deliberated what to do about situation, convinced this latest development was surely signal for first time of open Budapest persecution of Jews. We tried to plot some next plan of action to propose to Papa, Tamas and Mama when we got home.

"Just as we were preparing to stand up, we heard loud popping sounds ricocheting overhead, coming from further up on island? Or from upriver across the way? At first we thought, was this from vehicles backfiring? Or were these explosions? But no, we came to realize that these were rifle shots, many, many of them, bang bang bang bang following one after the other. But coming from where? What was happening?

It sounded like there were soldiers firing at random from the top of the Water Tower further north on the island.

We were terrified.

Bence grabbed my hand and we ran.

"We ran toward the linking bridge, we ran across Margaret Bridge toward the Buda side, we ran in direction of home, thinking only to run toward safety, not thinking we might be running directly toward danger!

"What were we doing? We were startled, we were not thinking.

"As we approached the Buda side, we saw in distance a straggling group of Arrow Cross soldiers making their way along the embankment from upriver, lurching and laughing loudly, jeering, pointing their guns toward the river, shooting into the water, and they were heading our way!

"We reached the far end of the bridge, jumped over the railing and scrambled down the face of the retaining wall till we reached the abutment underneath the bridge. One more level down was the river embankment.

"We could see a long shallow concavity where water had gouged out earth through erosion. We hung by our fingertips then dropped to river level. Into that depression, we pressed our backs to the wall of the outcropping.

"Upstream, at eye level, we saw strange forms drifting toward us on the black, swift-flowing water amid the floes of ice.

"At first I thought these were large black birds of some strange and foreign breed from the way their bodies rode low in the water like water-logged black swans, and from the way what seemed to be their feathered chests pushed the water aside in front of them in long rippling V-shapes. It seemed totally improbable, but I also thought perhaps they were giant injured bats because of the loosely flapping stiff cloth-like wings that rose up and down above them on the waves. Or perhaps those wings were attached to the ribs of half-folded or broken black umbrellas that were making their way downstream against all odds of neither floating nor sinking?

"The mind plays tricks when it does not and cannot believe what it is seeing.

"As these strange misshapen shapes drew closer in the chopped-up ice, we realized that they were human bodies, the black feathers their wet hair, the black wings their drenched clothing as they churned and turned in the water, and that the soldiers were following their progress down the river, taking pot shots at them like they were at a midway carnival arcade.

"Then Fanni's body floated out from under the bridge into open view, and drifted close enough to see her clearly. Her hair matted to her head, her black dress heavy and soaking wet, she coasted by lying on her side, her face turned toward us, her glazed eyes pried wide open in shocked disbelief, her mouth stretched open in a final agonizing howl of pain. Her blouse had been torn open, her gentle breasts mutilated, her tiny hands bludgeoned into unrecognizable pulp. Her little bare feet were distended from under her water-logged dress like stiff claws, like raw wooden clothes-pegs.

" 'Fanni!' I cried.

"Bence gripped me and put his hand over my mouth. He dug his forehead and jaw so tight into my forehead and chin that I could barely breathe. I realized that he too was trying not to scream.

273

"From above came men's voices. In German, we heard: "There's one who's not yet dead! She's still flinching!""

"A heart-tearing deafening round of shells ripped into Fanni's tiny body and pockmarked her from head to toe.

"We crouched under cover of the gouge in Margaret Bridge embankment for as long as we thought best.

"While we lingered, I found my eyes dwelled on a light brown sand pebble. It was embedded in the shale and rabble under distorted, yawning bubbles trapped underwater by a thin sheet of glassy ice.

"The stone seemed to be calling to me to hold it.

"I reached down and with icy fingertips, poked through the ice, and released it from its freezing-cold trap.

"The stone was soft and round, like a smooth flattened egg, a mere sandstone pebble. It was of an unusual light cinnamon-colour, marked with a thin, fine pinkish-tone thread running through the middle of it. I sensed its history. This stone could only have been ground perfectly smooth from being one of a mass of rocks smashing and tumbling in waters flowing downward from the mountains during the first glacial melt in distant European history.

"It was just the right size to fit into the palm of my hand and for my fingers to fold over it. It fit like proverbial hand in glove.

"It warmed me.

"I can't tell you how it warmed my heart or why it soothed me.

"I told Bence.

"He was not—is not—a religious or spiritual-inclined being. After all, remember! He is a scientist! But he surprised me, 'You found it right where Fanni died. She has sent you solace and comfort.'

"We held each other close and just swayed back and forth together in each others' arms, with the bridge sighing overhead and the icy Danube flowing by.

"Stiffly and somberly up we climbed, and then began our slow walk along the promenade toward home, opting not to follow the path of the blood-thirsty gang but to take a round-about way of getting home, heading upriver first with intentions of cutting toward Andrassy diagonally.

"Huge snowflakes the size of pancakes began floating aloft then plummeting down in bucketloads. 'Now Fanni is sending you latkas!' Bence whispered, hugging me around my waist. He made me smile. We both smiled softly, as softly down fell the snow.

"Then the weather transformed itself into an ugly assortment of sleet and pelting icy rain.

"We took shelter under the protective boughs of an old tree.

"Bence put his briefcase over his head and held it there with sopping wet gloves, water trickling up his sleeves.

"I pulled my coat collar up over my beret, and I bent over into the fierce gusts of wind, holding fast till the worst had passed.

"Further along the walkway we reached a low retaining wall between us and the dropoff into river.

"There were empty shoes lined up in a row along the top edge of the retaining wall— at least thirty, possibly forty pairs of shoes.

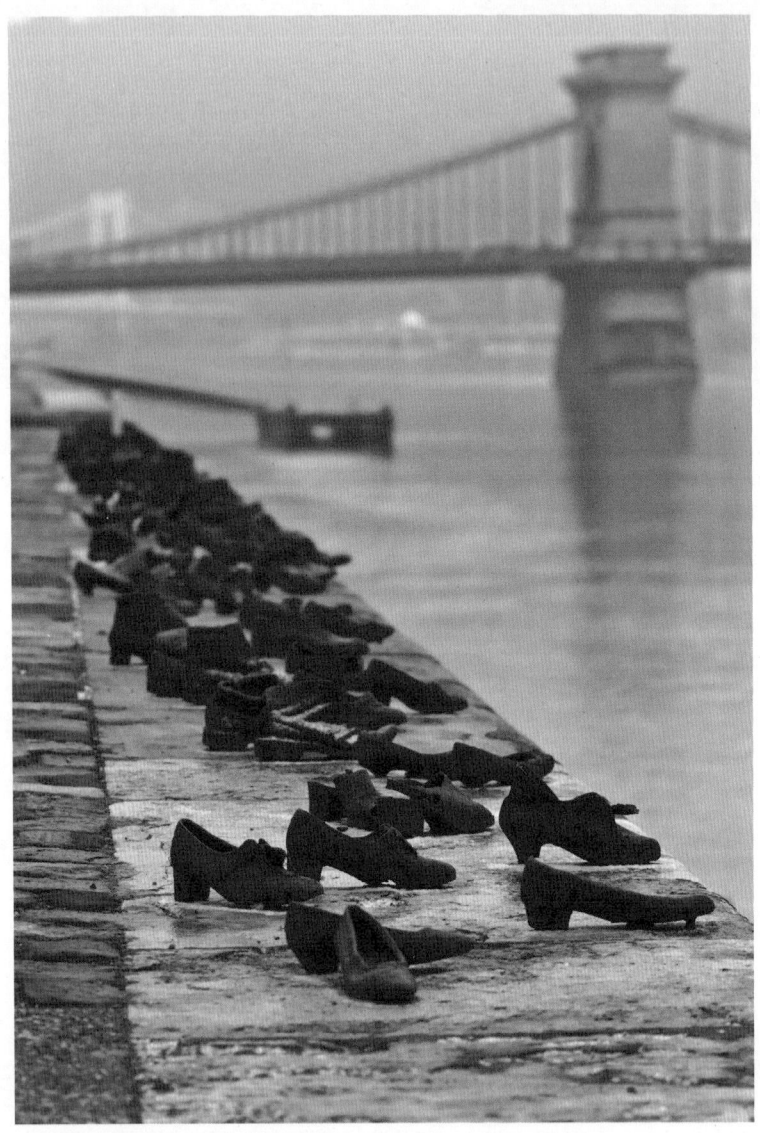

Shoes on the Danube Bank, Budapest

"Bence and I suddenly understood what were the popping sounds we had heard and what had just occurred.

"The owners of these shoes had been forced to line up side by side with others, stand facing outward toward the river, made to remove their shoes, then remain in place without budging, where they waited to be executed, their bodies dropping one by one into the rushing waters below.

"Among the shoes was a pair of woman's black sling-backs with little brilliants still glittering like diadems on the front tabs."

●

CHAPTER SEVEN
Unfinished Business

Sitting Ducks
7-1

Tuesday, October 15, 1957

7:30 a.m.

Chaque matin au petit déjeuner

Pétales de mais doré au four

I am pouring Kellogg's Corn Flakes into my bowl while absent-mindedly reading the French side of the box, when Father comes into the kitchen, his mouth yawning uvula-wide, stretching his arms over his head, and then scratching his chest through his housecoat and pyjamas.

He does this scratching bit to wake himself up.

Apparently, it's a mild form of self-flagellation to help stimulate his circulatory system.

I've tried it and it doesn't work for me.

Mother is following close on his heels.

"Well! Now I know why they call it Thanksgiving!" Father proclaims. "Thank God it's over!"

Mother smiles and wraps her arms around him from behind.

"Oh yes, the entire weekend was a total bother, wasn't it?"

"Let's put it this way. It is not something I would have planned, nor worked hard for, nor dreamt of. Your dinner was good though!"

He swivels around and pecks her on her forehead.

"So was the trip to Niagara Falls!" she says.

"Any chance of getting back to normal around here?" he asks, his eyes pleading.

"Not till after you've called the lawyer for Eszter!"

"Eszter! You've got to be kidding. You think I'm going to book an appointment with my solicitor to discuss Mrs. Molnar's problem, when I have the upcoming weight in Ottawa of representing Chief Fred King and the fate of all the Mississaugas on my shoulders?"

"Yes. Book enough time for both!"

"I'm heading off to shower."

"Why isn't Father at work?"

"He has a follow-up appointment this morning with the specialist."

I think: I hope it doesn't come down to salmonella or he'll blame Beetlebomb, and I'll never hear the end of it.

All ready to go, Mother sees me off at the front door.

With bicycle carrier loaded down with flute case, and my zipperbinder containing the precious manila envelope with my finished Burr Project, I push off with a wave.

"Good bye for now, Lois! And remember! When you see Mitsy, you've the bike ride planned with her for Saturday!"

Oh no, ruin my day.

I wobble and nearly fall off my bicycle.

"No way!" I yell.

Mother just nods cheerfully, then closes the door.

She's done her job. She's marshalled both Father and myself into facing obligations that she herself set up. Now she can relax and enjoy her day.

Mitsy the Menace
7-2

At the mere mention of Mitsy, let alone the fact that Mother made plans for the two of us, I ride on up the Main Artery with a craggy, pointy-edged rock turning sharp edges in my ribcage.

Mother thinks that Mitsy was an angel sent to me from heaven.

I'm convinced that she was sent to me as an envoy from hell.

When we moved here in the spring from Unionville, Mother was worried that I would not know anyone at school, and that come Fall, I would end up going back and forth from home alone.

It was Mother who set the two of us up by calling the school.

Why did it turn out that the only other girl my age who lived in Maplewood had to be her? She is a brat. She is rude and obnoxious. She is always cooking something up. When it comes to me, she is devious, has some trick up her sleeve. And she is always flaunting herself, deliberately finding ways to rub it in, that she has assets that I do not.

Father had already 'sauced her out'. But he has refused to defend me when she pulled her pranks in front of him. He could not take sides, he said, because it wouldn't be fair if it appeared as though we were ganging up on her. Besides, Mother wouldn't abide it.

Mitsy has a big bosom that she trots out like a status symbol wherever she goes. Initially, it was a big problem for me, something I'm still having to work through. I find myself in long, tortuous debates with myself, splitting hairs between degrees of jealousy and envy, and denial. If anything, I'm resentful. Other girls back in junior high, and now here in high school, have developed large busts, whereas I haven't. I have to work hard not to feel hurt and overlooked, if not punished, by an indifferent universe. It's not a handicap that I can hide. Mitsy has nothing to hide. She uses it to her advantage. She flirts shamelessly with the boys in our class, just as she did with the construction crew we passed every day en route to school—until the Neighbourhood Watch unknowingly put an end to it. She also made a play for Father, yes! When she ended up dancing to Glenn Miller with him as her partner, there she was in our very living room—shamelessly rubbing herself against him and trying to hold him tight. She pushed her assets to the max at the solo 'Teaserama' show she put on at the Big Culvert, where she flaunted herself and did everything but a full strip tease act.

Mother never heard about that, and I had to keep mum because I would be blamed for going to it. I had no idea what Mitsy was going to do until I was there, and found myself witnessing it all. But Mother thinks that Mitsy and I are total buddies, so if she ever found out, she'd presume that I must have known.

Bert rescued me, and it was afterward, when we escaped out the back exit-way, that he helped me with gathering burdock for the botany project from the other side of the highway. That turned out well for me. I had an excuse for arriving home late after school. I think that I also made a new friend.

My real godsend is Becky, nicknamed Bo, real name Boglarka, who plays flute with me in music class. We get along like a house on fire. She is very polite, and sensitive, and thoughtful, very intelligent and very talented. I adore her like a sister. Soon, we will be performing a duet for the school concert. I'm very nervous about it, but I trust Becky will pull us both through.

●

CHAPTER EIGHT
The Bike Ride

Tour de France
8-1

Saturday, October 19, 1957

10:30 a.m.

As soon as Mitsy rounds the corner, the fink takes off down the Main Artery like a shot. I'm pumping as hard as I can, but she has almost reached the highway before I've barely reached the last block.

I see her lift her arm to signal a left turn as she wheels across the highway and heads south.

I call out to her.

"Hey! Where are we going?" I pant.

"This way!"

"But that takes us toward the City!"

"Never mind! Follow me!" she yells, and then off she goes, the soles of her little blue-and-white saddle shoes in a whir.

Tagging along behind her, wobbling precariously on the edge of the pavement any time a car or truck whips by, I watch Mitsy up ahead, pedaling hard to beat the band, as though she's signed on for the Tour de France.

"Hey!" I shout, "Slow down a bit, will ya?" But she just beetles along, her head down and her neck craning forward, often standing on her pedals to gain more leverage.

This is no lazy saunter in the countryside.

This is some kind of freaky hundred-yard dash with no finish line in sight.

It's happening against all pleading and against all reason.

Just momentarily, it crosses my mind that I could just quit, turn round and go home. But that thought only lasts a split second before my Mother's words ring in my ears.

"You're going and that's that!" Mother said firmly.

"But what if I don't want to go?" I asked.

"You'll be glad you went once it's over," Mother said, applying her inscrutable logic.

"Why do you constantly fob Mitsy off on me?"

"Don't you get saucy with me, young lady!"

"But you force us together when I don't want anything to do with her!"

"What kind of attitude is that to have against a friend?"

"I have told you umpteen times, she is not my friend!"

"You will stop being so self-centred this instant, Lois! It's high time you realized that friendship is a two-way street."

"Not this one. This one is a three-way street: You, Mitsy, and Me!"

I reached for my last resort.

I blurted: "I thought you'd let me off the hook, now you know she was the one who sicked the RCMP on you!"

"Get off. Where did you get that notion?"

"She was the one who complained to the police about the Neighbourhood Watch and they forwarded the complaint to the 'feds'!"

"That is an outlandish, and a very incriminating accusation, young lady. I'm disappointed that you would sink so low as try to wing that one at me. How do you know that word 'feds' anyway?"

I was speechless. I couldn't find the words to fight back. Under high pressure from Mother, I didn't have the where-with-all to piece it all together, how to give Mother the condensed version of that day on the way to school when Mitsy was putting on an impromptu, flirtatious Annie Oakley act for the construction workers, how she didn't understand why nobody came out to watch her raunchy routine, until the foreman rushed out of his hut and told her not to bother the men anymore, and to 'Shoo!' How when I told Mitsy about the newly formed Neighbourhood Watch, she stormed off, ranting about the Gestapo and threatening to notify the authorities.

I panicked.

In a sudden burst of desperation, I switched tactics and blurted:

"I have the right to choose my own friends!"

"That, Lois, is where you're wrong. Choosing friends is a luxury. You will find that Life itself—more often than not—chooses your friends for you!"

"Not *my* life!" I replied, sticking out my chin.

Mother lifted her finger, a signal for me to shush, a signal that this exchange had drawn to an abrupt end, a signal as quietening and as powerful to me as if I were a trained monkey.

Father was no help at all.

I stomped into the living room and appealed to him, "Father! Mother is forcing me to go on this loony-tunes country bike ride with Ditsy-Mitsy and I do not want to go! Why should I?"

He just lifted his head from the morning paper and grunted.

I stormed off to my room to get changed. Decided to wear the yellow sleeveless blouse with my red pedal pushers.

While I was putting on my sneakers, my mind was in a blur.

Father knew she's a nuisance. And a menace. Fine ally he's turned out to be.

Come to think of it, he never promised to be an ally.

Well, he should be, not liking her very much himself, and knowing how much I detest her, knowing how little desire I have to go on this gosh-darned *#@&$%! bike ride.

I learned from the kids at school that those symbols are used to mean swear words in comic books.

When opening my bedroom door, I overheard him in the kitchen, saying something to Mother.

"Doesn't she have homework?"

There was her murmuring voice, and then Father said in return:

"It just strikes me as odd that the girl wants to go for a bike ride in the country, that's all. Her type would more likely want to be hanging out at the Mall with all the low-life and riff-raff on a Saturday!"

Mother had just finished slathering my face, arms and legs with suntan lotion when the doorbell rang and the front door burst open.

In came Mitsy, chomping at the bit, saying "Are you ready, teddy?" not coming any further than the landing and hopping from one foot to the other, jiggling her upper raft with unashamed abandon.

Mother was still holding the bottle of suntan lotion. She told her to stand still while she slathered her as well.

She handed both of us a thermos and a packed lunch to put in our knapsacks. "There's ice water in the thermos in case you get thirsty, and a sandwich for each of you along with a treat in your lunchbags!" Mother smiled.

"Oh thank you, Mrs. Michelsen, I never even thought of packing a lunch!" Mitsy carolled, knowing how to show jubilant appreciation for an eager recipient.

"Even teddy bears pack lunches for their picnic!" Mother smiled.

"Did you pack 'hamburglers'?" I asked.

I was being funny but serious. I love cold hamburgers with Kraft mayo and green relish on a hamburg bun.

"Maybe!"

"Whatdyamean 'hamburglers'?" Mitsy asked.

"You know, that's what Beaver calls them!"

"Oh that stupid programme," Mitsy said, throwing a wet blanket on my favourite television show, "Leave it to Beaver", that had just started this season.

I glared at Mother.

Mother mouthed: "Be Nice."

Mitsy had her lunch bag and thermos packed, and her knapsack slung on her back, in jig time. She was almost clawing at the front door like a pet dog eager to be let out.

I pulled the rim of my gob hat down over my ears.

Mother barely had time to help settle my knapsack on my back and give us her send-off: "Have fun!" and "Be sure to be home by supper-time!" when Itchy Mitsy was pushing off on her bike with a "So long!" and the toss of a waving hand over her shoulder.

Instead of the casual take-off to be expected of a relaxing, laid-back outing in the country, I found myself jumping on my bike and charging after her to catch up.

So here I am, chasing down the highway after her.

No matter how hard I try, I feel I'm steadily losing ground in the pedaling department. It's not so easy to pedal fast because I keep banging my knees against the handlebars, which should have been raised, or the seat lowered, from the outset when it was first new only weeks ago. I try to keep my knees apart, and I pedal like a bow-legged cowboy.

I'm also slowed down each time I have to clap my gob hat to my head when it almost flies away from the wind stirred up by passing traffic. I wish it had a chin-strap like Mr. Floyd's deerstalker.

With her green bandana tied gypsy-style to her head, her horizontally-striped green v-neck t-shirt and her lime-green capris,

Mitsy has become a horizontal stack of green, rapidly threatening to become just a green blob on the horizon.

Follow that Blob!

"Mind the traffic!" Mother had called out just after we pushed off.

"Traffic? What traffic?" I had thought. There'd be no traffic where we were going. We were heading for the country! At least, that's how Mitsy had enticed Mother into letting me go with her on this junket, by persuading her how "neat it would be" to explore the countryside, find a nice place to have a picnic. It would be "a gas and a half", as she put it.

This is how I had imagined our bike ride in the country would be: Mitsy and I would take the Main Artery to the highway then head north, past the pumpkin fields, pedal a bit further, then turn west into the network of criss-crossed sideroads leading into the countryside. There would be the woods, like last weekend, still ablaze with autumn colour. Eventually, having found an ideal spot for our picnic—on the banks of a slow-moving stream perhaps, we would stop to lounge and snack, perhaps even have an afternoon snooze under the sun-filtered, dappled shade of some grandmotherly weeping willow.

Obviously, this was not to be.

The fields along this highway are empty, stretching out for acres, most of them stripped and already turned over for fall or winter planting. Around the fringes, there are remnants of the original forest, the only vestiges of autumn the fiery oranges and yellows and reds glancing luminous in the sun. Closer to the fence line, there are the odd groupings of thin young maple trees with their sparse patches of autumn leaves still clinging. Closer to the road, usually on the banks, there is the occasional stand of sumacs—such a brilliant scarlet, they could take one's breath away if we were not moving so hard and so fast, they blend in with the passing blur.

We tear along, heading south down a two-lane highway, eventually cut west across another major road, pedal madly through a village.

After more huffing and puffing, we finally reach a T-intersection, where to my befuddlement, Mitsy turns south with me in tow, until we are barrelling full steam along a highway that a passing street sign reveals as Weston Road. Fortunately, it is mostly on a downhill grade.

I yearn for the relaxing, laid-back idyll that I had imagined! A day filled with fresh air and sunlight, browsing past stands of tall weeds growing in the side roads, drifting past deep grassy meadows.

Not to be! It is noisy, smelly, and hotter than Hades!

For the middle of October, it is another one of those hot Indian-summer days. The temperature can reach 80-90 degrees Fahrenheit with ease. Out in the full sun, despite the suntan lotion, I know that I am being burned to a crisp, as it is even hotter than normal from racing along like fury on steaming hot asphalt.

I am doing my utmost to keep up the pace with Mitsy, while the traffic becomes heavier and heavier. I am being doused with exhaust fumes, the smell of burning rubber and overworked brakes, buffeted by the slipstream from passing trucks, my ears assaulted by distant unidentifiable sounds that overtake me before I can tell the source or cause.

For instance, at one point in this grueling trial, in the far-off distance there is a high-pitched, whining, buzzing sound which had my eyes been closed, I might have thought to be a massive swarm of hornets. Up ahead, I see Mitsy tear off her head scarf, pull over onto the shoulder of the highway, turn her bicycle to face the road, plant her feet across the bike's frame, and rest her big bosom on the handlebars. There she waits, grinning widely, spinning her scarf in the air, her red tousled hair clearly visible, the V-neck in her green t-shirt revealing her ample cleavage.

The sound gets louder and louder. In total fright, I too pull off onto the shoulder. Roaring past me is a horde of black motorcycles. When the black-leathered, black-helmeted gang passes Mitsy, she lifts her hand with a royal wave and every motorcycle bleeps and blats their horns. As though on cue, the entire retinue slows down and turns around full circle. There, ranged in flight formation across both oncoming and ongoing lanes, the lumbering machines put on an improvised performance for her, riding round and round in a large circle, two- and three-abreast in front of her 'reviewing stand'.

The din of horns blatting and male voices shouting 'Hurrah', 'Bravo' and 'Howdy, Babe' fill the air as they salute her each time they pass by.

Mitsy kills herself laughing.

The gang's equivalent to the Mounties' Musical Ride doesn't break up until oncoming traffic forces the motorcycles back into a single lane, whereupon they fall back into formation and carry on south down the highway.

Mitsy is still doubled up in laughter when I pull up and hit the brakes.

"Wasn't that a hoot and a half?!" she shouts over the din of passing traffic.

I lift my eyebrows and purse my lips as though to say: "You think?"

"Oh, don't be such a Stick-In-The-Mud!" she gripes.

Shortly thereafter, we reach an overpass on Weston Road. At the crest, Mitsy pulls over and stops, dismounts, hauls her bike over the curb onto the ledge next to the railing, looks out into the distance, then down at the cars and trucks streaming below us on four lanes of traffic.

I follow suit.

"Where are we?" I ask.

"That is the extension for the new Highway 401 expressway," she says, with the air of a tour guide.

She roots about in her knapsack and brings out her thermos.

"What now, Brown Cow?" I ask.

"Just wanted to stop to have a look. This whole interchange completes the Toronto Bypass! It was only just opened up this week!"

"I'm sure I've driven over this bridge with Mother and Father!"

"No doubt. This bridge itself was completed in 1953. This is where the Toronto Bypass ended. See the brand-new bridge over the Humber River farther up there? The original one was washed out in Hurricane Hazel. They had to blow it up with dynamite and start over. All in all, completion of the entire east-west 401 system was delayed by four years!"

Now she sounds like a Grandpa sucking on a pipe.

"How do you know all that?"

"I read the newspaper for the news, not just the funnies."

She pours cold water into her thermos cup and takes a swig.

"The access roads for the overpass here had also been washed away. They had to be rebuilt. Huh! Only two after all that!" I have no idea what she is talking about.

"Eh?"

She breaks into song: "I'm looking over a two-leaf clover, da-da da de-da da de da!" does a little same-spot tap dance and laughs.

I am hot and thirsty, covered in dust, my feet are boiling in my sneakers, but I want to save my thermos water for lunchtime.

"Look. There are only two access and exit ramps. Cars coming west along the expressway have to go under the bridge to reach the exit ramp to go north or south. Cars coming east on the 401 have to go under the bridge for the same reason. Eventually, they will build two more ramps so it will look like a cloverleaf from overhead."

I nod, sagely, but to tell the truth, any interest in highway engineering is not one of my strong suits.

For my part, I find myself struggling to grasp the overall purpose of the interchange, let alone the expressway itself. Scanning from east to west, the entire project seems to have gobbled up a tremendous amount of land. What was here before? Why, and what for?

I can only relate to some events in the outside world if I take such enigmas from the objective to the subjective. I was told that this is typical of an immature mind with a narrow frame of reference. I say:

"When Father moved us to Centrewood, he said he wanted to be closer to work compared with the distance he had to drive from Unionville. This must be the highway that Father's been waiting to open, so it will be faster for him to get to work in Malton!"

"Terrific!" Mitsy grimaces, who is not at all interested, and is now hanging precariously over the railing on her belly to watch the cars zooming by underneath. She shouts, "See how they seem to go faster, the closer they are?"

This startles me. First, I never knew she followed the real news in the newspapers. And now she's being observant, talking science! I latch onto the opportunity to discuss something real, rather than the usual mindless chitchat.

"That has something to do with physics!" I call to her, "Like, it isn't the car that has sped up, it's your perception that makes it look that way—It's an optical illusion!"

That turns her right off. I see her eyes go blank. She looks annoyed. As though I butted in on her cleverness, put a puncture in her originality, dared to intrude on the superiority of her thinking.

My interpretation is correct.

"Thank you, Einstein!" she says.

She swings upright.

"Okay, let's go!" Mitsy exclaims, "Onward ho!"

"But where are we going?"

"Into Weston!"

"Why?"

"I want to show you something!"

She shouts this into the wind as she takes off.

Memory Lane
8-2

12:30 p.m.

Once inside the town proper, Mitsy points left and we turn off Main Street onto King Street, past the red-brick Weston Public Library on the corner, past a few more buildings, then we rattle our way across two sets of rusty, rough railroad tracks.

At the next corner, we pass a doctor's office in a one-storey yellow brick house. "That was our family doctor, Doctor Crane," she said, "I hated having my annual checkups."

"Why?"

"The only time I want to strip is for my own pleasure, thank you, not to give a doctor his jollies!"

"Why do you say that?"

"Well, Dr. Crane was a kind old man, so he wasn't really the bother. But he had a concern about my rapidly premature development, and was bound each annual checkup to refer me to the hospital for more extensive physicals. There was a specialist who loved to tweak my nipples like radio dials and maul my breasts like preparing bread dough."

Is there nothing she can do or say that won't shock me?

A few blocks farther along, Mitsy slows down at the Rosemount Avenue crossroad.

Like a tour guide, she indicates the parkette to the left:

"We'll stop for lunch here in a bit. But first, I want to show you something. Follow me just another couple of blocks!"

At the corner of King and Pine, Mitsy stops and points at a large old house with a mossy pitched roof and inset dormer windows, walls smothered in ivy, the front and side yards set deep in giant maple trees, and sweeping gardens filled with dense shiny periwinkle cover.

"That was my Grandmother Gardiner's house. That's where I lived before moving to Centrewood."

She looks wistful.

"It sure is a big house! Where was your bedroom?"

"Up in the attic. I had the whole top floor to myself. My bed was near the far right dormer window. It had a built-in padded window seat. The windows opened outward. See the low railing to prevent me from falling out? I would perch up there and pretend that I was a princess living in a palace, and that was my parapet. I could see all the way across Pine Street, and rule over all the children in the school yard a block away. See the school? Memorial School. That's where I went to elementary school."

"Where is your Grandmother now?"

"She died."

I feel uncomfortable. I sense sorrow breathing in the thick leaves.

"What is this—A trip down memory lane? Were you planning all along to bring me here today? Why did you tell Mother we were going for a ride in the country?"

Mitsy snaps out of her nostalgia and turns her back on the house.

"She'd never let us go this far away!"

She steps down on a pedal and starts coasting down the hill.

"Why must you always have something up your sleeve?"

"Come on, let's go to Chadwick's!"

We ride a long block down King Street until we reach a main thoroughfare Jane Street, where we turn left and pedal one short block to Church Street.

On the corner is a drugstore.

"Man, am I thirsty!" she calls out, dropping her bike and slamming through the shop door. Reaching her hand into the cold water of the pop cooler, she pulls out an Orange Crush. "What do you want?" she asks. "Don't tell me, you like Cream Soda, don't you!" She fishes one out for me.

A gentleman with snow-white hair, wearing a starched white lab coat, steps out and down from the dispensary.

"Hi, Mr. Chadwick!"

"Well, if it isn't Topsy-Mopsy Mitsy!" he says, working his lips around his mouth, "Long time no see!" He eyes her thoughtfully, then turned his gaze to me. "Double Trouble today?"

"Oh no, she's no trouble. She's my new friend!"

"And what can I do for you?"

"Oh, just these two pops. Lois and I have ridden our bikes all the way from nearly King City and we're two thirsty kiddos!"

"You living up in that neck of the woods now, are you?"

"Yes. Mother and I moved there last spring. She had a yen for life in a brand new house in suburbia for a change, so we moved to Centrewood, a 'Model Experiment in Modern Living,' " she says, air-quoting the billboard on the highway.

"I was sorry to hear about your Grandma's passing, Mitsy. She was a fine woman."

"Yes. She was."

There is a respectful pause.

I can smell antiseptic as he slips past us toward the snack rack facing the cashier's counter. He digs out two Neilson's milk chocolate bars with his spanking clean fingers and bleached fingernails.

He holds them out to Mitsy.

"Might as well give them to you now than miss them later! Here you go!"

She holds out her hand.

"Well now, that's mighty kind of you, Sir!" Mitsy says with a slight mock curtsy, and not entirely without sarcasm. "Allow me to pay for my two pops!"

"That I shall do. With pleasure! Then I shall escort you to the door, wish you well and bid you adieu!"

No bum's rush going on here!

She pays for both the pops, snaps the caps off both bottles at the cooler, takes a swig, hands me mine, then turning on her heel, says to me "Come!" like commanding a dog. She struts out the door past the threshold-hovering Mr. Chadwick, gets on her bike holding her drink with one hand, and heads back toward King Street on a wobble.

"We'll have our picnic lunch at that parkette we passed!"

***

I am boiling hot and drenched with sweat. The top of my head feels like a sizzling frying pan. I take off my gob hat, run it under the public drinking tap until it is soaking wet, wring it out a bit and plunk it back on my head so the cold water trickles over my face and ears and down my neck. Then I take a long suck from my pop bottle.

"Thanks for the pop," I say, and fling myself onto the cool shaded grass. I lie spread-eagled, waiting for the dampness from the freshly sprinkled lawn to seep into the back of my legs and my shirt.

Mitsy undoes the wet knot in her kerchief, shakes it out and rinses it at the tap, wrings it out, wraps it around her neck. She comes over and sits on the park bench next to me. She holds her sweat-drenched green t-shirt way out in front of her, and flaps it rhythmically to create a breeze.

Each time she flaps her top, she knows I can see those huge orbs underneath, encased in some kind of cross-stitched, reinforced bra.

She looks down on me with a veiled smirk, deliberately taunting me with assets I don't have. And in high probability, I never will.

Confidante
8-3

"My Father lived at my Grandmother's house, too, before he went to hospital and died," she says.

I prop myself up on one elbow.

"I thought your father was in California, serving as a pilot with the U.S. Air Force!"

"I lied."

"I see!" I say. Although I don't.

"Those two photographs on the mantel at my house? The one of the man in the American Air Force uniform is in actuality my uncle, my Mother's brother. He's the one who is testing U-2 spy planes for reconnaissance flights over Russia."

Now what's this? I ask myself, propping myself up on one elbow, looking away from her, holding up a hand to shield my eyes from revealing sheer distrust.

"The other Asian-looking man was my Father. He was born in Canada, but his family was born in Japan. He was first-generation Japanese-Canadian. My Mother met him while she was working as a doctor in Vancouver. His name was Kenta Hirano. He was a botanist at the university.

"Mother had an interest in botany. She took night courses from him. That's how they met. They fell in love. They were secretly married before the War, to spare his parents who expected him to marry a Japanese woman. And to spare my Grandmother, who had never met anyone Japanese before in her life.

"After Japan bombed Pearl Harbour and war was declared, all Japanese-Canadians were rounded up. Father was sent with his entire family to a detention camp in the interior of British Columbia. Mother moved back here. By then, she was expecting."

"Expecting what?"

"Me! I was born here in Weston. I did not see my Father until he was released and free to move here in 1949. He was not permitted to return home to Vancouver. Besides, the Hirano family home and all their possessions had been confiscated. He had a choice: to return to Japan or be evacuated further east from B.C. Naturally, he came here. I was almost six years old when he joined us."

"Why are you telling me all this?"

"Because it's time. I want you to know who I really am. Remember when we first met and I said that Mitsy was just a nickname? So it is. My real name is Mitsuko. Mitsuko Hirano."

"I don't believe a word you're saying, Mitsy Gardiner. This is just another giant fabrication, another one of your tall tales. I don't know why you bother. Is it just another ploy to get attention?"

"It's true, Lois! I'm not making it up! You know that silk kimono I wore at the 'Teaserama'?"

"You mean the shiny housecoat with the long sash? Yes, I do!"

"The sash is called an 'obi' in Japanese."

"Whatever you say!"

"That was my Mother's wedding dress. She keeps it stored in her cedar chest. When she finds out how soiled it is now, she'll be really, really, really mad at me! Pure silk is not easy to clean."

I just stare at her with disbelieving eyes.

She is looking aptly morose. What an actress she is!

"So why the big secret until now? Why didn't you just tell the truth from the beginning?"

"I couldn't. I'm forbidden."

"Who says?"

"My Mother. She is afraid that I'll be harassed, bullied, possibly physically attacked! People still hate the Japanese, you know!"

"But the War is over! Besides, your father was a Japanese-Canadian citizen, so how could he have anything to do with the War?"

"Ask the Government. Ask the authorities who stripped us all of our property and livelihoods, put us on cattle cars and left us to freeze in the interior of B.C. Ask those who still believe what they were told about us!"

"Wait a minute! You're saying 'us'! You weren't even there. Why are you including yourself?"

"Because I am half-Japanese, Lois! Look at me!!"

I had already slid my cold 'hamburgler' out of the waxed paper ice cream bag that Mother had used to keep it fresh, and had started to munch on it, ruminatively, like one of those black-and-white Holstein cows I'd seen chewing their cud in a pasture during the drive to Niagara Falls.

Slowly, reluctantly, I raise my eyes to look straight at her.

"Look at my eyes! They're slanted! I have hardly any upper eyelids—See? It's called the 'epicanthic fold' which is a trademark of Asian eyes! Why do you think I wear black eye liner? Why I draw cat eyes? Because I figure by accentuating my eyes, I draw attention away from them by drawing attention to them!

"Look at my nose! Is it a normal nose? No! It's flattened, there's no pronounced bridge!

"Look at the colour of my skin! This is more than tan! It's this colour all year round!"

"How would I know?" I say, "I've never seen an Japanese person! Do Japanese people also have green eyes and red frizzy hair?"

I think I've nailed her. But she slips right out from under me.

"No. Most of them have brown eyes and straight black hair."

"Well, there you are then!"

But there is always a curve:

"I'm told that some have red hair. But I got the red frizzies and the green eyes from my Mother, who is Caucasian."

"Okay then. All round, you probably look more like your Mother."

The next curve:

"Japanese women are flat-chested. I got my big boobs from my Mother."

"Anything else?" I say, trying not to be sarcastic.

"You believe me, then?"

"I might believe you after I meet your Mother," I say, "Who till now is a phantom. It's odd that I've never met her."

"Can I help it if she works long shifts at the hospital?"

"I heard she's a psychiatrist. Fathers says that explains why you're such a nut case."

I am happy to see Mitsy flinch.

Inside my brain, something twigs.

"Does my own Mother know about all this?" I ask.

"I don't know. Why?"

"She might have already known about your Father. It might explain why she doubted your story from the get-go about the 'bun-sigh' or whatever it's called."

"Bonsai." She spells: "B-o-n-s-a-i. Look it up. Learn something you don't want to know, for a change."

Mitsy bites into her 'hamburgler'.

"When you called me over at bedtime that night to see something exciting, you told her a lie. You said you'd received a *bonsai* from your Father who sent it from Vancouver while on leave from the Air Force in California."

"Yeah. But that was a lie."

"To cover up for the Rico event."

"Somehow, she found out I was lying. So I ran over to the Hub and bought one myself."

"Surprise, surprise. When we came over that day to pick you up and Mother asked to see it, she read the Centrewood flower shop label on the bottom of the pot."

"She was suspicious. I think she wondered how I knew about bonsais at all."

"How did you know about them? Hardly anyone in the world knows they exist, let alone someone like you who is only interested in playing pranks on people and causing trouble."

"There's a lot more that exists in this world than you are aware of, Lois."

"What do you mean?"

"Don't presume that what you don't know nobody else does."

Wow. She just called ME my own definition of a Know-It-All. What an eye-opener.

"My Father's specialty as a botanist was cultivation of the bonsai. He was internationally renowned for his expertise."

"You know, Mitsy, it's amazing how everyone you know is the biggest and the best. First, your so-called Father couldn't just be requisitioned from the Canadian Air Force to become a United States Air Force pilot, you had to claim he was a test pilot for U-2 spy planes. Now you've retracted that tale, you say your real Father was more than just a botanist, he was a world renowned bonsai expert. Why don't you stop boasting about anyone you claim to know?"

"You think you don't go on and on about your big-shot father who doesn't just work at Avro, he designed the Arrow?"

"Well, he did!"

"And you never let anyone forget it."

"Yes, but you always have to be on top, you are always exaggerating, trying to make an impression, making up stories, most of which are bald-faced lies. Everyone sees through you, you know. Why don't you give it up?"

"Quite frankly, I don't care if nobody believes me when I'm lying, although it does hurt when I'm telling the truth. But I must say that I have always felt guilty for saying that it was my Father who was in the Air Force and not my Uncle. When I told your Mother and Father that the Asian man in the photograph was an Asian friend of my Father's, I felt ashamed. I betrayed my very own Father when I told such a lie."

We have polished off Mother's homemade butterscotch cookies, and are lying on our sides on the cool grass under the deep shade of the maple trees.

I say, "I have no idea what has prompted you to be telling me all this now, as though I matter."

"I told you because I trust you now. It's taken a long time but now I do. You have to appreciate that it's hard for me to trust anyone."

"What led you to think you could trust me?"

"We-e-e-ll, I've told you about my rolls in the bed naked with Jimmy. I hooked you into coming into my backyard for that naked scene with Rico, and both times you didn't run home to tattle. You knew that I helped Joey swipe smut rags from Mr. McAssburn's porn rack. You never said a word to your Mother when I put on that Teaserama show at the Big Culvert—"

"But you covered for everything you did! You used me as your so-called 'shill' to steal those porn magazines. You lied to Mother about the bonsai, knowing I'd be too scared to tell her about the "scene" with Rico. You lied to her why you needed to borrow the apron, which was really for your Teaserama, and *not* for a home ec demonstraton!"

"Exactly! You've known all about my antics. And you never once ratted on me!"

"How could I when you set me up every time? You made sure I was implicated, and couldn't tell even if I wanted to?"

"I didn't really plan any of it. It just turned out that way."

"You're telling me that you pulled all those pranks just to test me?"

Mitsy laughs.

"Maybe!" Then she thinks a moment. "Maybe yes, maybe no!"

I lie on my back and try to empty my mind of Mitsy's nonsense, make a valiant attempt to regain some sense of myself.

"You know, Mitsy," I say after a while, "You went to great measures to test me, to see if you could trust me. But guess what. You overlooked one major factor."

"What's that?"

"Me. Because of all your antics, I don't trust you one bit."

We have already started packing up when Mitsy looks at her watch. "Holy Doodlebug!" she exclaims, "Look at the time! It's quarter past 1:00! We've got to go!"

"Why? What's the sudden rush?"

"Move it, move it, move it!"

She hustles to toss our garbage in the bin, and then heads for her bike.

I am clambering onto my bicycle and about to push off, when I stop in my tracks.

"Hang on! Waitaminnut! There's been something I've been wanting to ask. You scared me half to death at that Teaserama of yours when your boobs started to spill out of that bar-lady saloon-girl-type corset."

"My bustier?"

"If you say so! Underneath, there were two big round sequined circles the size of coasters stuck on your tips—"

"Tips or tits?"

"Tips," I said primly, "What were they?"

"Oh, those are called pasties. I found them at a Sex Shop in Mount Dennis!"

That flies right over my head. I don't ask. Probably because I don't want to know.

"How did you make them stick?"

"Oh, nothing like a good solid dollop of Elmer's Glue!"

She prepares to push off, pauses for a moment, and turns to say: "If you're interested, I also bought a set with tassels. Are you up for watching me practice putting on a good nipple-tassel-twirling burlesque show?"

"A what?" I ask.

"Come on," she snorts, "Let's get moving."

While we are riding along side by side, Mitsy asks, "Did you ever hear the fashion rule: 'Blue and green should never be seen?' "

"No I haven't," I respond, then reflect aloud, "I don't know why that should be a rule. I mean, the sky is blue and the trees are green. Don't they go together?"

"Good point. But it's why I didn't wear my blue t-shirt."

We ride a bit farther, still side by side and she says, "Did you ever hear the fashion tip: 'Be a good fellow, avoid red with yellow'?"

Suddenly, I feel self-conscious and blush as though I'd been caught committing a major crime.

"No. But it's just as stupid as the other one!" I muster.

Mitsy lets out a hoot.

By then, we are almost at Main Street, crossing the bumpy railroad tracks. Under her green t-shirt, Mitsy's bosom jiggles and jostles with every bump.

At the Fox
8-4

It is going on 1:30 when we empty out into the town proper at the corner of Main Street and King. Mitsy pulls over, plants her foot on the curb, points at the Weston Public Library on the corner to our left, and says:

"Let's stash the bikes here in that rack, then just mosey around a bit!"

We do that, chaining the bikes to a stand just outside the library, then we amble off a few steps to Main Street.

"I thought we were in a hurry!"

Instead of turning left toward the downtown stores, Mitsy steps off into the road and takes a diagonal right.

"Where are you going?" I ask.

Farther up to the right is a movie theatre.

"Let's walk over to the Fox and see what's showing!" she answers, "I like looking at the posters."

Suddenly, Mitsy is pointing at the marquee: "Look!" she exclaims, all bedazzled, " 'The Curse of Frankenstein' is playing! Hey, I'd like to see that! Let's see what time it starts!"

She scurries ahead of me, and reads the show times listed at the wicket. "Hey! We're in luck! There's an afternoon matinée! And it starts at 1:45! Let's go see it, why don't we?"

"What?" I squeak.

"What d'ya mean, 'what'?" she says, tugging on my arm, "Come on, let's go to the movies!"

"I'm not allowed to go to the movies on my own!"

"You won't be on your own, you'll be with me!"

"You know what I mean! I only go to the movies with my parents!"

"That was when you were a child. Not now, when you're in Grade 9, for Pete's sakes!"

"Still, I should ask permission. Besides, we still have to bike home! It took us well over two hours to get here! We will have to allow at least three hours to get back because it's all up-hill! And I'm already beat. Besides, my knees are wrecked from banging against those handlebars all that way."

"But the movie is only an hour and a half long!"

"Sure! Sure! That means if we go, we won't get out till going on 3:00. That means we wouldn't get back home till way after six and that will spell big trouble because you heard Mother, we're supposed to be home by suppertime!"

"No, you are supposed to be home by suppertime!"

"No way! What are you pulling now? We're in this together! Don't get cute with me, Mitsy!"

I manage to spill this out, while Mitsy is guiding me by my elbow up to the wicket.

"Oh phooey, we'll just say we went too far and didn't gauge how long it would take for us to get back!"

I yank her off my arm. She tugs back.

"And who's going to pay?"

Just then, amid our pushing and pulling and bickering back and forth, I sense two guys are approaching us. They are very tall, one of them much taller than Father, so he must be at least 6'4".

One is slender, has dark shellacked hair with a long slicked-back duck cut, like Elvis Presley. He even lifts one side of his upper lip to smile, as though putting on like he is the real McCoy.

The even taller one is built as solid as a warehouse, has brownish-coloured hair with a tall brush cut ladled with a thick gel to make it stand straight up in gooey spikes.

Both are wearing faded old denim jeans, white t-shirts, dusty black boots. Slung over their shoulders are black leather jackets covered with silver studs.

Even from that distance, they stink of nicotine and one of them reeks of some kind of men's cologne.

I hear one of them say, "Hey, would you dig those two chicks!" and I see MItsy's face light up as though she is witnessing the Second Coming.

Emitting a husky croak from the base of her throat, she utters "Hey, Daddy-Ohs! Give me five!" Then all three of them are slapping each other's hands, and guffawing about the amazing coincidence of bumping into each other like that. "Can ya dig it!" Then, whirling around toward me, as though suddenly remembering my presence, in a high-pitched tremolo, Mitsy squeaks:

"Guys! Meet my friend, Lois! Would you believe we just biked all the way into town today from Centrewood—which is almost as far away as King City."

"Ya don't say?"

"Hoo! Now that's one long way!"

"Y'know, Mitsy, I thought when I didn't see you around no more, they'd finally put you in the loony-bin!" mock-Elvis jeers, as he stands there with his thumbs hooked in his jeans pockets, feet spread apart.

"Hey, yeah! A crazy broad like you belongs in 999 Queen Street!"

Mitsy's eyes glitter.

"Never mind, you big jokers! Anyway, I'll tell you it sure is a long trek, much further than we reckoned, eh, Lois?" —as if I'd been involved in the planning of this outing, "Oh, this is Richie, and this is Corky!! We all lived on the same street in Weston when we were kids. Played baseball, summers, in a neighbour's empty lot. Winters, played shinny on the road with our own home-made goalie net. We grew up together. Right, boys?" Some more high fives.

To Corky, she says: "Man, I dig the flat top! Still wearing the Old Spice to draw the ladies, eh? you Dog, you!"

"Still keeping that slick duck's ass in line, eh?" This is to Richie who had slipped out a small black comb from his back pocket.

"So whatyadoin' nowadays? Still working for STUD-a-baker, you big Studs, you?"

"Yep," says Richie, puffing himself up like King Kong, "We're both working full shifts there now. Plant expanded. We drive into Hamilton for work in my—get this, babe!" tilting toward her for emphasis "Two-tone '55 V-8 souped-up Studebaker Speedster, wouldn't ya know?"

"Whoo-ee--ee!" Mitsy exclaims, clapping her hands together, "What I wouldn't give to have a ride in that hot roadster some time. What about you, Corky? What do you drive?"

"The same old pickup truck. But it comes in handy, let me tell you!"

"I can guess what for—" Mitsy slaps him on the shoulder, "Dairy Queen pickups? Eh? Eh? Ha ha ha!"

"You got that right!"

"These guys are in the money big time, Lois! They work shifts on the assembly line at one of the biggest automobile companies in Canada, and have the most big-paying jobs in the world right now. Big money! Set for life! Right, Corky? Right, Richie?"

"You gotcha!" Richie says, his chest once again swelling up with pride, at the same time as Corky says: "You betcha!" his eyes riveted on Mitsy's cleavage.

"Say," Richie says, "You girls thinking of taking in this movie?"

"No," I say. Bluntly.

"We were thinking about it," Mitsy says, "How about you?"

"Yep. But lookie here," he points at the poster, "It says PG—that means 'parental guidance'. Which means you can't get in if you're under 18 without adult accompaniment!"

"Well that settles it!" I say, turning away.

"Say!" Mitsy says, as though having a brainwave, "You're both 18, why don't you two take us in with you?"

"Could do that!" Richie says, still ogling Mitsy's breasts.

"Great, then! You're on! We're in!"

Mitsy hooks her arm in mine. "But oh dear! We don't have any bread!"—This said with a cutesy-pie pitiful singsong tone to her voice.

"No problem! Let it be our treat!" Richie says.

"Sure! You bet!" Corky agrees.

"Why you rich devils, you! Is that why they call you 'Richy', Richie?"

"Yes, ma'm, my success in life was foreordained."

"Groovy!" Mitsy purrs.

Without further ado, I have an arm wrapped round my waist, am squeezed tight to Mitsy's side, and am frog-shuffled up to the box office while the two big lugs buy our tickets. Then I am whisked through the main doors of the theatre into the lobby, where Mitsy and I are planted against the wall while they buy small boxes of buttered popcorn for us.

In line, I can tell they are in hot debate about something. "No way!" one of them says. "Way!" says the other.

I hear Corky say: "My gut says to follow the traffic signals."

"Follow what?"

"The stop lights. Red means Stop and Yellow means Caution, but Green means Go. So! You take the red and yellow, I'll take the green!"

"No frigging way!" Richie objects, "This is my gig, so I get first dibs!"

"So—why don't we share?"

Then they snigger.

When we enter the theatre, Mitsy says to Richie and Corky: "Let's sit in the back row."

I am worried about being stuck between these two big bozos. As it turns out, there is no need for me to do anything at all to allay my qualms, for the instant we reach the back row, we are all bumping into each other like lost molecules, as both Richie and Corky start jousting to get beside Mitsy. Waving all gallantry aside, Richie plunges into the back row first, grabbing Mitsy's hand and pulling her in after him. Then Corky knocks me out of the way and dives in next. I end up—through default—gratefully—ultimately—and with a big sigh of relief—in the aisle seat.

I toss my knapsack under my seat.

Mitsy is instantly all a-bubble and a-babble.

"Oh, I can't believe it! I'm so excited! Isn't it amazing bumping into you two guys like this? And outside the Fox! Just when a show is about to begin! I can't believe it! What a treat! What a coincidence! Oh, I love ya, Guys!"

"We love you too, Babe!"

"We miss you around here, Babe!"

"But this movie—it's going to be scary, isn't it? Isn't it a MONSTER movie? Oh, I hope I don't get too scared!" she whimpers, widening her eyes, fluttering her hands, and putting on her Betty Boop voice.

"Hey, just hold onto us and let us hold onto you, Babe, don't be scared, we'll take care of ya!" All so sugary and phony somehow, I think I'm going to barf.

I feel terribly uncomfortable at the prospect of sitting next to Corky. It is the first time that I've ever sat next to anyone other than family—aside from other kids at a children's matinée—let alone in a soon-to-be darkened theatre—beside someone like him. I plunge my hand into my popcorn. Out of the corner of my eye, I find myself sizing him up. In the dimmed lights, he has bulging eyes and a fat snout like a boxer dog, and his large bristly head looks threatening to me, like a porcupine. He has a thick neck like a bull. Unconcerned about anyone else needing a seat, he had thrown his leather jacket over the back of the seat in front of him. He is wearing a white t-shirt, in vogue these days, like James Dean in "Rebel Without A Cause". What astonishes me is the massive size of his arm muscles—the biceps, bulging large and round as Popeye's. Also unnerving are his enormously broad shoulders and thick bulky thighs. I am instinctively afraid of our shoulders or thighs touching, so I sit way over to the left side of my seat, and let him have all the shoulder- and elbow-room he seems to require, about which he has no reservations at all. It becomes evident that I am either totally invisible or I don't exist at all, for he immediately appropriates the arm rest and sits with his legs splayed apart, his closest knee and foot jutting well into my territory.

I look across Mitsy over to Richie. It becomes quite apparent even before the lights are dimmed that he has eyes only for Mitsy. He has already put his left arm around her. I could see his forearm and large hand draped over her shoulder.

Meanwhile, Corky is already shifting his body toward her, and his left arm is slowly reaching out toward her waist.

When the theatre is in total darkness and the raucous din from the audience has quietened down a notch, the screen show begins with a fanfare of recorded trumpets accompanied by flashing searchlights. There is the head of the big lion roaring, and then the rolling of the credits. After which, to a volley of excited, loud music, the preliminaries begin.

First, there are trailers for upcoming movies that provide clips of key scenes that must surely give away most of the plot.

Next, there is a Bugs Bunny and Elmer Fudd cartoon. I have never been able to tell what those two are saying to each other and this is no exception. There is always some reason for them to be chasing each other, yelling at one another as though gargling, and lying in ambush until hitting each other on the head.

The cartoon is followed by the newsreels. There is a clip of Elvis Presley wearing his gold lamé jumpsuit at Maple Leaf Gardens right here in Toronto this past April. There is Father's bugbear John Diefenbaker, taking over as Prime Minister from Louis St. Laurent in June. To my utter surprise, there is an overhead view of the Rollout of the Avro Arrow on October 4, taken, I'm sure, by the cameras I'd seen on the Avro roof overlooking the ceremony. While this was rolling, the camera pans the crowd. I spot myself sitting with Mother in the front row of honoured guests, facing the platform with all the dignitaries. I spot Father on the podium. I feel a sting of pride. I think: I was part of history!

This bit is quickly succeeded by a series of stills showing the launch of the ICBM by the USSR in August, and next, the launch of Sputnik on the same day as the Rollout, October 4. The narrator's voice is deep and burbly. He sounds like he is underwater, talking through a snorkel. He says the Russians used the same rocket as they used for one of their missile tests. I think: How could that be? Did they send a big net out into space to haul it back to earth? I'll have to ask Father. Oops, no I won't, he'll wonder how and where I learned this.

The newsreel wraps up with a reference to the space race and a depiction of the H-bomb exploding at Hiroshima in August 1945. The voice speculates that it will take more than twelve years for that atrocity to be forgotten.

Then the movie starts.

Feeling more secure with Corky's attentions focused elsewhere, I allow myself to become engrossed in the movie.

It is very smoky in here. Everyone is smoking, even Mitsy's two 'buddies'. I am conscious of all the cigarettes flickering throughout the theatre, like fireflies in the dark, and I sit there, desperately hoping to avoid any ashes falling from Corky's cigarette on my shirt or pants. I could never explain a burn in my clothing.

The stench of burning tobacco fills my nostrils.

The seat in front of me is empty.

I surprise myself by moving into it.

I grab my knapsack from under my seat then I leap one seat forward.

Despite the initial pitch-black darkness in the theatre, my eyes have become accustomed to the dark. The light cast from the screen illuminates the audience. It flicks across viewers' faces and across the fronts of their bodies. It is at one point during the movie—when Victor lopped the corpse's head off—that I glance back to see if Mitsy is disturbed or frightened by it all. It was then that I grasp the reason why she wanted to sit in the back row, because Richie, with his arm hooked around Mitsy's shoulders, had his hand plunged from above into her top and is firmly cupped on her right breast. Meanwhile Corkie, with his arm stretched across her midriff, had his hand slipped up under her top from below, firmly cupping her left breast. With one breast each to himself, both are fondling her enormous breasts, squeezing and caressing the nipples which are protruding between their fingers through the cloth of her top, standing out hard and high, like two mountain peaks in the Himalayas. Curiously, underneath her top, her bra seems to have disappeared.

Mitsy stuffs her mouth with popcorn, a sublime smile on her face, as though she is not perturbed at all, not by the movie, not by anything; in fact, as though she is caught in an entirely different world, and from her blissful smile, enjoying herself immensely.

Other than trying to brace myself for whatever the Creature in the movie might do, coupled with attempts to swallow the activity of the 'three-headed four-armed octopus' Creature behind me, I am fretting. How on earth are we going to be able to ride our bikes home in time for supper? Especially since my legs already ache, and I am so sunburnt I think I got heat stroke despite wearing my hat and the slathering of suntan lotion. Question is: would I be able to ride that far even if we had all night?

Eventually, the movie is over.

I glance back and happen to see Mitsy adjusting her bra straps which had slipped down almost to her elbows. Quickly, she is replacing her breasts in their Brunhilda cups and smoothing her top over both with expert hands.

After the three disengage, the four of us spill out into the lobby. Both Richie and Corky walk out across the lobby and through the main doors somewhat hunched over and slightly bow-legged, glancing from left to right, trying to look macho and blasé, as they excuse themselves to visit the men's room.

Outside once again, we stand in a little circle facing each other, idling, waiting to complete the pleasantries of parting, I presume. First, there has to be an exchange about the movie, then someone has to express regrets about going our separate ways.

"Hey, what a great movie!" Mitsy says.

"It sure was!" Richie and Corky agree, vigorously nodding their heads.

"I want to thank you for the treat—You guys are real pets!" Mitsy says.

"No, no, no!" Richie replies, "You're the treat—you're the pet!"

"Yessir, m'am," Corky adds, "It was a real feel-good afternoon all round at the movies!"

All three of them crack up laughing, as though this is an inside joke. Obviously, they think no one else knew what they were up to in there, that myself—and how many others in neighbouring seats—were oblivious.

"Listen guys, it was great seeing you again, what little I saw of you, but we, Lois and me, we've got to toodle off home!"

She looks at her watch and then at me, with consternation.

"It's almost 4:00! We're never going to make it home in time!" she exclaims.

I am instantly enraged.

"I see!" I counter, "Going into the movie, you said we'd have plenty of time. But now we're out, it dawns on you that we're going to be late?"

"The movie was supposed to be an hour and a half but with that other introductory garbage, it all added up," Mitsy sniffs.

"You're always so right until you're dead wrong, you dimwit," I snarl.

"Regardless, let's face it," she says, "It will take us at least three hours if not more because this time it's all mostly uphill—"

"Oh yeah! Sounds familiar!"

"It will take some mighty fast pedaling for us to be back at your place even by what? 7:00? 7:30?"

I can't believe my ears, and glower at her. "What are you, a parrot? That's exactly what I said to you!"

"What's your problem, Lois? Don't blame me! Isn't it time you took responsibility for your own actions?"

My blood starts to curdle in my brain.

"You witch!" I snarl, "Once again, you've tricked me—"

"As I recall, you came along quite willingly!"

"I did not! You pulled me up to the wicket and strong-armed me into the theatre. I'm sick and tired of you playing me for a fool!" I wheel around, and start to march off.

"Where are you going?"

"I'm going to find a pay phone and I'm calling Mother to fetch ME and you can find your own way home!"

The two oafs are standing there, watching us take turns going at it, like following a shuttlecock at a badminton game.

Richie steps forward. "Whoa, whoa, whoa, not so hasty! Why not let Corky and me drive you home?"

"What?" Mitsy asks, instantly all sparkly-eyed, "You would do that for us?"

"Of course we would!" Corky steps in, "It's the least we can do!"

I grind to a halt, confounded, instantly suspicious.

Is this a remarkable solution or just another trick?

"Well, tell me, what kind of vehicle are you driving that can handle two girls and two bikes?" Mitsy asks, suddenly the organizer.

"We'll use my truck!" Corky says, "But we'll have to go and fetch it. We came here in Richie's Studebaker. It's parked around the corner on King Street."

"Oo—oo—Nice! That's exactly where we left our bikes!"

I am not exactly sure but I think I see her wink at Richie.

At the Weston Central
8-5

4 p.m.

"Listen, girls, why don't you go to down to the Central for a milkshake, and wait for us while we fetch the truck?" Richie says.

"Leave yer bikes here and we can fetch them on the way out of town," Corky adds.

Mitsy agrees, waves them off.

"Tutty-bye!"

"No! Titty-bye!"

"Oh you guys!" She mock-scolds, shaking her finger at them.

I am left not knowing whether to fume or relax.

"Ease up! Come on! We're going to my favourite old greasy spoon where they have fabulous coke floats! My treat!"

I trudge along behind her.

"You can treat but you can't bribe!" I say, "And you can't change how I'm feeling. I'm furious and disgusted with you."

Undeterred, she now launches into her role as tourist guide.

"Here I am back in my old home town, on Main Street, one of my old hangouts!" she squeals, "On your left is Cruickshank Motors, the place run by the Mafia, where every crook gets his motor cranked. On your right is the Shave's Stationery Store, the shop that had to be bolted in place so it wouldn't drift away! That's a play on words—Get it? Let us pick up our step and stride quickly past Woolworth's, the place where red heart cinnamon candies are sold in open bins, begging for free-hand self-service—if you get my scoop! Across the way is Maher's shoe shop, the place where they give you one lone boot and lacing free, as a reward for previously swiping the mate, which they suspect but can't prove—and then they kick you out!"

I roll my eyes at her.

"Ah now, we have arrived at the Central Restaurant, Weston and region's famous diner, where waitresses Connie and Dale are bound to be still working, where Joan and her best friend Bonnie are bound to be found smoking in the far back booth while practicing their shorthand, both completing their last year in commercial at Weston High—hanging out here because this is the one place where their mothers will never dream of finding them!"

She barges in, leaving the door banging in my face. She calls out:

"Howdy-do! Look who's back—but not for long!"

Two women look up from their work. One is carrying a tray, the other is at the cash.

"Hell's bells, if it ain't the She-Devil of Satan's Choice, or is she the Belle of Hell's Angels?"

"Odd you should say—they passed us on the highway, gave me their biker rendition of the Musical Ride."

"You knew them?" I croak.

"Of course I knew them. Why else would they have done that routine?"

"And what unsuspecting soul is this that you have with you today?"

"Oh, this is my friend Lois!"

"Friend, eh? More's the pity!"

Mitsy trots down the aisle past several booths then swings into one of them, flinging her knapsack beside her on her seat. "I see you've reserved my favourite booth!"

"Oh yeah. Knew you were coming, baked a cake!"

"Wanna guess what we're ordering?"

"Two coke floats? Two hamburgers with fries?"

"Right on the first count. But hold the hamburgers and fries."

"Gotcha."

Mitsy puts her elbows on the table, squeezing her cleavage into full view. "That's Connie. The other one is Dale."

Connie has materialized once more at our table.

"Boss says, you want coke floats or anything else, you put your money up front on the table. Now."

Connie is staring at her point blank. Her chin is jutted out in an aggressive, almost rude way I'd never seen any woman do, except perhaps in the movies.

Mitsy lifts her head.

"Now that's not very cordial, Connie, do you realize I've travelled three hours from way north of Toronto just to savour your coke floats? I've been telling my friend Lois here all about your hospitality!"

"Did you tell her we always demand cash in advance from those known to slurp and dash?"

Unfazed, Mitsy replies: "Not yet!" She grubbles about in her knapsack and finds a two-dollar bill. Slapping it on the table, she sticks her own chin way out at Connie and says: "That do?"

"You leave it in full sight till you're finished and it'll do just fine!"

After the coke floats arrive, we sit sucking on our straws.

"That was quite the caper, wasn't it?" Mitsy grins.

I am so ticked off with Mitsy that my annoyance with her is bordering on being flabbergasted.

There's no point in nagging at her. Especially since we're getting a ride home—And with her friends.

Nonetheless, I am compelled to speak out.

I say in a calm voice: "I fail to see the reason behind your True Confessions in the Rosemount Park when another 'caper' was already in the works. How am I supposed to trust you after such a stunt?"

"You got it wrong. It's not a matter of you trusting me. I already explained it's all about me trusting you."

"I see," I reply, "Well then, once again, very cleverly, you've broken my trust. And you've pulled a number on me that I can never tell Mother and Father."

"Exactly!"

I allow my mind to drift away. I start thinking about the movie.

"Didn't Elizabeth have fabulous dresses?" I blurt out.

"You just saw a monster movie and your lasting impression is the lead actress's dresses?" Mitsy asks.

"Yes!"

"Me too!" she shrieks, and launches into a peal of laughter.

There is something infectious about Mitsy's laugh. It is hard to resist once she gets wound up. Despite myself, I fall into line. I show a crooked grin, then a tight smile, and then I too start to laugh. I can hear other customers start to titter.

Connie drifts by.

"You wanna keep it down? You're disturbing other customers! What the hell you two laughing at, seeing as we all now want to know!"

Mitsy mops her red face and says: "You want to share our good laugh, it'll cost ya!"— pointing at her two-dollar bill.

"My Lord in Heaven but you're quick! How does your Mother ever keep up with you?"

"She can't and she doesn't! She has no idea where I am today, let alone most days!"

"God spare her!" Connie replies, throwing her hands up in the air. The interruption had pricked our balloon of hilarity, but that exchange with Connie inflated another balloon, and made us burst out laughing again.

Time is passing by and still no sign of Richie and Corky. I'm getting more nervous by the minute. But what can I do?

"Can you count on those two jerks?" I ask.

"You bet! They may seem a bit sketchy but they'll turn up eventually, don't worry."

"It's the 'eventually' that worries me," I answer.

"So what did you really think about that movie?" Mitsy says.

"Well, it was scary in parts. I started to worry that Paul and Elizabeth were next in line to have their heads chopped off, but somehow I figured they wouldn't be killed."

"Huh! Why not? I wouldn't put anything past a man with an acid bath at his disposal!"

"Yeah, it was pretty gross when Victor chopped off the dead man's head and hands and threw them in the acid bath."

"At first I couldn't figure what he was doing in the town mortuary when he was stealing the eyes. But then I remembered at the very beginning, he told Paul that he wanted to create the perfect human being which would mean it would have to have the hands of an artist, the brains of the genius and a perfect body, so of course its eyes should have 20-20 vision. He could have used Elizabeth's but she was his fiancée.

"Maybe she was too shortsighted! ha ha."

"As for a brain, he could have used Paul's."

"True. But he needed him to help run the machine! Anyway, he'd sewn on new hands from a dead sculptor, and he had everything in place except for the brain when that brilliant old professor came to visit. Victor deliberately invited him!"

"Poor man! it was obvious from the outset that Victor had targeted him for his brain. He set him up!"

"Yeah, but I still don't see how he intended to bring his Creature back to life, since surely it had been dead a long time by the time he finished with his fetching and attaching of body parts, and all his other tinkering with the body! Anyway, at some point I didn't follow what happened after he 'did in' the old man."

"Paul caught him removing the old man's brain. Remember? He'd already put it in a jar. Paul came in and accosted him and knocked the jar out of his hand."

"But Victor still used it!"

"Yes, but after he ignited his 'life spark' and the creature came to life, it turned out he was a monster!"

"So he blamed Paul."

"Yeah, it never crossed his mind to blame himself for having initiated the horrible project in the first place. He said it was all Paul's fault. He had damaged the brain during their tussle! He made Paul feel guilty. And that's how he persuaded him to keep on helping him!"

"What's this 'life spark' business?" Mitsy ponders.

"Well, I think the author wrote the story of Frankenstein around the time that electricity had just been invented and scientists were trying to think of more ways to use it than for light bulbs and street lights!"

"How do you know all this?"

"I listen to intelligent conversations, instead of chasing after boys!"

"Touché!"

I hesitate. Watching that scene in the movie had made me think of Father. What I say next to Mitsy wants to spill out of me unchecked, as though I have Mitsy's confidence. Which intuitively, I know I don't. Despite lessons learned, I decide to share. Perhaps it's my vanity that compels me.

"I can tell you this now, because it's no longer under wraps. But can you keep it to yourself?"

"Huh?" Mitsy says, putting her open hand to her ear: "Is Miss Prim going to share a Secret?"

I dismiss her, flicking my fingers at her.

"The week that Father went to Toronto, it wasn't for business. He went to Toronto General Hospital for testing. They gave him ECGs and EEGs and all sorts of tests, which involve sending pulses of electricity through the heart and the brain to look for irregularities. That's how I know about at least one use of electricity. He told Mother and myself about it. Every time I saw the Creature on the slab, it reminded me of Father lying on the examination table. That was more overpowering than even following the movie."

"Wow. That's far out, Lois. I had no idea!"

"Just keep it under your hat, okay? It's not exactly a secret, but since the cause of Father's illness still has to be determined, do me a favour and don't mention this at all when you're at my place, right?"

"Right!"

"Hey there, chickie and chickadee, we're back and ready to boogie!"

Richie and Corky are standing there.

"Where did you get to, fellas? I thought you'd forgotten us!"

"Never!"

"But it's been well over an hour and now we're going to be in really big doo-doo—unless you're used to driving at 100 miles per hour?"

"On the wings of a jet, girlies, not to worry!"

"We had to go and tank up. Corky is such a skinflint, he fills up by the tablespoon," Richie says.

"You fellas want anything? If not, clear out!" Connie barks.

"Hey hey hey, we've come to pick up our broads, you mind?" He says to us, "Are you ready? Grab your gear and get out of here—the truck is idling right outside on the road, waiting for us!"

"Let us pay," Richie says, reaching to give Mitsy back her two-dollar bill.

Connie comes over and lays her hand flat on the money.

"No problem, lady, we'll pay for whatever these girls had! Put your money away, Mitsy!"

"Let me leave it as a tip," Mitry oozes graciously, shooting a vixen smile at Connie.

Richie slouches up to the front cash register, slips his bent, flattened wallet out of his back pocket, and takes care of the bill. The other lady named Dale completes the transaction, slams the drawer, and then stands there with arms folded, looking dour and sour.

The manager steps out from the kitchen, clenching and unclenching his fists.

At the far back booth, Joan and Connie pop their heads out to see what's causing the fuss.

Joan thumbs her nose at both of us, and Connie blows a smoke ring.

"So long, ladies! I lo-o-o-ve your coke floats!" Mitsy calls out to Connie and Dale as she reaches Corky, who is holding the door. When she steps out, she adds: "But there's not much lo-o-ove in my heart for you!"

The Pickup Truck
8-6

Sure enough, there is the truck waiting at the curb.

"Welcome to my '53 Ford F100 Flathead V8 pickup!" Corky says with a flourish.

"Flathead for a Flat Top, eh Corky? Sweet!" Mitsy jokes.

Corky hops in the driver's side. That leaves three of us to squish into a bucket seat meant for one.

"Skinny Minnie gets in first! Step up on the running board and climb in! You'll have to sit on the console between the seats and wrap both your gorgeous filly-like long legs around the gear shift!"

"Make sure he doesn't give you the shaft!" I hear Richie laugh.

I wrap my left leg around the gear stick, so my left foot rests on my right in the passenger well.

"I can just reach without hitting you with my elbow," Corkie says, his bulldog face treacherously close to mine, his bicep pressed into my ribcage.

Richie piles in next, grinning when Mitsy sits sideways on his lap and curls her legs over his.

He looks at Mitsy. "Good thinking to have a thin friend with a flat rack, or we'd never be able to do this! One of ya's would have to sit in the back with the bikes!"

He makes a move. "I gotta feeling this is another feel-good moment!" he declares, pulling her tight into his crotch and putting his hand plunk on her left breast.

"No way, not now-no how!" Mitsy objects, "Let's go. Fetch the bicycles!"

Corky pulls a U-ie in the middle of Main Street and guns it to the Library, hops out, yanks the bikes from the rack.

Mission accomplished. With bikes heaped in the flatbed of the pickup, off we drive.

Each time Corky stops, he jokingly puts his hand on my knee instead of on the gear stick knob.

"Oops! Sorry, my mistake!" he laughs, digging his elbow into my side.

"Once more, and you're a dead duck!" I glower.

"Lawdy-dee!" he cries, looking over my head at Mitsy and Richie, "The clothes peg speaks!"

"Mitsy," I say, "How come we forgot to lock the bikes? I always lock mine at school."

Mitsy says, "I dunno. I forgot, too. I guess we were out of town, so it didn't matter?" She lifts her shoulders, and adds, "Goes to show how 'New habits die fast'!"

"Imagine if they had been stolen," I reply, "Both were birthday gifts, too— We'd have been in real trouble."

Father and Mother had given me my trusty gold 'steed', Trigger, in advance of my birthday at the end of October, so that I could ride to school and bypass the construction. To my chagrin, they had arranged with Mitsy's Mother to buy a red bike for her, which she named 'Tonto', as a belated birthday present. At the time, I was elated, and then enraged. I thought I could escape her company until I found out she got a bike, too.

This may sound infantile to others, but I had been praying for some means of escape from her—the *deus machina* of real life. It was a plot device that I had learned about from Greek tragedy when studying a play by Euripedes in grade 8. The end result was that my faith in God had been seriously damaged.

As soon as we leave the town limits, Corky flicks the radio on to the local pop radio station—Mitsy insisting that it be CHUM— and pumps the music up high. Richie bursts into song, then Mitsy, followed by Corky, so the whole trip up Weston Road and onward becomes a jolly croon fest with loud groans when hitting wrong notes and horrendous attempts at bad harmony.

"Whatsamatter, Little One, didn't ya know that us guys dig these songs?"

"Is that why they call it 'Hard Rock' music?" I ask and the two guys roar laughing.

"Oh yeah, oh yeah, wait till ya see us hoods groovin' on American Grandstand! Step aside, Dick Clark, we're about to show ya how to boogie!"

"Boogie?" Mitsy pulls a face of scorn, "You get on American Bandstand, you do the twist!"

Going up the highway, it is freaky that all my favourite songs are being played back to back, and they are all this year's '57 songs according to the d.j.— Singing the Blues, Party Doll, Teddy Bear, Diana, That'll Be the Day, Wake Up Little Suzie. It turns out that I know the lyrics, too, so after some badgering, and downright bullying, I join in and add to the braying. To tell the truth, it is really fun! I am having a 'swell' time!

Without blinking an eye or with any instructions from Mitsy, Corky turns into the parking lot at the Big Culvert, swings in wildly and pulls a 'U-ie' just as wild, braking with a spray of gravel on the very brink of the turnoff and the highway. How did he know this road was here? Had he been here before?

"Look at you, Corky, majoring in U-turns today," Mitsy says, "You ever drive straight, Big Guy?"

"Someday I'll drive YOU straight, Little Lady," Richie whispers loud into Mitsy's ear.

"Out you get!" Corky commands and all four of us tumble out.

The guys haul the bikes out of the flatbed and set them in front of us.

"Now off you go!" Richie says.

"Wait! I have a thank you present from Mr. Chadwick!"

She hands them each one of the Neilson's milk chocolate bars.

Richie is suspicious: "You swipe these?"

Mitsy's quick retort: "No, the man is such a sharp old dude, the instant he saw me coming, he shot that idea down in a pile of cow dung."

"That true?" he asks me.

I nod.

"His favourite nickname for me was 'Sticky Fingers', Mitsy supplied, "Not quite as incriminating as 'Five Finger Pickup'!"

"While he forked them over, did he sing Move Along, Little Dogies?"

Meanwhile, Corkie has ripped off the wrapper. He bites off a chunk.

"Not bad chocolate," Corkie says, "Although I like my milk with nuts!"

With a bee-beep, they pull out and drive off down the highway.

The Brawl
8-7

Mitsy and I pull into my driveway on our bikes at 6:45 p.m.

"Phew! Are you happy now? We made it!"

"We made it how? Safe and sound, yes. In time for supper, no!"

"Oh don't be such a drag!"

I yell at her, "You set me up, you witch!"

"What are you saying?"

"You planned this whole 'country picnic' outing way in advance!"

"What are you talking about?"

"The bikers. Taking off like a jackrabbit and charging along fast enough not to miss that motorcycle 'fly-by' which you must have arranged, it was just too coincidental. You knew they were coming!"

"Oh fuddle-duddle." Pause. "How did you cotton on?"

"That waitress who greeted you at the Central. She called you on it. Said you were one of the Hell's Angels."

"Well, she was wrong, all right? The guys I know are with Satan's Choice!"

I rolled my eyes.

"And the movie. You tore off from our picnic, so you would be at the Fox by 1:30. Really! It was all too pat for words, you just happening to bump into those two goof-balls."

"Well, I did!"

"Guess what. I was suspicious but later, when they arrived to pick us up, I recognized the truck! It was the same one that escaped with all your props at the end of your 'Teaserama'. That clinched it. You had no intentions from the very beginning, of going on a nice bike ride in the country!"

Mitsy doesn't miss a beat.

"Okay, you're right, you win! But we had a great time, right? Admit to me that you had fun!"

"When I need an event planner, it won't be you that I hire. Get it? I don't need you to plan OR provide 'fun' for me! Besides, I was the last person you had in mind when you cooked this one up!"

"You didn't enjoy the movie? You didn't get a kick out of burning rubber up the highway singing rock'n'roll songs, going well over the speed limit? I swear at one point, Corky was hitting 80 miles an hour!"

"Don't you ever ever ever do this to me again! Don't you ever ever ever swindle me into another one of your shenanigans!! YOU USED ME! By the way, I saw you letting those two dorks feel you up all through the movie! You think nobody else saw?? You were the only one in the dark. You are a shameless, vulgar tramp! A hussy! A-a—a—very bad bad bad person, Mitsy Gardiner—or should I say Mitsuko Hirano?"

"How dare you, you dirty double-crosser!"

"Oh, shoes on other foot, eh? Now you know how it feels, eh eh eh???"

Mitsy punches me in the nose. I feel the bridge of my nose crunch. I sock her in the eye.

She bludgeons me on my upper right arm.

I throw out my closed fist and catch her on the chin.

By the time Mother opens the front door, we are knotted limbs rolling around on the front grass, slapping and biting and kicking.

"So there you are!" Mother says, hands on hips. "Where do you think you've been? It's almost seven o'clock! You are late! Your Father and I have already eaten!"

She strides right into our tangle and drags me out by the sore arm.

"You get inside, Lois Michelsen!" Whirling, she points at my foe: "And you—Mitsy Gardiner, go home!! Right now!!"

Both of us are still so enraged, we hesitate.

"Do as you're told! Both of you!!"

I stand up full height and wipe blood off my upper lip.

Mitsy stands up and clobbers me on the side of my head as she limps to her bike. I fall to my knees. I hear carillon bells chiming and Big Ben bonging. Now I understand how it feels to be 'clocked'.

I leave my bike on the lawn.

Indoors, I go to face another kind of music.

Father is waiting for me.

"When was suppertime ever 6:45 p.m.? Certainly not today, or anyday! You will be sorry to learn, Miss, that we are going to the movies. We are going to see The Curse of Frankenstein. We were going to take you. But now we are not going to do so!"

Mother is draping her jacket over her shoulders and reaching for her purse.

"Your supper is in the warmer oven. You will have no dessert. After you have eaten, you will take a bath and clean yourself up! Then you will go to your room where you will go to bed and find yourself fast asleep by the time we return."

Father puts on his windbreaker. "What were you two doing out there on the lawn? Did I see fisticuffs? Who do you two think you are? Gorgeous George? Whipper Billy Watson? Let me make myself clear, Miss! Girls don't brawl! And young ladies don't wrestle!" Almost as an afterthought, he adds: "When did you start doing that??"

They are at the front door.

Father rattles his keys.

"Lock the door behind us."

Frankenstein
8-8

Sunday, October 20, 1957

I have a tough time at breakfast.

Neither Father nor Mother greets me.

Neither of them asks me directly about the front lawn fracas yesterday, despite the fat puffy nose I am wearing in the middle of my face. I don't think they even took the time to notice the large welt expanding black and blue on my right upper arm.

They make comments to each other like: "Somebody got 'gressive' yesterday!"

"Yes, I saw! I'm wondering why they didn't resort to black chewing gum to get attention instead of beating each other to a pulp!"

They, of course, are obliquely mocking me while ignoring me, by referring to Episode 3 of Leave it to Beaver, which we had watched last night on TV.

In that episode, Beaver had come home with a black eye, and his Father had scolded him for not fighting back, but then, he didn't know the source had been a girl, Violet Rutherford. His Father told him he had to stand his ground, be more aggressive. So Beaver went over to Violet's house and asked her if she felt like being more 'gressive'. They ended up having a milkshake together at the local ice cream parlour, and then buying black chewing gum. When the Fathers finally found them, they were sitting on Violet's front stoop sticking the black gum to their front teeth. "You look a lot better without teeth," Beaver said to Violet.

After these blatant rounds of teasing, still not acknowledging me in any way, it gets worse when they start discussing the movie.

"I've always thought that Frankenstein was the monster," Mother says.

"Me, too!" I want to say, but bite my lip.

"Come to think of it, the doctor was a monster in his own right," Father says.

"Ain't that the truth," I withhold.

"The movie critics say that doesn't hold a candle to the 1931 version with Boris Karloff."

"Strikes me it was an entirely different script. Are they allowed to take liberties with the original story? I'm inclined to unearth it from my library to read it again!"

"There were some real moments of terror. I really thought it was Victor who shot Elizabeth when she went out on the balcony!" Mother says.

I want to leap into the conversation. I want to say: "Me, too! So did I!"

Mother says, "The whole notion of reconstructing a human body by assembling body parts from elsewhere was brilliant, really. You have to hand it to Mary Shelley for her imagination. But the notion is so preposterous, it could never happen in real life."

I think: I could do with some replacement parts myself. My arms and lower back were strained from hanging onto the handlebars, which simultaneously gave my knees a solid beating from all the hectic pedalling. I had come into the kitchen limping.

I could also do with a new forehead and a new nose.

I think of Mitsy and smirk, hoping she has a black eye. No, two black eyes! One each for those jugheads from Weston she calls her 'buddies'. And one each for the liberties she let them take with her twin boobs.

I keep my chin in my cereal bowl, ladling in the milk with my spoon.

Father says: "It was clever how they portrayed Frankenstein's machine that he devised to activate the Creature while laid out on that slab. All those whirring, crackling electrical sounds! My own torture on that damned ECG gurney at Toronto General came to mind!'"

I had mentioned this very thing to Mitsy! I almost say: "Me too!"

When Father says: "Victor met his come-uppance because he dared to meddle with the origin of life. He dared to snatch the last spark of life from a dying corpse and use that to create his own idea of a perfect man!"

Mother says: "He dared to play God!"

I want to interject, to say that what brought about Victor's downfall wasn't so much that he offended God by trying to create life, it was his betrayal of the maid Justine! He had led her on into believing that he loved her, but as soon as Elizabeth turned up, he ditched her! The true evil he committed was by deliberately luring Justine into the Creature's den to be killed. Victor murdered her, whether he wanted to admit it or not!

But I keep my head down and my thoughts to myself.

God help me if they ever find out what I did yesterday! I'll be even more bandaged up than the Creature.

Oh boo hoo hoo, I think, then, suddenly finding it funny, almost snork out loud.

I must keep a sober face.

I must continue to look as though I'm sulking.

Actually, I am still sulking.

Proving you can indeed do two things at once.

At one point, Father musee: "I wonder why Victor Frankenstein didn't try to build a perfect woman! That's what I'd do!" He cocks an eyebrow at Mother, knowing that will razz her.

"You?" Mother laughs, "That's so typical of a man. You don't know what you've already got!"

I get up from the table and leave the room. Don't ask permission. Don't announce my departure. Just hobble out with as much dignity as I can muster.

I go back into my bedroom.

I try to orient myself to my day, and the coming week.

***

It is Sunday and I have so much homework backed up from the week before, and even more piled up from this past week, I am glad to have a whole day to get on top of it all.

It is critical that I do so, especially with so many more disruptions in the offing this coming week:

Tomorrow after school, Mother and I are traveling into Toronto with Mrs. Molnar and Becky as planned. Becky has her weekly Monday after-school flute lesson at the Royal Conservatory.

I will have to leave early morning and ride my bike over to Becky's. Then we'll walk to school together. When school is out, Mrs. Molnar will pick up Mother first, then Becky and myself.

After Becky's lesson, we plan on going to Diana Sweets for supper. Mother will have left a casserole and some dessert for Father.

After our outing, Mother will be dropped off at home, and I will continue on to Becky's for two overnights.

That's because on Tuesday, Father and Mother are flying to Ottawa with the AVRO Admin delegation and other CEO wives, for two whole days. They will be staying at the Chateau Laurier, which I gather by the tone of Mother's voice is a very swank hotel. Mother told me the name of it as though I should know it. A clear case of fruitless name-dropping.

Separate appointments to address both the life of the Arrow and the RCMP abuses of civil liberties have been booked with the Solicitor General, former Prime Minister Louis St. Laurent, MPs of the Opposition and some members of the Privy Council. As well, Father has a private appointment with the Governor General to discuss Chief Fred's land claim. I'm not sure if he will be dealing with Mrs. Molnar's missing family in Hungary. At this point in time,

I don't think even he himself is sure. I heard him discussing it with Mother, saying he would be short on time, and it would have to be as an aside, as it really wasn't Avro business, yet it would end up on Avro's tab.

Thursday is the night for our Doppler Flute Duo concert, so staying at Becky's will give us two solid nights to practice leading up to the performance.

***

I stand at my window, looking out across the Main Artery, out over the pastureland.

There is the tall Dutch elm tree standing with its regal arms uplifted as though praising life and its own existence. It was the only tall tree in the middle of the field. I could picture in olden days, that was where the cows would settle down in the grass, lounging like bit fat old ladies at a picnic, after drinking at the stream nearby.

There is an old woman emerging from the stand of willow trees down by the stream. She is dressed all in earth tones, head and shoulders wrapped in a clay-coloured shawl, a tan cloth belt wrapped around her midriff over a long dark brown loosely-woven blouse and skirt.

She is carrying a basket-load of burrs.

She seems to be wiping her eyes in sorrow.

In slow motion, as though time is being slowed down and is now suspended, she looks up and stares directly across the pastureland, across the Main Artery, straight at my window, directly at me.

Aunt Ani! I gasp.

Then she vanishes.

●

CHAPTER NINE
Philosopher's Walk

The Funk
9-1

Monday, October 21, 1957

School is out for the day. According to plan, I am standing next to the main entrance to Centrewood Collegiate Institute.

Leaning against the yellow brick wall that is soaking in the soothing warmth of the sun's rays, I am lost in thought, head down, just studying the pavement, when I find myself suddenly enveloped in shade.

I lift my head just a bit to see Bert Sanderfield deliberately blocking the sun, smiling at me.

"Lost your bike?"

"No. It's at Becky's. I'm waiting for her to come out—And for our mothers to pick us up. We're driving into Toronto together for supper after Becky's flute lesson."

Bert looks more closely at me.

"I noticed Mitsy has quite the shiner today. From the looks of that schnozz of yours, I have a feeling you were the one who finally plowed her one! Good show! Power to you!"

I turn my face away.

"Huh!" That was all I could muster.

"Hurt much?"

"Well, ya!"

"Try some Watkin's Medicated Ointment to draw the bruising out. Take it from me! I've majored in many a socked nose in my day— Not from beating up girls, mind you—Mostly from playing sports. I don't recall one single sport where I didn't get slammed in the face. Baseball. Hockey. Football. Tennis. You name it."

"You're a guy. Everyone probably congratulated you."

"You're right there. The way I see it, your job will be to drum up an explanation. My suggestion, for the nosy parkers, is the old standby: running into a door. One thing for sure, if it was Mitsy you plowed, don't feel apologetic or embarrassed about it! Feel proud! Gotta go. Hope you feel better, okay?" Then he wheels around and takes off, taking his shadow with him. Along the walkway, he stops and says: "How about Wizard of Oz? I'm thinking of dressing up as the Scarecrow. You wanta be Dorothy?"

Oh. He's talking costumes for the Hallowe'en Dance. Which is the last thing on my mind—so much so, that I had forgotten about it entirely.

"I'll think about it. Thanks. But what will I wear? As far as I know, I have a hair bow and a basket!"

"Good start!"

"Maybe I'll go as the Tin Man, then I won't have to worry about my face!"

"She starts beating up on you again, all you have to do is call me!"

"Hey! Thanks!"

Eventually, Becky shows up. Shortly after, Mrs. Molnar pulls up in her car with Mother.

Becky and I pile into the back seat. She looks at my nose and frowns. She mouths, 'Are you okay?' and pats my hand. She doesn't look surprised. She must have heard about it.

I am still not talking to Mother. Or technically speaking, not to Father either!

***

Yesterday, I got up early and stayed in my room.

I concentrated on homework as best I could while breathing through my mouth and sipping water to wet my whistle. There was a lot of vocabulary to be learned for both French and Latin. In both cases, there were lists of new words with definitions, then passages to be read, followed by 'fill in the blanks' exercises. With the words already supplied, the latter suited my tired brain quite well.

Next, I worked on an assignment on the copula verb for English grammar

The introduction provided three tips:

* A complete sentence must have both a nomination and a predicate.

* The copula (or copular) verb is part of the predicate

* It is not an action verb.

The assignment had two parts:

1) If the four major word classes are nouns, verbs, adjective and adverbs, which class follows a copula verb?

2) Complete sentences with the nouns and copula verbs supplied in the appended list.

I decided to tackle 2) first.

This was not the kind of assignment to ask of an addled brain and a swollen nose. I sat at my desk with second and third fingers of my left hand supporting my forehead, fourth finger and thumb supporting the bridge of my nose. My right hand clutched my pencil, hoping it would self-activate and move along independently.

There was some horrible block in my head that stopped me from constructing the assigned sentences with any of the natural ease I thought I could summon. I laboured over each sentence till I was sweating bullets.

To my chagrin, I had to admit to myself that I didn't know what I was doing.

It was then I realized that I had to crack open 1) in order to complete 2)

I looked at all the words I had used to complete the sentences using the assigned copula verbs.

The question is: what class do these copula verbs take?

It struck me suddenly that all the words for the copula verb were adjectives.

So the nominative is the subject, the copula verb is the bridge, and the predicate has to be an adjective!

I liked the thought of the copula verb as a link between the subject and a descriptor. I drifted off for a bit, thinking about its role as being neither active nor passive but neutral. Also, if this was even relevant.

My mind went round and round in circles.

Finally, I reviewed the required ten sentences with copula verbs:

>Smell, taste, seem, grow, look, proves, remain, run, become, be

>The rose smells heavenly.

>My ice cream tastes delicious.

>That dog seems lazy.

>Old men grow weary.

>That lady looks smart.

>The attempt proves unsuccessful.

>He remains silent.

>Rivers run downward.

The sunset becomes brilliant red.

Be prepared.

My nose was howling (Is that a copula verb or a past progressive tense? Oh no, not another quiz, this time self-assigned!)

I had shooting pains across my cheekbones and up into my forehead.

I picked up my flute, and tackled one passage of the Doppler that still bugged me. It was the transition from the Andante to the Rondo. To me, it shouldn't stop entirely, then start up again. Instead, the end of the Andante should slow down to a diminuendo, and flow into the Rondo without a break in breathing.

I worked over that section repeatedly, watching my fingering while enjoying a renewed confidence in musical expression.

When it got close to noon and I started feeling hungry, I opened my bedroom door a slot. I could hear Father and Mother having an intense discussion behind their closed bedroom door, so I went to the kitchen, prepared myself a peanut butter and jam sandwich, and took it back to my room with a glass of milk.

I couldn't care less if they were arguing about me, or the price of tea in China.

Later when Mother called me for lunch, I ignored her.

Then she was standing at my door.

"Come for lunch," she said.

I pointed to my empty milk glass and my plate with vestigial crumbs and smears of jam, and then turned my back on her, went back to my studies.

She came up to me from behind, held me firmly on both sides of my head with two hands, and forced my face toward her.

She frowned, and then left the room.

A while later, she brought me some ice wrapped in a wet face cloth.

I took it from her and draped it over the bridge of my nose, held it there with my left hand but said nothing. It was a bit awkward holding onto it with one hand, but I carried on using the other to write and hold open a page of my "Basics of Algebra" text book. At this beginning stage, we were dealing with "unknown variables" using "values" like a, b, c. I had a feeling that if these were the basics, I had a long, rocky road ahead of me.

When it came round to suppertime, again the call, and again I ignored it.

Father turned up without knocking, with a plateload of food in his hands, and hunkered there beside me at my desk.

"You know, all Mother and I are expecting is an apology."

"You won't get one." Tersely.

"You think you don't owe us one?"

"No. You both owe me one."

"How do you figure that?"

"One, you didn't ask me why I was late, you just lambasted me instead. Two, you didn't ask me why I was fighting with Mitsy, you just tore into me. Three, I didn't ask to go for a bike ride with Mitsy, Mother made me go. Four, you both ganged up on me at the breakfast table, pulled the silent treatment, pretended I wasn't there. That is rude and doesn't work on me, it just makes me mad! Five, thanks to a botched so-called 'bike ride and picnic', when I finally stood up for myself, I have a punched nose. I can hardly breathe. I have a bruised arm. I can hardly lift it. And who has to play the flute at a performance on Thursday? So no, I don't owe anyone any apologies!"

Father hovered there for a few more seconds.

"What do you think you are playing at? You think you're going to stay in your room forever?"

I shrugged.

I figured, monkey see, monkey do. He had already proven himself recently in the silent treatment department. If he could play that game, so could I.

***

Early this morning, I got up on my own. Dressed. Poured my own cereal and orange juice. Packed my own lunch.

Before leaving, I placed the manilla envelope on the breakfast table. It held Father's research at the Victoria University archives and all the relevant treaties, maps and land claims Father discussed at New Credit with Chief Fred. That was a hint that he should take it with him to Ottawa.

I left the house half an hour early. I had to ride to Becky's first to drop off my bike. I had to leave enough time for us to walk to school from her place.

"See you with Mrs. Molnar after school!" Mother called to me as I was opening the front door, "I'll have your overnight bag packed for you by then!"

I didn't say a word, kept my back to her, turned my head away while closing the door.

It isn't that I'm not grateful, but I'm mad because I'm supposed to be. It keeps me beholden to her.

I've been so fed up with Mother expecting me, without any consideration, to go traipsing around, following through on plans she makes for me. No consultation. Just: this is what you're doing. And that's that.

Then when I start making my own friends, she invites herself along on plans I made all on my own. Way back, when Mrs. Molnar suggested this trip, I thought it was a great idea. I wanted to go into Toronto with Becky and Mrs. Molnar. I wouldn't mind going to Toronto even now, if I wasn't so furious with Mother for horning in—and if I didn't have so much homework—as well as practicing to do. Lots of it.

Mother doesn't understand. Father doesn't either. They think you just pick up an instrument and it plays itself, like a player piano. They don't get that pieces of music, especially serious ones like the

Doppler, cannot be played mechanically. They think practicing is all about hitting the right notes, and keeping the beat without blundering. Playing an advanced piece is not the same as playing the bass drum in a brass band to a straight 4/4 rhythm.

This is how Mr. Maxwell explained the Doppler at one of our after-hours practice sessions: "This piece," he said, "Requires considerable technical skill. However, proficiency is but the beginning. It is not enough just to be able to play every note, if the end result sounds robotic. Mind, it is essential to have the tools at hand so you are equipped to go one major notch further without being hampered by any mechanical difficulty. Once you have acquired those essential tools, you must become deeply acquainted with the music itself. True musical expression occurs when you achieve the inner balance of mind and spirit to free up your sensibility and allow it to express itself—like a butterfly emerging from its chrysalis, and then effortlessly floating out to fill the air!"

Such a beautiful image! I thought at the time: I can only hope to acquire the technical skills plus musical expression by recital time to make that happen!

Mr. Maxwell seems to believe I have the talent to pull this off. Becky seems to believe in me as well. I have grave doubts. From the outset, I have been terribly worried about the technical demands the Doppler makes on me, not so much in the Andante but especially in the Rondo section. As for musical expression, well, that is something new to me. It means not only knowing the music, but expressing it. Worse, I don't know if I can hold up this bruised right arm of mine, let alone breathe through this swollen, bruised nose.

I could just cry.

Flute Lesson at the RCM
9-2

October 21, 1957

Mrs. Molnar is a terrific tour guide. She deliberately chooses to drive into downtown Toronto along Lawrence Avenue, south on Avenue Road, and then jog through Forest Hill, so we can see Casa Loma.

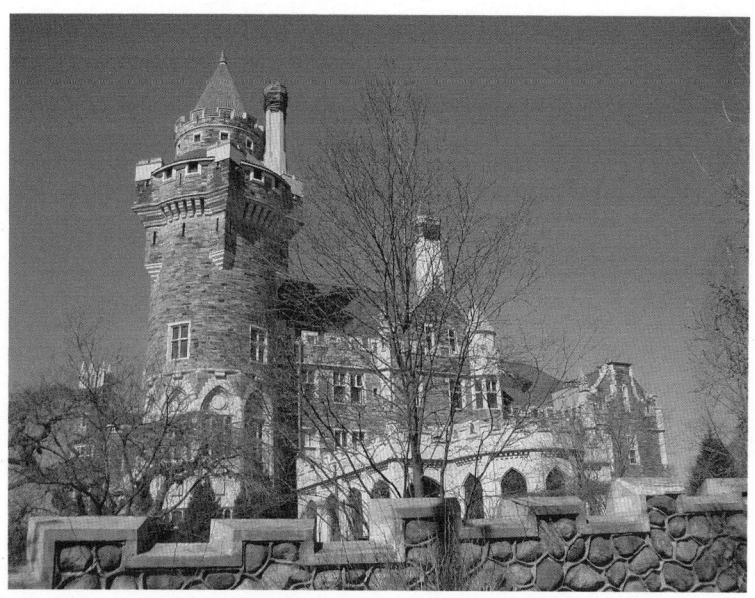

Casa Loma, Toronto, Ontario

I have never seen a real-live castle before. Mother has seen castles in Great Britain, but has no idea there is one right here in Toronto. It is Mrs. Molnar who had come all the way from Hungary who discovered it, and relates its history to us.

She tells us that Casa Loma was never intended to be a real fort, like Fort York. It was built long after the War of 1812 by a self-made Toronto millionaire, a Sir Henry Pellatt, who made his fortune from

343

building the first privately established electric company in Toronto. He built the castle for his wife Mary. He went bankrupt due to his extravagant furnishings after living in the castle for only ten years, and his wife died shortly thereafter.

Mother says, "I can guess what happened. When his wife Mary learned that her husband was daft enough to blow his whole fortune on a blinking castle, she probably shot him with a *pellet* gun!"

I'm the only one who 'gets' it, but refuse to humour her with a laugh.

Mrs. Molnar says you can't fault a man for trying to realize his dreams.

"There's no reward for dreams that are pie-in-the-sky," Mother replies.

I think about Father and the Arrow. Were his dreams also "pie-in-the-sky"?

***

Becky's flute lessons take place at the Royal Conservatory of Music, which is located on Bloor Street at the north end of the University's campus.

Royal Conservatory of Music Building, Bloor Street, Toronto

To get there, we have to park on a narrow street off Bloor called Devonshire Place. We walk along a wide sidewalk under a long row of columns that support the seats overhead for Varsity Stadium. This takes us up to Bloor Street. Then we turn east to walk as far as the Conservatory.

It is an aging red brick building. Its stones are seamed with soot, most likely accumulated since the industrial age. Its grime looks the same as the old factories on the outskirts of Unionville, my childhood town, although I don't see any railway tracks nearby to account for it.

We climb up the old, foot-worn stone steps, and enter through idark-stained swinging doors to the entrance hall with its flag-stoned floor. It has a very solemn air inside, more funereal than academic. I surmise that playing music is very serious business here!

We leave Becky on her own to climb a few flights up the narrow, winding staircase to the left as far as the lesson rooms on high where she will be meeting her teacher.

When we leave the building, I am happy to escape the fusty air.

Directly adjacent to the Conservatory is the gateway to Philosopher's Walk. It turns out that the Walk is not swarming as I had imagined with sage old men strolling about in togas and sandals, stroking their long grey beards while ruminating on a philosophical syllogism or two. On the contrary. There is not a soul in sight. The "Walk" is a long, wide, gently winding paved path leading from Bloor Street through a narrow park into the heart of the University of Toronto campus. It is filled with an assortment of trees that are all changing colour with the season, and up to their ankles in fallen leaves.

A few paces along the path, we come to a park bench surrounded by huge, mature maple trees, their orange leaves catching the light, ablaze with a luminous glow only seen in autumn.

"Isn't it beautiful?" Mother exudes, "If only autumn could last forever! You see many of the leaves have already fallen. How decent of the trees to wait for us to enjoy, before they drop them altogether!"

"Sit! We only have to wait one moment, and then we will hear lesson start!"

There we sit facing the side brick wall of the Conservatory. This is where Mrs. Molnar tells us she likes to sits and listen to the sound of Becky's flute pouring out of one of the small casement windows, way up high from the third storey of the building.

Out of small, latticed windows, most of them propped open, there are the sounds of other lessons going on. A soprano is singing part of an aria over and over again, working on what? Her breathing? Her enunciation? Her articulation? I listen how she modulates her voice when reaching the crest of a crescendo? A clarinet is also busy, methodically working its way up and down two octaves of a scale note by note. There is a piano thundering up the keyboard in progressions of arpeggios, with someone shouting, Count! Count! Count! I think I hear a guitar as well, very gentle in comparison with the other instruments, but what is it doing playing classical music? This strikes me as odd, having only heard guitar-strumming accompaniment to pop songs.

"Yes!" Mrs. Molnar interrupts, "Now you can hear Bo play a few bars, and then the teacher tapping her baton on music stand—hear her? Teacher is humming along and giving instructions. Now we hear Bo's flute starting up again with the teacher's tapping and the counting!"

Sure enough, we can hear the lesson in progress.

Becky is working on a very difficult advanced piece of music in preparation for her "ARCT", which she explained to me will make her an Associate of the Royal Conservatory. After she achieves that level, she will be qualified to teach music herself. The "T" stands for Teacher. We hear some repeated passages from that piece and the teacher's murmured commentary.

Suddenly, miraculously, a familiar passage from the Doppler Flute Duet issues forth, with Becky's flute soft and plaintive, floating towards us, and then fanning out overhead like long combed swirls of cirrus clouds.

Tap, tap, tapping. The flute stops. What follows is a lot of talking.

Becky starts up again and her teacher is shouting out her instructions, bidding her to think about each rest! "Pay attention! There is meaning held inside each rest—a rest is a pause for breath, yes? Now you please start again at beginning of same phrase, while you treat each rest like a comma." Becky resumes playing until she is stopped again. Tap tap tap. "Now I want you to consider tempo which is *andante con espresso* but dynamics change for loudness/softness. Tempo remains same, but sound level modulates from *p*—*pianissimo* down to *pp*—*double pianissmo* and then up with *crescendo* to *forte*! —Is very good!! Go back to start with *pianissimo* then build again to the *crescendo, again to forte*! Loud, soft, loud—Yes, but not the pace!

Tap tap tap. Yes, is difficult not to speed up, the louder you get! But it remains same pace! I ask you now, as you play again, to feel the pulse. Do you sense the mounting urgency—what is this urgency? Play! Tap tap tap I ask you now: What you want to tell us with your song, with your music? What is your interpretation? Tell me why would there be these mounting series of crescendos? Think! You are not the composer of this music, but you are now its interpreter! You know now the source of the music! Do you copy someone else's voice, or do you dare to speak for yourself through your flute? What is your story?"

Her teacher must have come from somewhere else in Europe. Like Mrs Molnar, she speaks with a strong accent, in a strangely fractured English. She doesn't use the progressive verb properly, butchering anything ending with 'ing', and she blunts all words beginning with 'th' to sound it out as a hard 't', like a pick-axe hitting a knot in wood. Or she drops using any article at all. She also indulges in long juicy rolls of her R's, which I envy as my tongue will not cooperate at all in doing that. Amazingly, she has a large vocabulary and her diction is so impeccably clear, I can practically hear her every word, as though she is right here beside me on the park bench. Perhaps sound travels farther through open, elevated windows on clear, calm days such as this.

I don't like how she shouts at Becky while she is playing, but I can appreciate why she does so. I understand that she is calling out to her, cajoling her to "reach inside" herself for the "hidden strength of the music," "the backbone of its structure", discover its "hidden mystery", the secret behind its "continuous flow"! Tap tap tap.

There follows a low-keyed talk. The teacher is quietly explaining something to her, philosophizing about the piece, laying another foundation, perhaps? Something about a key signature signalling the mood, same as a modulation from major to minor key, and how certain passages change the tense, as in in a sentence. I can hear murmurs from Becky, and occasionally her voice piping up like a little bird, a fledgling taking seeds of knowledge from its parent's beak.

The practicing starts up again. "Good! Good! No—Stop!" Tap tap tap. "Again—play! Think Nom-in-a-tive, Co-pu-la, Pre-di-cate, you see? You see? Composer provided everything for you—structure, phrasing, incidentals, all to help you tell story! Is grammar to assist you with musical conversation! Yes, yes! Carry on!"

Tap, tap, tap

"Again!"

Becky stops, asks a question. The teacher answers, "Now we are getting into t' soul of t' music, now you feel t' difference between music learned only by rote and knowing t' music deeply! From t' heart!"

Nominative? Copula? Predicate?

What an odd coincidence, for me to be doing that English grammar exercise only yesterday, and then to hear these words in an entirely different context, with music and not words!

Whether from this distance my ears had betrayed me, whether her teacher was actually saying these words, the notion swept me away, triggered thoughts about likening the whole concept of a piece of music to a piece of writing, of music being just as complex a set of paragraphs with its own grammatical rules as any essay written in words. Now I see it—of course it is! But it has not been so patently obvious until now. After all, I think with a jolt of recognition, works of music and literature are both called compositions for a reason!

I drift off, lost in thought, comparing words strung in a sentence with notes strung in a line of music, trying to draw more parallels, wondering if there is an analogy in the rhythm of writing to the key signature, the time measure, the rests? I find myself asking: Is there a way that the writer controls the pace and the tone in the same way that the composer provides indications for the tempo and sound level, and if so, how? Also, do the commas serve the same purpose as rests, as notations for phrasing, and does the period or full stop signifying the end comparable with the double bar line?

Then I set to wondering: If one regards the Andante as the Nominative and the Rondo as the Predicate, is there something equivalent to the copula verb that serves as the bridge between the Andante and the Rondo? Does the Rondo serve an adjectival purpose? Ever since my exposure to the Doppler, I've wondered what links the first part of the piece to the second part, when the two parts seem to me to be so distinctly different. Is there a basic principle that determines how a "Predicate" is chosen as an appropriate companion for an "Andante"? I mean, surely you can't just compose an Andante and then slap off anything to be attached to it without reason! In this instance, the Rondo does not seem to be at all similar to the Andante. But in the end, it merges with the same central theme to have the same adjectival or descriptive 'flavour' after all.

Turning to writing, say a novel, does the author know from the outset what will tie the entire work together? Is it sheer serendipity how one event follows the other and how the story is resolved, or is the foundation laid from the outset to ensure that the entire composition is knitted together and draws to a satisfying conclusion?

Did Doppler know from the beginning where the Andante was heading, and that a Rondo would follow? Did he deliberately build a 'bridge' to connect the former and the latter by using some kind of musical equivalent to a 'copula?'

And so forth and so on.

Like a fly on the wall, I realize that Mrs. Molnar is asking Mother about me.

"Whatever happened?"

"I don't know, she isn't talking."

"Whyever not?"

"We reprimanded her and she shut down like a trap."

"Good lesson not yet learned: ask first, then reprimand! What you gave her for the blow? She must surely be in pain. You give her aspirin?"

"I gave her an ice pack."

"I tell you, she has glassy eyes—This happened on Saturday? But she still has look as if in shock. She needs sedative. Also, she needs ointment for bruising. I tell you, I show you this, which I always carry with me—" She rustles around in her handbag and draws out a little tube. "It is not from pharmacy. It is from homeopath. But is not drug! Is natural product, called Arnica. Please! You will permit me to administer to her? Apply only a thin coat now and it will relieve her distress, I assure you! And here—" She roots out a little bottle, "We will give her Rescue Remedy right now, right away, okay?"

"Oh, I don't think so!"

"Emily, I know so! The girl must be in shock from such a blow to nose. Shock affects the brain. The brain is not so far from nose not to be affected!"

"You're telling me that our brain knows what our nose knows? Or that our nose knows what our brain knows? Which is it?"

Trust Mother to make light of everything and anything, even when it doesn't warrant levity.

It takes a moment for Mrs. Molnar to comprehend, and then she laughs, "Oh, now you are being silly!"

The Mothers titter.

Mrs. Molnar slips her arm through Mother's, so they sit close and snug, almost like lovers.

Becky once told me that linking arms is a custom of European women. I told her you'd never see two Canadian women—except perhaps middle-aged sisters, or two tottery old women holding each other up—getting along in this way.

I pretend I haven't been listening.

Mother must have given the nod, because suddenly Mrs. Molnar stands up and is bent over me, saying, "Lo-iss, I want that I give you something to relieve pain in nose. This is like liniment. Is for bruising and swelling. I apply just a wee bit. Will smoothe it over entire top of nose."

I let her do her bidding.

"Now you take this. Open your mouth." She sprinkles a few tiny, round, white crystals into her palm. "Lift your tongue. I put these under your tongue. Now close mouth and let them melt."

I can feel them dissolving.

"You rest. We will wait a few moments. Then we take a wee walk down path and back, okay? Relax. Try to breathe deep. Nice fresh air! Then we have a little exercise!"

I nod.

I find myself constructing sentences with copula verbs to describe Becky playing the first passage of the Doppler. When it opens, *the music sounds carefree,* like a bird in summer singing joyfully from a tree. *The air tastes yellow as lemon, smells green as tall pine, is blue as a cornflower.* As the bird lifts its wings and leaves its perch on the branch, the air *turns fresh and crispy.* The bird calls out. Its calls *grow louder*, its *pleas become larger.*

I realize that I had been listening to the Doppler in an entirely different light. I have no idea what was behind the teacher's intent of the lesson itself. But I know that reaching for adjectives to describe the opening passage has shifted my understanding of the work to another indefinable level.

Soon the most delicious music unfurls from on high. Two flutes! The teacher has joined Becky with her own flute, and they are playing the Doppler duet together, working all the way through the Andante, from the first lone call to the antiphonal responses, through the intertwining and cascading, lifting and lilting, rejoining, and then dividing into separate waves that come together again, and then part ways.

On one occasion, the teacher stops on a breath to say: "Two flutes, two voices having discussion, two voices with different opinions— hear them? The first one to speak presents the idea, the second voice rejects it, and then along comes another idea, see? Until difference of opinions is reconciled. Think of this music as a dispute, as a situation where no words will do, where thoughts transcend words and can only be expressed in music. See?"

I am transfixed.

"Come, we walk now," Mrs. Molnar commands, interrupting my reverie.

I stand up and let my body be hauled away. Part of me holds back as long as I can resist. The rest of me follows behind the two mothers, dragging my heels, with Mrs. Molnar talking, talking, talking, pointing to left and to right, her arm still linked with Mother's.

They pause for a spell when Mrs. Molnar says something and Mother puts her hand to her head. I hear her say: "My Lord, I never thought of that! Oh no!!" and Mrs. Molnar is patting her on the forearm, protesting, "No, no, no, of course! Of course! You have been so busy. But I take care of it! Let me do it! I am happy to help in this way!" and Mother is saying: "Dear me! Whatever was I thinking? or NOT thinking?" with Mrs. Molnar replying, "You cannot think of everything! It is OKAY! I do it for both our girls, and all is well!"

As we walk along Philosopher's Walk, we learn about the adjacent buildings. Immediately behind where we were sitting is the back wall of the Royal Ontario Museum. Further along on the left is a large empty space, next followed by a large building on the corner of Hoskin Avenue, the Faculty of Law.

"Bo's teacher tells us of new University Faculty of Music building to be built in that big space, but is still on drawing board. Slated for 1962. Bo will be long graduated from university by then! But she might just be faculty teacher there, so?"

The Trinity College playing field is on our right, we learn, next to the grey stone buildings of the College itself.

Mother feels it seems strange to be given a tour by someone from a faraway country. "My goodness, I have been in Canada much longer than yourself, Eszter. It strikes me as odd that you are the one giving us a tour of Toronto!"

"We only learn about the outside world when we have a purpose," Mrs. Molnar replies.

Taddle Creek
9-3

Lost Rivers map

As we stroll along, to our left I notice a peculiarly artificial dip in the lie-of-the-land running the entire length between the path and the adjacent row of buildings. I need not go much farther for an explanation, as it is handily provided by a plaque that had been erected at the juncture of the Walk with Hoskin Avenue.

'Lost river'

This naturalistic ravine park setting known as Philosopher's Walk was once host to Taddle Creek which over time has become 'lost' to Toronto citizens. Taddle Creek flowed south for approximately 6 km from its source area on the edge of the old Glacial Lake Iroquois shoreline near St. Clair Avenue where it joined the Don River as it entered Toronto harbour near the Distillery District. Water quality was maintained by natural vegetation covering the watershed and aquatic organisms in the stream course. Taddle Creek provided habitat for fish and wildlife and a gathering place for Toronto's early inhabitants, notably the Ojibway and later, the Mississauga.

As a result of the damming of McCaul's Pond to the south, impeding the natural flow of Taddle Creek, and contamination that polluted the river and brought about the risk of typhus and other disease, the creek was buried south of College Street by the 1850s and north of Bloor Street by the 1870's. The old town of York had grown and the surrounding neighbourhoods had intensified, making an underground sanitation and sewage system a priority. The part of Taddle Creek remaining at the surface on University lands was diverted to this subterranean system and buried by 1884. The topography of this ravine remains as a tangible reminder of Taddle Creek, with the dips and valleys defining the original riverbanks and the walkway itself following much the same path as the 'lost river'.

We three stand together while Mother reads the entire contents out loud.

Rage pours into my brain. I blurt,

"Mother, this is one of the creeks Chief Peter Jones was fighting for! His tribe was one of the Ojibway! Chief Fred himself told us about this. There were at least sixteen streams and rivulets that travelled through Toronto and poured into Lake Ontario. I know! I saw the old maps, I remember! Chief Fred mentioned Taddle Creek and Philosopher's Walk to us when we were there!"

"When we were where? What are you talking about, dear?" she says, looking at me with warning daggers in her eyes, "Chief Fred? Who is that?"

"You know full well who he is! Chief Fred King! At the First Nations New Credit Reserve! He spoke to us of how the settlers took away their fishing and hunting rights even though promised to them in their own Magna Carta."

"Magna Carta?" Mother says, tossing her hand in the air, "I hardly think the British were around here in 1215!"

I cry out: "King George III signed the Indians their own Magna Carta in 1763. There were later treaties, which guaranteed them access to their lands and rivers, and forbade the white settlers from driving them off. So *this* is how the Indians were cheated of their rights! They *buried* their rivers and streams! That's disgusting!"

"Well, not all of them. There is still the Humber and the Don and the Etobicoke left. And some others," is Mother's retort.

"How *can* you be so—so—*blasé* about this, Mother, especially after hearing the truth from a real live Mississauga Chief! I thought you *sympathized* with him. I hope when you tell Father where we were today, he will take this more to heart! I hope he's more serious than you sound, about taking the issue of the land claim to the Governor General when you go to Ottawa tomorrow, that's all I can say!"

Mrs. Molnar is looking from one of us to the other as though in a complete fog.

"I have no idea what she is going on about," Mother says to her.

Then something strikes me like a lightning bolt:

"You know what, Mother? All the flooding that happened during Hurricane Hazel— They said it was due to the heavy downpour of rain. They didn't mention the sixteen creeks that are buried underneath Toronto. You know what I think, Mother? I think the creeks backed up and rebelled, that's what they did. They saw an opportunity to get back at people who came to this land and did not respect it, who had the gall to rearrange things to their own liking, who didn't care one whit for the people who lived here before them OR for all the nature that they so wickedly destroyed! Imagine burying all those creeks and streams, and polluting them, and turning them into sewers!

"I am so disgusted, Mother, that I hope there's another almighty great flood that will get back at EVERYONE who thinks they can get away with this! I hope whoever is responsible for this—this— travesty— all drown and get swept away into Lake Ontario by old, bursting, rebellious sewer pipes!"

Mother commands, "Lois, get a grip on yourself. Right now."

"I hate it! I really do! I don't want any part of a world that is so crass and cruel!"

I am choking back tears, gulping and swallowing sobs as I speak.

I have had my say.

Then I start to cry.

Then my nose starts to bleed.

"Lois! See what you've done!" Mother says, sternly.

Mrs. Molnar reaches into her bag for a handkerchief, and says: "That is sign of girl still in shock."

"Nonsense!"

I start to walk away from them, back up the path toward the Conservatory building, pressing the handkerchief against each nostril.

"You get right back here and apologize to Mrs. Molnar, Lois!"

"No. No. You let her go. The girl speaks her truth. And acts on it."

I keep on going. I hope I will find Becky at the main door, waiting for us. Surely she will finally be finished with her class by now. If not, I will wait for her there.

***

We pile back in the car on Devonshire Place and drive down Yonge Street, where a parking space is found close to Diana Sweets.

In the restaurant, Mother chats chirpily with Mrs. Molnar.

Becky and I sit side by side across from them. Becky seems 'spacey'. I feel drained.

"You played magnificently, Becky, you really did!" I tell Becky.

"Did you hear teacher Mrs. Boyko playing your part for the Duo?"

"Yes, I did! It was beautiful! Perhaps we should get her to do the same for Thursday, eh?"

"Oh no, you'll do fine!"—after a long pause, adding: "*Won't* you?"

"Pray for miracles, Becky! At least we have two full nights to practice together!"

Becky nods, trying not to look glum.

"Your teacher, was she shouting 'Copula" at you? I'm sure I heard her coaxing you with 'Nominative', 'Predicate' and then 'Copula, Copula!'"

Becky looks thoughtful.

"Sometimes it is difficult for a Polish lady and a Hungarian girl to communicate well with English as the common language. To be truthful, I am not quite sure at times what she is meaning! It is often only when demonstrating on flute that I 'get her', if that is correct way to say?

"Once, she stopped my playing and asked me how I would define music. I said music was made of many notes put together, but she talked further about what is *real* music. She talked about the use of notes in a string to make a melody."

"Melody! Of course! What good is music without melody!"

This sets me back somewhat. How could I have overlooked this important ingredient? A piece of music must have a melody. So how does that compare with what a piece of writing must have? A melody is a theme. Writing has themes. Of course! It is the theme that ties both musical and writing compositions together.

"But what could she be saying when she called out 'copula'?"

"I do not know at what time in lesson to what you are referring," Becky replies, "Perhaps you refer later on when she was describing how two separate lines of music seem to function independently until eventually they come together. Whether apart or united, they do so through harmony. When the two lines do come together, it seems as though they merge. It is at that point they resolve into the cadence. She then pointed to end of the Rondo and the repeated 'Cadence'. Could that be it? She adds many syllables to some ordinary words."

."A cadence?" I ask, "The word hardly sounds like 'copula'."

"For meaning, Mrs. Boyko asked me to think of how to join two ribbons to make a bow. Like a bow, the cadence ties the two lines together."

"So it's the cadence in music that serves the same purpose as the copula verb in a sentence! One ribbon is the nominative and the other ribbon is the predicate? And the copula links them together! The cadence is the link!"

Becky indicates with a shrug that she doesn't know.

"All I know is, she asked me to notice in a descant how the lower line sings longer, more sustained notes and the upper line sings rapidly strung-together notes. She asked me to pay attention to the spaces that widened and narrowed between the two lines, as that was critical, to best express the music."

"What does all that have to do with the nominative and the predicate, let alone the copula verb?"

"Only heaven knows, Lois!" Becky laughs kindly, "I think you're stuck way back in grammar homework, and have copulas like worms wriggling about in your brain!"

This makes me laugh. Correction: snort. Oh, my nose is so sore, with nostrils now caked way up inside with blood from the latest nosebleed. Nonetheless, she is right. And she makes giggle.

Laughter feels good. Like a tonic. Like a salve. Like a poultice.

It is getting to be sundown when we head back to Centrewood.

"We take different route home. We go new way, now new interchange of highway is open," Mrs. Molnar says. She asks if we would mind. If it is faster—and it should be faster—this is how she will drive to and from Toronto for the lessons at the RCM from now on. She hadn't wanted to explore it on her own, in case she missed the turnoff. But if she gets lost today, we can all get lost together.

"Please don't," Mother urges.

We are on an expressway, but it isn't until I see the sign for the Weston Road turnoff that I realize where we are, and where we are going.

We drive under the big double bridge where Mitsy and I had stopped above on our bikes only two days ago, then up the off-ramp to the stop-lights which had turned red. They hold us back until we can turn left onto Weston Road and head north.

"This extension to the 401 just opened last week!" Mother says, "At long last! Graham is thrilled! He can finally get to work faster!"

We come in via the highway onto the Main Artery and drop Mother off at the house.

Father's car is not there. He has gone to a meeting with Mr. Smye and the Avro team, preparing for the Ottawa session. I hope he has had time to prepare for a meeting with the Minister of Indian Affairs.

Mother comes back out with my knapsack. I wind down my car window, and toss the bag between Becky and myself. Mother bends over to say goodbye. Her arms reach in. I feel them wrapping around my shoulders, then her hands cupping my face.

She says:

"You be good now! Buckle down! Mind your manners! Practice hard!"

"Mnff," I snort.

"Give me a kiss goodbye, Lois, I won't see you until Thursday! We'll be home by supper with lots of time before your recital! Shall I say goodbye to your Father for you?"

I shrug and fold my arms.

She leans in closer and her voice turns harsh as she whispers in my ear: "You mind that we have told NO ONE about our visit to see Chief Fred OR about your Chief Peter Jones! Not a word about it, you understand?"

"I'm sick and tired of secrets, Mother," I reply.

"Nonetheless, it is Father's orders!"

"Well," I pronounce loudly, "You tell him he'd better help Chief Fred and Chief Peter Jones while he is in Ottawa, or his stupid orders will mean nothing to me!"

Mother withdraws and begins to turn away.

"Oh and Mother, just in case HE has forgotten, remind him with these two words--" I yell at her:

"TEN SHILLINGS!"

"Lois!"

"I'm not your puppet, Mother. Not any more!"

Ten shillings

Mrs. Molnar drives us out to the highway the way we came in, because she needs to fill up at the gas station farther down the highway. When we return to Becky's, we take a concession road that approaches Centrewood from the opposite direction.

Hospice
9-4

Monday evening, October 21, 1957

I have had a hot bath steeped in a fragrance that Mrs. Molnar called 'essential oil of lavender'. It is meant to soothe and relax me, and has certainly achieved its purpose, for now I am feeling all rubbery inside and out. I am wearing my favourite three-piece baby-blue baby dolls, which are light cotton, and cool to the skin.

Mrs. Molnar applies an ice-cold poultice of grated potato skin on the big black-and-blue bruise on my upper arm. Then she wraps the whole works in gauze which she tapes to my arm at one end, and splits lengthwise at the other end, tying off in a knot. She is now applying more potato poultice across the bridge of my nose with white surgical tape.

"I've never heard of a potato poultice!"

"Is old European remedy. Are many uses for potato! Boils, sprains, spider bites!"

"I always thought potatoes were just food—boiled, baked, fried, mashed or roasted. But not smushed up raw and used for cures!"

"Only potato skin itself is used as medication. You see, you can heal with potato, and eat the rest, too!"

"Not like cake," I reply, "You can't have your cake and eat it, too!"

Becky is in attendance. She smiles and asks, "Perhaps the icing is the skin? In my opinion, is best to eat both!"

"Both icing and cake? I'm with you, there!" I say.

I ask her: "Do you know where potatoes grow?"

She shakes her head no.

"In the heels of worn-out socks!"

Becky thinks about this for a moment, and then bursts out laughing. Mrs. Molnar does not.

Ignoring my attempt to be pleasant company despite my mood, Mrs. Molnar says solemnly, "Cold potato poultice draws heat out of soreness. When it gets warm, we put back in freezer compartment, then take out and apply again! We do this till your bedtime!"

"Mrs. Molnar, Becky and I have to practice! But first, she and I, we need to talk! From what I learned today, listening to Becky and her teacher play, I have an idea how the piece should be played!"

"Ah, you have new inspiration for the music? Even listening from afar on park bench?"

"Oh yes, listening to the Doppler played by two professionals was inspirational, it truly was!"

"Professionals! You mean me?" Becky muses. "Hardly!"

We have set up our flutes and music stands in the kitchen, where Mrs. Molnar can come in from the living room, and tend to me while we have our talk and then play. She promises she will not disturb us, she will just tiptoe in and out, so we can do our work.

As soon as we are all set and ready to go, I look at Becky and say:

"You know what, Becky? This piece, I don't think I understood it until now!"

"What do you mean?"

"We are playing the notes but do either of us really know what the music means? During your lesson, I heard your teacher calling out: What is your story? What story do you try to tell with your flute? Do you remember her saying that?"

Becky looks doleful, "Yes, I do! Her story is that two people are arguing or what did she say: 'discussing'. To her, the discussion goes on until difference in opinion is resolved."

"I don't like that interpretation, do you?"

"No, it is too heavy for the lightness of the music."

"Exactly!"

"So?"

"Well, I didn't realize that I had a story in mind all along. Whenever practicing, I've imagined the setting for the piece as taking place on a bright and sunny summer's day down by the stream. It is very peaceful and calm. There are two 'common yellow-throat warblers' flitting through the trees, dipping in and out of the dense foliage, suddenly soaring up high and doing cartwheels in the air.

"Whenever one bird lands on a treetop and the other can't see where the other one went, it calls out:

wichety-wichety-wichety!

Becky bellows out a laugh. "You are a very good birdsong maker!"

"In response, the other bird calls out and they keep calling to each other until they find each other again!"

"But what is this—this common yellow t'roat worry-bler?"

"War-bler. It is a tiny bird with yellow feathers and a black mask that sings its heart out, warbling. There were oodles of them in the marsh down by Willow Creek this summer!"

"Oodles? What is that?"

"It means a whole lot of something—But here I am now defining 'oodles' when I have something pressing to say!"

"Sorry— Why is this called a warbler? Sounds like something that 'wobbles'?"

"No, but its voice does. A warbler is a songbird with a voice that wobbles!"

"Lois, I know only one kind of little birds that talk to each other. Mine are chubby little brown birds with black cap and black bib that I see hopping about in back garden."

"You must mean the chickadees? They are named after their call. When they are talking to each other, they repeatedly say:

chicka-dee-dee-dee"

"Yes! Oh, very good reproduction!" she admires, "I vow they seem to chit-chat with each other while pecking around on ground!"

"I think they do that call to keep tabs on one another because as soon as their chief scout gives a warning signal, they all take off as one and fly away together!"

"That is so true!"

I thought: Here I am, having a conversation about birds with a friend! Is this a first or what? Had I died and gone to heaven!?

I am so pleased, I am 'tickled pink', as Mother would say.

"What I propose is that we start off playing the Andante with our two birds in mind, either with my yellowthroats, or with your chickadees, no matter."

"Forget the chickadees—They are very cute, but too chubby for the job, I like better your yellow warbler-birds for this music—I picture them light and graceful as they flit about!"

"Great! But before we play, I have more to say, okay? Can we look at the music first?"

Becky nods.

"After the preamble, are we agreed that it is your flute says that says Hello, hello are you there. And my flute answers, Yes! I'm over here. And then the two little birds start flying about. Eventually they find each other, they celebrate together, singing and swooping and diving, sweeping up into the air, taking playful nose-dives then soaring once more high into the heavens. But—" and then I stop.

I eye her sheepishly, anxiously hang-doggish.

"But what, Lois? Tell me what you see now!"

"Well, here's the thing: After listening to you and your teacher play this piece together, I realized that it all starts off with that image I just described, but it doesn't end up that way! Instead, through various stages which I suppose are the variations, I have to say that in the end, the overall feeling is not one of exhilaration and happiness. May I tell what I think this might be all about?"

"Yes, of course!"

"May I begin all over again? I think it starts out with the two birds together, they go off and they are playing together, flying and flitting about, doing aerial gymnastics and zooming from tree to tree, and they celebrating, true, but almost immediately, I'm sure you've noticed this? there is a darker tone. It is almost as though a cloud passes over the sun. The pitch of joy and excitement is replaced by a brooding mood that builds in stages. The first time, there is a sounding of alarm, followed by a sense of urgency, which intensifies until it reaches a pitch close to panic before it subsides! That occurs at the first set of crescendos in the Andante. Each time the main melody sounds, the mood invades and there is greater tension in the air.

"Becky, if we can identify when the melody surfaces with this brooding undercurrent, and then understand the following stages where the alarm sounds and it gets more pressing, we will have cracked it!"

"Cracked it?"

"We will have broken through! Solved the mystery! Found the way to tie the entire piece together! You see, I'm thinking that there is a progression of moods that ranges at first from exuberance and celebration, but slowly there is a sense of denial, then dread, loss, then longing. Becky, I can't quite put my finger on it, but I think this music is not just about the joy of friends reuniting, it is also about sadness and loss—it starts out with longing but it ends with anxiety, with the fear of losing the friend again! After all, if it happened once, why not twice? You see what I mean?"

I feel horribly nervous. Frightened even. I look down and away.

Becky has fallen silent.

I am afraid to look at her.

Finally, I force myself to look at her.

Becky's face has turned white, pale, almost as fragile and transparent as porcelain.

"Becky?"

Becky's soft deep dark-brown eyes plunge into my heart.

"You think I'm being a goofball?" I stammer.

"No, no, Lois, not at all!"

"I just feel so certain about this!"

"You are correct."

More silence.

"Teacher Boyko was also correct. But I did not want to tell her my story through my flute."

"Why not?"

"Is too painful. I am not comfortable to express my feelings with teacher. I do not know her well enough."

"Well enough how?"

"To entrust to her."

We sit together without saying a word.

Mrs. Molnar calls out: "What is it that is happening? I hear no music! I hear no work going on!"

"Leave us, Mama, we are working, just a different kind of work!"

"There is something else, Becky!"

"What is that then?"

"The tempo, the pace. I think Mr. Maxwell set us off on the wrong track!"

"How so?"

"His interpretation of 'Andante' is too chipper, too upbeat. He directed us to start off playing jauntily, like a rowboat rocking. Well, I looked up the definition of 'andante' in the music dictionary, which says: 'walking pace'.

"You see, I was listening closely when you and your teacher were playing the duet together. Sure, it is quite possible that your teacher set the tempo the way she did because you were practicing. But Becky, I think it was the right tempo!

"This is how I see it! It should begin with a gentle lilt, like a soft breeze lifting the willows. It should be like water caught in an eddy along the shoreline, quietly lapping against the sand. It should start off calm, the tempo evenly paced, so that the melody has a chance to be truly lyrical!"

Becky nods at me. She is looking at me with a different cast in her eye, as though in a new light.

"Very good! I agree. Let us start now. We shall play Andante that way, and we shall look for times when melody surfaces, see if also increase of stages as you described—"

She puts her flute into position, and by lifting her elbows up and down, establishes the 4/4 beat with a tempo long, steady and measured.

I couldn't express the relief if I tried.

The bridge of my nose hurts like the dickens, my rebellious dry nostrils start taking in air, I fill my lungs and lower lungs to capacity, set my lower lip over the embouchure hole of my flute, and just when Becky began the lead part, I say:

"I feel like that butterfly, Becky, emerging from my chrysalis!"

After we reach the end, we put our flutes down and stare at each other.

"Let's talk more about the Rondo," Becky ventures.

"Okay."

"I think Mr. Maxwell started us off on the wrong foot with it as well!"

"How do you mean?"

"He said a Rondo was a gypsy jig, and that explained the lop-sided rhythm!"

"Well, there is Irish jig and American jig. But I think he did not know word for European-style jig, one type of which would be the 'Czardas', which is really Hungarian folk dance!"

"What's that, a shard-ass?"

"No, no, iss pronounced like this: 'char'dash'!"

"Spell it."

Becky does so.

"Say it again, please?"

"Char-dash."

I try again. Becky shakes her head.

"Golly, it still sounds like Shard Ass to me!" I say.

We laugh. We don't know why exactly. Except it sounds rude.

"Okay, so! How is it different from a jig—As though I would know!"

"Jig is played very fast. But Czardas? It is true that Roma gypsies made this dance popular, but it came from Hungarian music played in taverns—what you call 'pubs'? It has structure and conventional rhythms, usually in 4/4 then 2/2 time! It starts out slowly then tempo speeds up!"

"Why, that is our piece!"

"Yes, it is. I not say anything to Mr. Maxwell. For our purpose, it makes no difference!"

"But it does! Well, it makes a difference to me because you are saying a 'Shard-ass' starts out slowly!"

Becky frowns, but lets my deliberately bad pronunciation go.

"Yes, compared with Mr. Maxwell's instruction, yes!"

"Listen, can 'Rondo' also mean the same as a 'round'? You know the song 'Row, row row your boat? That is sung 'in a round.'

I demonstrate to her by singing the first two lines then making her join in from the start.

"To me, when the second flute leaps in, it is singing a round to the first flute's song!"

"Yes, I see! You mean, each time the melody or refrain appears, the two flutes play it like a round! Very good, Lois!"

"But what is all the stuff in between each refrain?"

"I would say that the Rondo is entirely separate piece of music, but the 'stuff' is variations of melody from the Andante that keep on turning up!"

"You think the Rondo is a set of variations on the melody or refrain established in the Andante?"

"Yes."

"That clinches it. The Rondo is the 'adjectival' predicate following the cadence-copula link!"

Poor Becky. It is clear that she was not in my mind while I was doing my grammar homework, and was not sitting on the bench with me while my thoughts about the copula vis-à-vis the Doppler were percolating.

To her relief, I switch topics.

"This Hungarian 'Shard'ass'. Does it always have a rhythm that sounds like someone dancing a jig with a peg leg?"

"In the 'czardas', all dancers are doing same steps in what you say? a syncopated rhythm and as they dance, there is extremely increased tempo until it seems like total frenetic madness takes over! But with the Doppler, it is different. There is that idyllic scene! I see now that despite the attempts to take over tempo and go faster, that the same melody surfaces as before!"

"Yes, the lyrical passages resurface!"

"Shall we try the Rondo now?"

"Not quite yet, Lois. Now it is myself that has something to say. I need to add to our discussion that some czardas are round dances that usually include a 'grand chain' where all dancers form a big circle, men on outside, ladies on inside, then when music starts they must swing 'loop the loop' in opposite directions left, right, left, right—and when the music stops, they must dance with that dancing partner with whom they last swung!"

"So with every round, they ended up with a new partner?"

"Exactly."

"Shall we practice the Rondo now?"

"No. First we will ask Mama to bring dessert. Then I will tell my story."

It is late. Becky has told her story.

I see how she couldn't really share it with just anyone, because she was very proud, and would have needed to control her emotions with a stranger.

She did not want to cry in front of her teacher.

By the time she has finished, she has tears rolling down her cheeks.

"This time we play Andante and Rondo together as one whole continuing piece of music!" Becky orders.

Once more we lift our flutes and play.

When we finish, we fall into each other's arms.

"We did it! We found it! We're ready!" Becky cries, "Let's see if we can do it again!"

But Mrs. Molnar 's voice says: "Enough!"

She startles us with her presence.

"I sit outside kitchen door to listen."

Her eyes are filled with tears.

"I weep for your talent! I hear you improve by leaps and bounds! You both play so beautifully together, I am so proud of you both!"

The poultices are removed.

A long, rubbery, spiky stalk from a house plant called 'aloe vera' is slit down its shaft by a paring knife, and the gooey juices are applied gently to my upper arm and nose.

"I wrap arm loose with gauze then tape it down so it doesn't stick to sheet. But nose, that I cannot do. You try to sleep on back, okay?"

"As far as I can remember from last night, Mrs. Molnar, that's the only way I can breathe when lying down!"

She chuckles.

Mrs. Molnar leads the way upstairs. Becky and I clamber after her.

"There's something else Mr. Maxwell told us that is not true, Becky!"

"What is that, then?"

"Doppler was not Hungarian, he was Polish!"

"So, so," Becky replies, "When he was born, it was in Poland. After Hitler, it became Ukraine. Then he lived long time in Vienna, Austria. Later, for a very long time in Budapest. All were part of Austro-Hungarian Empire. He helped found Hungarian Philharmonic Orchestra and wrote five or six Hungarian operas. So to me, and all Hungarians, he was Hungarian enough!"

"Well, that's that then!" I respond, laughing.

Once again, I have been given my own room. This time, the window is open. A light breeze sifts the light, white cotton curtains up and down ever so gently.

The sheets are fresh and smell sweet from having been hung in the fresh air to dry, which is Mrs. Molnar's wont. She has a dryer but prefers to use the clothesline when the weather is fair.

The bedside table lamp is the last to be turned off.

Mrs. Molnar bends over and kisses me on my forehead.

She tucks the pillow under my head so it supports my neck.

"I am as soft and smooth all over as cream cheese, and I smell like a delicious garden!" I say to her, "Thank you!"

She chuckles.

"Lavender help! You sleep well, okay?"

I can hear her say good night to Becky, "Good night, *Edes angyal!*"

That is Mrs. Molnar's term of endearment, which Becky says means 'Darling Angel' in English.

"Good night, Mama!"

"I leave door open a bit, in case Lo-iss needs help, okay?"

"Yes, Mama!"

There is the sound of her footfall on the stairs as she heads back down.

Across the way, Becky waits until her Mother has gone downstairs. Then she calls out:

"Good night, Doppler!"

And I call back:

"Good night, Double Doppler!"

We giggle and that's all I remember.

Darling Angel
9-5

My story is one of separation, sadness, longing and loss. Always, since earliest time of my life in Budapest, there has been change. With change came most often great distress, tension, danger.

Sometimes came relief, sometimes celebration, more often than not, hard blows. And loss.

You shared with me your Father's theory of the building blocks, his admiration of geometric forms, his reverence for the stability of the circle and his advice about triangles which are prone to falling apart. My life has been one of many triangles that formed, broke apart, then became new triangles.

Mama, Papa, Bo.

Bo, Auntie Szofia and Uncle Tamas.

Bo, Mama and Grandpa Gyorgy.

First was my life so happy with Papa and Mama in the big house in Budapest. I knew love of two devoted parents back then. They loved me and adored me. We three were always together, at least in my memory.

They called me their 'Edes Angyal' which means in Hungarian 'Darling Angel' and would gather me up in their arms, would kiss me and hug me tight. They loved how I would chortle with delight. I would bask in their love.

I learned too how special is the family circle, which bound all of us together. Always in background there was my mother's sister Aunt Szofia and her husband, Uncle Tamas, who loved me as their own.

Also in background there were my grandparents. There was my father's father, my Grandfather Gyorgy Molnar and Grandmother Borka. They left for Canada in 1944 when I was only one year old, but I felt the gap and how my entire family missed them.

There was my mother's father, my Grandfather Mihaly Nemeth and Grandmother Cathalin. I remember them clearly even though they died when I was two years old in warehouse fire during 1945 Siege of Budapest. I remember crying and crying for them. I felt my Mama's pain to lose her own Mama and Papa.

By the time I was ten years old, only my aunt and uncle were left with us in Budapest. It was 1953 and again, Hungary found itself in great danger with threat of Communism. Papa and Mama feared for my safety so they sent me with Aunt Szofia and Uncle Tamas to Canada, to be with Uncle Gyorgy and Grandmother Borka. So then it was Bo without Mama or Papa.

In 1956, on edge of Revolution, Mama came alone to Canada. She came on Papa's orders. So then it was Boglarka and Mama—with Aunt and Uncle and Grandfather Gyorgy—but no Papa. But then in same year 1956, my aunt and uncle returned to Hungary to find Papa.

Now was left Boglarka and Mama and Grandfather until this past May when Grandfather Gyorgy died.

This month of October we learn that Uncle Tamas had died.

Now, it is only Mama and Boglarka left in Canada. For where is Papa and Auntie, we do not know. We are alone.

That is bare bones of my story.

It is a story of uncertainty, confusion and loss.

Every time there was happiness, sorrow was soon to follow.

I miss my Papa. Mama misses him, too.

Mama says that I must live my life fully, whether I know where Papa is or not, whether he is alive or not. For otherwise, I would be wasting my precious life in waiting for word of him.

I try hard to follow her advice. But I confess that despite my best efforts, I often feel as though I am holding my breath.

Now I tell you my interpretation for this piece of music which we are bound to play very soon, but is not too late for review and revision!

Yes! I like the image of two yellow birds with black masks calling out to each other, and that they are of a species that flocks and forages together.

I see how one is left on its own, perched on a fragile willow branch. It wonders where the others have gone. It calls out, saying, Oh dear, I wonder where everyone went, is anyone there? To me, this bird's song begins first with the fear of abandonment, and dread of loss! Then when there is a response from another bird followed by reunion, there is joyful celebration.

This is what I want to note:

Despite the joy, there is a sorrowful tone of reflection throughout the main melody or refrain, for the bird is cautious, from having tasted loss before!

Each refrain expresses loss, fear, expectation and longing in the midst of celebration.

I have hinted, but now I will ask you forthright: what if each time there is played the refrain, it is a different bird that lands on the branch? That would be true to my own story, which I have just told you. Every time I turned around, I was being minded by someone different. Every time that happened, I would cry out for the one gone missing. I would get used to new situation, only for another change to come along.

To me, the refrain becomes a description of what happens over time in one's soul, when sorrow of separation strikes again and again. To be rejoined then parted. To know how it is to find love again then suffer loss once more!

I suggest to you now that by the time the music comes to conclusion, the birds do not only sing in joy as much as they sing in lament.

Divine Retribution
9-6

Tuesday, October 22, 1957

Bert is waiting for me behind the lockers. He leaps out and pounces at me, fists clenched.

"Dukes up!" he cries.

"What the—?! What are you doing?!"

"Back off! puff puff I am the bearer of good news! puff puff!"

He hops from one foot to the other, takes imaginary punches in the air.

"What am I doing? puff puff I am your next contender! There's the bell to start Round Two! Watch out, Sanderfield! Not so hasty! Plan your next attack!"

He jogs in one spot, eyeing me, "Hm! If I want to knock her out, I can't just look at her! Boof! Boof!" he pokes at me playfully with his fists, as though I'm his sparring partner. "He's making his move, he's jabbing at the undercut, trying to bring his left hook upstairs! He's finding it difficult to throw, has to get in closer, pity I have only my hands to block!"

"Watch my shoulder, my arm!" I beg.

He stands back, apprises himself of my nose and arm. "Learned your lesson, Michelsen, or are you still cruisin' for a bruisin'?" he laughs.

"So what's your good news?" I ask.

"We-e-e-e-llllll, it turns out that Mitsy has not only one doozer of a shiner, she has a 'posterior dislocation of the TMJ' —otherwise known as the temporomandicular joint—a condition which is commonly called a dislocated jaw!" He leaps at me again with his 'dukes up', then he pretends to pant heavily while running on the spot. "I ought'er know better, every time I land one punch, I get two back!"

"So tell me more!"

"Well, her Royal Doulton Highness arrived for band practice this morning, but was in so much pain —she couldn't open her mouth to even put her saxophone in place, let alone blow into it —that she was sent off to the Pacifier's office" (that's the nurse's nickname) "Who couldn't work on the problem alone. Who summoned Colonel Strebig, what with his military experience in the field and all. Transpired that neither of them together could make the adjustment. Which involved two parties putting their thumbs into the mouth at both sides of the jaw and simultaneously pulling down then pushing, or is it the other way around? I forget! She almost bit the nurse's thumb off! Principal Beamish was summoned. Who sent her off to Butch (the gym teacher) with the Colonel—and because he had a class but she had a spare, Butch herself is taking her to hospital emergency! Apparently, the condition is such that it requires medical intervention, meaning, a sedative of some sort, to relax the jaw before it can be manipulated!"

"Wow! That is news all right!"

"Good news, right? To me, it serves her right. Fate is getting back at her for being such a royal nuisance. Yes, that is what she is!"

"I didn't mean to hurt her. But I'm not sorry. Not yet. She has been a thorn in my side ever since school began. Nevertheless, the score is even!"

"I like the way you're taking it! I do not detect compassion or regret! It means she has less of a hold on you. And that's good!"

"Sez who?"

"Sez me. Lois, I suggest you don't have anything more to do with her. She's bad news! Recently, word has it she's been seen hanging out with a couple of hoods from Weston. Apparently, she used to be part of their gang, one of their "molls". Remember that pickup truck we saw after the Teaserama at the Big Culvert, hauling away her props? Yes, those jerks! They shouldn't be coming near her, they are a lot older than her, and she is still underage, but just begging for trouble!"

Didn't I know *exactly* who Bert was talking about!

"Good advice! Thanks for the tip, Bert!"

"Hey! I realize you didn't come out unscathed. How's that nose? How's that shoulder?"

"Could be better, could be worse! The upper arm and shoulder are getting better. But my nose is really a bother. My nostrils are all caked with dried blood way up inside, it still bleeds now and then, and it's hard to breathe without wincing."

What I also want to say is how worried I am that it might start bleeding again in the middle of our concert.

The Run-Through
9-7

After classes are out, Becky and I wait in line to speak with Mr. Maxwell at his desk. When it is our turn, Becky does the speaking.

"Mr. Maxwell, Lois and I have made exciting discovery with the Doppler, we wish to request ten minutes of your time to share with us our progress!"

"I'll hear you both in twenty minutes for full string rehearsal!"

"No, no, we wish you to hear us before rehearsal!"

"Not necessary! Do go off now!"

"Mr. Maxwell, I wish to inform you that I myself will be prime conductor and you will be co-conductor. I wish to demonstrate to you our reason why!"

"Sure, and pigs can fly! It is too late to make major changes now, Becky! The concert is the day after tomorrow, this is our last strings-only run-through, so neither the strings nor I could possible adjust!"

"Oh but you must, because Lois and I will be playing the Doppler in an entirely different way, with a very different approach!"

"You think so?"

"Yes, Sir!"

"Give me one good reason why!"

"Lois attended my flute lesson at Conservatory. Teacher Mrs. Boyko put forth challenge to find the real meaning behind the music in the Duet. She asked what story we tell? Last night, Lois and I worked hard to answer that question. I feel strongly that we have made huge breakthrough—late yes, but not too late to play it the way we feel it should be played!"

"No."

Becky rocks on her heels.

"Pardon me, Sir?"

"I said: No."

She looks hard at him. I can see she is gauging him against her own mettle.

"Then you are no more a Kil*roy*, Sir, you are a Kill *Joy!*" She is referring to the class nickname for him, which he had accepted at beginning of term with good humour. Now, not so much.

Mr. Maxwell's expression changes from indifference to surprise to indignation, to brief cogitation, and then to resignation. He lowers his shoulders, points toward the piano, and says: "After you, Mes Demoiselles!"

Quickly setting up our music stands and our music, we take our positions with Becky aligned, so that she faces him, with me standing beside her.

She sets the rhythm by tapping her foot. 1+ 2+ 3+ 4+

She nods to him, he plays the introductory bars then we are in full swing. Every transition, every mutation, it is Becky who conducts using her elbows. Amazingly, Mr. Maxwell goes along with her leadership, complies with each nod of her head. At the slower pace then the cadence leading into the Rondo, again she establishes the beat 1+2+ 1+2+ and he supports us all the way through to the climactic ending.

When we finish, Mr. Maxwell sits still, shoulders slumped, absorbing the impact, looking straight ahead.

We wait.

"Ladies," he says, "That was brilliant! You're on!"

Becky and I break into a jig then hug each other.

"We did it, we did it!" we sing.

The strings who are waiting outside the door in the corridor file in, and take their places. We play through the entire Duo flawlessly, accompanied by strings instead of by piano, for Mr. Maxwell has taken his rightful place as conductor on the podium, but cordially defers to Becky one hundred percent, co-conducting the orchestra accordingly.

The Makeover
9-8

Wednesday, October 23, 1957

This afternoon, the full rehearsal for the entire Centrewood Music Concert starts at 1:00 p.m. It is a full programme estimated to take two hours. Attendance for the duration of the show is mandatory. If everyone manages to get on and off-stage briskly today, it means we will all be let go for the day at 3:00 p.m.

I study the programme.

First the choir will perform—a group of about twenty earnest ninth- and tenth-grade students led by a teacher who is purported to have expertise in choral work. He is a minister at a local church. Here he teaches a course in Religious Knowledge. I have been totally unaware of this man to date, let alone the existence of an extracurricular choir. Where did they practice? Who knew there is a course in Religious Knowledge? Does Mother know about it? Oh, please don't give her any ideas!

Next, there will be a performance by a grade 13 pianist, playing Prelude in D Flat by Glière, to be followed by an encore with Claire de Lune by Debussy. What gives? She plays two pieces and we only play one? Then I remembered. The Doppler really is two pieces in one. Besides, that is quite enough. How nerve-wracking would it be to have to play two whole Dopplers?

There will be a ten-minute intermission.

After the intermission, it will be the band's turn. First they are slated to play Seventy-Six Trombones. The programme has the caption: "a very popular song from the Music Man now playing in Broadway". In italics under this entry, there is a caveat that the audience should prepare itself for a surprise.

This will be followed by Sousa's Hands Across the Sea. There is an asterisk stating that Mr. Maxwell will be playing the sousaphone. He will provide a briefing about the instrument before the piece is performed.

Our Doppler flute duet is the last item on the programme. Oh, how I wish it could be first, so it would be over and done with!

We file into the auditorium ranged in order of performance, and are relegated to seats in separate rows in the middle of the hall.

Mr. Maxwell raps his lectern and calls for Item Number 1.

The Religious Knowledge choir members troop out in single file from both wings back stage, and are ready to sing their hearts out in a jiffy. They sing a medley starting out with a camp song This Little Light of Mine, which breaks out in a cacophony of multitudinous ear-splitting rounds, merges into voices singing in unison the hymn What Star is This That Shines so Bright, and progresses into full four-part wobbly harmony for the first verse of All Things Bright and Beautiful. I get the clever theme but wish they would just sing the hymns, instead of starting off with that hokey juvenile-level selection. How old does the minister think we are? Or our parents?

Then comes the pianist. I've seen her around. She looks very mature which makes sense because she is a senior and is most likely close to seventeen years old. She has incredibly slender hands with long tapered fingers. She plays beautifully. Becky leans over and whispers that we should get her to accompany us at the next concert in the spring. I nod enthusiastically.

Mr. Maxwell asks the choir and the pianist to return to the back of the auditorium and be seated. They are not permitted to leave until the rest of us have performed.

To simulate Intermission, he announces that we will take a ten-minute break.

The band members object. They want to get on with it, so they can get out of school early. They 'boo' and shout out: Overruled! Objection! This is Overt Anti-Reedism! This is Bass Prejudice! Brass Discrimination! The cymbalist brings the greatest cheer when he shouts: Blatant Anti-Cymbalism! Obviously not wanting to annoy Mr. Maxwell to the extent that it backfires and they are all issued detentions, they try to ensure that the protest is done in jest with great mock-jeering and cheering.

Becky and I decide to stay put in our assigned aisle seats in the tenth row. Neither of us feels compelled to visit the washroom which will be jam-packed with line-ups for the toilets, and girls maniacally applying lipstick and making kissy-kissy faces to themselves in the mirror, back-combing their hair into bee-hives, and filling the confined space with clouds of hair spray.

Holding his bassoon, Bert leans over from the seat behind us, and hands me a package.

"What's this?" I ask.

"I told my Mother about your nose and she prepared a saline spray solution for you. It has non-iodized salt diluted with baking soda in boiled water that she poured into a sterilized bottle. She included a medicine dropper. You are to lean back and squirt that stuff up each nostril gently, one at a time—over the sink, mind you— Let it drain, and don't blow your nose hard until after letting it swill awhile. It will wash away any caked blood and should clear up overnight!"

I am totally taken aback, and sit, as Mother would say, with 'my gob open'.

"Thank him, Lois!" Becky says, nudging me.

"Oh my goodness, yes! That is so very kind, Bert! Please thank your Mother—and thank you!"

"Hey, no sweat! Us Avro family folks gotta look out for each other!"

"Well, you sure do that!" I smile, "You've saved my skin more than once—Bert to the rescue!" I say, showing him the V for Victory sign with one hand, and toasting him with the parcel in the other hand.

"Oops! There's our signal! Gotta go!"

He scoots away.

Becky asks: "How else did he save your skin?"

"Uh, well, um—"

Saved by a drum roll. Becky knows nothing about the Teaserama.

From the back of the hall, the drum roll starts up, then down the aisle arranged in order of division comes the band led by the bass drum, the percussion, the reeds, and then the brass, including trombones—six or seven of them. Not Seventy-Six. But enough to make a blaringly impressive entrance. Coming in from the rear— That is the surprise and a good one! All are playing their instruments as they march along. There goes Bert with the other woodwinds honking into his bass bassoon, all of them gaining the stage steps in single file, then falling into line in front of their chairs where they remain standing.

That is no easy feat. They must have memorized their parts because they are not carrying any music racks with them! Those of us who have returned to our seats rise up in unison and roar with applause.

That isn't the only surprise.

Mitsy is there. But she is not playing her beloved saxophone.

She is marching with the percussionists, playing the triangle. That scourge 'James Dean' wannabe, Joey Sutherland, is with her, but why? Who knows? That jerk doesn't even take music, so what's he doing in the band?

After the band has finished, Becky and I are next.

As soon as we've had our run-through, which went really well I think, with the rehearsal now over for everyone, Becky and I step out into the corridor.

The rest of the detainees are now pouring out of the auditorium.

Inevitably, along comes Mitsy holding her triangle. She pulls in close and snarls: "Break another Nose, why don't cha?" and I respond: "Lock another Jaw, Shit Face!"

Joey is slithering along next to her.

"What's Joey doing with you? Holding your triangle?"

"No, Smart Ass, he's carrying my music, it's a new part and I don't know it well enough to go solo—"

"So you need a 'page' to turn the pages for you! Why isn't he dressed like a court jester?"

"Ever see someone play the triangle with both hands, and read music at the same time?"

"Poke a music stand in your cleavage, why don't cha? You've got a big enough rack to do the job! Or did you forget to wear your Wonder Woman Lift-Up Bra?"

"You are one hell of a Bitch, Michelsen!"

"Right back atcha, Titsy Mitsy! Or is it Puke-o *Mitsuko* now?"

"Why you—"

Wow, I am really perking!

"I hope you make sure you 'ting' instead of 'ding', you scrag," I sneer.

"Oh go blow it up your arse!" Mitsy snarls.

Bert turns up. He speaks.

To Mitsy, he says: "Wow, Mitsy, you've got a real mouth on you. Makes sense it got smashed up. Ever heard of karma?" He points his finger at her, and says, "Back off and leave Lois alone."

To me, he says, loud enough for her to hear, "I'll make sure tomorrow night that there is lot of distance kept between you and the Mad Moron of Maplewood!"

While I simmer down, Becky sidles in close: "I never thought you had it in you! OR those words!"

"Becky, I'm so spitting mad, don't let anyone else cross me!"

The Makeover
9-9

Mrs. Molnar is sitting outside on a bench waiting for us.

Without further ado, she stands up and says: "At last you come out! Now we must hurry to hairdresser's. Then we must be at dressmaker's by 5:00 for fitting!"

"What?"

"Why?"

"Huh?"

Off we are rushed.

"But I don't want my hair cut, Mama!"

"I don't want my hair cut either, Mrs. Molnar!"

"My hair is just fine the way it is!"

"So is mine! I can turn it under now with a curling iron—I finally got it growing long enough not to look as though Mother cut it with a salad bowl!" I turn to Becky. "That's what someone once told me." (I chose not to name the pariah Mitsy)

"How mean."

"We go. No more to be said. You want to look nice for concert, don't you? After that, we look at matching dresses I found for you both."

"Dresses? I was just going to wear a white blouse with my black skirt, Mrs. Molnar!"

"Me too, Mama! I need to be comfortable when I play! My blouse and skirt will do just fine!"

Later that evening, after supper, shortly after flushing out my nostrils à la Mrs. Sanderfield method, the phone rang.

Mrs. Molnar answered it in the front hallway.

I heard her talking for a while, so I presumed that the call was for her. Eventually, however, Mrs. Molnar called me:

"It ees for you, Lois! It ees your Mother!"

Now I was mad at her too, why did her choppy accent suddenly annoy me so much?

I took the phone, closed the adjoining doors to the livingroom, and crawled under the front hall side table where I sat on the tiles across from the hall mat with its shoes and guest slippers.

"Hello dear, how did your rehearsal go?"

Pause. It was impossible to say absolutely nothing. But I didn't want her to think I wasn't mad at her anymore, enough to answer her question. I asked, "Where are you?"

"Why, we're still in Ottawa, darling."

I cut straight to the chase:

"Did Father solve the land claim issue?"

"Oh, I doubt it. Rome can't be built in a day, Lois."

Pause.

"Are you having a good time, dear?"

"Not entirely. Well, I am because I'm with Becky."

Mother said in a low voice: "I can't exactly say that I am having a good time. Remember that hoity-toity woman in the brown suit at the Rollout who didn't deign to say hello to us when we were being seated? Well, it turns out that it is Mr. Gordon's wife. I've had the misfortune to be paired off with her through the day, whilst the men are in their meetings. She is one bossy-cow of a woman, with a deadpan sense of humour, and no other interests while in Ottawa other than shopping for Eskimo sculptures depicting sealers and seals carved out of a grey stone— It's becoming quite the trend these days but it's not to my taste, I must say! Other than that, she loves haunting the Hudson's Bay Store to no end, along with hunting down every fur store in the city for seal collars, seal hats, seal muffs, seal gloves, and she still hasn't found her ideal black seal coat! I'd do anything to wander off and explore on my own, but I'm trapped!"

"Now you know what it's like to have someone foisted on you," I said, making a blunt reference to Mitsy, but Mother disregarded my comment, and talked on regardless.

"Never mind, it's been extremely difficult to hold my own against her, so just let me say I'm glad the ordeal is almost over."

"Will you be back in time for the concert?"

"Of course! We'll be there when you get home from school!"

Pause.

"Mother," I whispered, "Did you know Mrs. Molnar was going to take me to have my hair cut along with Becky?"

"Well yes, I thought it was a good idea, so I agreed when she asked me!"

"Is that so?" I hissed into the receiver, "Well, now I look like one of the Three Stooges. I have bangs cut straight across my forehead plastered down with some goop so they don't fly away, and a so-called 'page boy' cut that is so short, there's not a hope in hell of getting a curling iron underneath it to turn it under, so it's bound to flip up!"

"Which Stooge do you have in mind? Did I just hear you use a swear word?"

"Becky got the same cut. She's just as furious. All her beautiful wavy hair is now straightened and wrestled into submission! How can we play the Doppler, knowing we look like a couple of vaude-ville dorks?"

"It can't be that bad!"

·"Oh, it's bad, and it's gotten worse. You should see the dresses she bought for us! Oh—my—God, Mother, they are exactly the same— and identically atrocious!"

"Tell me about them!"

"She says they are modern prom dresses. Huh! They are so fuddy duddy, no one would wear them nowadays, ever. I doubt anyone would wear such a horror even back in your day!"

"Horror? Really, Lois, you mustn't exaggerate!"

"Mother, only a creepy woman in Dracula would be caught wearing one!"

"Because?"

"First of all, they are an indescribable metallic blue."

"Powder blue?"

"No, bright, neon Crayola-crayon blue!"

"Oh, that's good, that colour blue would suit you!"

"The basic dress is made of some kind of shiny plastic material that the dressmaker said was called 'acetate' and which I call 'assinine'!"

"Lois! Language!"

"Ugly blue netting covers the bodice and the skirt entirely. Yes, netting!! not bridal voile or even drapery sheer, but netting! Tacked on just above the waistband is a shiny blue acetate cumberbund! and here's a crippler: there are wide, pleated, shiny-blue, capped sleeves binding the shoulders that the dressmaker called 'shawl sleeves' made of the same acetate garbage crap!"

"Lo-is!"

"To add insult to injury, Mo-ther, get this for the final decorative touch! Running around the scoop neck is a strand of drab blue artificial flowers that look like they came from Woolworth's rummage bin!"

"Oh good, I'm glad the neckline is scooped. Not too low?"

"No!"

"And your shoulders are covered. So it isn't strapless like a cocktail dress?"

"Are you there, Mother, are you listening? I hate my hair. I hate that dress. I am going to shear off my hair so I look like Joan of Arc. And I am going to tear that dress to shreds!"

With that, I hung up.

●

CHAPTER TEN
Old Pinewood

Rebels With Due Cause
10-1

Thursday, October 24, 1957

8 a.m.

"Girls, girls, girls!"

It is Mrs. Molnar frantically calling up the stairwell to us.

Becky and I are in the bathroom wrestling with our hair and bemoaning the dreadful fate that awaits us: having to wear those atrocious dresses and facing the whole world with these wretched bangs and page boy haircuts.

"I feel like Friar Tuck without the bald pate!" I said.

"Whoever that is and whatever that is, me too!" Becky moans, leaning against me.

It seems so unfair for us to have unravelled the Doppler with such resounding success, only to be confronted by this monstrous prospect where our entire performance is bound to be ruined by our appearance!

Then Mrs. Molnar is calling again: "Girls, girls, girls!"

We bite our lips, and head downstairs.

"We have forgotten something very essential! Lo-iss, do you have black dressup shoes?"

"No."

"Bo also does not have!"

"All I have is my pair of black 'nickel' loafers," I reply, "I could wear those!"

"No, no, no! Not with formal dress, never! Not acceptable! Well then, never you two mind, I will go to store while you are in school. I shall find something for you both!"

"Oh please don't bother, Mrs. Molnar!" I plead, doubting she'll ever find shoes large enough to fit me, and dreading playing the Doppler in shoes that are too tight or too large—or too high.

"But I must! I promised your Mother I would take care of both your presentations!"

She is kneading her hands and starting to dither about.

"Mama, calm down! You are the one who should be helping us stay calm. Instead, you are all wound up like a top and it is upsetting!!!"

"Yes, yes!! Of course!!"

I am grateful to Becky for this intervention, because her Mother is really starting to get on my nerves.

Mrs. Molnar reaches for the newspaper and pulls out the front page.

"Put foot on this newspaper, Lo-iss," she commands, "I not know your size so I will trace!"

Will this nightmare never end? Now there's this business of shoes! Drats!

As for those blinking dresses, Becky and I had privately discussed the logistics of sneaking our blouses and black skirts to our lockers, and changing into them behind our mothers' backs. If we did, we could just wear our regular shoes and know they didn't pinch.

Along comes Mrs. Molnar's next obsession:

"I lay awake all night thinking: what to be worn underneath the dresses? You cannot wear only bras. Dress lining is too transparent. Under stage lights, will be too 'see-through', you see? You will both need full—what you call them? Slips? I must go shop for them too, and measure so they do not show above the neck line or below the hem!"

"Mama! Enough! Just let us wear our bras and forget about slips!"

"Absolutely not! It is not right!"

As I will be going directly home once school is let out, I opt to walk my bicycle, so Becky and I can go to school together. On the way, we plot how not to wear those dresses, but we can't figure out how to pull it off.

Both of us are chewing our bottom lips. We are so nervous about the performance tonight that butterflies are already fluttering about big time in our stomachs. Thankfully, we are both furious at Becky's Mother. I reserve due spill-over of wrath on my part for my own Mother for going away, and not tending to this herself! Fine time not to be lording it over me!

When botany class is let out, Bert is waiting for me.

"Hey! Good mark on your Burr Project! I'm glad that Mr. Gladstone passed the best ones around for all of us to view!"

"Why, thank you! Although I admit I did have some help from my friends!"

"Nah! Not with what counted!"

"How did you do with your milkweed project?"

"Not worth mentioning! But listen, you have a great talent for drawing botanical plants! And excellent scientific-looking penmanship—Did you study calligraphy with someone? You got it from your father, I bet—He's a draftsman par excellence. You have a knack for precision in your descriptive content as well. Have you ever considered going through as a botanist? You sure love nature and it shows in your work!"

"Me a botanist? I'm a girl, Bert. The only choices I have when I grow up are teacher, nurse or airline stewardess—and the last is eliminated due to my height!"

"They say that girls can be anything they want nowadays! Weren't you in the same guidance class as the rest of us?"

"Yeah. But I think it was just to fill the classes. Anything I chose, was nixed. Like, I chose to join the RCAF and be a fighter pilot. The counsellor hauled in my parents! No way, José!"

"Well—hm, I can't see you chasing down Russian fighter planes, you don't have the grit. Or a mean bone in your body. Any other followup choices?"

I lift my shoulders and roll my eyes.

"How's your nose coming along?"

"Oh your mother's nasal spray concoction has worked wonders! I can still feel the bruising way up there but the blood clotting is gone! I think I can breathe again—enough to get through the concert! Thank your Mother for me! I am truly grateful!"

"What do you think about Mitsy being reduced to playing the triangle?" He digs his elbow into my side, "EH? EH? Serves her right, doesn't it? She had it coming! She's such a ding-a-ling!"

I pretend I'm tapping a triangle. "A ding ding ding?" I smile.

"Good one!" he says, "So you are all set for tonight?"

"Musically, yes. As much as I can be. But for the concert itself, how can I be with this hairdo? Becky's Mother hauled us off and had the hairdresser give us the exact same cut. We feel like two lowly tribunes being sent to the Forum on the Ides of March!"

"Hey! What don't you like about your hair? I think you look cute, and pretty! Really! Listen, every time I've gone to the barber's, I feel like I've been scalped. But only because it's different from what I had gotten used to!"

"How very generous of you to say that. But—Did you have to give a performance in front of a hundred people right after being scalped?"

"Not that I recall! But say, if you both hate it that much, why don't the tribunes step up a few notches in Roman society, and make yourselves laurel wreaths?"

"Oh that's so funny! YOU are funny! Thanks for making me laugh, Bert!"

"No problem! You're the bees' knees and we aim to please!"

"Is that a compliment?"

"It's flapper-talk for 'excellent', or 'gro-o-oovy'!"

"That's all right then!"

Becky and I have time to talk a bit more at lunch break. It's a toss-up whether it's the horrid dress or our plastered-down bangs that bring us the most grief.

Thanks to Bert, we think we've come up with a plan for the bangs!

As for the bras and slips quandary, I hesitate to give Mitsy any tip of the hat, but I must give her credit for our other plan.

Around suppertime, Mrs. Molnar will be dropping off my overnight bag at my place, along with the dress with the new shoes and slip. Before that, I will have time to get at it.

Becky plans to do as much as she can from her place before she joins me.

Fall Out
10-2

Thursday, October 24, 1957

In light of the concert tonight, school has been let out early at 3:00 p.m.

I'm riding my bike home.

My mind is completely engrossed in how to manage my part in solving the problems caused by the stupid dress, shoes, and bangs.

Becky and I are agreed on what we will do about it. It's just a matter of execution.

As soon as I arrive home, I will have a lot of scrambling to do. Find Mother's roll of white surgical tape, her fine manicure scissors, at least four bobby pins. What else?

I hope Mrs. Molnar has come and gone with my knapsack and the other recital paraphernalia—God forbid I forget my flute and music! So I can get to work as quickly as possible—and so that both Becky and I can be ready in time to leave early for the show.

The question is: have Mother and Father arrived home yet? They better have, is all I have to say!

I reach the stop sign at the top of the hill and prepare to turn left onto the Main Artery.

Before I even make my turn, I can tell out of the corner of my left eye that something is wrong. Very wrong!

I look up, and Eagle is wheeling about overhead, farther away from his eyrie by the main highway that I have ever seen him.

He lets out a cry. My shoulders stiffen.

I pull out onto the Main Artery and cross to the other side. Then I put my foot out to brace myself against the far curb.

What on earth has happened?

At the foot of the hill, at the Small Culvert, oversized backhoes are lifting their enormous hinged shovels in the air, tap their foreheads against the earth and gnawing into the channel outlet like hungry mechanical beasts—These are the pterodactyls and other prehistoric animals that I had seen in my waking vision!

Looking across the stretch called Old Pinewood, I see that the pastureland is being torn up. The entire tract of land is being mawed and pawed, huge mounds of churned-up soil are being pushed, shoved, rearranged, the very shape of the landscape is being re-contoured, re-engineered with artificial swoops and sweeps, with steep inclines serving as ramps for the heavy machinery.

The sweet fields with their yellow buttercups and blue cornflowers, Indian paintbrush and queen anne's lace, wild grasses and daisies, mullein and thistles have all been turned over.

The silo and the foundation for the old farmhouse are in heaps of concrete rubble, and the adjacent lilac bushes have been torn out.

The magnificent tall stand of 'whispering' pines that once served as a wind break leading up to the old homestead has been felled, the branches being sawn in even lengths to build cords of wood to be hauled away as firewood.

The tall Dutch elm tree that stood alone in the pasture is gone.

***

Willow Creek is no more.

The weeping willow trees have been chopped down. Where once they quietly dipped their long graceful fronds in the water, their stumps have been plucked out of the earth like old teeth, and now lie upended in a jumbled heap along the bank.

What was once my beloved, lazy, gentle, winding stream is now a straightened mucky trench into which huge concrete pipes are being laid, connected end to end, bending south parallel to the highway toward the berm in the distance.

The marsh is gone.

The little waterfall is gone.

The maple bush, the thicket and the mixed woods are gone.

At the far end, close to the highway, the great oaks— and the Eagle's own eyrie in the far scotch pines— have been unceremoniously clear cut, their stumps yanked and their massive roots upended, tossed upside down, and exposed to the world.

Trimmed of their branches, naked, aged trunks are being sawn up to length, dumped in organized heaps for removal by a line-up of logging trucks.

***

The destruction of the landscape is still in full sway. There are lumbering bulldozers and busybody backhoes beetling about like crazy everywhere, like beetles, slugs and earwigs unearthed by removal of a huge rock.

Wherever the desecration and levelling has been completed, there are already surveyors scuttling about with their theodolites on tripods, mapping in roadways and new property lines. Derek, the surveyor—that's what he said was going to happen—so it really was true, what he was doing in Pinewood that day! White stakes are being driven into clods of barren clay where there was once fertile soil now stripped of all its richness.

This is why the Skinned Rabbit charged straight at me from way across the field! It was trying to warn me!

This explains the 'zipline' running diagonally across the pastureland. It too was a sign of the destruction to come.

The undulating quilt with all its fall colours—it too was a premonition of this upcoming upheaval. It was that same day we stopped by the pasture that Eagle came looking for me when I was in Father's car. I thought he was trying to protect me from Father, but was he trying to tell me that Pinewood—and his home—was in danger?

Is this why Aunt Ani stepped out of the thicket and appeared to me only last week?

A tremendous pain rips through my whole body. A horrific howl pours from my mouth. Blinded by tears, I push off on my bicycle down the hill.

Reaching my street and turning the corner, there are Mother and Father at their car.

I roar up to them and fly off my bike, ditching it behind me. One stride and I tear into Father with my arms flailing like a windmill, punching and scratching and clawing and kicking, screeching, "You promised me! You promised me!"

"Lois! Lois!" I hear Mother crying out.

It is all Father can do to ward off my blows. He lifts his forearms, but that just exposes his chest and stomach. He reaches out to grab my arms, but that just exposes his chest and his face.

Mother cries out my name again.

I turn on her, elbows back.

"You knew! You knew this was going to happen!"

"But—"

I don't let her finish.

I am bawling my eyes out, I feel as though I am sinking, losing ground, as though the earth is giving away beneath my feet. I hurt so badly inside my chest, that I might as well have been slugged by a sledgehammer.

"I hate you both for what you've done! I hate you!"

I let off with the punching, and haul open the front door. I can see they have just arrived home. Some of their luggage has been set inside the door. Other bags are on the landing.

Father lunges after me. He comes through the front door, and is reaching out toward me, to catch me going up the stairs.

"Go away! Go away! Leave me alone!" I scream, still crying. I wheel around and kick him in the gut. He doubles up, and staggers backward down the stairs.

I kick at the luggage and each suitcase takes flight, then topples down the stairs.

I run to my bedroom, close my door, throw myself on the bed face down, and keep on sobbing so hard, I can't stop.

Just when I think I might be calming down, I hear a woman's voice calling "Yoo-hoo! Yoo-hoo!" from the front door. I know it is Mrs. Molnar come to deliver her crumby dress, slip and shoes.

I can hear Mother greeting her ever so politely and thanking her profusely. Her voice is calm and courteous, ever the poised and pleasant hostess.

Now Mother is calling me. Obviously, she hasn't told Mrs. Molnar what's just happened.

"Lois! Lois! Mrs. Molnar is here! Come out now!"

I stay put.

Mother and Mrs. Molnar are murmuring and muttering together in the hallway.

Soon Mrs. Molnar raps on my door, and then enters without a welcome. She comes to my bedside and tries to turn me over, to pat me, to give me a hug.

I remain wooden and unreceptive.

"What has happened, my poor Angyal? Oh my, oh dear, oh my, I saw what they do to your farm land! I know why you are upset, my dear girl!"

I say through the pillow:

"Go away, Mrs. Molnar, please! You're just as much to blame, you also belong to the Ratepayer's, so you must have known all along with Mother and Father that this was going to happen! You all lied to me!"

"No, no, they say might possibly do next spring or summer, my darlink, that was my understanding!"

Mother is standing at the open door.

"It's true, Lois! We really did not know they would be doing this immediately!"

I wheel over and shout at Mother: "What are you telling me? That you knew it was going to happen sometime?"

"I tried to have Father tell you a couple of weeks ago!"

"But he didn't, did he? The way I see it, you both lied to me!"

"Not really, dear. Pinewood really was slated for a public park when Centrewood was first planned. When the developers started to build Upper Pinewood, the request by the Ratepayers to retain Old Pinewood as a park hadn't yet been finalized!"

"How can you mince words, Mother? All of Pinewood was supposed to be a public park!! A nature reserve! Old Pinewood!! A preserve of nature—just like the communal green spaces public in your country, Mrs. Molnar, reserved for generations! You all got rooked, don't you see? Hood-winked! Pinewood was meant to be protected. Not destroyed by stupid, greedy, ignorant, mismanaging, cheating lying developers!!"

I flop on my back and keep sobbing, choking for air.

"Go away!"

My nose is throbbing badly. I feel myself starting to panic. I cannot breathe. Instinct takes over, tells me I must calm down.

I stare at the ceiling.

The blankness of the ceiling is all that makes sense to me. It somehow reassures me, soothes me.

Time disappears.

I must have fallen asleep. Or passed out.

I open my eyes.

Mrs. Molnar is no longer in the room.

Mother is standing by me with a cold washcloth, folding it up length-wise, placing it on my forehead.

She hands me a handkerchief.

"Here, honey, blow your nose, it looks like it's still bleeding?"

OH GREAT!! Just what I need!

I look Mother in the eye.

"Mother," I ask, "Did Father make time to talk to the Governor General while he was in Ottawa?"

"What about, dear?"

"On behalf of Chief Fred, about Chief Peter Jones's land claim?"

Her mouth opens, and forms around the words she will choose:

"Well now, he and Mr. Smye spent almost all their time with the Attorney General and other officials regarding the Avro's future, and the problem with the RCMP."

"He didn't do anything about the Ten Shillings, did he?"

"Well, no dear, not really, there wasn't enough time!"

"He had enough time to deal with his own concerns, but not with Chief Fred's, not even mine?"

"Yours? What do you mean—yours?"

"The Eagle—AND Chief Jones came to me, Mother, asking for help. That's why it's my concern!"

"Darling, none of that is really our immediate concern!"

A jagged line of hot fury crashes through my brain.

"Get out!" I scream, "Get out!"

I leap up and push her out of the room.

"Go away!" I bawl, slamming the bedroom door behind her.

***

Around suppertime, it is Becky who knocks on my door. She opens it. I am lying face down on my bed, my face smushed into my pillow with tissues stuffed up my nostrils just in case I bleed on the pillowcase.

"Lois? You let me come in?" she peeps. "You not mad at me!"

"No, I'm not mad at you!"

"Mama fetched me. I saw during ride what has been done to your beloved fields and river. I am so sorry, Lois!"

I turn my head to look at her. She is bearing a tray. She lowers it, so I can see there are a few strips of chicken, a glob of red jelly and some potato salad on a plate. There is also a small glass of tomato juice.

She places the tray on my desk, comes to my bedside, sits on the edge of the mattress, and takes my hand, strokes it.

"You let me hold your hand? You let me stroke your back, your head, your arms?"

Not even the kindness of human touch can reach me. I ache inside and out. There is a tremor throughout my body. I feel a pain deep in my gut.

"Is necessary you try to eat a bit of this food. You sit up now, okay? I give you tray!"

I do as I am told. She helps me sit up, puts my legs over the edge of the bed, and plants my feet on the floor. I feel nothing. I am numb from head to toe.

Becky places the tray on my lap.

She is the last person in this world that I still trust. I let her spoonfeed me some potato salad, a bit of jelly. I take a small piece of chicken into my mouth but cannot swallow it. I feel like wretching. I let her lift the tomato juice to my lips, I take it from her, take a few sips, wash down the chicken.

"You still want to play at concert, yes? You must! Not say quit now! We have a lot to do, Lo-iss! I brought all parts and pieces for our 'costumes' so we get ready here together! Dress, slip, shoes. Now I am here with gear, that means we can *prepare* together, yes?"

I smile at the secretive way she put emphasis on the 'prepare'.

I watch as Becky unpacks the Maher's shoebox and the Reitman's lingerie box.

"Here, first we try on new shoes!"

Unlike what I envisioned, that is, some clompy heels with bows, these are a surprise! They are soft black-leather ballet slippers with black suede leather soles. A thin band of elastic grips the entire inside edge and holds the shoe on. Miraculously, despite my huge feet, they fit me, for which I am grateful, although without any arch support I find my feet flap along when I try walking across the floor. At any rate, Becky's slippers fit, too! They aren't very stylish but that's one major dilemma out of the way.

Becky picks up scissors and white surgical tape.

"How many strips should I cut off?"

"Three strips for each."

She attaches the ends of twelve strips to the edge of my desk.

"Now we turn our backs, take off tops then bras, and stick them on!"

This is the plan we had concocted:

We knew from our fittings at the dressmaker's that our thick, wide bra straps would show above the cut of the dresses due to the shape of the neckline and the cap sleeves. What could be done? Not wear our bras at all? We knew that the only way we could do so would be if the tips of our boobs did not show. It is considered to be very vulgar if a lady's nipples show through her top. In fact, that was most likely one of the major reasons women in our culture started wearing bras. Without, was it considered too *tit*-illating? All this fixation over breasts, I still fail to understand why.

It was agreed that we would dare not to wear bras. Instead, we would cover the tips of our breasts with surgical tape! I got the idea from Mitsy's Teaserama pasties. I don't tell Becky that.

We turn our backs to each other. Off go the bras. On go three criss-crossed strips of white tape covering the tips of our boobs.

It reminds me of the universal symbol that Father showed me, it seems so long ago: three radiating spokes depicting the wheel of life.

Out of the Reitman's box come the white slips. Each one followed the scoop of the dress neckline. But each slip had thin ribbon straps, not as wide or blaringly white as bra straps but still, visible and ugly. We decided we would use small golden safety pins to tack each strap under each cap sleeve where they would be concealed. I rooted about in Mother's sewing box for the pins. We can't do that until we have put on the dresses. Nonetheless, that eliminated major dilemmas one and two.

Becky turns to the dresses that had been stored on hangers, covered with tissue paper and thin plastic. Out come the dresses. On they go.

Next: we check the length of the slip in the full-length mirror.

Relief: It is short enough not to show below the dress hem.

Now for our bangs. We comb our cap cuts forward and spray the hair with water to make it lie down flat.

Then we set to work.

Using Mother's small sewing scissors and her tiny razor used for snipping fine stitches, we carefully remove the ugly blue Woolworth's artificial flowers from each scooped bodice.

Fortunately, each flower comes off attached in a continuous strand, so all we have to do is bobby-pin the entire string of flowers straight across our bangs and around past the ears.

"We will look like twenties flappers with headbands!" Becky says.

"I think we will look like Julius Caesar, except our wreaths have artificial flowers instead of laurel," I say, and turn to her to share the source of the idea:

"It was Bert who mentioned laurel leaves. These will have to do!!" I crow.

We stand side by side to look in the mirror.

The sight sends us both into reams of laughter.

The sound of jollity sends both Mothers into heights of confusion.

They open the bedroom door and rush in.

"Bo!"

"Lois!"

"What you do?"

"What have you done?"

Mrs. Molnar works herself up into a royal hissy-fit, and reprimands her Bo for ruining her dress, now with the ragged broken stitches across the neckline.

Mother disagrees, and says it's an all-round improvement and a brilliant idea.

"Give both the dresses to me!" Mother commands, "I have some cornflower-blue rickrack which will cover the pulled stitches and will do just fine!"

Off she runs to her sewing machine.

We are left standing in our slips and black dance slippers.

We eye each other.

So far, neither Mother nor Becky's Mother has noticed our bra-less white-criss-crossed-tape state.

Fingers crossed!

Once the dresses have been repaired and we have asked to put them on in private, Becky and I help pin each others' slip straps under the cap sleeves.

We consider ourselves ready.

We permit the Mothers entry once more.

Mrs. Molnar is rooting about in her handbag. She pulls out a small flat jewellery box.

"Lois, where is your blue sodalite pendant we give you for advance birthday gift? You find it now, please, and put it on!"

While I extricate it from my dresser drawer and Becky helps me with the clasp, Mrs. Molnar has opened the jewellery box and is affixing Becky's white opal pendant around her neck.

"This will complete your presentation! Now iss perfect!" Mrs. Molnar says proudly.

Well, at least our necks aren't bare naked, I think, liking the pendants but still not willing to give an inch.

At any rate, aside from blond and dark brown hair, with our blue and white stone pendants, we aren't totally "perfectly-matched identical twins"!

Theoretically, we are ready to go.

Except my face is all blotched and my eyes are blood-shot from crying.

Mrs. Molnar has Murine in her bottomless handbag and helps me with eye drops. Becky runs the washcloth under the tap so I have a cold compress alternating on my forehead and across my nose.

We four go to the living room.

All this time, Father has been nowhere to be seen.

Getting on to the witching hour, Father materializes from downstairs. He has showered, is wearing a suit and tie. He has long scratches across his forehead, down each cheek.

When the Mothers express concern and pity for him, he says we should see the ones on the rest of his body, good thing he has to wear a suit!

Mother fetches rubbing alcohol and starts dabbing at the scratches with a cotton swab.

"First Lois with punched nose, now you looking as though you too were in big fight, I hope school authorities won't suspect child abuse of any sort!" Mrs. Molnar says, quite seriously.

"Eszter! For Petey's sake!" Mother admonishes her, "Nothing like tossing another iron into the fire!"

Father pooh-poohs her concern.

"But what happened?" Mrs. Molnar persists. He tells her he got caught in the blackthorn thicket across the way, chasing after a neighbour's dog that was chasing a coyote.

It's a blatant lie, of course. He's forgotten that along with the rest of all the trees, bushes and any other natural growth, the thicket is no more.

"If I'm worried at all, I'm hoping that the Avro staff at the plant will buy it, along with the CEOs, more than anyone at the school," I hear Father say to Mother.

Mother suggests, "If you're that worried what your staff think, you could tell them that you had a royal dust-up with Diefenbaker while in Ottawa!"

"Ah, is that the truth?" Mrs. Molnar asks.

Mother continues, "As for the CEOs, they will have to be as gull-ible as Mrs. Molnar!"

"Gullible. What means 'gullible'?"

"For Pete's sake, Eszter, give it up!" Mother croaks.

We have to leave for the school in separate cars.

Initially, I refuse to go with Mother and Father.

"I'm going with Becky," I say.

They'll have nothing of it.

"Get in the car," Mother orders.

She opens the back door.

Good thing I have to sit in the back where I have room, other-wise I'll crumple the stupid dress. The stiff slippery acetate feels like wearing hardened aluminum foil. What idiot ever thought this synthetic material would be suitable for women's wear? Would you ever see a man wearing a suit made of this—I have to say it—crap? Only Liberace, I bet! Only phony, plastic Liberace.

Not a word has been said so far between Father and myself. We are at an impasse.

To get to the school, we have to drive past the carnage that used to be my beloved pastureland and stream. From the backseat window, all I can see is destruction across the fields as far as the berm.

That brings on another round of choked sobs.

"I'll have no more of that nonsense, young lady," Mother com-mands, "It's time for you to pull yourself together and bring your very best self forward! You have a concert to give!"

I guess it's Mother's belief that only so much time can be allotted for any given major upset. Then I suppose it's pick up where you left off and let heart-ache, heart-sickness, anger be damned! Oh my, did I hear myself say "damned"?

2

ANDANTE ET RONDO

FRANÇOIS DOPPLER Op.25.

Stich und Druck von B.SCHOTT'S SÖHNEN in MAINZ.　21264.

Doppler, Franz. Duet for Two Flutes. Andante.

CHAPTER ELEVEN
Flute Concert

Double Bubbles
11-1

Thursday, October 24, 1957

7:00 p.m.

When we arrive at the school, I still have a tremendous pain in my chest and a stab in the pit of my stomach. I feel dizzy. There is a persistent tremor running throughout my body. I am breathing in deeply then holding my breath, trying to 'will' it away, hoping if I am patient and if I can ignore it, it will vanish.

The entire 'cast of thousands' has been instructed to collect in the corridor backstage behind the auditorium. We are to arrange ourselves in sequence according to the programme. There is one exception: once the hall is filled, the band is to gather in the main foyer, at the two entranceways at the back. Once each group has been assembled, we are to wait in sequence until we are called to perform.

Theoretically, we should find ourselves at the end of the line.

This means that every performer who has not yet arrived is obliged to pass us to get to their respective group. Eventually, every number seems to be in place except when—

The grade-thirteener pianist glides by—or should I say 'Glieres' by? looking for all the world like Grace Kelly, with her professionally shaped blond hair, matching turquoise-stone earring- and necklace set, and her long, turquoise satiny dress. I guess she wanted to make an entrance. Taking our breath away, she did!

The wait seems endless.

It has to be past opening time because the choir evaporates ahead of us.

After a brief duration, we presume they must have finished because we can hear applause.

Bit by bit, the performers shuffle forward.

"Least they could do is provide chairs for the last of us!" I mutter.

"And a toilet!" Becky whispers, "I have to pee!"

That gets us giggling, imagining both of us wetting our pants in the open corridor because we are so nervous, with no time to make a beeline for the washroom. We beg each other to stop laughing, as "It only makes the need worse!" I say, "Or more pressing!" Becky says, and then we are engulfed again.

"Thanks for making me laugh!" I say, hugging Becky with my free arm.

It is Grace Kelly, the pianist's turn: distant muffled sounds of piano keys rippling, then enthusiastic applause.

Now there's a louder roar, and we can hear the mumble-jumble of people talking and pouring out from the auditorium, so we know that the pianist has had her day.

It is intermission time.

When you're up next, you can't stand waiting for one more second. You want it to begin. But terror reigns. Every molecule in the blood stream is utterly paralyzed when you know your time is nigh.

I imagine how Anne Boleyn must have felt: forewarned, with time to pray, but heading to the guillotine, still believing in her heart that she will be spared, she wants it all to be over.

We could hear the band's grand entrance from the rear of the auditorium and the roar of the surprised audience who joined in and stomped their feet, clapped their hands to the numbers they played.

"Hope we're not 'also rans'," I whisper.

"Hm, I am thinking same thing! What if the whole audience has had a good enough time, goes home, and does not bother to wait to listen to us?"

"Oh, now there's a thought!" I grimace.

Due to poor foresight by whomever was responsible for staging, everyone in our entire accompanying string orchestra, along with ourselves, is requested to press against the wall while the band members pass us in single file. Someone had forgotten to accommodate their exit— via the back stage emergency exit out into the parking lot, perhaps? after arranging for their entrance through the audience from the back of the hall!

Inevitably, along comes Mitsy and her triangle with that scourge Joey Sutherland.

Through clenched lips, Mitsy focuses her Cat-eyes in our direction and wiggles her bosom at us: "Well, well, well, if it isn't the Boobless Twins! Say, get a load of those matching glitzy-glossy raz-ma-tazz dresses! Was there a pre-Hallowe'en costume special on at McAssburns?"

"Get lost, Mitsy!" I growl.

Joey says: "Hey, hey, if it isn't Little Lulu! Listen up! With all that-there net in which yore drownin', ya wanna go fishin' with me after the concert? Promise you we could score us a Big One!"

Mitsy shimmies her cleavage some more and says: "Good luck tonight with your flutey toots! What key is this Doppler-thing in? B Flat!?"

I wince and glower.

"I see that not even having your jaw wired together can stop you from mouthing off, you blubber-faced loser!"

"Loser? A socked nose trumps a dislocated jaw anytime!"

"Oh sure! Make up your own rules! You always have and always will, you jerk-faced donkey!"

The mood is bristling.

Mitsy lifts a fist and gets set to land it on me, aiming for my face: "You want another broken nose, you Namby-Pamby Suck of a Mommy's Girl?"

Guys from the band move in and stand between us, shoulder to shoulder.

Bert steps up.

"Wow, Lois. You are really pumping it out! Good on you!"

Mitsy is holding the triangle over her head, threatening to bash him with it.

He turns to Mitsy: "Get lost, you Ringling-Circus Ding-a-Ling! Leave Lois alone!"

Becky has turned pale. She is unnerved by all the hostility. Bert notices.

"Same goes for Becky! You'd bet lay off both of them, or I'll sick the rest of the band on you."

Mitsy moves off.

"We're with you two. We are going to make sure you are both safe and sound."

"Thanks," we say. Then suddenly self-conscious, we both look at our feet.

The eternity is over. We are waiting in the wings with the strings.

Mr. Maxwell appears before us, lifts a finger for us to wait a moment, and then indicates to the strings to follow after him.

The strings move in single file away from us.

Mr. Maxwell goes next.

From the wings, we can see the strings taking their seats and we listen to their final frenetic tune-up in A using the first violin's tuning fork for lack of an oboe.

Once settled, Mr. Maxwell strides out onto the podium.

He delivers an effusive speech, extolling our talents both impressive (Becky's) and modest (mine), describes our own musical journey in discovery of the Doppler, explains how it came about that Becky will be conducting, while he will be co-conducting, lauds our creativity and 'moxie' then he calls us onstage to an enthusiastic applause.

We step out and take our positions.

Becky signals Mr. Maxwell with a slight nod, who lifts his baton to the orchestra.

Becky establishes the tempo by tapping her foot while gently lifting and lowering her elbows.

She nods. This prompts the strings to launch into the brief four-bar preamble. Becky joins in with the soulful song of her solo introit. I join her with the echo of her call, and we are off into the surreal realm of the flitting yellow-throated warbler who calls out for a lost friend, is joined by same, the two soar in the air with joy then, then, then—the successive crescendos —1, 2, 3 that reach a peak of anxiety, panic, fright. Then follows sorrowful loss. Again, back to a peaceful spell before another succession of crescendos brings heartbreak and desolation.

The cadence ending the Andante and providing the bridge to the Rondo is suffocatingly prolonged and poignant. It is so intense and I am feeling so tense, that the tendons in my arms ache, and it seems that my heart stops beating. For here comes the change in tempo. Here comes the upbeat with the gypsy who dances his jig with his peg leg. Here come the variations that complement, but do not seem to relate to the lyrical calling of the soulful refrain until it surfaces again, entangles itself, then eludes, and dives once more into the ether.

I cannot pinpoint when it happens but somewhere during the Rondo, I find myself floating off, transcendent, losing touch with the world of substance, merged within an indescribably surreal brilliantly golden skein of being that contains an intricate blend of all emotions in the range of human existence. Joy, sorrow, loss, longing, fear, anger—the whole gamut intricately interwoven.

I look over at Becky.

She has tears streaming down her cheeks.

When she looks up to signal me, she sees that I too have tears streaming down my cheeks.

When we finish, the entire audience rises to their feet calling out "Bravo! Bravo!" and "Encore! Encore!"

The applause goes on and on and on.

We bow together in unison.

We face to hug each other.

"I wept for my lost Papa!"

"I wept for my lost Pinewood!"

We hug each other again, console each other, strengthen each other.

Then we turn to the audience again and bow.

Mr. Maxwell cajoles the audience: "Give it up for the Doppler Twins!" he shouts with pride, evoking another wave of applause.

He takes us by our arms and leads us off-stage.

"Kleenex, I need Kleenex!" Becky pleads from a lady standing in the wings who carries a large handbag. "Me, too!" I say, hoping that my nose is not bloody.

The lady seems to be prepared with exactly what we need. She has tissues on the ready for both of us, also a thicker pack of gauze for me in case I need it.

We thank her profusely.

Rescued, we blow our noses and start wiping the tears off our faces.

"I was so afraid that my nose would run down over my upper lip so I could not play!"

"Me, too!" I answer.

"When I was breathing in and out, I had bubble in my nose!" Becky says under her breath.

"You! I had double bubbles in MY nose!"

Becky looks at me with astonishment. I can see her trying to imagine what I had just said. Then her gurgling laugh pours out.

We are once again immersed in laughter when Father and Mother with Mrs. Molnar find us. They are smiling broadly. The Mothers have our cardigans draped over their forearms.

"Congratulations, you two!" Mother and Father exclaim, proudly.

"Yes, yes, my two Darling Angels! Very well done!" Mrs. Molnar exclaims.

After Becky and I have finally calmed down, we pause.

We look at each other with exultation and disbelief.

"We did it!" we cry, "We did it!"

Then we dance a jig of joy, reversing arms to go round in a circle one way, then the other. Never have I ever experienced the intensity of pleasure that can come from such a triumph.

"Csardas!" Becky calls out.

"Shard Ass!" I call back.

Neither of us knows why our exchange is funny, but it makes us collapse into giggles. I suspect it is very rude. I have no idea what 'Shard' means in Hungarian, but do know it is a daring way of getting away with saying 'Ass' in English.

Doppler Twin Salute
11-2

Thursday, October 24
9:30 p.m.

Father announces after the concert that he is taking all of us out. We will celebrate "Our Doppler Twins" and their successful performance by going to "Bertie's and Gertie's", a tavern and country restaurant on the highway. It is one of the few places in the whole area that is open '24/7'. Outside on the highway there are flashing neon signs: "Open All Day Every Day" and "We Doze But Never Cloze".

"You two must be famished!" Mother says.

"It takes very much energy to play so well! You can also have any dessert you want—my treat!" Mrs. Molnar says.

Father puts her straight, "Waitaminnut now, not so generous, Mrs. Molnar, this is on me, so I'm the one to decide who gets dessert—and what!"

"Oh Graham! He's just teasing, Eszter! You must be back in good humour, Dear! He can be such a card!" Mother titters.

Or a cad, I mutter to myself, figuring he probably means it!

I would rather go to "Ab's Diner" and have fish and chips with pickled beets. Or "Ethel's Olde Englande Home Cooking" for roast beef and Yorkshire pudding. But who am I to say? It's not up to Becky or myself to decide the ideal treat for all our efforts and success. We are merely the honourees.

I think: when I grow up, I will go anywhere I want, treat myself to anything I want, never be told ever again where to go or what to order.

Feeling so hateful toward Father twists a corkscrew in the heart. It is self-evident that I am still fuming, and struggling against guilt. It is my duty to love my Father unconditionally. Yet how can I resurrect my love for him after he has betrayed me so badly?

We find ourselves being led to a large round table set for eight. Father insists he had reserved a table for that number. Mother and Mrs. Molner launch into a head count, which they seem to think if repeated several times will rectify Father's alleged miscount, as there are five of us. A lot of squabbling takes place—until Father gets a word in edgewise and says, "What you don't know won't hurt you!" This stops them in their tracks. It is then that Bert, his own Father, plus the backstage lady with the tissues and big handbag enter the dining area and join us. Bert is grinning and pointing over the lady's head from her to himself. I quickly gather from his antics who she is.

"You are Bert's mother?" I exclaim, "You were the lady waiting off stage with tissues on hand, just for us?"

"Well, let's say 'Just for you', in case you had a nose bleed in the middle of the concert!" the lady smiles, "I hadn't anticipated that you would both be crying!"

"Oh, thank you so much for doing that, Mrs. Sanderfield! And thank you for the other treatments you sent with Bert—"

"What treatments? What are you talking about?" Mother interrupts, never to miss a beat when it comes to her daughter.

"You see?" Father says, "You see? This was supposed to be a surprise!"

"It still is!" Mother says, beaming her hostess smile.

Introductions all round. Father explains the Sandersons' presence, something to do with the bond formed between the two Fathers while in Ottawa, and the fact that Bert was also in the concert, he was in the band and was the one who marched up the aisle playing the bassoon without any music, so he too deserved a reward, and then Bert comes to stand with Becky and myself until the table is ready. The restaurant owner, Bertie, I presume, rushes around completing the table for eight. A woman's head and shoulders, like a bust on a mantel piece, peers through the serving window behind the main counter. I decide that must be Gertie. If he's the host, then she must be the cook.

We are seated round a larger table according to Father's directives.

Father and Mr. Sanderfield sit together with Mrs. Sanderfield next to her husband, then Bert. Next to Father there's Mother then Mrs. Molnar then Becky. That leaves myself sitting directly across the big round table from Father, with Bert to my right and Becky to my left.

Everyone—meaning Mother, Mrs. Molnar, and Mrs. Sanderfield versus Father and Mr. Sanderfield, is talking at once, with two entirely different conversations going on.

I learned a new word recently and can now apply it: cacophony.

I turn to Bert and ask, "Why wasn't your Mother at the Avro Rollout?"

"She was unable to attend. She has just been released from the sanatorium!"

"Oh! How long was she in there?"

"A long time. Six months. Iron lung. Terrible!"

"Oh! I am so sorry, Bert!"

Then it dawns on me. I blurt, "That explains a lot!"

"What do you mean?"

"You are kind. Considerate. Civil. You have compassion. You don't talk down to me, or smirk at me when I talk just because I'm a girl— You are not like other guys in our class!"

"Well, on that note alone, I certainly hope not!" Bert laughs.

"Your Mother—She took the time to send me her home-made nasal spray, just in time for me to breathe again. Then she waited in the wings with tissue in case I got a nose bleed and needed it! How very thoughtful, especially considering she has been so ill. Has she fully recuperated?"

"Not really. She tires easily."

It comes round to placing our order, and I am surprised to hear Father ordering fish and chips for me! He also remembers to order extra tartar sauce. "Oh boy—Yum!" I say. But I'm still not up to any further pleasantries, like saying "thank you".

"You're the one who's turning out to be a real tartar!" Bert says quietly, winking at me, "You sure aren't taking any guff from Mitsy anymore! Good for you!"

"What's that?" Father says from across the table. "Did you just mention Mitsy?"

"Yes, Sir, I did!"

"What's with that cockamamie cuckoo anyway? The first time we met, it was when I caught her defacing Diefenbaker's portrait in the foyer of Centrewood's Public Library.

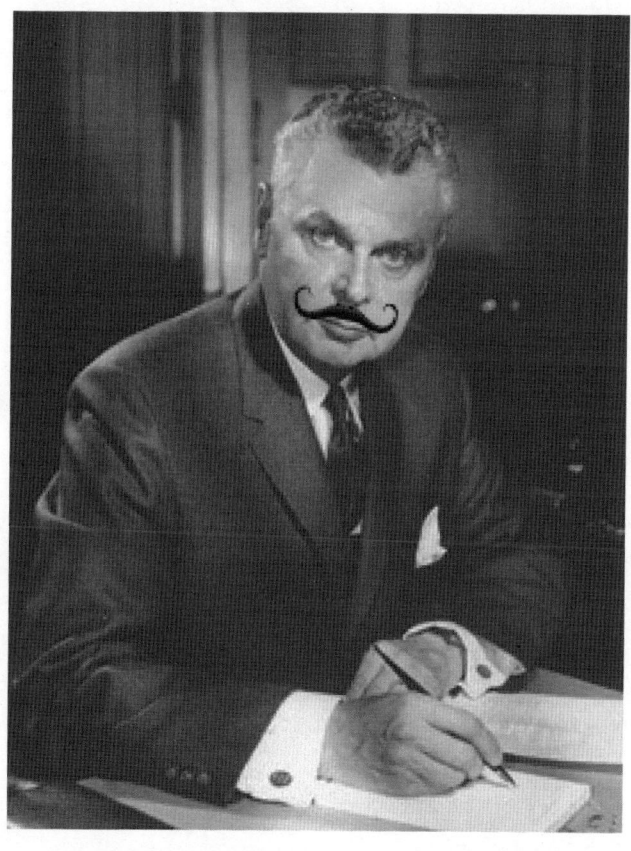

Defaced photograph of Prime Minister John Diefenbaker.
Moustache added by minxy Mitsy Gardiner.

Later, she told us that her father was a pilot flying spy missions for the U.S. Air Force. Methinks she is prone to telling tall tales. When she was at the house, she told us she played the saxophone! But there she was in the band, playing the *triangle!* Of all the cheek! Hmph!"

Bert, Becky and I look down at our placemats. None of us chooses to enlighten him. For which I'm grateful. Because I know if Father finds out Mitsy couldn't play the sax because she got a dislocated jaw and had to have her jaw wired, they would instantly want to know how she got it, it was bound to be my fault somehow, and I'd be up that proverbial creek again without the paddle.

Out of the corner of "one ear", I overhear Mr. Sanderfield asking Father how he got those scratches on his face: Did he tangle with Revenue Canada while he was in Ottawa—did he suffer a claw-back on his taxes? with Father saying a neighbour's cat got loose in the house, and naturally as the Man of the House, he was the one who had to catch it. Mr. Sanderfield says that on first sight, he wondered if they had unwittingly unleashed Sasquatch when they started tearing down Pinewood. I can barely discern what they say next for the women all talking at once. I know that the men are discussing the revised plans. "Surprise" "So soon!" "Sooner than planned." "Daughter not pleased."

Then Father's words ring clear, are distinctly discernible. I hear him say:

"But she'll come round when she learns that! She'll have to admit there's some compensation for losing Pinewood." Mr. Sanderfield asks, "It's settled then?" And Father replies,"Oh yes! The thing is, when the Olympic Pool is built, she won't be that far away from the house at all! She will be amazed how strategically well placed we are, in terms of access to both the Collegiate *and* the Olympic Pool!"

Despite my conviction never to speak to me again, I hear Me, Miss Big-Ears, butt in:

"Excuse me, Father? Have plans for the Olympic Pool been finalized?"

"Well, yes, they have, Lois," Father says curtly, this being the first time he has spoken to me since I almost clawed him to death. In fact, his hand almost reflexively strokes the deepest gash on his face, "It is going to be built between the berm and the Main Artery on this side of the highway!"

"That is not where you said it would be built. I still have your sketch of Pinewood where you placed it on the other side of the highway!"

Father replies, "Oh yes, that was the original plan for it. But this way, it will be just around the corner from you!"

"Are you saying that I should regard the demolition of Willow Creek, the destruction of the marsh, the bush, the little waterfall *and* my Eagle's home at the top of the tallest trees near the highway as an acceptable trade-off for an Olympic Pool?"

Bert intercedes: "Gee whiz, Lois, from where you live, you'll only have to walk a couple of blocks from your house, and you'll be there!"

My whole body starts to weep, involuntarily. Tears start to pour down my cheeks and my body is filled with tremors, as though a dark electrical current is flowing up and down from head to toe through heart and gut inside me. My feet and hands turn to ice. I am suddenly terribly cold.

To entice me into moving away from Unionville, Father had told me there would be an Olympic Pool at Centrewood. I had been doing very well with my swimming lessons, and my dream had been to be Canada's next Marilyn Bell. But when we moved in, there was no such pool, and that the plans had been suspended.

Meanwhile, to compensate for losing all my friends and having the whole summer to occupy myself, I had ventured across the road and explored a new world, Pinewood. I found wild plants that rivalled domestic plants for their unusual shapes and colours, a wide variety of trees that had different bark and character from the ubiquitous city maple, and creatures that I had no idea existed, like

Beetlebomb, my baby turtle, found scrambling down the slope to reach Willow Creek before being trampled to death by its brothers and sisters. There was also the Red Eft, the poisonous salamander, and Eagle, who came to my rescue.

Why do I have to give up my beloved Pinewood with all its beauty and its innocent little creatures, in exchange for one of my life dreams?

I want both! I want both!

Father leaps at the opportunity to start rattling on to Bert:

"See? That's the beauty of Centrewood—the magic of living in the first place in North America with a plan based on the circle! Lois will see how direct her path will be, when the new Pinewood plans are completed and the extensions to ring roads three to eight are opened. She'll be going back and forth to school, and to swimming, in a jiffy!"

I hear Bert saying, "Centrewood is not the first place based on the circle, Mr. Michelsen! Washington, D.C. has a 'wedges and corridors' master plan also based on the wheel and spoke model! Apparently, it is not turning out so well! There is chaos at peak times, such as during rush hour!"

"There won't be traffic jams in Centrewood," Father asserts, huffily, "All the traffic to and from the downtown core can be readily dispersed by cars taking any one of the ring roads and turning onto one of the radials."

If Bert isn't careful, he will learn and no one should dare to challenge Father's intense loyalty to Centrewood. If suburban wars broke out, would he swear fealty and bear arms?

Who cares. I am too distraught to listen closely.

It is Mrs. Sanderfield who first notices that I am weeping and trembling.

She stands up discreetly and slowly comes round the table to me, shelters me from view by her body and her arm when she bends over to me, "You look so miserable! For a young lady who conquered a very difficult piece of music, I would expect you to be a radiant sunbeam. What's wrong, my dear?"

"Pinewood. They have torn up my pasture, destroyed my trees and wild flowers and all the little creatures that live there. They're burying my stream in underground pipes. They lied to me!" I gulp, "They told me Pinewood was not going to be developed. But they severed Upper Pinewood for development. Now this. I was promised an Olympic Pool before we even moved here because I want to train as a long-distance swimmer like Marilyn Bell, but when we moved, it wasn't even in the plans. Now I have to say goodbye to my stream and my Eagle and all the natural beauty across the way from me and be happy in exchange? Why couldn't I have had both?"

I know I am babbling but I cannot stop.

Mrs. Sanderfield listens closely to every word.

She draws several tissues from her large handbag and mops my face for me, helps me blow my nose gently.

She reaches out and takes my ice water, pours some on a napkin, applies the cold wet fabric to my forehead.

Meanwhile, I sense that I have created a spectacle. Everyone at the table has stopped talking. All-life-as-we-know-it has come to a standstill.

"This girl is in a state of shock," Mrs. Sanderson announces, "She's shaking and she is starting to turn blue. Bert, honey, take Dad's car keys, run to the car and fetch the motor rug, would you please? Would either of you happen to have another blanket for Becky?"

"Oh, she be all right, she has sweater!" Mrs. Molnar says.

"Don't fuss over her, Mrs. Sanderfield, she's just fine!" Mother says.

Father, Mr. Sanderfield, Mother, Mrs. Molnar: they all sit there like wooden soldiers, arms tight to their sides.

Becky has drawn in closer to my side.

Father is frowning in a dark cloud of disapproval. He doesn't like theatrics. Or setbacks. He doesn't like anyone at all rattling his cage, let alone me. After inviting everyone to this celebration, is his daughter going to be a troublemaker and rain on this parade?

Bert materializes with the 'motor rug', which is not the usual itchy grey wool army-issue type blanket with the thin red stripes that we have in the back of our car. It is an enormous thick and cuddly off-white Hudson Bay blanket with wide black, green, red and yellow stripes at each end.

I hear Mrs. Sanderfield instructing Bert, "Spread it out first if you can. That's it. Now let's lay half of it over her lap, then her legs and feet and tuck her in!

"We'll leave your hands free so you can eat, honey!" she laughs, then she says: "Becky! There's plenty of blanket left over for you too, dear, if you wish!"

I hear Becky's voice and feel her clutching my hand:

"I wish to come too into blanket as I am Lois's Doppler Siamese Twin!"

Bert says: "Say, is there room for an honorary triplet?"

"Get away with you!" Mrs. Sanderfield says, chuckling.

It is Mr. Sanderfield who saves the day and is most chivalrous.

He summons Bertie the waiter, and orders glasses of white wine for the ladies, two beers for Father and himself, a coke for Bert, and!—two Shirley Temples "on the double" for the "pretty damsels in blue".

The drinks have arrived by the time Becky and I are both 'tucked in' and wiped our eyes.

Mr. Sanderfield stands up and clinks his wine glass with his butter knife.

"Young ladies," he says across the table to Becky and myself, "When I saw the programme this evening, I thought there was a piece of music being played in my honour! That is because I am responsible at Avro for the radar tracking system! Have you seen those big radar dishes set out like saucers on the Malton airfield? The biggest and most advanced dishes ever before installed are being used for the first time to track the Avro Arrow! Why am I telling you this? Ironically, because they are called "Doppler" dishes, not after your famous composer Franz Doppler but after the renowned physicist Christian Doppler. He is the scientist who noticed that when tracking an object, be it a heavenly or manmade body, the frequency of an approaching object is higher than that of the object receding. That is called the 'Doppler Effect'. Have you learned about that in science class yet?"

We shake our heads no.

Father interjects: "I told Lois all about the Doppler Effect leading up to Avro Arrow Rollout Day!"

"Indeed? Well now, may I propose a toast to the Doppler Duo who had quite a Doppler Effect on *me* tonight?" he says, and we all laugh. "I for one can assure you that I am a Doppler Twins fan! You are going to be stars! I will be tracking your flute careers well into the future!" He turns to everyone around the table, "A toast to the girls! Well done, well done!"

To which everyone else responds, "Hear, hear!" with a clinking of glasses and a round of applause.

When we all step out into the wide-open countryside of "Bertie and Gertie's" parking lot, the sun has gone down completely. It is not entirely dark yet. Instead, the skyline, the trees, the outbuildings, the night with all its other silhouettes is cloaked in a velvety darkness in gradations from black to shades of blue directly overhead. The deep cerulean-blue sky is clear, filled with stars.

We are still draped in Mrs. Sanderson's Hudson's Bay "motor rug", which she left for us temporarily.

"Look!" Becky says, pointing at a black disc of a moon floating high above us, almost completely covered except for its pearly-white luminous rim, "A New Moon!" She draws me close and we stand with arms linked looking up at the sky, "Lois, I shall never again play Doppler Duo the way I played tonight with you! Our performance, it was—how is it said in English? It could happen only 'Once in a New Moon!'"

New Moon

"I like it!" I laugh, hugging her closer while we stand side by side, looking up at the sky. "Although I believe the actual expression is really 'Once in a Blue Moon'."

"What is a blue moon?" she asks.

"It's when two full moons fall inside one calendar month."

"Oh! Let us keep watch for it. When does that happen next? Then you and I, we can have one full moon each in same month!"

"Great idea! But for the moment, Becky, let's stick to your expression for tonight's moon—It's brilliant!"

Hubba-Hubba's
11-3

Sunday October 27, 1957

Since I launched my own personal collection of collective nouns—a 'bale' of turtles, a 'clowder of cats', by way of example—I became increasingly aware of another collective 'entity', which is not a collective noun per se, but a collective pronoun. It is in the third person plural, and therefore impersonal and, most worrisome, anonymous.

I am referring to the ubiquitous 'They', which seems to have a tremendous amount of power and influence, and seems to be in charge of many aspects of life. Yet since this entity 'They' is invisible, and no one seems to know who or where 'They' are, it seems that their decisions cannot be challenged, are not subject to repeal, are irrevocable, and yet can affect us all.

Whenever 'They' are invoked, that is the end of any discussion: that is that.

'They' know best.

'They' are in control.

Leave it up to 'Them'.

***

This entity 'They' figured large during the Avro delegation's time in Ottawa.

There had been not a word about that trip, until we were in the car and heading for the Hub. Father seemed to be in a more communicative mood. Perhaps the low-keyed conversation he had with Mother in the bedroom this morning put him in a change of mood. He was still not pleased with my behaviour, but he was willing to put his best foot forward.

In the course of the drive, Father divulged some of what had happened while they were away.

The appeal to Leon Balcer, Solicitor General of Canada, against RCMP violations of Father's civil liberties and its unwarranted harassment of other respected Avro CEOs had gained results. He agreed to intercede with the RCMP Commissioner Stuart Wood to restrain the Secret Service from any and all further indiscretions involving Avro employees. Any further complaints, the Solicitor General ensured the committee of CEOs chaired by Mr. Smye, that 'They' would take care of it.

The entity 'They' also figured largely when Father took his appeal to the Governor General Vincent Massey concerning the Mississauga land claim. The 'GG' was not prepared to entertain any action concerning the way in which First Nations treaties had been negotiated by the Crown. Father told us it was par for the course with a man who was a 'toady', which he explained was a person more loyal to protecting his own position than upsetting any apple-cart. He told Father that the matter would have to be addressed to the Department of Indian Affairs where 'They' would handle it.

From the backseat, I contributed my nugget of wisdom:

"During my ride from the Pancake House in his Blue Pierce Arrow convertible, Mr. Floyd told me you needn't bother with the Department of Indian Affairs. They are just civil servants bound to enforce the Indian Act. He also said the Governor General would be a lost cause, but I didn't have a chance to ask him why. Did you discuss the issue further with Mr. Floyd at all, Father?"

Nothing from Father.

I tacked on my opinion:

"I should expect the Governor General could appeal to Queen Elizabeth, just as Peter Jones himself went directly to London and appealed to the Crown way back when. After all, the Governor General is the Crown's representative in Canada. It was the Crown that signed what the Mississaugas regard as their own 'Magna Carta' in 1763. It was the Crown who promised to protect their land from colonial malfeasance. So why won't he act on the Mississaugas' behalf?"

No answer.

I asked: "Did you tell him about the 'Ten Shillings', Father?"

Silence.

"Is this where it ends? Chief Fred asked for your help!"

It was Mother who shot a curt response over the seat: "Your Father managed to gain an audience with the Governor General himself. That was the best he could do."

"Is that all then? Just one question, one exchange, but nothing more? The Governor General let you say your piece and that was the end of it?"

Silence.

"Mr. Floyd said your best resort would be the Supreme Court. Will you be helping the Mississaugas to appeal?"

Mother intercedes once more as Father's self-ordained representative on earth:

"I should think you would be pleased that the delegation was able to appeal the RCMP violations and get assurances we won't be treated with such disrespect in the future," Mother said.

"But the Mississauga have been treated with disrespect for almost a century! Now you know how it feels, clearly it's now time to fight for Chief Fred and Chief Peter Jones!"

"Your Father's primary responsibility was to look after our own interests first, Lois!"

"That's not how I see it! You can look after tending to your own interests, and still make attempts to help someone else! What will Chief Fred think? You went to him for help, and he put time aside for us. He even called you 'Uncle'. You called him 'Son'. It was as though you made a sacred pact with him."

"He made a pact, Lois. It is blasphemous to call such a deal 'sacred'," Mother shoots back.

"What is your next step? Are you going to tell Chief Fred what 'They' said? Did you ever consider going to Ottawa again and taking Chief Fred with you?"

"No," Father finally spoke.

"How will Aunt Ani feel? Now I know why she appeared outside my bedroom window only just last week!"

"She what?" Father slammed on the brakes, and pulled over to the curb.

When we visited the New Credit Reserve, it was Aunt Ani who brought the photograph that clinched my description of Chief Peter Jones, chief of the Mississaugas, who had appeared to me during the Arrow Rollout. She said my waking visions were a "special gift" not understood by religion-controlled people in our society. She was very knowledgeable about native history, also about nature, and helped me solve a major stickler with my burr project, while the men discussed the Mississauga treaties. By the time we said goodbye, we had formed a special bond. Unbeknownst to Mother, she gave me her phone number, in case I wanted to contact her.

"I saw Aunt Ani in Pinewood, walking out of the thicket, coming across the pasture toward me."

"What the heck did she want?" Father asked.

"She was carrying a basket of burrs. She must have known something bad was about to happen. She came to warn me. Just like the skinned rabbit, I know now he wasn't chasing me, he came to alert me that something dire was about to happen—Its whole world was about to be stripped. Just like the zipper that crossed all of Pinewood on a diagonal and opened up the earth into a big gash. My friend the Eagle—He too tried to appeal to you, Father! He landed on the hood of your car to protect me, yes, but also to ask you to save Pinewood! Now his own home atop the trees in the forest is destroyed! Couldn't they at least have left the tall scotch pines alone? Did they have to decimate everything?"

"That's enough, Lois!" Father said, "What's done is done. You will put all of it behind you. Leave it all in the past. That includes your 'Aunt Ani', do you hear?"

"Was seeing Aunt Ani another one of your waking visions, dear?" Mother asked, stating the obvious.

"Remember what Chief Fred said, Father! 'What goes round, comes round'."

It was almost fortuitous that there was only just enough time for Father to broach another big Elephant in the Room before it was too late. We had turned up the ramp into the parking garage above the Hub on our way to Hubba-Hubba's.

"Your Mother and I still have not yet heard about your day with Mitsy. We have gathered from your comportment, that more than just a pleasant bike ride and a picnic in the countryside transpired?"

I thought: Wouldn't you just like to know! And: Too late now, you missed your chance.

I bit my lip and buttoned up.

***

As for Mrs. Molnar's dilemma, it turned out that Father's lawyer had put the wheels in motion to determine the whereabouts of Becky's father in Hungary, also to clear his name of any anti-democratic activities.

He had also found out which procedures had to be followed in order for Father to become Mrs. Molnar's 'interim' Executor and Power of Attorney.

Accordingly, the necessary paperwork had been prepared during Father's absence in Ottawa. It was this past Friday, the morning after the concert, that Father met with Mrs. Molnar at the lawyer's office, to sign the papers.

***

For this reason, Mrs. Molnar has invited us out to Hubba-Hubba's on the upper level of the Hub for the much-touted "All-Day Open Buffet Sunday Breakfast" to express her gratitude to him.

"To Mr. Michelsen, my new P.O.A., a noble knight in shining armour who comes to rescue maidens in times of duress! Now I can relax, knowing my Bo will be okay, if anything should happen to me before husband Bence comes home," Mrs. Molnar says, lifting her glass of apple juice.

We raise our juice glasses and clink all round.

She lifts her glass again:

"Oh! Now I can offer my own toast to the girls, our pride and joy, the Doppler Twins!"

"Aye, aye," Father and Mother cheer, clinking their tomato juice glasses, "To the Twins!"

We shuffle off to the buffet laid out on a long table laden with salads, pasta dishes, steamed vegetables, bacon—both peameal (Canadian or British, my favourite) or "back bacon" (American word for the former) and ordinary old American bacon (it tastes like fatty dried wood to me) that is served in crispy strips on the plate, or used to bind together a wad of "real" meat such as pork tenderloin, and every type of egg dish imaginable.

***

"Hey," Becky says as a quiet aside to me, "Did you watch 'Beaver' on Friday night?"

"Ye-es, I did!" I reply, my voice equally low, "How's that for a coincidence? Beaver also got a haircut!"

We have watched every episode so far.

In the recent episode of Leave it to Beaver, Beaver kept losing his lunch money, was reprimanded, then he lost the money his Father had given him for a haircut. He decided he would cut his own hair. Brother Wally's attempt to patch a botched job made it even worse.

Becky laughed, "I know! I thought our haircuts were bad!"

"Ours are even worse! At least he didn't end up with bangs!"

"Ha ha! True! And we can't use artificial flowers every day!"

"He has bald spots where he cut right down to his scalp!"

"It will take much longer time for his hairs to grow back!"

"Hair, Becky, Hair. The word 'hair' in the singular is used as the collective noun."

"Yes, yes. Although makes no sense. In English, one single hair is a hair. Hair altogether on head is hair. Not as in Hungarian, which if plural, is hairs!" she sighs, "Then so should it be 'bang' not bangs, yes?"

"No. But you're right. It makes no sense."

"Who decided all that?"

"I don't know, Becky. Somewhere, at some time, 'They' decided!"

***

While Father slices into his eggs benedict, he reminds us all to change our clocks before we go to bed tonight. It is time for the big switch from Daylight Savings Time to Eastern Standard Time. "Spring forward, Fall back!" he sums up.

"Why should we? It's ridiculous, just when we need the light, that's when the time change comes along." That was me. Choosing once again to speak up.

"Don't be so ornery, Lois," Mother says, "It is what it is." This stymies the conversation, so she adds, "I'm reminded of the famous quotation by Churchill: it's always darkest before—DST!!"

"That proves my point, exactly!" I rejoin, "It doesn't pay to be clever, Mother, if you're trying to score a point for the opposite side."

"Well, pardon me for living," Mother says, another one of her inscrutable comebacks. After completing the next fork-load of her eggs, she adds, "Perhaps we have to soak up enough darkness over winter, so we can appreciate more light when it finally comes!"

I say, "I remember last year when we converted to Standard Time. It got dark so quickly, like a blind being dropped, that there was hardly enough time to get home after school, let alone do anything outdoors before suppertime!"

Father says, "That's because 7:00 DST is really 6:00 EST. By this time of the year, the natural light even on DST is darker, at least more so than during the summer months, lest we all forget that the earth is tilting away from the sun."

He reminds us, "Just remember that it will be harder to get up in the morning when it is still dark," and to observe the maxim: "Less light in morning—Peeping Tom's warning!"

"What—Why?" Mother asks, instantly clutching her hands to her bosom, and looking wary.

"Think before you open your drapes in the morning. If you've turned the bedroom light on without first putting on your dressing gown, there might be someone lurking outside, waiting for the chance to peek in your window!"

"Oh, Gra-ham!" Mother titters, "You made that up. You're in fine form today. You must be feeling better!"

"Why can't 'They' leave things well enough alone?" I ask, "Whoever was the bright bunny that decided to plunge us all back into darkness, just when we need more light?"

"We can only assume that 'They' thought it best to do it this way," Mother answers primly, with an air that she has confidence in anonymous wisdom.

"It might have been implemented in wartime for energy savings," Father says, "As a trade-off between the need to reduce electricity use and lower heating costs. Or perhaps to provide the farmers more light for early spring planting. Regardless, it seems they knew what 'They' were doing when they launched the whole scheme," Father says, sagely.

"Is anyone sure of its usefulness any more? Or will it continue just because it's always been?"

Becky asks, "It seems beneficial to have more light both morning and evening. Why not leave it at Daylight Saving Time all year round?"

"That is so much an excellent idea, Becky," Mrs. Molnar says.

"Who is this invisible entity called 'They' anyway?" I ask.

"Why, 'They' are the authorities, Dear!"

"Who are these authorities, I'd like to know?"

" 'They' are the government, or more specifically, the branch that has to do with issues that affect the public interest," Father says.

"How would a citizen go about finding out which branch is responsible so it can be repealed? There must be tons of people wanting to dispense with it!"

"That's enough, Lois. You've made your point," Father has indulged me quite enough, and finally puts an end to it.

I switch topics, and raise the next unsolicited topic for discussion:

"There is another major 'They' in my books. It is the 'They' who allowed the developers to retract the original plans made for Centrewood, and who wangled their way into using more of the land for development at the expense of retaining a natural space for public enjoyment."

Father stiffens, but does not reprimand me. Instead, he wipes his mouth with his napkin, glances at Mother, and opts to respond, not entirely eagerly.

As we daintily spread our patties of butter on our toast, as we genteelly pick up fork and knife and slice into a stack of pancakes drooling with maple syrup (Becky), bacon and eggs with steamed beans and home fries (Mrs. Molnar), tossed scrambled eggs with sliced tomato and french fries (Mother), or in my instance, sedimentary layers of cheese omelette with peameal bacon, asparagus and onion, Father presents his rationale for the preposterous bludgeoning of my pastureland.

According to Father, it was necessary for the developers to do what they did since they were running behind costs. They saw the best way to solve the dilemma would be to build more houses than planned.

"As it was, it was fortuitous that technology had caught up with them.

"Originally, at the inception of planning for Centrewood, there was a reason why most of the Pinewood tract was designated as parkland. It lies in a flood plain! As it was, its grade was perilously close to the water table, and was not suitable for housing, particularly houses with basements. However, since the recent advent of more solutions in modern engineering, it is now possible to build homes if the streams are laid deeper underground. With Pinewood, it was determined that with the surrounding elevations as support and with scientifically-based re-engineering of the land, only an additional berm would be required to serve as a retainer in case of flooding. A drainage pipe through that berm will empty out into a concrete gulch to handle the overflow. After which, it will run through a large culvert under the highway to rejoin its natural path into a deep ravine where the Humber River flows south to Lake Ontario."

"There won't be a stream or marsh or open fields anymore."

"No."

"There are no plans for a large public park anymore."

"No. But to compensate, certain smaller areas have been designated throughout the whole of Centrewood for local parks. Instead of a larger public park, inside each subdivision, there will be smaller parks."

I look at Father almost speechless with scorn. "If you're talking about ones like the parkette next to the Municipal Building, I don't see how that comes close to being a real park! It is just a small, flat faceless patch of sun-shocked grass mowed to within an inch of its life, with a spindly privet hedge around the edge, and a twiggy little sapling plunked next to just one bench! Oh, don't let's forget the shrivelled, unwatered marigolds planted under that tree. Call that a park? It's just a place where people let their dogs run around off-leash for a pee"—"Lois!" Mother exclaims in reprimand— "Not to mention anything else they might get up to!" I had those coupling chihuahuas in mind, but how could anyone at the table know exactly what I was thinking?

"What do you consider to be an ideal park, Lois?" Mrs. Molnar asks me. I appreciate her courtesy.

"A real park would be like Pinewood, a large tract of land with a bush and a natural stream running through it, and large trees like weeping willows hanging over the water. There would be small wooden foot bridges that cross over to the other side where people can explore the amazing variety of plants and creatures that abound in nature. There would be places on the banks of the stream where people can picnic on fields of natural grasses, or sit in the shade to relax, maybe read a book!"

I turn back to Father. "You know the section of Pinewood on the other side of the berm? That is now supposedly a park. There is a large drainage pipe through the berm that will handle any overflow from what was once Willow Creek, then an ugly poured-concrete trough that to guide the water to the Big Culvert and under the highway. On the edge of the trough, 'They' have plunked a token picnic table and a bench next to a struggling sapling. That 'park' is hardly an inviting place to relax, without a real tree for shade, with no breeze, and a place to sit out in the steaming sun with hot concrete radiating heat till it's burning your face and the soles of your feet! You know how it's being used? By boys and their roller boards. They use the berm for propulsion! —Anything man-made like a concrete trough can never be a genuine park!"

Father throws his hands up in exasperation.

"Remember that this is all brand new, Lois!" he enjoins, "You are judging all of Centrewood by its bare bones. Come enough time, all the trees that have been planted will grow tall. All the new local parks sprinkled around Centrewood will be quite pleasant.

"This summer, the grass was parched and unsightly after a hot summer and the new little saplings did not flourish, but with a better season, the grass will take hold and grow greener and the trees will be taller. You never know, there might even be fountains or splash pads! Everything is in the throes of planning right now!"

"The difference between your perspective and mine, Father, is you see it the way it will be, Meanwhile, I'm stuck living in it the way it is."

"Good point, Graham," Mother offers.

"And what about all the wildlife? What about the field animals— the mice and the shrews, the rabbits and the gophers? What about the birds—the owls, the swallows, the bluebirds, the pheasants and the partridge? What about my Eagle? Where is he to go? What about the insects and snakes and wild flowers? the tadpoles, the frogs and the trout? What about the blue skimmers and the green darner dragonflies? What will happen to them, Father? This was their home first!"

Father ponders a bit then says:

"They'll just have to find somewhere else to go, I suppose."

"Spoken like a true colonialist," is my retort. It takes some strength not to add a caustic remark about "White Man's" attitude toward the Indians.

Father flinches. I can see that this remark has stung. But he does nothing to change his stance.

I had never seen this side of him before. The side where his only defense is a hard defense. He is willing to explain away my loss and my grief, but it is clear that he has had no intention from the outset, of fighting on my behalf to save it all from destruction. He has no intention to defend me or represent me. He supports the developers' plans, and he doesn't give a fig about nature or the wildlife. Or me.

I scowl at him.

"There's more to nature than meets the eye, Father! It feeds the human spirit. It stimulates creativity. It delivers more sustenance than a swing or a slide can do. May I inform you that Becky and I found our inspiration for unravelling the Doppler music from the habits of the common yellow-throated warbler? Am I right, Becky?" Becky nods. "Flocks of them inhabitedWillow Creek! They would call out, fly off, and flit about until they found each other again. We would never have been able to interpret Doppler's music without observing nature!"

Father thinks he's come up with a smart retort:

"Think what you will have in its stead, Lois! Brand new first class facilities! Your own Olympic Pool!"

I sulk.

I mutter under my breath to Becky: "Shard Ass!"

Becky digs her elbow into my side, presumably as reinforcement.

"Don't you think they've designed and built a perfect Eden here?" Father asks, turning to Mrs. Molnar to extol the virtues of

Centrewood. It is like preaching to the converted, since she too chose to move here, didn't she!

I can see that he is winding up and veering toward his long-winded worship of the Circle when I interrupt him:

"I know how much you treasure Centrewood and why, Father!" I say. "What I can't understand is why the Centrewood Ratepayers— that includes you, and Mother, and yourself, Mrs. Molnar, allowed the developers to break their contract and forge ahead with changes that were not in the original agreement. The developers gave you their reason for doing what did. They claimed overruns in spending. But I say that it was really just so they could squeeze some more houses into Centrewood, and make more money out of the entire project! Why didn't you stop them?"

"Your Father has given you every reason for forging ahead with Pinewood," Mother says.

"Developers have the right to use their land anyway they want," Father says, "On condition their plans are ratified."

"But that's just it! Why do they have that right? Surely there should be a higher 'They' that could check them!

"Can developers present plans, have them ratified, and then do whatever they want? Obviously, they can if nobody stops them. As a result, this is what 'They' did: 'They' dug a long deep trench and buried my sweet lazy winding stream. 'They' hid Willow Creek from everyone's sight, forced it to flow underground through huge pipes. 'They' retracted their plans for a large public park, as though green space is a luxury, not a vital necessity. 'They' modelled everyone's needs after their own pathetic values, the fact they live most of their hours indoors, presuming people don't need nature, as though 'They' had the right to decide what a human being needs to feel whole. 'They' decided that wildlife should thrive elsewhere, along with all the trees and plants that sustain them. Eventually, will there be no free-running waterways at all?"

Father's next rebuttal does nothing to placate.

He has the audacity to admit that to developers, natural waterways like streams and rivulets coursing through a land site are just a nuisance and a headache. They occupy valuable land where developers could otherwise build.

"I suppose dutch elms, weeping willows, and the woods are also nuisances, they get in the way, as do the marsh, the frogs, and the reeds? And the pasture lands, with little creatures inhabiting the stones to the tall scotch pines where my Eagle dwelled? They are all nuisances?" I ask.

"Naturally," Father continues, "Mostly, because they don't fit into the greater picture, having grown at random as everything in nature does. It is part and parcel of a common sense approach to development, that any trees and marshes that stand in the way have to go."

"But why? Other towns and villages have the tall, original trees, and rivers that run right through them that didn't have to be buried OR rerouted!"

"Ah! Well, in earlier times, up till very recently, they had to do so! Changing the course of a river posed an enormous challenge. Besides, it wasn't necessary. You probably learned from your history lessons that towns were built wherever there was a river with a current strong enough for a dam to be built, that being the source of both power for the town, and lumber mills. The rivers were essential to the life of a town. Now they aren't."

"But why does the water from creeks such as Willow Creek have to be buried?"

"Every new house that is built and every new road that is paved stops the rain from going into the ground the way it was used to going. When the water doesn't have anywhere to go, all the runoff due to new building just builds up, causing flooding and erosion. The common sense solution is to pipe the rivers underground and control the direction of all the runoff to the main tributaries, like the Humber.

"Fortunately, the manufacture of huge earth-moving machines has meant that the entire grade of a landscape can be changed. Advanced water engineering has coincided with the growth of demand for large housing developments, making all this miraculously possible."

"Depends on what you consider to be miraculous," I respond. "I think it is Short-sighted. Destructive. And Criminal."

I lean across the table.

"This is my wish, Father! Deep down in my heart, I fervently hope that sometime in the future, Willow Creek and all other rivers, winding streams and rivulets that have been buried alive will once again see the light of day! That includes all the precious rivers and streams that belonged to the Ojibway, including Taddle Creek—I saw the plaque for that on Philosopher's Walk, did Mother tell you?—that have been buried under most of Toronto. You will recall Chief Fred mentioned them."

"Lois proclaimed that the rivers will all rise up and rebel," Mother says, rolling her tongue over her teeth.

"You think someday all the buried streams and rivers will return in some kind of reprisal?" Father asks, making a pooh-poohing sound.

"Yes, and then a future, wiser 'They' will dig them up, unearth and retrieve them, and revive them," I say.

"Don't hold your breath!" Father smirks, turning first to Mother and then to Mrs. Molnar to have them join in with his mockery.

I notice they do not laugh.

On the other hand, they were not nodding in agreement OR with approval.

I think I am shocking them for speaking my truth.

I lift my chin:

"Perhaps I myself will never see that day, Father. However, you yourself are fond of saying: 'Time will tell.' Well, there is something we both know, and that is: nothing lasts forever. In due time those underground pipes will crack, crumble and disintegrate. Under duress just from annual freezing and thawing alone, they will start leaking, and then they will burst! The buried waters of Willow Creek and all the other natural streams that 'They' have had the unmitigated gall to meddle with, will rise up in rebellion for being treated so disrespectfully!"

"Not in my lifetime, at any rate!"

"Never mind, future house owners will find themselves knee-deep in basement water, not knowing that a river lies buried underneath their very homes!"

"Nah. 'They' have taken care of that. Ever since Hurricane Hazel, the whole waterways system is being revamped, so that kind of flooding cannot happen again!"

"Perhaps not now. Perhaps not soon. But some day, records will be lost about what's underneath people's homes. Come one day, it will rain so hard that there will be uncontrollable flooding, water will fill houses to the rooftops, and whole backyards and whole houses will be washed away!"

"I doubt it very much," Father asserts.

"It is then that I hope someone of my own ilk, a person with a spirit like my own, will stand up to those parties you call 'They', to those who only respect making money, the city engineers and developers and investors who want to perpetuate this travesty, those who only know how to apply your so-called 'common sense' solutions. Someone will say: why were those rivers ever buried? Now they insist on resurfacing all on their own, what should we do? Do we spend money digging everything up only to replace them with more pipes so this kind of disaster can happen again? Why not revert to what was already there and respect nature? Why not have streams again, and let fresh waters flow along the foot of backyards and under little bridges, where trout can flourish and minnows can dash about like darting silver living reflexes at the slightest hint of movement from above, where sinewy willow trees can drape the tips of their branches in the waters and where human beings can dip their toes to be refreshed, can sit on a river bank in their own back yards, on sweet natural grasses, can smell the green in the trees and the earth underneath, can have a moment's tranquillity. Not the way it is now—with concrete troughs conducting runoff like it's surplus waste instead of a precious necessity!!"

Father has his elbows on the table, his chin resting on his folded hands. Now he is spreading his hands, spreading his fingers wide.

"What do we have here? Another Denton Massey in the making? Only this is not your Canadian bible-thumping evangelist! Folks, we've got a sweet-talking, nature-thumping, tree-hugging bard in our midst!" Father laughs.

"Go ahead and laugh at me, Father! You went ahead and bought me all those nature books to encourage my interest. Every discovery I made, you supported me by expanding my library. I will urge you to think of the baby wild turtle Beetlebomb— I thought you loved him as much as I did. Now I see that you were hoping he was just a stop gap distraction for me, a cute little hobby to keep me occupied for the summer!"

"Not true! I enjoyed our sojourn with the little fellow!"

"When I found him, that wee turtle was doing everything he could to reach the water's edge even when being trampled."

"That's what turtles are meant to do!"

"Not just turtles, Father! People know in their hearts what they need to flourish! People are also naturally drawn to water!"

"Not if it impedes progress!"

"It is those who don't know any different deride the importance of water, have ulterior motives and brainwash others and use their almighty authority to persuade others to see it their way!" I state, firmly, "And I object to being called a tree hugger, which is a derogatory term for someone like myself."

The tone of our conversation is making both Mother and Mrs. Molnar uncomfortable.

"Now, now, it's time that everyone be nice," Mother says.

Mrs. Molnar nods nervously, "Of course!"

In this case, I can grant them some leeway since they both witnessed the end results of Thursday's fracas. They might be worrying about another outburst of rage. Father's scratches on his face are still visible.

After a considerable duration of silence has ensued, predictably Mother asks:

"Have you two stopped arguing now?"

I sigh.

"We are not arguing, Mother, we are discussing!"

"Well, I can't stand it, so you can end it now."

I don't end it. I push further.

"In my opinion, there have only been two good things that Centrewood had going for it. One was Pinewood—and the other, thanks to my one lucky star: you, Becky! Your friendship, your arriving in my life has been a wonderful blessing. BUT! As far as Centrewood itself goes, I've told Mother umpteen times since we moved here, and I'm telling it to you all now: I HATE living here! The only saving grace for me was Pinewood—the pastureland, the birds, Willow Creek and Eagle. Otherwise, I state categorically that the rest of this place is arid and synthetic— and it STINKS!"

"Surely you don't mean that!" Mother says, clasping her hands.

"I do!"

Mother turns to Mrs. Molnar: "She's young and romantic. Teenagers are prone to being extreme," she explains, discounting my feelings as juvenile.

"Well, this was not what I expect by way of P.O.A. celebration," says Mrs. Molnar, sniffing in her Hungarian aristocratic way, which can be either endearing or off-putting, depending on my own mood. Why does she irritate me so much after having become so fond of her?

"But I suppose is best to clear the air. With all of us present to hear debate, now we all know what has caused so much heartache!"

I say: "What has caused so much heartache is the fact that Father betrayed me."

This causes a prolonged silence. Both Father's face and knuckles turn white. In contrast, Mother's face flushes. She rallies. She knows how to pivot.

"Eszter, I am sure that Lois and Becky want to thank you for putting so much time and energy into getting them ready for their concert. I know I really appreciated all your hard work! I would truly apologize for being away, but my absence could not be helped!"

I think of those atrocious shiny blue dresses. And the bangs.

"Yes, Mama," Becky volunteers, "You did good job. Thank you!"

I open my mouth but nothing comes out.

"Lois?" Mother says, glaring at me to speak.

"Next time, Mrs. Molnar, I would prefer to choose my own dress and haircut and shoes. I know you did what you thought best. But---"

"Lo-is!" Mother interjects, peremptorily.

"Okay, well, if I have to thank you: thank you then!"

"What—is—the—matter with you?" Mother hisses, "What was wrong with that dress?"

"I looked like a Capital D Dork!" I hiss back, "I felt like a Great Big Gawky Blue Heron in Black Flippers!"

"You—looked—lovely!"

"If you say so, Mother!"

"Doggone it, let's all drink a toast to our Benefactor!" Father exclaims, vivaciously lifting his glass: "To Mrs. Molnar, for a delectable brunch at Hubba-Hubba's!"

"Hubba hubba!" Mother cheers, glad for the relief, lifting her vessel and toasting her as well.

"Three cheers again for my Executor—thank you, Mr. Michelsen!" Mrs. Molnar says, standing up and clinking her glass against his.

"Oh for the love of Mike," Mother says, "Tell her to call you Graham, Graham!"

"Right!"

Father agrees. But I bet he never does.

Rendez-Vous Corral
11-4

Monday October 28, 1957

3:30 p.m.

When school is let out, and we all come pouring through the main doors, Mrs. Molnar is standing beside her car, which she had parked in the circular drive.

I walk over to her.

"Hello, Mrs. Molnar!" I say.

"Hello, my Darlink, I come waiting for Bo to take to flute lesson at Conservatory but I stand here watching for you!"

"For me?"

"Yes, I hope to talk to you before Bo arrives!"

I lift my eyebrows as if to say: what for?

"Lo-iss, I need hear you say you forgive me for concert outfit. You hated that dress—and the slippers, yes?"

I nod, glumly.

"Lois, there are times when best intentions get in way of end result! Here is good example of such a situation!"

"Yes, Mrs. Molnar."

I look at her. She seems so contrite, so sorely apologetic, that the overlay ogre image I have of her softens somewhat. I had been so fond of her, had felt at times that I loved her more than Mother herself. But that was before she got so bossy and high-handed, and treated me like she would a—a—a daughter!

"Yes, well, that's okay, Mrs. Molnar!" I say this politely, but with not one iota of feeling.

She reaches out to hold me, and is pecking me on both cheeks in the European style when Becky emerges.

"Hi, Mama! You have been waiting long time for me?"

"No, no, Edes Angyal! I just arrive!"

We three stand by the car, facing each other.

"Bo, I was apologizing to Lo-iss for making her wear something she did not like!"

Becky's mouth turns downward.

"I didn't like it either, Ma!"

"Yes, yes, so I already apologized to you, yes? I see now you both had right to wear what was for you comfortable, so you could concentrate on making beautiful music, to dress for yourselves not for audience!"

"Well, it wasn't a dance recital, Mama! It was a music performance!"

"That I know now. But I so wanted you both to look nice!"

Becky and I look at each other, wondering what which one of us will say.

"And the hair cut, Mama! You went too far!"

"Yes, yes, the bang!"

"The bangs!" I correct her.

"Yes!" Becky repeats, wincing for the two of them, "The bangs!"

Mrs. Molnar folds us both into her arms. Half of Becky's face is pressed next to mine. One of her large, dark chocolate eyes looks at me up close before she closes her eyelid with the long thick black lashes and tips her forehead into the nape of her Mother's neck.

I let Mrs. Molnar embrace me.

I know she meant well.

I have to try to forgive her.

Mrs. Molnar slides back behind the wheel.

I walk Becky around to the other side of the car. She opens the passenger side door and turns to face me. We give each other a hug.

"Bye for now, Doppler Sister!"

"See ya soon, Doppler Twin!"

With a lump of pure joy from this amazing, precious friendship rising in my throat, I stand there to wave them off.

Day and night. Night and day. For just as the Molnar's car pulls away and I am heading to the bike rack, Mitsy materializes.

"Hey!" she says.

I continue walking over to my bike, and then focus on my padlock.

"I got the wires removed! M-wow, m-wam, m-hruh!" she says, working her jaw, "You'll be pleased to know I can talk again—freely, unimpeded, unhindered, unchecked!"

"Hm!"

"So, Joe Shmoe, how's it go— Or how goes, and how's your nose?" she asks, thinking she's so 'with it' with her rhyming hipster talk.

I pay her no mind.

I haul the bicycle out of the rack and back it up, prepare to climb on. She throws one leg over the front wheel facing me, grabs the handlebars, blocks my way.

Leaning forward, she grins impishly up at me.

As usual, her deep cleavage is eminently visible through her scarlet V-neck pullover, her boobs hanging in the carrier basket.

"What do you think you're doing? Giving your over-the-shoulder-boulder-holder another fitting—or a major lift test?"

"Ha ha! Good one!" she laughs.

I give the bicycle a solid shove and she backs up with it, not letting go.

"I want to talk to you!" she says.

"Too bad! I have no wish to talk to you—ever!"

"I need to tell you something. You and Becky, you played that flute duet so beautifully, you know what? I started crying at the same time that you two started crying! The depth of the music really hit home, Lois! It was so-o-o amazingly moving!"

What is she up to now? I think. But when I look into her liquid, lake-green eyes, I see something soft and molten, an expression not seen before. Could it be warmth?

"I mean it, Lois!"

"Well, well," I say, dryly, not wanting to indicate in any way that I have been moved or impressed by her compliments, "You learn something new every day!"

"Well, yes, you do!" Mitsy picked up right away, "I'll tell you what I learned! That you really can't tell a book by its cover. That someone like you, with your blonde hair, your blue eyes, your statuesque height—hey! you're not destined to be just a poster girl or a fashion model, for behind—and despite of—all your natural beauty, you're a very sensitive, artistic, and dare I say—intelligent? soul with great potential for being a great, even famous musician!"

Whew!

This sets me back on my heels momentarily.

"Have you been to Ireland since I last saw you tapping on that triangle, Mitsy?"

"What'd-ya mean?"

"Either you've kissed the Blarney Stone, or a leprauchan taught you a new way to shovel a cartload of shit! Get out of my way!"

I shove hard. Then harder. The wheel goes into her crotch. There is now a vertical black tire mark down the front of her skirt.

But she holds her ground.

"Not till you tell me we're friends again!" she rejoins.

"Fat chance of that! I hate you for being so crass and crude, for being such a liar and a manipulator, and for causing so much trouble between me and my parents! How could we ever be friends again?"

"Easy!"

She releases her hold on the bike and steps off, steps away.

"As easy as that! Hey! Wait up for me!"

I ride off without waiting for her. I know she will be fetching her own bike from the host of other bikes in the racks and by the time she unlocks it, she will be trailing far behind.

I don't look back.

I set out toward home with her remarks ringing in my ears, then clanging around through my inner chambers like a loose brass bell.

I have never been so revolted by someone as I have been by the likes of Mitsy, nor so vindicated. Yet I feel my hatred for her burning a hole in my socket. I was taught it was a sin to say you 'hated' someone. Now I am beginning to reckon with the reason why.

I had been so angry with Mrs. Molnar, it had doused my original, devoted, sun-filled affection for her, and clouded my ability to set it all aside, for despite her apology I was still seething from the humiliation she had caused me, by sending me up to that stage looking like a freak. I still hated her for it.

I see how my rancour with Mrs. Molnar lingers on despite her apology, and that if I am ever asked for forgiveness by Father and Mother, they will be the hardest to forgive because I have always loved them so much, and they have let me down.

This continues to niggle at me: How easy is it to let go of anger and resentment?

Mitsy said it was "easy". Is it as easy as that?

As I am turning out of Upper Pinewood onto the crest of the Main Artery, not wanting to look downward to the left where the carnage continues on throughout stream and pasture, I turn my eyes to the sky,which from this vantage point facing west is large, wide and high. The horizon is far off. It is here that I see a phenomenon that I have never seen before.

I am transfixed. I stop my bike and watch the sky.

There are two distinct layers of clouds, one layer flowing fast at a slightly lower altitude than the other. The clouds at the higher altitude are running in long streams, moving equally as fast. But what strikes me most is that these two separate layers of clouds, moving at an equally fast clip, are flowing in opposite directions: the lower pouring across the sky from the north and sliding under the upper, the upper flowing from the south over the lower in a long trail toward the north.

The southward-bound layer is made up of long battalions of puffy grey cotton balls that seem to know their destination and are heading there with a hell-bent-for leather, come-hell-or-high-water determination, bunching up at times then spreading apart, only to collect themselves and rampage on.

But it is the northward-bound stream which is most remarkable, first breaking into a pattern that resembles a long stretch of raked white sand which coalesces, expands and becomes a fish fillet which then transforms itself into a human ribcage on either side of a human spine. It loses speed, as though having arrived at its intended station.

Gradually, a pair of wispy shoulders and a human skull takes form, then the arms, legs, feet, all the limbs of a human skeleton align themselves, and fall into place complete until even now they are to be seen floating lifeless overhead as on an endlessly-blue inflated raft.

The grey puffy clouds heading south have reached the horizon and have disappeared from sight.

Time is suspended.

I am immobilized by a sense of dread that descends into my core without explanation.

Filled with wonder, I look around and realize that I am the only one to bear witness to this sight.

◉

CHAPTER TWELVE
Pumpkin Raid

Hot Rod
12-1

Monday, October 28, 1957

7:30 p.m.

Mother and I are doing the dishes together, side by side, and she says, "You couldn't have hurt your Father more if you tried."

I am taken aback and say, "Why? How?"

"When you attacked Centrewood. You drove your point right into his core."

"That's too bad. I only spoke my piece."

"What you need is a change in attitude, young lady."

"Which way?"

"You could be less self-centred. You think there is only one way to look at something because it's your way. But you could just as easily be wrong."

"Can you be more specific?"

"I told your Father what Mrs. Molnar gave to me as advice. She told me if there's a problem, first of all we should listen to you and find out what's been happening, before deciding whether or not to punish you."

A few more plates are soaped then rinsed. They clatter against each other when placed one by one in the rack.

"I doubt we will ever learn now what went wrong on your picnic for you to deserve a punch in the nose."

What a clumsy opener. What a hook. I am dumbfounded.

"Sounds to me like we're dealing with two different issues: the so-called 'picnic', and my opinions concerning Centrewood. I have nothing to say about the former since you both judged me without a trial. As for Pinewood AND Centrewood, I had my say. No retractions."

"Just remember what I said about Attitude. Okay?"

Mother wrings out the dishcloth, folds it, and drapes it over the rack.

"Carry on," she says, "It's time for me to go."

***

I am finishing off the dishes and putting away pots and pans, when the doorbell rings.

I hear Father say: "Who the heck can that be?"

Mother has already left the house for a Ratepayers' Association meeting, and Father is in the living room playing chess with Mr. Sanderfield.

It looks like a friendship is forming between the two Avro men.

This chess business is a new development. Tonight is their second "chess tournament" after getting together on the evening Mother and I went to Toronto. They'd had such a good time, they agreed to another match.

Mr. Sanderfield is a very funny man. He likes to do impressions. Right now he is pretending to be Foster Hewitt, the broadcaster for the National Hockey League. With a nasal voice, he is giving a play-by-play of his next move. "Here comes Sanderfield down the far left wing of the board. He deliberates, he thinks, he ponders, eyes his opponent's cornered king, now he takes the rook in hand—he shoots, he castles, he scores!"

"Dang-blast it!" Father roars, and laughs a hearty har har har, a laugh very rarely heard in these parts lately.

When the doorbell rings again, he says: "Get that door, will you please, Lois?"

I answer the door.

Mitsy has already opened the storm door. She puts one foot inside the house the moment I open the main door, "Quick, quick, come on! Grab your jacket and come out!"

"What for?"

"Go, go!" she urges.

"I don't think so!" I say, "Go away!"

Mitsy pushes past me and opens the front hall closet door, hauls out my windbreaker. "This is yours, right?" Then she grabs my running shoes. "Kick off those slippers, kiddo, and let's go!"

Rushing past me on her way out, she grabs me by the arm and hauls me out through the front door. After stumbling on the threshold and almost falling, I find myself hurled onto the front lawn, my slippers flying.

There is a car idling in the driveway, headlights off, that I don't recognize. Flung into profile from the rays of the porch light, there is the silhouette of a guy at the wheel of a low-slung, two-tone boat of a sedan. It looks sleek and sharky in the dark and it sounds ominous with its motor revving, the driver tapping the accelerator to make it sound like it's just itching to get going.

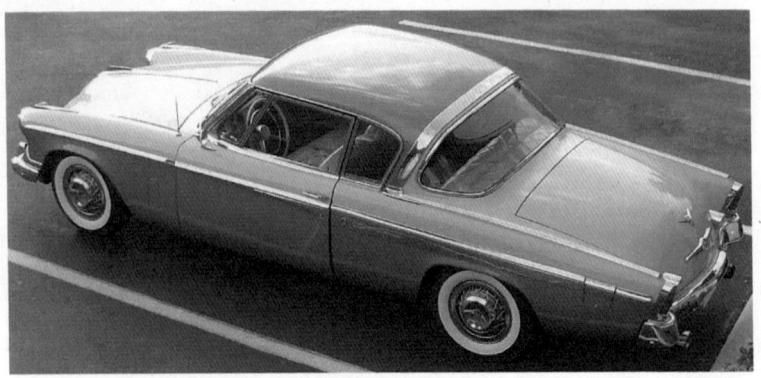

Hot Rod

"Wanna go for a joy ride in a hot rod, ba-by?" she says.

Suddenly the passenger door pops open, the passenger seat folds double, and someone with long legs is getting out from the back.

"Who's that?" I ask, "Who's there?"

"Look over there!" Mitsy points over the rooftop.

I turn to glance in that direction, only too late to realize she has deked me out.

"Get in—Quick!" she conjures.

A strong arm catches me from behind, I feel myself being hoisted up by my armpits, flipped, grabbed underneath my knees and tossed over the flapped-forward front seat into the plush fake-fur cover on the back seat of the car.

My stocking feet catch on metal as I fly.

I cry out "Ow!"

"Welcome to my Stud-a-baker!" It's Richie, snorting amused from the driver's seat, "Ready for some cruisin'?"

"No!" I reply, defiantly.

Mitsy clambers into the front beside him.

"Come into my parlour, sez the spider to the fly!" says the guy who hauled me in, and who now more than occupies the back seat with me. He doesn't share it, he hogs it, his thick thighs and knees bunched up for lack of room to stretch, each of his huge shoes filling the well behind both the driver and the front seat passenger, leaving me no place to put my own feet.

I can smell him before I recognize him by the nicotine and the cologne.

It's Corkie.

"Let me out! I'm not going anywhere with any of you!" I yell.

"No use, sweet bitty titties, you're goin' for a joy ride!"

Richie throws the car into reverse, backs out into the street without headlights on, cranks the gear shift into Drive and takes off in a din of muffler roar and exhaust fumes. The car reaches the stop sign with a screel of its brakes, and then spins its wheels as it whips out onto the Main Artery burning rubber. Hitting the green light at the intersection, Richie tears out of Centrewood with a right-hand turn and careens off up the highway "hog-tied to hell" and "faster than a speeding bullet".

Two running shoes land in my lap, thrown over from the front seat.

Mitsy says: "Here. Put your shoes on."

It is really dark out.

It really does get darker, now that Daylight Savings Time is over.

Set the clock back one hour, and it makes it seem as though the whole earth has been tilted much more drastically than just one notch toward north.

Only the dim headlights cast criss-crossed beams to show the way up ahead.

"Put on your high beams, Richie, or we might hit a moose!" Mitsy says.

"Ha. Deer maybe. There ain't no moose in these parts!" says Richie.

"The only one around here with a big rack is You-Know-Who!" Corkie says.

"No, who?" Mitsy replies.

They all laugh, thinking they're immensely funny.

Richie laughs (snorts) through his nose.

Corky goes "numph, numph, numph" and sounds like a first class dolt.

I think: According to Mitsy, both these guys are loaded, they work full-time. I wonder if you have to be smart to make a lot of money.

Richie at control plays Mr. Big Shot, the Smoothie, chest inflated with his right arm stretched out across the back of his seat and Mitsy tucked all snug-like in his armpit, and with his left elbow hanging out of his driver's side window as he "hoo-haws!" his way along. He starts zigzagging, jerking the car from right to left across the centre line. With every twist and turn of the wheel, I am flung like a rag doll from side to side. Not wanting to be touching Corkie, I hang onto the window handle with all my might. Whenever Richie hits the gas, "pedal to the metal, man!" I am plastered against the back seat from the brute force of the accelerator.

One lone passing vehicle approaches. It has only one headlight.

"Padiddle!" Corky calls out. Then he turns to me and tells me: "First one to spot a paddidle gets to kiss the girl beside him!"

"Not this girl!" I say. But he grabs me by both cheeks and presses his wet lips onto mine. This is followed by a slathering tongue travelling up and down my face and chin as far as my throat.

"Ugh! Ugh! Stop that!" I cry.

"Whatchadoin' already, Corky? Cantchawait till she warms up a little?"

Warms up for what? I wonder.

Mitsy is up front there twittering and gabbling and doing her "oh gee" and "golly gee whiz" number, urging Richie to speed up even more, to "gun it, man!" while squealing "ohhhhhhh eeeeeeeeee!" and "yipp-eeeeeeeeeeee", at one point reaching out for the wheel shouting "Gimmeeee those reins" and bouncing up and down like a cowgirl on a bronco, no doubt jiggling those big bazoomies of hers to Richie's great delight.

Meanwhile, Mr. Won't-Take-A-Back-Seat-to-Nobody has one arm looped around my shoulder, his one hand groping downward for a grip on one of my pointy little breasts as though to cover his odds, which I keep smacking away, and his other arm reaching over the front seat, gesturing with his hand in Mitsy's face, poking his right finger in the air, doing everything possible to draw Mitsy's attention to everything he said: "Hey Mitz, didn't we promise you, Babe? eh eh eh? Didn't we say we'd come out and give ya a spin in the STUD-a-baker? Can ya believe it? Here we are again, all four of us together and out for a goooooooood time! Yeah, yeah, yeah!"— all the while trying to grab a feel of her breasts while doing so.

We are roaring down the highway at such a tilt that if it had been a convertible with the top down, my hair would have been horizontal in the wind. As it is, the full blast of air rushing in from Richie's wound-down window is playing havoc with my bangs. I'm sure my hair is sticking straight out sideways like baled hay. I think: I am the one who should go to the Hallowe'en party as the Scarecrow, not Bert!

I can hear the engine whining as though doubting it should be pushed to go so fast. I wonder if engines are like hearts that just keep going until they sputter and die from old age, or if they can fail early in life due to misuse and abuse. If the latter, Richie's souped-up Stud-a-baker is destined to live a short life.

A solid piece up the highway, I hear Mitsy say: "Up here on the right."

Richie hits the brakes, slows down, starts to patrol, headlights seeking out an opening and soon he veers onto a side road in a spray of gravel.

"Hey, man!" Corky shouts, "Ease up a little, you wanna spare the paint job!"

"What's it to you, Corky?" Mitsy asks, "It ain't your car!"

"No, but it's in mint condition, he oughta want to keep it in good shape!"

"Why is that?"

"Limited edition."

"How so?"

"By the colour of the paint job—Like it?" Richie asks.

"Like I can see it in the dark," Mitsy says.

"It's two-tone lime-and-lemon! Only the 55' Speedsters have this combo! So it's very special!"

"Yeah, so special, being one-of-a-kind makes it stand out like a sore thumb!" Corky numphs. I can see his boxer-dog profile as he keeps jawing on, "There are so few of these on the road, you gotta make sure you don't do nothin' wrong while driving it!"

Then it strikes him where we are.

"Say, Richie, this is a mistake! If we're really gonna pull off this caper, we shoulda taken the pickup!"

Caper, what caper?

"Who in their right mind decided on painting your car lemon and lime, Richie?"

"They did, the Head Honcho's at Studebaker's!"

"Are they a big family?" Mitsy asks, innocently.

"No," Corky interrupts, "They're a bunch of lemons, just like their cars!"

"What's got into you, Corky? Sour grapes just because I won the toss?" Richie asks.

"You think you won the jackpot tonight? Think again! Give it up, man! The night is young!"

Richie has slowed down somewhat, and is proceeding at a relatively cautious pace. It is stone cold pitch black out there, no matter which window I look out of.

"Where are we going?" I venture, feeling queasy and extremely nervous.

"There!" Mitsy shouts.

Then Mr. Big Shot hollers: "Hang on!" and into nowhere we whip between two white painted fence posts grazed by the headlights, then a hard right and bumpety bumpety bump we rollick over an untilled field giving out onto a narrow lane. Farther down the lane, Richie turns off into what seems like some woods, but lower branches scrabbling at the doors and thunking on the roof tells me is an apple orchard. Richie dowses the lights and we sit awhile until our eyes become accustomed to the dark. Then he shifts the car into first gear and we drift down a slope, slowly lump and slump into a field of tall grasses till we pitch to a halt.

"So much for your paint job AND your fenders, Ass Hole!" Corky says.

"Sounds like you love this car more than the owner!" Mitsy comments.

"Where are we?" I cry out.

"Sh-h-h!!! Keep your voice down. In fact, button up!" says one of the guys.

"Yeah, Lois, button up!" Mitsy echoes.

Car doors open, Richie and Mitsy get out. Then Corky.

It is so pitch dark, it is impossible to tell if my eyes are open or shut.

Corky has been pressing the overhead light button and also holding the front seat forward for me to get out. He grabs me by the arm and grunts: "Come on, come on!" and I am pulled forward, pitched head first into the dark. Somebody grabs me by the wrist and I find myself heading out blind into total blackness over lumpy rough terrain. We are all stumbling and tripping over broken branches and sharp stumps, losing our balance from sudden depressions in the earth, our shoes snagged by creeping vines and low-lying roots.

I hear Corky wince: has he sprained his ankle?

"Holy crap, man! I'm killing myself here!" Corky says, "Let's stop for a bit and wait till our eyes clear."

We do what he suggests while he rubs the gash in his leg, then tastes the blood with a fingertip. "Yep! I'm claiming Workman's Compensation! I've got a bleeding scratch here!"

After a while, my eyes adjust, and I can make out the silhouettes of trees off to one side and more clearly, the mess of brambles underfoot.

"Good scouting, you Zits! You couldn't find an easier track in?"

"Nah, we wanted to test your survival skills, Corky! You know, for the next big war!"

"Thank God, Korea's over and they can't send me anywhere—yet!" Corky numphs.

"You know where we're going?!" I blurt.

"Been here earlier to scout it out!" Richie affirms. "Call us the Advance Patrol, right, Mitsy?"

So this was planned. But for what?

The sky becomes more legible. There are great masses of heavy charcoal-grey clouds lumbering tight overhead. They resemble thick, fat pigeons' wings, slightly illuminated from behind by feeble rays from the sliver of a moon that casts some light through.

"Come on then, follow me!"

The four of us troop single file into the trees, then over some ruts that signal the edge of an unharvested corn field. We slip along between rows of tall corn silently, like Indians.

Eventually, the sea of corn rows ends and we step through a clearing into an open field dotted with rounded shapes of all sizes, large and small, some perfectly rotund and some elongated, almost oval.

I know what this is: it is a field of pumpkins.

Pumpkin at sundown

"Know where we are, Lois?" I don't ask, so she tells me anyway. "Remember our first bike ride past a field with all the tiny baby pumpkins? Well, there they are now, all big grownup! Didn't I say that we should come back and pick some for ourselves once they were bigger? We drove all the way around along the back section roads to find the best way to get here that's farthest from the farmhouse. Well, here we are—and we're goin' to take some of them-thar dag-nabbed soo-veneers for ourselves! Okay, guys, let's get organized and get picking while the going's good!"

"Take me home, Mitsy, I don't want to be here!"

"Ah," Corky whines, "And leave me alone with these two? Nah, please don't go home! Stay by me!" Corky slings his arm around me and hooks my neck with his elbow. His arms are massive. "Come on, gimme another kiss!"

"I never gave you a first one!"

"Well, well, at least I've got you talking sooner than the last time we were together! Was it all the rollicking singing that warmed you up?"

"Nothing about you warmed me up, Corky!"

"She's a tough one, Cork!" Richie teases.

"All the better when she comes round!" Corky jeers.

Richie leads the contingent, followed by Mitsy. I am assigned a position behind Mitsy, and it is Corky who pulls up the rear. It is now an "all into together" gang as we start systematically raiding the pumpkin patch. At first, I am reluctant to participate and I dig in my heels, refusing the pumpkins Mitsy tosses to me. But common sense wins out when Mitsy says the sooner we do this, the sooner we'll be out of here. With that as incentive, as well as being a chore-oriented type—and feeling a surge of relief that this was all the mission was about—I tuck right into the project with the others. We form a chain gang, working in a shift, tromping back and forth, systematically transferring the load along the way that leads from the pumpkin field through the woods to the grasses where the car is hidden. The trunk lid is raised and pumpkins start being tossed in.

For some reason, only pumpkins of a certain size are being selected for the load. Why they didn't control all that before we schlepped so many to the car is beyond me. But then, my co-workers here are not the sparky-est spark plugs in the universe, are they!

I suppose we let up on our cover, presuming the darkness and our mostly mute actions would serve us, but we are wrong, for just after we return to the field for a final relay since the trunk has space for some smaller ones, gunshots ring out.

To my surprise, I do what I've seen cowboys do in the movies: I bite the dust, drop straight down on my face and play dead while all around me, I hear a man's loud, angry calls, the bark of a distant dog and a frightened "Yip!" from Mitsy who is a piece beyond me.

To my horror, in the dim light I see dirty rolled-up cuffs of workman's pant legs and stomping workboots working their way toward me, pass me, circle about, stop only yards from my prone body, then prowl on.

All is silent.

Out of nowhere, Corky is scrambling on all fours toward me.

He lies face down in the furrow on top of me, spread-eagled.

He covers my head with his huge hand. It fits like a tuque.

"You okay?" he whispers.

I move my head up and down as though that would help.

"Listen, let's just be real quiet till they've gone!— Je-sus!" he croaks.

I can feel the nerve ends running the length of his trembling body—He is braced, ready for action!

Meanwhile, I am trembling from fright.

He wraps his arms around me in a very protective way, and we lie there together, like a club sandwich, on the wet ground.

"Don't be scared, I'll get us out of this!" he croons reassuringly, more like an older brother than like someone who tried to kiss me with a whole long wet tongue.

We lie there breathless, the blood in my head pumping like all getout, until the footfalls recede and all time suspends itself.

Total quiet reigns.

Only the dense, black-feathered sky, and the orange incandescent glow of the surrounding pumpkins standing like weird, overweight sentinels in the night, are guarding us in the silent field.

"Where's Mitsy?" I whisper.

"I dunno," Corky says, "Let's go look."

He helps me up. I am still shaking from fright.

He puts my hand in his big mitt of a hand and pats it.

Off we go, crouched low, canvassing up and down the tilled rows of the pumpkin field, criss-crossing the whole pasture, tripping over and crushing smaller pumpkins, bumping into larger ones, trying our best to be quiet and not to panic.

We move as one unit.

The search takes us weaving to and fro until I am afraid we have become disoriented.

I have two concerns:

Would we be able to find our way back to the car?

And:

Where are Mitsy and Richie?

We come across them in a patch of long sedge grass on the edge of the pasture just as some quick activity has just ended between them, just when in the dim light of the dark clouds I spot Mitsy rolling out from under Richie then flopping on her back.

Richie remains face down, pants to his knees, breathing hard, his buttocks in spasms, exposed like smooth, twin quartz boulders.

Arms stretched above her head, Mitsy lies mouth open on her back, her legs spread apart exposing her thatch, her huge marble-white, round bare bosoms now seen naked in all their enormity with their fat nipples pointing upward toward the sky.

It is as though the night is on stage. For almost on cue, out from behind the splitting furrow of dark-feathered clouds there emerges, clear and solemn in the inky night sky, the slender waxing crescent moon illuminating Mitsy's glistening white orbs.

"Sh! Sh!" whispers Corky, "Let's leave them alone for a moment! Follow me!" Creeping closer to the car, he leads me by the hand into the nearby bank of tall grasses. He stops, holds up a hand to signal stop, whirls around as though hearing something. "Sh! Did you hear that? He's back! He's back!"

Corky crouches low.

"Who?"

"Lie down!"

I don't hear a thing, but I obey him.

I throw myself face down into the bed of tall grasses. My nose is pressed into what I know is Indian sweetgrass, for there is a strong perfume emanating from the blades that I've crushed. But there is a mix of other weeds—bluestem, cord grass, wild rye? Some of them have prickles and some have serrated edges. Sedge. Cut grass.

"There it is again! A gunshot!"

"I didn't hear anything!"

Corky lies on top of me.

We remain still.

But what is he doing, what is happening?

He is rummaging about underneath me, his hand is searching along my denim's waistband for the button. He half-rolls over, is lifting me up by my stomach and unbuttoning, unzipping my jeans. At the same time, he is turning me over, pulling at my jacket, unzipping it, yanking up my sweatshirt, reaching behind, undoing my brassiere, feeling for my breasts.

"Stop! No!" I yelp.

But his hands are broad. He presses down on my back. And he weighs a ton.

In seconds my top is over my head, my pants are around my ankles and he is pulling them off.

"Help! Help!"

But he is gathering me up and laying me on my belly over an old rotten log. I can smell the moss on it.

With one hand pinning me down, I hear him unzipping his own pants.

Then he lifts me up onto my knees and spreads my legs.

There is a prodding, jabbing and poking with what feels like a blunt wooden mallet while he pants hard, muttering encouraging words to himself.

He grunts: "I found it!"

The force of a long hard thick rod shoved way up inside me sends sparks of pain into the back of my head.

I cry out but he reaches around and puts his hand over my mouth.

"Don't! Don't!" I choke, trying to bite his hand. I know I am repeating this over and over as he slams the rod harder and harder into me, rhythmically rocking then pulsing, the way that chihuahua in the parkette and his own hard pink popsicle prodded inside the other little underdog.

My face is smushed into the bark, I feel the bark grazing my cheeks, back and forth, back and forth, I turn my head to the side, I am being smothered alive!

Limp with shock, my insides howling with sharp stabs of pain, I sense he is now turning me over, like a cork screw, keeping his rod still jammed inside me, then sliding it partially out, again like the male chihuahua with its penis still connected for all the heavens to see.

He has flipped me. He lifts me up by my bottom, hooks my legs around his hips and leans back on his knees, looks down on me and the connection with a look of satisfaction and completion on his face. Another expression comes over his face in a wave. He urgently reaches down and grasps my little breasts in his hands, rubbing the nipples, wanting something from them. He wants something more!

"Make them stand up, make them stiff!" he pleads hoarsely, "Oh you little vixen! I'm coming, I'm coming, I'm coming again!"

And he is pounding once more on top of me, his great muscular arms like the frets of an iron bridge strung over me, and I am pinned.

"Get up, Fat Arse!" I hear Richie bark. He is kicking Corky in the butt. Then he is hauling him off me, leaving me stark naked and exposed.

"Lois!" I hear Mitsy's shocked voice. One look and she knows I am devastated, was not a willing partner.

"What have you done, Corky? I didn't set you up for a fuck, you Fuck Head. You know she's a minor, you prick! If you've caused her any damage, you're in real trouble now, you mean, sick Jerkoff!!"

"Get back to the car, you fucking shit-mouthed little hussy!" I hear Richie say to Mitsy, "You're a real freak, you are, pimping out your best friend! How warped and twisted can you get?"

"Don't lay it all on me! You are as much responsible for this as I am, Richie!"

"You get back to the car, too, Cork!" who had been fitting his junk back into his pants and was now combing up his flat top with his fat fingers.

What had Mitsy done? Had she really set me up for this?

Mitsy's voice recedes as she returns to the car. I hear her berating Corky:

"This was just supposed to be a jolly outing! We brought Lois just to round out the foursome. Don't you know how to just PET, you filthy pig?"

I am shattered.

I close my eyes.

I lie there naked and bruised and utterly, utterly defenseless.

I have a terrible feeling that more of something bad is about to happen.

I sense someone overhead, smell more fresh Indian sweet grass being crushed.

I open my eyes. Focus.

Richie is standing over me.

"Oh please!" I beg, lifting myself up on my elbows. "Please don't you hurt me too! Please help me! Let me go! I want to go home!" and I start to bawl my eyes out.

Richie is very gentle and circumspect. He finds my clothes and shakes them out, hands each piece to me one by one, helps me put them back on, avoids touching me.

I am tender 'down there' when he helps me with my panties.

Before I pull up my jeans, he fishes out a clean handkerchief from his pants pocket and gives it to me, pointing between my crotch.

"Use this to wipe yourself down. I suggest you leave it wadded in there. If you need more, I'm sure there are more clean rags in the car that I use for detailing and buffing. Come on, let's go! Let's get out of here!"

He pulls me up by both hands, plants me on my feet and leads me to the car.

"Get in the back with Lois, Mitsy," he commands, and Mitsy complies.

"Get up in the front seat with me," he says to Corky, "You big useless baboon you!"

Corky is smirking.

I hear him say in a low voice: "I popped her cherry, buddy, it was awesome!"

In the front seat, I can see Richie shaking his head.

"We've gotta have a talk, man!"

Duh-h-h! What a couple of lugs! They sound like a "stupider" version of Dr. Frankenstein and his gullible accomplice doctor friend of his, what's-his-name.

I wonder: why are these two lump heads friends? Just because they grew up on the same street, have been friends for ages, does that mean they are destined to be friends forever? Or is there a point in every friendship when the spell is broken, when a line has been crossed, when there will come a disruption that means the end of friendship for them, too?

I think: this spells the absolute end for me and Mitsy. Once again I have been her patsy and an innocent victim of another one of her pranks gone sour. She just wanted me to round out a 'foursome'?! Why? To get Corky off her back—or Richie up front? So I end up an accomplice to theft as well as being—attacked, assaulted, and terrorized.

I watch my mind trying to wend its way through the horrors of the evening, but it collapses into a dizzifying vortex of confusion. I see loose and lost threads of reason undulating in a hollow space, the collapse of any ability to think clearly suddenly gone AWOL, and my consciousness being sucked into a black hole.

I realize that I am not only totally unable to think, I have also lost all connection with my wracked body. I am unable to relate to it. I know my insides have been torn apart and sullied. And that I am bruised all over, it seems. On my back, on my belly, under my arms and inside my legs. On my chest, my breasts, my pummelled nipples, my grazed face. But I know all that with some other awareness than my brain.

"Man, it's a good thing that old geezer didn't find the car, buddy! He could have flattened the tires or laid a tire iron against your pristine paint job!"

"Never mind, he could have blown us to smithereens with that shot gun!"

Gradually, the car lumps and thumps and bumps its way in reverse out of the deep grasses the way it came in, then it backs out onto the laneway, finds its way forward onto the gravel side road with lights off—all of us crouched low, like fugitives—until arriving at the black asphalt tarmac peel of the highway.

"You've sure got a lot of polishing and detailing to do!" Corky says, as though the evening is behind him. "Tell ya what. Both of us'll take it to a car wash first thing, rinse the mud and grass off the wheels, put it up on the hoist and detail the underbody!"

"Think that will wash away all traces of *your* crime, Corky?" Mitsy asks, eyes closed, still in a huff, her head uninvited lying on my lap.

"You are taking me home now, aren't you!" I say, with pleading eyes.

Nobody answers.

The Bridge
12-2

Monday, October 28, 1957
10:00 p.m.

They are not taking me home. As we careen south along the highway and approach the Centrewood turnoff, I brace myself for being flung from one side of the seat to the other by Richie's crazy driving, expecting him to turn left onto the Main Artery. But we sail right through, and he takes the next right turn farther down the highway at Major Mackenzie so hard, Mitsy and I are flung against the door like limp puppets, so hard that the handle grazes my left hip. I cry out from the pain, and Mitsy says from the floor where she's been tossed: "You call this a *joy* ride?"

I look down at her.

"It's late, Mitsy! I really have to go home!"

My appeal falls on deaf ears.

Blasting down the length of the highway, barrelling pell-mell as far as Weston Road, turning left and tearing south like a bat out of hell, the car roars each time that Richie guns its engine, and revs his 'dual exhaust mufflers' to the hilt.

"Faster than a flying bullet!" Corky yells, window down, hanging out on the doorsill with his arms flung to nowhere. "No shit!" Richie calls, weaving back and forth, making like he wants to shake him loose.

There seems to be another agenda in the wind. I sense that the others have a destination in mind, but I am left out in the cold. I don't have a clue what is happening, even when we approach the Weston Road overpass for the 401 and I can see the intermittent stream of cars passing underneath, white headlights in one direction, red taillights in the other.

At the crest of the bridge, Richie brakes, pulls a U-ee so we're facing north, pulls over onto the side strip of pavement next to the railing, and screeches to a halt.

He stops the car and hollers:

"Everybody out! Okay, ladies and gents, the fun begins! Step up to the wicket and buy your tickets now!"

"Beats the midway at the CNE any day!"

"Come one, come all! Pick your target, choose your prize!"

The other three pile out.

I am still very sore, feel very weak, pummelled, and I don't get out.

Through the back window, I see Richie lifting the trunk lid.

I see all three of them start taking pumpkins out, one by one, and then I see them, torsos hanging over the railing, tossing pumpkins one by one, down onto the stream of cars passing underneath. I'm in a fog. At first I don't get it. But only too soon do I realize what they are doing.

An arm reaches in and grabs me.

It's Corky.

"Get out," he says, "Right now."

He drags me out of the car, props me up against the railing and tries to hand me a pumpkin.

"No way!" I say. I turn and grip the railing with all my might.

I can hear the pumpkins smashing and smacking on the pavement below.

"Take it! Take it and toss it!" Corky grabs me from behind by my crotch, "If not, you want to fly, too? I suppose you'd like to BE a pumpkin, go for a short flight yourself?"

I can hear Richie and Mitsy really getting into it, letting out war whoops, calling out "Ha! almost gotcha!" and "Missed! Too bad!!" and "Oops! Almost!"

"You better git in the groove and join in!" Corky says, trying to unlatch me.

"What's it to you?"

He hooks me by the neck and clamps down with his other arm. "Hey, it's you and me now, get it? Since we did it together, we're a team, see? So you and me, we're going to throw these dumb-ass pumpkins together!"

"I will not!"

He releases my fingers, and drags me over to join the others, supplies the four of us with one pumpkin each.

"Okay then! On the count of three, all of us pitch together! One—two—three—GO!"

I do it. Or did I? I'm pretty sure I didn't. Did I do it? I can't remember. I'm not sure. I recall thinking: I should throw it over my head behind me onto the bridge. But I'm afraid of Corky, what if he catches me cheating, so—no, I don't think so. Did I or didn't I? I honestly can't remember.

What I do remember is looking over at the oncoming stream of traffic, and then a blur of orange spheres tumbling down against the glare of the headlights, seeing the pumpkins falling, were there three or four? Four— yes? Or no? If yes, one of those must have been mine?

What happens next on the other side of the bridge is a sickening sound, the 'whump' of crushed glass, then the ear-splitting screech of swerving, braking tires followed by a colossal horrific metallic crash.

Then Richie is shouting, "Holy Fuck, man, let's get out of here!"

Corky is pushing me, shoving me to the car, stuffing me into the back seat, shouting, "Get in, get in, get in!"

Mitsy is standing at the railing, shrieking at the top of her lungs, her hands on her cheeks, her elbows pressed down and digging into her bosom, her eyes wide and white as headlights.

I hear Richie call out to her, see him rush over and scoop her, pick her up, carry her like a raggedy ann doll.

I edge over as she is dumped head first into the back seat beside me where she remains sprawled, her head landing in my lap.

"Holy shit, man, holy shit! What have we done?!!" Richie keeps repeating.

"It was your bright idea, Richie—Man up!" Corky moans.

"No it wasn't, it was Mitsy's!"

I sit ramrod rigid with my hands stuck to my sides.

Tears are running down my cheeks.

I have no strength or inner stuffing to cry.

My body is sobbing for me.

Home Base
12-3

Monday, October 28, 1957

11:00 p.m.

When the Studebaker hauls into the drive, Mr. Sanderfield's car is still parked at the curb.

Corky steps out on his passenger side and flaps back the front seat for me, so I can get out. He holds out a hand to help me.

I hurt so much inside that I am grateful for any assistance. Even his.

"Good night, Sweet Stuff!" he whispers in my ear.

"Go fuck yourself!" I hear myself say. (Wow. That's new!)

My slippers are still strewn on the front lawn.

The front door is still open.

These facts mean two things: one, Mother is not yet home (besides, Father's car is not in the driveway so that was a good enough hint); and two, I could have been kidnapped and sold somewhere for ransom before Father or Mother found out! (Besides, I WAS kidnapped! I certainly did not go voluntarily)

"See you tomorrow at school!" Mitsy calls out, cheerily.

I open the storm door without looking back and enter.

Father calls out: "Is that you, Lois?"

"Yes, Father!"

"Do you know what time it is? Where have you been?"

I have no choice, but climb the stairs and enter the living room.

I know that my hair is matted, my face is grazed from the bark, my jacket and jeans are covered in mud and grass stains.

"What the—?" Father says, looking up from his chess game.

Mr. Sanderfield's eyebrows shoot up to his hairline. He looks equally surprised.

"What have you been up to, Lois?" Father demanded.

"Rolling up and down the berm," I reply. I am amazed at my inventiveness.

"Who with?"

"A bunch of friends."

"Who do you know owns a car? I heard a car out there!"

I say nothing.

"You'd better get to the back and clean yourself up before your Mother comes home!"

I am more than happy to comply.

In my room, I strip down, put on my bathrobe, take all my dirty clothes with me, go into the bathroom, start running a bath, throw my top, jacket, brassiere, jeans and red-stained underwear into the bath, will scrub them as best I can after I've finished washing myself.

I am desperately anxious about what is up inside of me and have no idea how to flush it out, so I climb in with my dirty clothes and lie submerged in the bath with my legs open, and I rub everywhere down there with ordinary soap, but am thinking perhaps Javex would be better? But how to get it in there? With a meat syringe?

The water stings when I lower myself into the bath but not half so much as my innards which I did not know I had until tonight.

I lie back in the water and shampoo my hair.

When I turn over on my knees to rinse my hair under the tap, I wince from the pain. All the way up inside, I feel as though I've been sliced by a thousand exacto blades, my private parts shredded by a giant spiral vegetable cutter.

I get out of the bath to do the clothes scrubbing.

With a bar of Sunlight soap in hand from under the sink, I bend over the tub and concentrate first on the soiled crotch of my underwear.

The crotch of my denims is also stained. The denims are doing a dead man's float in the tub, their legs partially submerged and askew. They are brand new. They are smeared with grass stains. Mother is going to kill me.

Concentrating on the scrubbing, I don't notice till now that blood is trickling down inside my thighs.

I am panic-stricken, sit on the toilet, try to think.

You can't pull one over on Mother. She has eyes like a red-tailed hawk and the nose of a beagle hound.

In the morning, she is prodding me awake, whispering:

"Lois, did you get your monthly last night?"

"Huh?" I grope, non-committal.

She continues to whisper.

"I saw that my sewing machine cubby-hole had been left open, and that a certain someone had raided my stock of some sanitary napkins in the night!"

"Mm-hm," I answer.

"There is also wet clothing hanging in the hall closet, dripping everywhere, soaking the carpet!"

"Oh!" Not being able to get past Father in the living room with a clutch of wet clothing, I had thought to hide the culprits on hangers in the front closet till morning. I forgot about the fact that they were still sopping wet when I hung them there!

"Oh well, never you mind!" she says.

Mother then proceeds to do something extraordinary. She reaches into the bedclothes, sits me up and hugs me!

"Congratulations, darling," she said, "You're now a woman!"

Mandatory Orders
12-4

Tuesday, October 29, 1957
10:40 a.m.

At school during homeroom, we are informed via the PA system that some young hooligans throwing pumpkins off the 401 overpass at Weston Road had hit the windshield of a car, causing it to veer off the highway and crash. If anyone in the student population knows who might be responsible, they are to report to the principal's office immediately.

Bert connects with me in the corridor. As soon as he looks at me, he bursts out laughing.

"Look at your face!! I hear you were "Berm Rolling" last night!"

I look at him, blankly. How would he know?

"My Father told us at breakfast. He said you'd come in covered with mud and grass—he thought it was hilarious. You might have started a new craze!"

"Yeah, well-l-l-l—" I reply.

"You're turning out to be quite the tomboy! First our young lady the concert flautist gets a punched nose, and now we see the marks of another battle—a 'berm battle', that is!"

I had totally forgotten about the grazes on my cheek and forehead.

"Listen, have you seen Becky today?" I ask him, adding, "Not that I care!"

"No, I haven't!"

"That's strange. She wasn't in homeroom this morning."

"Maybe she's just late. If she's in math next class, I'll let her know you're looking for her. See ya later!"

During the move from class to class, Mitsy catches up to me, drags me into a cubicle in the girl's washroom and hisses: "You keep your mouth shut, you hear? You know nothing about the bridge, get it? I've called the guys, they've booked off sick, I'm cutting out and I'm riding over to meet them at The Big Culvert right now. I just hope the cops don't track them down before I get to them first. Or you, for that matter! You understand? Are you listening? You—know—nothing!"

She is a coiled snake, a cobra with glinting slitted green eyes and a stabbing forked tongue. She has gripped me by my upper arms and is shaking me.

"But--"

She hisses:

"Listen, as far as I'm concerned—and the guys will agree—you were not there on that bridge. Got it? Yes, you were at the pumpkin raid, there's no getting around that, but we drove you straight home after we left that farm. We dropped you off at *10 o'clock*! Do you understand?"

She throws her arms around me abruptly, and presses her face into mine. Her green cat eyes are swimming with tears.

"I'm so sorry, Lois, I truly am. About Corky and all. It wasn't your idea to raid that farm, it wasn't my idea that he do that to you, and it wasn't your idea to go to the bridge. Just let the three of us deal with it, okay?"

Then she is gone.

Next class, I am called to the principal's office and without explanation, I am sent home. I am terrified.

Consequences
12-5

11:30 a.m.

Riding my bike home, there is good reason to become even more terrified. When I arrive at the house, Father's car is in the drive, and there is a black-and-white squad car parked against the curb.

Blood draining from my cheeks, legs buckling, I stash my bike in the garage and step into the house.

Mother comes to the front door, faces me, takes me by both cheeks, kisses me on the lips, then puts her arm around my waist.

We walk together into the living room.

Father is sitting stiff, haggard and grim-faced, in his easy chair.

Two police officers are seated on the chesterfield. They put down their notebooks on the coffee table and stand up as we enter.

"Lois Michelsen?" the taller of the officers asks.

I nod.

"We have some questions."

I start to shake.

Mother says: "It's okay, dear, Mitsy has told them everything."

Horrified, I turn to Mother. "Everything?"

"Yes," Mother adds, "She and her two male friends contacted the police only about an hour ago or so, and they have confessed. All three of them."

"Just as well since that neon lime-green-and-yellow car they were driving stands out like a sore thumb. We already had a call out for it!" one of the officers says. After a pause, he adds:

"They said you had nothing to do with it."

"With what?" I am surprised with myself, how swift and coy my reflexes kick in!

The officer speaks: "Miss Michelsen, we understand that last night prior to the tragic car accident, you participated in a raid on Farmer Leo Stiles' pumpkin patch. This occurred on or about 8:30 p.m., which is the approximate time Mr. Stiles claims to have heard trespassers on his property. Is that correct?"

"Yes, Sir."

I hang my head. I feel sheepish but am equally anxious. I shrink into Mother's side. I am afraid to look at Father, dread what he might do.

"You are aware of the fact that an accident occurred last evening at the Weston Road 401 overpass?"

"But those other three said you had nothing to do with it!" Mother intervenes. "After the pumpkin raid, they said they brought you directly home. At 10 o'clock!"

"Witnesses have corroborated that the accident occurred at approximately 10:30 p.m. Would you concur with that time estimate?" the officer says.

Mother morphs in a split second from energetic and eager-to-placate Yorkshire Terrier to Ferocious Lioness. She shoots a look so defiant, protective and deadly, that it would make any predator's heart cringe.

"She knows nothing about that! Your Father and I have confirmed with the officers that you arrived home at 10 p.m."

"But I WAS in the farmer's field, I helped pick those pumpkins, Mother!" I reply.

"And for that you will pay your dues, young lady," I hear my Father's gruff voice, as though he is choking on his pipe smoke.

The other officer clears his throat. "You are obviously a good girl, Miss, and you are an honest one at that, for willingly admitting to your participation in the pumpkin raid. It is apparent that you played no part in the subsequent tragedy. Nonetheless, we are obliged to subject you to further questioning—" he glances at the filthy look on Father's face and back to me, "We must ask to you to testify to the names of the key participants."

"Tragedy?" I stammer. "Testify?"

"Answer the officer's question, Lois," Father orders me, sternly.

"Um—there was Mitsy, and two of her friends, Richie and Corky."

"How the heck did you get involved with those two losers?" Father explodes, "You have a lot of explaining to do, Miss!"

Mother speaks: "Lois, dear, I must ask you to sit down—here—next to me."

She takes my hand: "Lois, the officer referred to a tragedy. We—we all—have something to tell you that will upset you terribly. Father was called from work by the police early this morning, and he came directly home, not to punish you, so much as he too wanted to be here with me to console you—"

I look at Father. "Console me?"

"Miss Michelsen," the tall officer says, "You are aware that an accident occurred last evening on or about 10:30 p.m. at Highway 401 and Weston Road, caused by vandals throwing pumpkins onto the highway off the Weston Road bridge. You might not yet be aware that one of those pumpkins struck a car passing under the bridge, causing the vehicle to lose control. Two persons were killed in the vehicle. From artifacts found in the car driver's possession, the victims of the accident have been positively identified. It was ascertained that immediate next of kin are out of country.

Consequently, the appropriate authorities legally responsible for their affairs were notified. Accordingly, we are now able to release the names of the victims."

Mother squeezes my hand tight.

"The two persons killed in last night's car accident were Mrs. Eszter Molnar and her daughter Boglarka, known to you and her schoolmates as Becky."

Sets of overlapping, undulating sine waves of electrical shock fill the space between the officer and myself, travelling ever so slowly toward me, until they reach me, envelop me, and strike at my brain, rattling around like tiny ball bearings inside my skull.

"No!— No!" Are there words to express the shock that hits me?

Mother sits me down and holds me tight.

"Darling, they were coming back from dinner last night after Becky's flute lesson at the Royal Conservatory. The police found the restaurant chit for Diana Sweets in Mrs. Molnar's wallet. Becky's fall appointments with her music teacher were listed on a Conservatory memo pad with her flute and music in her briefcase. That's how the police know where they had been, and by contacting Diana Sweets, were able to confirm the timing which explained why they were on the highway at that hour on a weekday evening!"

***

I can't remember what happened next.

I think I might have passed out, or was there an exchange with Father? When did the officers leave? I'm not sure.

I woke up sometime in the middle of the night already in my nightgown with a glass of warm milk beside me on my night table.

Each time I came to after that, I tried to come to grips with what I had been told, with what happened, tried to add it all up. But none of it made sense. And none of it, surely, could be true!

Mull Time
12-6

Wednesday, October 30

Early morning, Mother wakes me up, tells me that I am not going to school today. She leaves me with a cup of tea, a ritual normally performed by Father.

I lie in bed, going over yesterday's events from beginning to end, then my thoughts run adrift, delving further back to beyond the pumpkin raid, with blotted orange flashes of the bridge but inevitably coming back to the few things that I can remember; namely, Mitsy in the school washroom, then Mother with the policemen, followed by something Father did after they left but what was it? What was it?

My mind turns around Mitsy. Her swimming green eyes steeped in tears. What she said when she collared me. It comes to me that Mitsy had done something astounding, something totally unexpected—out of character, really. She had apologized, had said she was sorry. That was remarkable in itself. But she did something else as well. God in heaven, she had persuaded Richie and Corky to take the rap along with herself alone— She had covered for me!

Then there was Mother who had stood by me like a lioness and stalwartly protected me, even lied to the police, albeit unwittingly. She was not there when I came home, but they presumed she was and didn't ask point blank, did they, so she said she knew the time when I arrived home. She didn't know the actual time at all. She lied for me. This was a staggering show of her love for me. My poor battered self is shaken to its roots by her loyalty and devotion.

Then there was Father. Something about Father.

Last evening comes to me in a rush.

He knew. He knew.

It comes back to me, yesterday after the policemen left.

We three were left sitting numbly and dumbly in the living room.

I am perched on the edge of the chesterfield facing the bay window. I can see the squad car backing out of the driveway, then pulling away.

Then Father said:

"You, young lady, go to your room. You will stay there until your Mother and I have had time to talk this over."

Father's face is beet red. I glance at Mother who sits in the armchair, her face white as porcelain. She is fiddling with her wedding rings.

She ventures: "Graham, dear, be gentle--the girl is in shock!"

Graham says: "No more in shock than I am. I am shocked— utterly and totally shocked! that my own daughter would be mixed up in such a mess! And—and—to have the police at our door! What will the neighbours think? She has disgraced the Michelsen name!"

I remain seated.

"But she didn't do anything wrong! She wasn't with those ruffians when it happened!"

Father strides over to me. He takes me by the chin with thumb and forefinger. He forces me to look at him. He looks directly into my eyes. I endeavour to return his gaze. But I look away. I can feel the burning rising steadily from deep inside my heart, creeping up my neck until my face floods with crimson.

He knows. Mother presumes she knows all but she does not.

By their complicity, Mother lying for me, and Father lying for both our sakes, they have protected me.

By her actions, by covering for me, Mitsy has redeemed herself.

But what do I have to redeem myself?

Somehow, through no fault of her own—I cannot believe it— Becky is gone. Somehow and I do not know how, or even if I really did, no matter how it falls, by my own actions, whether through my fault or not, I have lost Becky.

Oh my God! Becky! Beautiful person, beautiful friend!

Tell me none of this is true.

Tell me I had nothing to do with this!

Mrs. Molnar is gone as well?? In my mind's eye, I see her face, looking at me so fondly. Such a kind, loving woman who adored her Bo, who went through such hell in Hungary, whose husband and sister are lost, who lost her parents and her brother-in-law, who escaped to Canada to build a new life, only to be killed in a senseless car accident. She loved me like another daughter. How cruel I was to her over that stupid blue prom dress! Why couldn't I have just accepted it as her wish to make us happy?

After moving here, I had no true friends. Then I had one. Now I have none.

●

CHAPTER THIRTEEN
Banished

Bud Longford Scoops Again
13-1

Centrewood Weekly

SPECIAL EDITION

WEDNESDAY OCTOBER 30, 1957
HORRIFIC HALLOWE'EN CRASH

by Jason "Bud" Longford

What began as a misguided Hallowe'en prank at the Weston Road and Highway 401 overpass resulted in the deaths of two highly respected and beloved members of the Centrewood community.

On Monday, October 28 at approximately 10:30 p.m., Mrs. Eszter Molnar and her daughter Boglarka were traveling west on the 401 from Toronto preparing to take the turnoff onto Weston Road when their car was struck from above by a volley of pumpkins thrown from the bridge by mischief-makers old enough to know better. One of the pumpkins landed square in the middle of the windshield, smashing the glass to smithereens. Highway passersby attested that upon impact, the driver of the car lost control, veered wildly from side to side then careened into the abutment, killing two occupants instantly.

Mrs. Zsofia Molnar fled the uprising in Budapest, Hungary, arriving in Toronto in 1956. There she joined her daughter, sister and brother-in-law who had come to Canada earlier, and her father-in-law, Gyorgy Molnar, who was already established in the successful operation of his Bancroft mining endeavours. Mrs. Molnar had assumed full directorship upon his demise only this past spring.

The community will remember her talented daughter Boglarka Molnar, known as Becky to her school chums, as the lead flautist in the Doppler flute duet played to great acclaim at Centrewood Collegiate's recent fall music concert.

Unconfirmed rumour has it that her close friend and fellow flautist of the duo, Centrewood student Lois Michelsen, 14-year-old daughter of eminent Avro Arrow aeronautical engineer, Graham Michelsen, was indirectly involved by allegedly participating in the pumpkin raid which took place earlier that night at a farm further north, preceding the subsequent violence that occurred at the bridge.

Facing two counts of involuntary manslaughter in adult court are Riordan (Richie) O'Sullivan, 21, and Declan (Corky) Callaghan, 21, both of Weston, Ontario, both second-generation descendants of émigrés from Cork, Ireland.

A charge of reckless endangerment leading to death was also laid against 14-year-old Centrewood student Mitsy Gardiner.

All three have previous records and have been summarily held without bail. The two men have previously served time for break-and-enter, assault and battery. Miss Gardiner has committed several infractions, was never incarcerated, but was currently on parole for previous misdemeanours involving petty theft and shoplifting. The two men are being held in the Weston Jail without bail where they await court hearing, trial and ultimate sentencing. The young lady has been sent to the Ontario Training School for Girls in Galt, a reform school for incorrigible and delinquent girls aged 12 to 18. There she will await assessment and possible committal with dire consequences. If committed, she will become a ward of the state. Miss Gardiner is the daughter of psychiatrist Dr. Fiona Gardiner currently working at Sunnybrook Veterans Hospital.

Interment at the Hungarian cemetery in Toronto will be a private ceremony. There will be no memorial service.

Disappeared
13-2

I had forgotten this moment.

Father is gripping my chin, is towering over me.

"I am ordering you right now—Do not say a word. I told you to go to your room. I will not tell you again!" Father glowers.

I pull away from his grip and stand up.

Next moment that I recall, I am crouched on the floor, listening from my room with the bedroom door slightly ajar. I'm feeling the lowest of the low, like a grub curled up under a grey stone. My mind is frantically trying to grasp what has happened. And can't. I am too frightened and too stunned to cry. My chest alone is sobbing without making a sound.

Father is ranting like a deranged general, pacing back and forth past the living room doorway. His voice fades, gets louder, fades as he does. I picture him shaking his finger at Mother as he delivers his edict:

"You, Emily, will find a suitable private school for her. Not co-ed. For girls only. Try Alma College in St. Thomas first. It has a good reputation. You will contact Alma College and if they have an opening, you will arrange to have her transferred immediately," he states.

"I will do no such thing," says Mother.

"Emily, Lois cannot and will not return to Centrewood Collegiate."

"Give me a good reason why not!"

"Her stay at that school has been ruined. She could never bear the shame."

"Is it Lois who couldn't bear the shame—or you, Graham?"

"I am her father. I know what's best for her."

"And her mother has no say?"

"Not under these circumstances."

There is such a long silence, Lois hopes they have kissed and made up but I know better. This is a face-off. They are holding each other at bay in a wordless duel.

" 'Absence speaks louder than words', Graham. How can you be sure that her absence might not just incriminate her more than if she turned up and carried on as normal?"

" 'Carry on as normal', Emily? What on earth would that be like? Normal?"

Silence.

"If you send her away, you will be punishing me, too. What did I do wrong to deserve this?"

"Nothing. Except perhaps for encouraging her to 'go out and play' with 'her little friend' —with that no-good little tramp, to be more accurate!"

"Graham, that is not like you at all. If you are referring to Mitsy, that girl needed guidance and attention. I thought we both agreed on that score."

"You have been so eager to be the do-gooder, you were compelled to take in a stray—At our expense, both Lois's and mine!"

"Well, now that's going a bit too far! You are really off the rails, aren't you— To say that I would risk my own family's well-being! To even dare say such a thing to me!"

"That is the truth, Em. Truth hurts. I asked you several times to reconsider and not push Lois so hard into spending time with her. It was obvious from the get-go that she is nothing but a common slut—and now, by the looks of it, a hard-core juvenile delinquent!"

"Graham, that is quite enough!! Have you finished?"

"No! No, Emily, I've not finished. That girl has always been bad news! You claimed her 'more mature behaviour' was due to the fact that she was six months older than Lois. You maintained that girls develop at different rates. That she only seemed more sexualized because she was older and maturing faster. Well, guess what!! Since school started, Lois has continued to conduct herself as a good and proper young lady. Sure, she's had her lapses in the impudence and temper tantrum departments, however, I accept that's all part of finding one's voice, of growing up. But that one? she has become wilder than ever. You've noticed her behaviour yourself—acting like a vamp—Who knows how far she goes with that seducing act she pulls with every Tom, Dick and Harry? You saw her—she even came on to me that time we had Glenn Miller playing, trying to teach them to dance. Even if she is too young to appreciate what she is doing, she still behaves like a right little hussy. I asked you time and again, and I told you umpteen times, that I wanted Lois to have nothing more to do with her!"

"That is very harsh."

"Lois will leave this place and have nothing more to do with any of it. She will start afresh."

"I always thought we were a team. Now I know we're only a team when it suits you."

"Look at it this way, Emily. Not only has this travesty shamed Lois, it threatens to shame both you and me—Ruin us! Not only could it sully the Michelsen name right here in Centrewood, it could very easily jeopardize my position at Avro, and my career!"

"You are telling me that you would send away your only child in the off chance that your position might be in jeopardy? That you only retain your position at AVRO on condition that your name is not tarnished, and not on the basis of your God-given abilities?"

"You've got it!" This said almost gnashing his teeth.

"Graham, what happened has nothing to do with you and your name or your job!"

"Oh yes it does, Emily, that's where you are wrong. You know very well that it does! First of all, this age we're living in—this damned Cold War, this horrendous Red Scare that has been destroying the fabric of American AND as we've just discovered, now Canadian society—"

"Graham! Are you still stuck on that old saw?"

"You'd better believe it. You have seen how what McCarthy started as a Communist witch-hunt is backfiring on everyone in the so-called 'free' world. Even in Canada here!"

"I thought that's why we went to Ottawa, to clear up any possibility of its interfering with our lives!"

"Believe you me, Emily, we might have lodged our protest, we might have received reassurances, with the result we will not be subjected to overt harassment, but we will all continue to be under surveillance—each and everyone of us will be subject to the same kind of scrutiny! The slightest misdemeanour can damage us!"

"You honestly believe that Lois being involved in a teen prank of raiding a pumpkin patch could give us a black mark us as Communists? Get away with you!"

"Emily, it's being even peripherally involved in a criminal offense that threatens to damage us! My name and by extension my family's reputation is tied to Avro's public reputation. By being shamed, through innuendo and insinuation Avro could be shamed. For that, Avro could give me the sack!"

"Graham, you are frightening me. How on earth would Avro even remotely think their status would have anything to do with an employee's child's caper in a pumpkin patch? Don't all teenagers end up pulling these kinds of pranks? This is just one that went sour—Lois wasn't even part of the worst part! I can't believe either the RCMP or Avro would go as far as you fear!"

Father goes quiet. He says:

"I can't believe my own daughter is nothing but a common thief!"

I can hear Father choke on his words when he says this.

I sense that Mother has come close to him, is face to face with him, holding him by his collar or is gripping his shoulders: "Graham, listen to me! Get a grip on yourself! I can see why you are panicking, really! really! Yes you are!! But we need help with this!" He must have pushed her away, because she says: "Don't shuck me off—Yes, we do! Tell me: is there anyone from Avro we can call right now that we could trust? Do you know someone with whom we could confide? We need some objective ears so we can air the options! I know! How about Bert Sanderfield?"

Father pounces on that idea, almost snarling, "Absolutely not!"

No, because Mr. Sanderfield knows the real time I got in last night! He daren't let Mother know! He would spill the beans.

"How about Crawford Gordon and his wife?" Mother asks, "Although I must say from being flung together with her in Ottawa, I'm not sure she could be a very good confidante, she's most likely prone to being judgmental, she's such a snob! If I had to spend one more day with all her hair-tossing and skirt-smoothing and her sundry other affectations, I thought I'd scream! She's a pretentious twit! So why not just Crawford Gordon alone?"

"Emily, you just made your own case. There is no one from Avro who would be eligible. You can't possibly be expected to know the climate at work! Yes, we work close together as a team, and we got tight when it came around to dealing with the FBI threat, yet day to day, you have no idea how fierce is the competition, or how much mileage the slightest bit of gossip could have to impugn someone's reputation and ruin their chances for promotion. There are some in that group who would consider themselves to be entitled enough to use whatever they can if it means clawing their own way up the ladder."

"You're referring to all the Avro CEOs?"

"Yes."

"Surely not you as well, Graham."

"I try to cut a low profile and keep my nose clean. I do my work and avoid gossip at all costs. Meanwhile, now the main bulk of my role on the Arrow is done, I must jockey for a new position. I'm so close to a really important advancement that this whole thing could blow up in my face, and very easily leave me out in the cold."

"You think this could affect your promotion?"

"It could ruin my chances!"

"Won't people still talk, whether you send Lois away or not?"

"I doubt it. As long as Lois is kept out of the public spotlight, any suspicions about her direct involvement with the accident will soon evaporate. The press will have no reason to get at the girl and badger her with questions when there is nothing more to be said. We'll keep her home for now, away from the fray. Her transfer to another school will just look like a coincidence. You, Emily, will keep your own counsel and not discuss this matter with anyone."

"You feel that handling it this way, the whole matter will soon be forgotten?"

"Yes. By everyone. Including us, Emily. Once Lois is removed from this scene, it will be as though it never happened, and even we will need never mention this again."

"Not even notice that she is no longer at home? You are talking about our daughter, Graham!"

I had no idea, really, what this conversation was all about. I heard the certainty in Father's voice, the vulnerability in Mother's. I could grasp Father's rationale behind keeping me at home for a while until it blew over. But transferring me to some other school called Alma College was ludicrous— it was Father just spouting off. I've heard him rant and rave and blow his bolt before, only to come round in the new light of day.

I felt dizzy and sore, hurt and stunned so I crawled into bed, and resolved to stay there forever.

What remained in my system long after I found comfort in my flannelette sheets and familiar old quilt was the certainty that some sort of change was in the air. Father had sounded so firm in his conviction, I pictured him going to sleep lying on his back, arms behind his head, convinced and confident. As the man of the house and master of the family, he could rest easy knowing that he had made the best decision, rest assured he was right. Even if he changed his mind in the morning.

Hallowe'en Prank
13-3

Thursday, October 31, 1957

I am at home. I have been grounded. I am not to leave the house under any circumstances.

Mother is in the living room with her sewing box, mending. She has spent most of her time crying, while sorting and packing my things. For some reason, my luggage is restricted to two suitcases, one carry-all duffel bag, one makeup bag and one carton.

Father is smoking his pipe and watching the hockey game. He is not talking to me, will not even look at me. His anger had escalated when the man he calls "The Muckraker" came out with his Special Edition mid-week broadsheet. Father has forbidden me from reading the article. I gather from his ranting that my name was mentioned in an "incriminating" fashion, so consequently his family name is now permanently stained. He wants nothing more to do with me. I have been banished from his existence even before I leave home.

It is dark outside. I am coming up from the lower level with a basket of folded towels, am fetching laundry from the dryer as Mother had requested.

There is a knock at the door and someone calling in a high voice: "Shell out, shell out!"

I open the front door a crack.

There is Bert, dressed—or as best he could—as the Scarecrow. He's wearing a Batman black face mask, his Mother's lime-green floor mop on top of his head under an old, flattened brown fedora, and he's tied a collar of jagged newspaper around his neck with some frayed rope.

He opens the storm door and starts to sing in falsetto:

"I would while away the hours

Conferrin' with the flowers

IF I ONLY HAD A BRAIN!"

while hopping bowlegged into a sideways dance.

I put my finger to my lips: "Shhh!"

He takes me by the arm and whispers: "Are you okay?"

I shake my head no.

He continues in falsetto:

"I'd unravel every riddle

For every individ'l

IF I ONLY HAD A BRAIN!"

He puts on a really high, squeaky voice again and shouts:
"SHELL OUT, SHELL OUT!"

Father calls out from the living room:

"Who's that squawking?"

Mother calls out:

"Give the child some candy, Lois, and close the door!"

Bert beckons to me and I step out, close the front door firmly behind me.

"What's up?" he whispers, "I haven't seen you at school!"

"I've been grounded," I whisper back.

"What happened?"

"They're sending me away."

"Where?"

"A private girls' school called Alma College in St. Thomas."

"When?"

"I go the day after tomorrow. I'd be going tomorrow except tomorrow happens to be my birthday. It also happens to be the day for the funeral."

"I didn't see anything about it in the obituary."

"Right. It's just going to be a cremation ceremony."

"Is there no other family?"

"No. Nobody."

We continue to whisper.

"But why are you being sent away? You didn't do anything wrong! It was Mitsy and those other jerks who caused the accident! You weren't even there! They've all been charged, you know! Richie and Corky are being held in Weston jail waiting for their trial. They're going to be tried in adult court! Mitsy has been sent to the juvenile reformatory in Guelph for her hearing. If charged, she could be in the slammer for five years or more for involuntary manslaughter!"

"I didn't know that."

"So if you were at all guilty, you'd be in the clink with her, right?"

I lean against the storm door.

"I guess since you're going away, this is a moot point: I've come to tell you that I can't go to the Hallowe'en dance on Saturday night. My Father has nixed it!"

"I see. You say I'm not guilty. But I'm guilty through association?"

"Something like that. I just said that I myself don't think you're guilty. I won't say what Father thinks."

No, I think, because he knows more than Bert thinks.

"My Father is afraid I've tarnished the Michelsen name—and put a black mark on Avro."

"Yeah. That's what my Father says as well. He's really disturbed about it all. He doesn't want me being friends with you anymore. And he feels he can't play chess or watch hockey with your Father, just in case it tarnishes his own name!"

Oh my god, I think, what have I done.

Bert splays his hands. "All because of a pumpkin raid—Really! Mother said it's a rite of passage for youths to steal pumpkins!"

"But not to drive to an overpass afterwards and toss them on passing cars," I whisper, bitterly.

"Mother is on your side. She admitted there was no excuse for it. But since the 'boys will be boys' argument is used to defend boys, she will stand up for girls, in that hey have the same right to raid a pumpkin patch as boys do!"

Was it because I am a girl? Is it that Father's daughters don't do such things? But then I remember, it isn't just the pumpkin stealing that has alienated Father.

"Listen, why don't we go shell out together?"

"What? Now?"

"Yeah!"

"I told you I can't go out. Besides, I don't have a costume!"

"Oh yes you do!" he smiles, broadly.

I didn't notice that he was carrying a large duffel bag with him. He bends over and unzips it.

Out comes a black long-sleeved turtleneck sweater and black socks. He tells me what to fetch from the house, he'll wait out back on the patio.

Once inside, I slip past the living room with the laundry basket, and deposit it the master bedroom without incident.

I go into my bedroom, change into black slacks, and grab what I've been told to bring.

I meet Bert at the back patio door and step out. He helps me pull the turtleneck over my top. I pull on his black socks. Then I slip my feet into the black ballet slippers.

While we smother our chuckles, he helps pull the horrid blue prom dress over my head and zips it up for me as far as the zipper would allow. I bobbypin the string of artificial flowers across my bangs.

"No point in your needing a mask—as though certain folks would ever guess who you are anyway! Namely your parents!" he laughs.

"Hm! Here's hoping they stay in place, and don't go for an evening drive!" I rejoin.

We head out up the dark street with the duffel bag for our loot. The odd front porch light is on, signalling readiness from indoors for trick-or-treaters.

"Let's go over and hit Oakwood where no one knows us!"

As we walk, he talks. He tells me how shocked he was to learn that it was Mrs. Molnar and Becky who had died in the accident. So tragic, and such a great loss. Becky was such a nice girl—and so talented! How terribly sad! After absorbing the news, his thoughts had turned to me. He was concerned about me, was wondering how I would be able to handle such a catastrophe, he knew losing Becky would be like losing a sister, he knew how close we were!

"Peas in a pod," he says.

I feel tears squirt into my eyes, but bat them back and stare straight ahead.

"I talked the whole thing through with Mother. She said she hoped you had someone to talk with, and that although psychology is still mostly pooh-poohed nowadays—despite all the soldiers coming back from the front in shell-shock— and people still think no matter what the trauma, that a person should just 'get over it' and move on— you will probably need counseling. If not immediately, then some time in the future, you will need it. To help you cope with the shock."

"It's true I have had no one to talk with about this," I confess, "Father is not talking to me and Mother skirts about, just tends to essentials, doesn't want to hear about it—there's no molly-coddling from her!!"

We make it to Oakwood but do not knock on any doors.

The Mopsy Scarecrow and Dipsy Dorothy just keep on wandering up and down the stupid curved crescent streets, sometimes getting caught in a cul-de-sac, just like in Maplewood. I recognize the pattern, but with different street names, I still can't figure how to get out. Eventually, I know I'm lost. I'm hoping Bert isn't.

"I don't have a clue where we are, do you?" Bert asks.

"No, but sure as dickens if we keep walking and don't retrace our steps, we're bound to find a main artery at some point!"

"Hm. You're right. The key lies in 'not retracing our steps'. Otherwise, we'll just go round in circles!"

"My Father thinks this Centrewood plan is brilliant. He stands by the Circle, his number one favourite form for a town plan. Myself, I prefer the grid plan."

"Me too!" Bert responds, enthusiastically. "There's nothing more practical for getting from point A to point B than an alignment of streets running in parallel, and that intersect at right angles with parallel rows of streets running in the opposite direction!"

"Yes, indeed," I agree, thinking how clearly he had expressed a simple concept that is no small feat to describe. I look at him sidelong, with appreciation. Bert is a stable, sober, steady-he-goes kind of guy. Even if Father were to label him as a square, Bert is a good sort, and there is a major plus— he's against circle plans—I like him!

It is good to be outside.

The crisp fall air is fresh on my face. There is the occasional colder breeze that blows straight through me, but otherwise it's tolerable.

Bert stops and looks up at the pitch black sky, points out the stars, asks about the moon. It is almost equally divided. Half dark, half light.

"What kind of a moon is that, do you know, Lois? Would you call it a half moon?"

"No. There's no such thing as a half moon even though it sure looks like one!"

"What is it then?"

"It's the first quarter."

"Is there such a moon as a last quarter?"

"No. The only other time it looks half and half is called a third quarter."

"So which way is it going? From darker to lighter, or vice versa?"

"It's getting lighter. Next week there will be a full moon."

"How do you know? How can you tell?"

"I only know at the moment because the night of our concert, it was a New Moon. It was a solid black disc with a barely perceptible thin ring of light glinting around the rim."

I pause and think of Becky standing there that night outside the restaurant, whispering it was a "Once in a New Moon" performance, and adding that she would never play the Doppler again the way she played it with me at the concert that night.

My throat tightens, forcing me to swallow hard. Tears squirt into my eyes. I choke back a sob.

"On Monday night, the moon was only a thin bright curve on the right side, like a luminous pared fingernail-clipping. From where it was only a few nights before, I knew it had to be a Waxing Crescent. Otherwise, from month to month, I forget too, which way the moon grows."

Bert falls quiet.

He says: "Monday night. You mean—"

I nod.

"Lois, do you want to tell me what happened? I promise I won't tell a soul!"

A ragtag bunch of kids rushes by in home-made costumes, one dressed as the Lone Ranger, another as Superman, and one who comes right up to us dressed in a white sheet with holes for eyes who says: "Whooooo! Boooo!"

We pretend to shudder with fright. "Oh-h-h-h!" we cry. We have to laugh.

When the street is quiet again, I say: "I didn't go willingly, Bert! I was snatched!"

"What?"

"Yes, right off the front porch! I answered the doorbell, the storm door was already open and there was Mitsy. She grabbed me, reached into the hall closet for my jacket and runners, and pushed me outside. Corky got out of the car, and threw me in the back seat! They even left the front door wide open and my slippers on the front lawn!"

"Didn't your parents notice you were gone?"

"No! Mother was at a Ratepayers' meeting and Father was playing chess with your father in the living room. When they finally brought me back home, the front door was still wide open and my slippers were still lying there on the grass, Mother wasn't home yet and the fathers were still playing chess!"

"That's preposterous! So you were kidnapped!"

"Yes, I suppose I was!"

After a pause, Bert asks: "Where did they take you?"

"Oh, on a wild and scary so-called 'joy ride' up the highway in Richie's 'hot rod'—he calls it his 'STUD-a-baker'—" to which Bert groans—"He drove like a maniac, weaving back and forth all over the road. Showing off, you know. Trying to impress Mitsy. Acting like the Big Shot, right?"

"And then?"

"He pulled off into a section road, drove in a bit of a ways, then slammed through some bush and buried the car in deep grass."

"Did he know where he was going?"

"From what I gathered, he and Mitsy had scouted out the place before, so yes, they knew their way in."

"That's when the pumpkin field was raided?"

"Yes."

"All four of you?"

"Yes. I refused at first, but Mitsy twisted my arm into going along with the caper, the reasoning being that the sooner they picked enough pumpkins, the sooner we'd be able to leave."

"Good thinking."

"But the farmer came along, fired off his gun in the air, took us by surprise, started stalking us. I laid down flat on my face. At one point, his big boots stomped right past me!"

"Where were the others?"

"Well, that was the next question after the farmer seemed to be gone. I knew where Corky was. He had thrown himself over me, as protection, while the farmer paced back and forth with his shotgun.

Corky even put his hands on my head to cover my blond hair from what little moonlight there was that night. I thought then that he was very valiant, willing to take a bullet for me! So I knew where Corky was. But Mitsy and Richie? That was another story."

"Did you find them?"

"Yes, after wandering around for ages, we came across them. They were—um, they were--"

"Making out?"

"Ummm —"

"Having sex?"

"Yes. I think so. Richie was lying face down with his pants around his ankles. Mitsy had just rolled out from underneath him stark naked. She lay there on her back with her bare breasts showing."

"My lord, Lois! How awful for you!"

"I was mostly stunned and disgusted, Bert. I didn't know what to think about it. I just wanted to go home."

"No kidding! So was that it? Did they finally take you home?"

"No."

Bert and I walk along a bit further. My face is now almost frozen solid from the wind and I'm starting to shiver from the cold. I'm also torn. Should I have just said 'Yes' and that would be the end of my story?

But I had said 'No' and Bert was waiting.

"Corky pulled me away as though to spare me the sight. Then when we were far enough away, he said he heard the farmer again and told me to lie down. I was frightened and did what I was told. So I lay down on my face again. Corky lay on top of me. Then he raped me."

"What?"

"Yes. He tore off all my clothes and raped me. Twice."

"Lois! My god!! No!!"

He reaches out to me, and asks gently: "May I please hold you? Let me hold you, Lois!"

I let him slowly put his arms around me and hug me. He holds me close and he begins to sway, like you would to soothe a baby.

He says quietly, "Does your Mother know?"

"No. No one. Other than Mitsy. Now just you."

I whimper. Then I start to cry.

"Oh my god, Lois, oh my god, I'm so sorry, I'm soooooo sorry!"

As I burble and sob, I tell him how grateful I am that he asked first if he could hold me, and I think while he is holding me, how relieved I was that he didn't say: "Poor thing!" as I have hated that expression since forever, and vowed I would never be able to tolerate being called a 'poor thing', as it's so condescending, and degrading.

"Lois, I think I'd better get you back home before you are missed. I sure wish I could take you home with me! I know Mother would know what best to do and how to help you! Is there some way that you can get away again, so that we can both help you in any way?"

I shake my head.

"It would only enrage them more, Bert, if they found out. But I do thank you. You are a very special person!"

We are back on the back patio and I am taking off the headband of artificial flower, he helps with the prom dress and the black pull-over. I remove the black slippers to take off his socks.

"These are deliciously warm thick socks, Bert! You planning on taking an expedition to the Arctic?"

"No, but if I have to walk all the way to St. Thomas to see you, Lois, I will wear them!"

"Would you really do that?"

"We-l-l-l— Perhaps Mother will drive me, we could both take you out, and she could talk to you about what happened?"

"I'd like that."

"Meanwhile, I won't tell her or anyone. My lips are sealed."

There is an awkward pause. Bert still has something to say:

"Lois, don't you think you should see a doctor?"

"What for?"

Bert looks tongue-tied.

"Well, to get a check-up!"

"Hey, I'm okay. Just a few bangs and bruises, that's all."

Bert looks away.

"Promise me you'll see a nurse at your new school!"

"That won't be necessary."

"Well, sometimes, after someone has been—well, what you've been through, there can be a—a delay, you know? I mean, some symptoms might take a month or two to show up, and some not at all. What I'm saying is, you might want to ask someone there for help, and you must be sure to tell that person everything you told me. Promise?"

I shrug, look dubious.

"Here, your feet must be freezing cold—keep the socks!"

"I can't wear them in. But I could wear them to bed!"

He stuffs them into my prom dress to hide them.

"Can I say something corny?"

I look down. "I suppose!"

"Perhaps to cheer yourself up a bit, you can think of that First Quarter moon."

"How so?"

"Well, call it what you want, it looks like a Half Moon to me. You said it's waxing? Well, let's face it, the prospects are good, since as you said, it's getting brighter all the time!"

I smile at him. "I like that! Thank you, Bert!"

I look down again.

"I could never quite figure you out. Now I see that basically, you're very shy, aren't you?"

"Is that an improvement over your original assessment?"

He chuckles, swamped in my humour.

"Lois. This new school. How are you going to manage?"

"I don't know. I'm thinking if I don't like it, I'll run away!"

"Now don't do anything foolish, Lois! Where would you run?"

"To my Aunt Ani in Ohswegen. I have her phone number. I'll call her and ask if she could find a way to rescue me."

"Where is Ohswegen, I've never heard of it?"

"It's um—near Brantford," then I decided to go further: "Close to the New Credit Indian reserve."

"You have an aunt who is an Indian?" Bert asks, as if the whole notion has raised his hair on end and blown his mind. I picture him with an Iroquois cut.

"She's a real Indian but not a real aunt. But all in all, she and I are kindred spirits. She looked into my heart and knows I am a good person. At the same time, I looked into her heart and saw a kind, beautiful person who I can trust. As she would say, 'we're of the same ilk'. Aunt Ani is someone who truly loves me, no matter what."

The Sepia Seed
13-4

Friday, November 1, 1957

Today's my birthday.

Today is also the day of the funeral.

There's been nothing left for me to do but just welter time away in my room.

No point in doing any more homework. Shove it.

I've already packed or stacked in the corner what I intend to take with me:

- Claire's 45 rpm turntable with 45s, still in same box as she packed it for me
- all Little Lulu comic books
- zipperbinder with eagle feather
- nature books, especially birds, turtles, trees, insects
- Kodak Brownie camera and flashes
- my art supplies tool box

- pencil case, coloured pencils and magic markers
- Grandfather's compass in its old case
- blank Hilroy exercise books
- paper of all sorts for sketching
- botany exercise book (with Aunt Ani's contact info)
- front page from the Centrewood Weekly special edition (slipped from a heap of newspapers left in the living room on the ottoman)
- Bert's heavy socks

I am not taking my flute or my music, or any of my textbooks, journals, or other notebooks. I've tossed the whole works into a carton labelled GARBAGE. In back of my desk drawer, I came across crumpled balls of angry words written about Mitsy. I tossed them into the carton as well. If it is a 'fresh beginning', as Mother calls it, it can darn well start out completely fresh!

Mother has been busy packing the rest of my things. She made it quite clear that "no consultation would be required from me, young lady", that she can decide which clothes I need, which pair of shoes and boots, which jacket and coat, which tops: one of each--light, heavy, short sleeved, long sleeved, turtleneck, cardigan.

She has to anticipate three seasons: warm, cool, cold. It's been quite mild lately, for end of October. I was melting at the beginning of the week. Hallowe'en night, the wind turned cold. Yesterday, with the window open for a bit, I could tell it was brisk outside. There was a nip in the air. Soon it will turn windy, wet and nasty, then it will be bitter cold. I will need mittens, hat, scarf. Boots. Leggings?

Seeing that everything I will need has to be shipped along with me, "The logistics are daunting." Those are her words.

***

Ever since I've been under virtual 'house arrest', I've stayed in my room with the door closed.

Mother has brought me in my meals.

She has only the bare essentials to say.

A few times she has placed her hand on my shoulder, but I have shrugged it off, keeping my back turned to her.

There have been times when both Father and Mother have left the house— Such as Wednesday, the day after the police were here, when they left to both Mrs. Molnar's house and Father's lawyer's offices to sign legal papers, then get the key to the Molnar house.

That same afternoon, they returned from the Molnar's with as many loaded cartons as they could fit into the car. These cartons contain personal Molnar business-related files that Father, as Power of Attorney and now as Executor will have to sift through. They are heaped up in random, like building blocks, in the unfinished basement, the empty area with the bare concrete walls and poured concrete floor that was meant to be the 'rec room' where I would throw all my 'glam' teen parties as Centrewood's most lovely debutante.

When they left, I crept out like the little 'thief' I am, and sneaked Ritz crackers with chunks of Velveeta cheese back to my nest.

I'm drinking a lot of Pepsi.

May my face break out in a billion zits.

***

Much of my time has been spent tinkering with Grandpa's compass. First, I just practice making circles, using the same centre point as anchor, then making larger and larger circles—one inside the other—yes, concentric circles, expanding as far as the edge of the paper would permit.

I see these circles as the ripples a stone would make when plopped in water.

I call it the Plopper Effect, and grin. I recall Father using the same image to describe the Doppler Effect. Then I think of Becky and our own Doppler Effect, and I start to cry. I cry while I carry on, describing my sorrow with each circle.

***

Wednesday evening, I start tackling the exercise given me by Father back on Labour Day weekend: the Seed of Life.

It took some time to get the hang of it but I managed to produce several creditable versions of various sizes.

It's relatively simple. The secret lies in determining the initial point for push-off and most critically, understanding the underlying principle. The pattern can only be begun and completed in one particular direction or the other. There are no shortcuts, no druthers. Once you've made your choice, that's it, you're committed and you're in it for the long haul.

***

Yesterday afternoon, while sorting through my supply of craft paper, I came across an 8"X10" sheet of sturdy linen stock left over from a school project. It had the faintest hint of a weave but to the touch, an ultra-silky smooth nap, as soft and rubbery as a tulip petal, with opposite edges that looked as though torn apart with precision, not cut away with a blade.

Suddenly, I was inspired.

I chose a fine nib for the pen holder, loaded it with India ink and set myself to drawing the Seed of Life, careful not to drag the edge of my palm in the black wet curved lines, blowing gently and waiting patiently for each part to dry as I progressed through each stage.

With great satisfaction, I leaned back and beheld the final product.

It was perfect.

It was beautifully done.

It was an achievement I had doubted only weeks ago while watching Father's careful rendering, that I could ever accomplish.

I felt immensely proud, elated, almost liberated.

An idea came to me.

Rooting about in my art supply box, I found a bottle of sepia ink, selected another nib, slightly fatter, inserted it into the pen holder and loaded it.

Then I carefully, meticulously, filled in the six florets that make up the seed with the reddish-brown liquid pigment.

At the head of the page, I wrote an inscription.

I found a manilla envelope, slid the drawing into it, sealed it and inscribed it on the outside with a black magic marker, simply as:

Father

The Opal
13-5

Friday, November 1, 1957

I wake up early.

Happy Birthday to Me
Happy Birthday to Me
Happy Birthday, dear Lois!
Happy Birthday to Me

May as well sing it to myself because nobody else will!

Yes, it's my 14th birthday. Whoopee!

I lie in bed and think about how Mother and Father came to choose my name. How I heard tell how cute a baby I was, as proven in the photos taken at my christening.

"You were a little doll! Perfection itself!"

November 1, 1943. Lois Margaret.

Named Lois after Mother's Mother Lois, who I never met because she died in the blitz at Coventry. Middle name Margaret after the Queen of Norway, not Princess Margaret, the sister of Queen Elizabeth of England, which Father was always quick to emphasize.

I do not yet hear any rustling of life abroad in the Michelsen home.

I get up and open the bedroom curtains, then the blinds.

Straight across the Main Artery lies the horrific decimation of Willow Creek, the tornup pastureland and destroyed woods.

I try not to cast my eyes across all the carnage.

I only look upward at the sky.

***

So much for pathetic fallacy, Mr. Shakespeare. It's a beautiful day! Mister Sun has climbed out of the eastern smear like an iridescent gold coin, has ascended gracefully and is now shining bright as a glinting silver dime, slipping ever higher into a clear blue sky. No sign of a cloud anywhere, only one lone star visible, wish I knew what it was. Is it a planet? I should get out my astronomy charts. Could it be Venus? Or is it Becky, hovering above to say hello before she travels further on out into the heavens?

Becky.

I decide to visit the washroom while the going is good.

When I emerge, I can hear Mother talking with Father in their bedroom. Their door is slightly ajar. Now I can see Father holding on to the doorknob. His back is to me.

"But she was her best friend!"

"Nonetheless, she's not going."

"But Graham! How else can she say good-bye?"

"She'll have to find a way to do that on her own. There is no need for her to be there!"

Mother has more to say on the subject, so he decides to close the door again.

His voice sounds quite stern.

I wait in my room.

Finally, around 7:30, Mother arrives with a tray of orange juice, a bowl of cereal, a small jug of milk, sliced peaches and a cup of tea.

There is also a cupcake with pink icing and sprinkles with a candle stuck in it, already lit and burning its way down to the quick.

"Happy Birthday, Darling!" Mother says.

She sits down on the edge of the bed.

She places the tray on my desk, keeping her face turned away from me.

I can tell that her eyes are puffy. She has been crying.

"Father says that you are not getting another birthday present. You already got your bicycle. That was your present. Remember?"

I nod.

I think: big deal.

"It's true that you can't take it with you. But it will be in the garage and you will be able to ride it when you come home for the breaks. Probably not in the snow at Christmas, of course! But in the spring! And throughout all next summer!"

I doubt it, I think. As far as I'm concerned, I'm never coming back here— Never!

Mother unnerves me by handing me a small package wrapped in white tissue paper and bound with a thin strand of white ribbon.

"I thought you should have this," she says, softly.

After I remove the wrapping and lift the lid on the long thin jeweller's box, I catch the glint of a silver chain in the double layer of cotton batten. I push the cotton wool back with my forefinger until I see what it is: attached to a familiar silver chain is Becky's white Hungarian opal pendant.

"All the Molnar jewellery has been stored in a safety deposit box, saved 'in escrow' just in case a member of Becky's family comes to

Canada to claim their belongings. Even Mrs. Molnar's engagement ring—the green malachite, remember?— and her treasured yellow citrine necklace and earring set have been stored there."

I lift the pendant out of the box and hold it in my hand.

Suddenly, my palm turns warm.

"Becky!" I whisper silently to myself, "Becky!"

Mother continues to sit there. I sense she has more to say.

With a broken voice, out it comes:

"You won't be going to the funeral, Lois. Father says."

I have never been to a funeral before.

I don't know whether to be relieved or angry.

"It will be a very brief ceremony delivered in Hungarian by a Hungarian-speaking priest and his one altar boy. Their bod—uh, they have been cremated. Their ashes will be buried in two separate urns in the same grave as the urn for the grandfather Gyorgy."

I think: cremated! What is that? The bodies are burned? How is that done? I've never heard of it before. Except when the Hurons burned Brulé?

"Becky's body—Burned?!" My voice cracks. The thought of it is horrid.

"I know, I know. It is not a custom here. We bury our dead. But this is what Eszter stipulated in her will."

So, her will be done.

"The funeral takes place at eleven o'clock this morning. Lois, I want you to keep an eye on the clock and when it turns eleven, I want you to get down on your knees at your bedside, and pray from your heart for Becky's soul and for Eszt--Mrs. Molnar's soul. I want you to pray for—"

Surely she is not going to say 'forgiveness' or I shall cry!

"Pray for peace in their hearts. Pray that their family will be reunited in heaven. That Becky's father Bence will find them. That Becky's aunt Zsofia and uncle Tamas will find them. Next—"

I braced myself but the guilt trip did not come. Instead, Mother said: "You might consider humming the tune for 'Praise God From Whom All Blessings Flow.'"

I glance up at her.

Tears are flowing down her cheeks.

Yes, I think. After all, she lost a friend, too!

***

After they've left the house, I stay in my room, watching the clock.

I find this an unnerving activity. Unnerving, how simple and easy a task it is. Yet what torture! Unnerving to witness the inner battle between acquiescence and impatience, letting the second hand make its journey round the face of the clock, watching the minute hand jerk forward. Unnerving to involuntarily allow both the pace of the second and minute hand, yet still wanting to meddle, interfere, speed them up, find some way to make them get a wiggle on, stop dawdling!

When it finally turns eleven o'clock, I do what Mother told me: I get down on my knees on my little bedside floor mat, rest my elbows on the bed, place the palms of my hands together, close my eyes and pray.

But I don't know how to pray 'from my heart'. I only know how to pray with prayers already learned.

Mother told me what to say, that's fine for her to say, it feels phoney, insincere, too theatrical, not real enough for me.

How do you pray for a soul anyway, when you don't know what one looks like, you don't even know where it's lodged! I need to visualize it, need to picture something before I pray for it!

Helplessly, I whisper:

"Dear God, please bless Mrs. Molnar's soul and Becky's soul. I hope their family finds them. I hope you love them and take them up into heaven."

But then I'm stuck.

Suddenly I am stricken by a searing pain the size of a bullet in the middle of my breast bone, burning a molten hole into my heart.

In a reflex to back away from the pain, I push myself backward onto my feet. I can hardly breathe. I am frightened. Am I having a heart attack? Do 14-year old girls have heart attacks? Do they have them on their birthday?

I back up, whirl around, searching for rescue.

On my desk there is the long blue jewellery box holding Becky's opal.

I reach for it.

As I do, I see the cause of the pain, I know it now. I understand what I have been unable to face until now. I see that having been unwilling to go to *it*, *it* has come to me.

The pain worsens, a smoldering hot blood-red eye of intense flame.

"Oh Dear God," I say, facing the window, arms outstretched toward the sky, "Please tell me that I was not the one who threw the pumpkin that killed my friend Becky! Please, please, please God! If you are punishing me for anything I did in the past, if this is your punishment, I ask you to forgive me! Please tell me that this horrible, horrible event did not happen, it did not come to pass!"

I manage to hang on to the edge of my desk.

I reach for the opal.

I grasp the opal in my hand.

A torrent of pain pours out of my eyes, my heart, my body, my whole being. Shuddering, I collapse face down on the bed and cry so hard, so loud, so helplessly, that everything around me disappears into vapour, and I am alone in a hollow void of just me, bearing this terrible seed in my heart, an inner voice repeating like a mantra:

Was I the one who killed my best friend?

Was I the one who killed my best friend?

Was I the one who killed my best friend?

"Becky!" I cry, "Becky!"

In desperation, I press the opal into the kernel of hot pain burning in my heart.

A flood of warmth surges through me.

Time passes.

I feel weak. Lost. Thirsty.

I haul myself up out of bed. Take another kleenex. Wipe my nose again and again. Blot my eyes. Trundle out into the hallway. Head for the kitchen.

But wait.

As I pull around through the kitchen opening, I see someone. Is that someone leaning with one shoulder on the door jamb, now pressing their face and hands against the sliding door?

The light shines from behind.

All I can see is the silhouette.

I go to the door.

The person is no longer there!

In the back corner of the back yard, I see something different, something new.

Why, it's Mrs. Molnar's birdbath, the one with the statue of the girl holding the bowl on her shoulder! Father and Mother must have decided to bring it here with them to keep it safe, must have brought it here unbeknownst to me, while I was in my room where I have stayed put, except when visiting the bathroom, or sneaking into the kitchen for food. But then, I was too intent on slapping together a snack to look out the window.

I slide open the door and walk across the patio into the garden— If you can call it that. It's just a row of cedars along the back fence. And some large pots of geraniums—not a *real* garden like Mrs. Molnar's!

As I approach, it seems that the statue is rotating slowly on some sort of turntable. I didn't notice that there was some kind of mechanism to make it do that, last time when we were visiting!

The statue has its back to me.

There is a peculiar slant to the bowl, it seems to be knocked askew. I suppose Father will fix it when he gets around to filling it with water.

As the statue turns toward me, so does the bowl, which weighs heavy on the statue's shoulders. I see now that the bowl is bearing a massive bouquet of fresh white calla lilies. That explains its tilt!

I had never seen the statue up close, only from Mrs. Molnar's back window.

Now it has turned enough for me to see its face.

Her eyes are a dark, chocolate brown, warm and full of life.

Her brown hair is wavy, somewhat windblown, with strangely cut bangs that frame her face, they have been cut too short but still, on the whole, they make her look rather cute. Cherubic.

Her mouth is soft and kind.

Recognizing me, it breaks into a wide smile.

Her eyes dance.

"Becky! I'm so sorry! Please forgive me!"

My cry pours out spontaneously from my heart.

I fall to my knees, crouch there, bent, head down.

Now I understand Mourning.

***

When I lift my eyes, the bowl, and the statue are gone.

***

Going on four o'clock, I find I am ravenously hungry. I make myself a cold 'hamburgler' sandwich, rustle out some raisin and oatmeal cookies from the jar on the counter, decide against Pepsi, pour myself a glass of milk. Even if I was being held prisoner, Mother made sure that I didn't starve to death. I never heard a peep from her about filching food. There was no need to keep inventory. She knew I was the one who was helping myself when they weren't around, or after their bedtime if I couldn't sleep. Who else could it be, who padded through these hallowed halls, silent and slippery in the night?

Just when I'm heading back to my room with my plate load, I hear the car doors slam and the front door open.

They are discussing this and that.

I hear Father say: "Yes, I do blame you for all this. If you hadn't forced that girl on her, there would have been neither a pumpkin raid nor an accident! But you also befriended Mrs. Molnar! Why couldn't you have just left the girls to make friends with each other, instead of cozying up with that woman, inviting them both over for dinner, and ultimately landing me with this whole goddam POA and Executor job when I already have enough on my plate!"

"Graham, if I could do it, I would. But women don't have legal authority, remember? I can't even have my own bank account or share title to this house because I'm a lowly, insignificant non-person, nothing but an incompetent woman in the eyes of the law! So don't you dare complain to me unless you're ready to fight for women's rights and my full legal status!"

"You won your right to vote! Isn't that enough? You wouldn't know the first thing how to handle this!"

"Not any more than you did before the lawyer instructed you!"

By that time they were in the kitchen.

There is a long, agonizing silence.

"Is this what happens when a family is fractured? The couple starts to pick on each other? Tear each other apart? Stop it, Graham, right now!"

"Stop what?"

"Oh, for the love of God, grow up!"

The Road to Alma
13-6

November 2, 1957

I'm looking at brochures touting the school where I'm being hauled.

Alma Ladies College, St. Thomas, Ontario

Mother is driving, I'm in the passenger seat.

I have my envelope for Father in my zipper case on my lap.

Father did not say good-bye. He did not come with us.

The prospect looks grim for yours truly. This Alma College looks like Miss Havisham's gruesome mansion in Great Expectations. It's a drab, ivy-covered, three-and-a-half storey, ancient Victorian building with dormers on top projecting like little green cardboard hats all the way across the front. I bet that's the dormitory, I think. Put the students up there where it's drafty and they can all die from pneumonia. Pocket the tuition. Bring in a new raft of freshies.

"I'm not happy about this arrangement, you know," Mother says.

"Who is?" is my retort.

"Don't me saucy with me, Lois, I won't be able to take it!"

Poor you, I think. Poor frail little woman.

All she has to do is deliver me. Then she can go home. To her familiar surroundings. Buff her beloved teak furniture. Experiment with her Cuisinart. Play with her new automatic washer and dryer. Attend her Ratepayers' meetings. Plan on burying another stream and destroying another pasture without having to consult anyone at all! I'm the one who won't be able to take it!

"Have you always been a 'good girl', Mother? Always done what you're told?"

"I don't have any choice, Lois!"

Oh yes you do. You could have refused.

It's as though she can hear my cogs grinding.

She says: "Father could have sent you even further away, where I wouldn't be able to see you at all!"

As we approach the signs for Hamilton, Mother takes an unexpected turn off the main highway.

"Why are you going to Hamilton? Wasn't that the sign for St. Thomas?"

"Yes, it was, but I'm not driving you all the way to St. Thomas, Dear, you'll be taking a train the rest of the way. The big train, then you'll be transferring to another little one, that takes you right to Alma College's doorstep!"

You've got to me kidding me, I think.

But no, Mother takes out a street map from the glove compartment, and starts conferring with it as we stop-start through downtown Hamilton intersections.

Hamilton is all recognizable blocks but seems to be riddled with one-way streets. We get tangled up more than once and have to double back. Talk about a screwed-up grid plan.

"You might be surprised to find someone you know when you arrive at Alma," Mother says, casually.

"Who might that be?" I ask.

"Your cousin Claire."

"What? Claire? How come? I thought she was in Montreal, 'studying French with the nuns'!"— the latter phrase said in 'air quotes'.

"So you knew! How did you find out?"

"My 'little friend' Mitsy enlightened me!" I answer, sarcastically.

We shunt along a few more blocks.

"She lost the baby," Mother says.

"Lost the baby?" I exclaim, "Oh my God, Mother! Where?"

Mother puts on her indicator and pulls the car over to the curb.

"The term 'losing a baby' is a euphemism for 'miscarriage', dear!"

"She was yanked away from home and sent to Montreal to deliberately lose her baby?" I shriek.

"No no no! A miscarriage is not the same as an abortion! She went to Montreal to have the baby, not to have it aborted! But it aborted itself! Lord love a duck!" Mother says, wiping her brow with the back of her hand.

"So why didn't she just go back home? With no baby, there's no disgrace. Is there? She could just carry on as before. Couldn't she? In fact, she'd only lose a year of school. We'd be in the same grade!"

"Lois. Lois. Lois." Mother keeps interrupting me in my rambles, and says: "She couldn't go back home. She couldn't and she can't."

"Why-ever not?"

Mother stares at me as though viewing craters on the moon.

"You have no idea, do you!?"

"What are you talking about, Mother? I have no idea about what?"

"Claire didn't tell you when you both talked in your room on Father's birthday?"

"She didn't tell me anything! She just said she was being sent away to a school in Montreal to learn French. That's all!"

Mother sighs.

"Gordon. It was Cousin Gordon."

What a blow.

It takes time to digest.

My mind is reeling.

Gordon!

"Why didn't they send *him* away?"

"Don't be ridiculous!"

Sure enough, we arrive at the Hamilton railway station.

The porter removes my luggage and other belongings from the trunk, and trundles it off to the loading area.

Mother gives me my ticket, and points out that the ultimate destination is ALMA COLLEGE not St. Thomas, which is where I get off. Someone will show me where to wait for the next train to transfer to Alma.

"It's just literally a little toot from the St. Thomas station, Dear. You'll love it! It's a tiny little train with a little locomotive and runs on a smaller gauge track! Dedicated to transporting only Alma College students back and forth. It even has its own little station!"

Oh goody gumdrops! A toy train!! This from a Mother whose daughter is now supposedly old enough to go out into the world alone.

The train has pulled in, is hissing and puffing, chomping at the bit to get going.

We stand together on the platform. Mother has her handkerchief in her hand, touches it to her nose, eyes me sidelong occasionally, looks away.

She pulls two envelopes out of her handbag. "Here. Take these. This one is addressed to the headmistress. It contains your school records and transfer papers, also a cheque to cover your monthly spending money so you can buy an occasional treat from the tuck shop there. There's also enough to cover any planned outings. They'll put whatever you purchase on your chit. Mind you budget wisely because there will be no more coming between now and the turn of December."

She neglects to tell me how much.

Then she leans forward as though to tell me a secret, "I've put stationery with envelopes and some postage stamps in this separate envelope for you to write me, if you wish."

But is she planning on writing me? I'm afraid to ask.

I prepare to board the train.

I hand the manilla envelope to Mother.

"What's this?" Mother says, arching her thin-penciled eyebrows, "Something for Father?"

"Just give it to him, okay?" I say, then add: "Please."

I watch the porter load my belongings in the luggage rack.

Two suitcases. A smallish carton (the 45s record-player)

One humungously huge carton.

One carry-on makeup case. I'm carrying my knapsack.

At least if Cousin Claire really is there, we can read our little Lulus and listen to our '45s together, just like old times.

From the window, I can see the back of Mother's head. She is walking slowly along the platform. She had given up waiting for the train to leave, and had started to walk away.

Absentmindedly, she turns to wave to me then looks back down at the sheet of paper in her hand.

She has already opened the envelope even though it was not addressed to her.

As the train approaches her, draws parallel to her, then slowly slides by, the glimpse I have of my Mother's face from the train window sends a shock through me.

Etched in her pale immobile face are seams that had not been there before, freshly carved, like crosswinds at cross purposes, a riddle of contradictory opposing grooves, one pair running in tandem in an undulating wave across her forehead, the other one a deeply incised crease cutting vertically through mid-forehead, travelling in a jagged line between her brows then on a diagonal down the left side of her nose, seeking, finding then double-scoring into a scar what would normally be the parenthesis of her smile. Surely it took more than five days, more than the trials of this past week, to trace these seams on her marble face.

I note that she is reading the inscription on my drawing of the Seed of Life:

To Father

From

Your Bad Seed

Smoke Signal
13-7

To Aunt Ani

c/o Chief Fred King

New Credit I.R.

Ohswegen, Ontario

Friday, November 15, 1957

Dear Aunt Ani,

I hope you will remember me when I visited Chief Fred with my Father and Mother mid-October. At that time, you gave me your phone number and said I was to call you if I ever needed your help. As I am unable to place long distance calls—or any outgoing calls, for that matter—I am sending my message to you c/o Chief Fred King. Even his address is a long shot, but there has to be only one person with his name and title at the New Credit Reserve, so I have to trust that this letter will reach you.

Lots of bad things have happened.

My pet wild turtle Beetlebomb was dead when we got home. I realized later that was the first bad sign. After that, it got even worse.

They destroyed my beloved pastureland, buried Willow Creek and tore down Eagle's lookout in the tall scotch pines to make way for more development. Pinewood was promised to me as a public park. But they lied.

Most painful of all, I lost my best friend Becky. We had performed our Doppler flute duo to public acclaim. Little did I know that would be the pinnacle of our cherished friendship.

I have been sent away to Alma College, a girls' school near St. Thomas. From a map, I can see that it doesn't seem to be too far away from you.

My cousin Claire was supposed to be here, but she isn't.

Could you please come visit me? I need your help and advice.

Please say hello to Chief Fred for me.

Sincerely,

Lois Michelsen

P.S. #1. I still have the eagle feather with me.

P.S. #2. Father was unable to persuade the Governor General to help you when he went to Ottawa. I don't know how hard he tried after that. Since then, he too has had one problem after the other—myself, being one of them.

P.S. #3. When I grow up, I promise I will help fight for your people.

●

EPILOGUE

**1959-1
Emily Reflects**

Black Friday: February 20, 1959

Nancy Warren

Obituary

Michelsen, *Graham Christian Frederick Jacob Michelsen, of Centrewood, Vaughan Township, Toronto. Died suddenly on Black Friday, Feb. 20, 1959. Dear husband of Emily (nee Watson), father of Lois Margaret. Born 1919 in St. Thomas, Ont. to Peter Christian Fridtjof Joakim Michelsen (1887-1952), of Christiana (later Oslo), Norway, Southwestern Ontario shipping magnate and railroad czar, founder of WSE Rail Lines. Mr. Michelsen's career began first as aeronautical engineer at DeHavilland Canada in both Mount Dennis and Downsview campuses, then at the parent company DeHavilland in Hatfield, England as a member of team developing the Mosquito for the war effort. After the War, he was seconded by Avro at Malton where he served with distinction as lead aeronautical engineer. He was directly instrumental in the design and completion of the Avro Arrow.*

Graham is gone now. Died on Black Friday, the day the Arrow was cancelled. It was a black day for him, an even blacker day for me. Formal diagnosis gave cause of death as stroke coupled with sudden cardiac arrest. Call it what you will, it was no accident that death struck him both in his head and in his heart. I know he died from a brain unable to process the news, and from a broken heart. Both mind and soul shattered from the shock when he heard that the Arrow was cancelled. It was his pride and joy, the very seat of his life force. His whole sense of self was invested in its accomplishment. He had given his whole heart to the project.

Graham had suffered from several dreadful repercussive blows that came in quick succession. First, when the Sputnik upstaged the Arrow, it pierced his heart. Normally blessed with a hardy constitution, it was then that he started to weaken. He said it himself: he felt like a punctured medicine ball. He didn't know what to do with his anger. He was infuriated.

Coming in quick succession, there was the unlikely event of that long-deceased Indian Chief appearing to Lois in a 'waking vision' during the Arrow Rollout. That too stole his thunder. He took the

vision as a personal attack. To believe it happened was totally preposterous and inane, but his dogged determination to discount it
as nonsense unnerved him, it worked its way like a worm into his
marrow. When he fell ill, I truly believe that was the first sign of
him cracking.

Oh yes, he was indignant. On two counts.

He was indignant when facts piled up that proved she could not
have invented her 'waking vision'. He dragged us all the way to New
Credit First Nations with the hope of finding a loophole in Lois's
tale. His indignation then shifted against Canada's founders when he
learned that the Mississaugas had been treated so shabbily. As a first
generation arrival in the 'New World', he had taken pride in his family's adopted nation and had absorbed all its carefully reconstructed
history like a dutiful sponge.

Meanwhile, the spectre arose of a rogue Special Branch of the
RCMP on the loose. Avro CEOs were being waylaid and interrogated by officers behaving very much like Secret Police. It seemed
that CEO's names were being added to a Black List. No one could
have been more surprised than Graham to see RCMP officers parked
in our driveway! Initially, they were after Graham for alleged illegal
possession of Avro Arrow aeronautical plans. When these charges
resulted in a standoff, they switched tactics and attempted to arrest
me with a trumped up charge of running a Communist sleeper cell
under the guise of Neighbourhood Watch, and named him as an
accomplice. Graham's intense sense of patriotic pride was stung to
the quick when his worst apprehensions about RCMP corruption
were confirmed. For all the hours he had spent day and night in
dedication to the Avro project, for all his efforts working himself
thin and running himself ragged to meet the Arrow deadline, he was
horrified to learn that RCMP 'dogs', as he started to call them, had
indeed been sicced on him, allegedly as a threat to National Security.
He could never really relax after the existence of the Special Branch
was confirmed. He was anxious that something even more dire

might happen to his beloved country, and to himself, lord knows why or what he might have done to deserve it. His paranoeia was so out of character for him, I was worried but had no idea what to do.

The prospect of the Arrow losing government funding weighed heavily on his shoulders.

After the Rollout, an Avro CEO delegation was sent to Ottawa to make representations to the Government for continued support of the Arrow. Avro delegates (Smye, Gordon, Sanderson, Graham, and three others, all with wives in tow) went to Ottawa mid-October. The men fanned out upon arrival and managed to beseech every possible source of influence in the civil service, the Opposition, the Privy Council and the former Prime Minister Louis St. Laurent. The key factor was the new Prime Minister John Diefenbaker who obliged them an audience. He gave no assurances. Nor to Smye's regret, did Minister of Defence Pearkes who had been instrumental when despatching the rogue RCMP agents from our driveway, but who sided with the P.M. in expressing doubts about the continued support of the Arrow due to logarithmically rising costs. The men also appealed to the Solicitor General concerning a suspected rogue unit within the RCMP that was functioning like Secret Police. These representations were received with great skepticism, although perfunctory assurances were given for further investigation. Nonetheless, Graham's name was blacklisted along with the other Avro men who had been interrogated, and nothing could be done to remove their names. It was crushing to him that he was being watched, and the RCMP suspected him as a spy.

Results of the tireless intensive efforts spent in Ottawa drew a big zero, leaving the men downcast and fit to be tied. The ride home for all of us was spent in a cloud of doom and gloom.

To add to his burden, Lois's friend's mother, Eszter Molnar, asked Graham to be Power of Attorney for herself and daughter, Boglarka. It was the last thing he wanted to do. Graham hated it when life got in his way. He preferred to control his own agenda.

That he was suddenly saddled as POA for the Molnars did nothing to improve his humour. He didn't have the time, inclination or the capacity to be valiant, to fulfil his role as an upstanding man in the community, to take on that role. He resented being boxed in, cornered.

Then came the pumpkin raid the same night there was the accident at the bridge. Even though he knew Lois was not directly involved with that tragic event, it enraged him that her name was even peripherally connected. As far as he was concerned, she was implicated by participating in the pumpkin raid, therefore she was a 'bad apple'. In his opinion, she had brought shame to the family name. No offspring of his would ever dare become entangled with the law, let alone risk coming close to being charged as an offender. Therefore, he felt he had no choice but ban her from his life. His decision was so swift and irreversible, it frightened me. I did not like what I saw. It bordered on the barbaric. I found myself wondering how close was his blood to the line of brutal Visigoths and Vikings from which he stemmed, to be so judgmental and cruel.

This was borne out after her departure for Alma College. He was totally indifferent to my sorrow. He seemed to have lost all compassion.

The fate of the Arrow weighed on Graham's spirits throughout all other pressing concerns. Even before the Arrow's maiden flight, rumours had started to spread about Diefenbaker's collusion with the United States and the prospect of abandoning jet fighters in favour of ICBMs. The BOMARC missile project had begun that same year, almost simultaneously with completion and rollout of the Arrow. The first launch of an ICBM happened in the May of '57, and in an innovative strike, the Russians had used that same rocket to launch the Sputnik. This had given everyone the jitters. Including Graham. At the mere thought of the edge Russia might have over the West, his long face would blanch and his jaw would start to judder. Little did we know that this was the beginning of the Cold War "Space Race".

When word arrived that the Arrow had been cancelled, Graham took it totally to heart. He was dumbfounded. He looked stunned and stricken. His head turned away in disbelief, as though clipped broad-side on the jaw by a huge, invisible fist. He doubled up, clutching his stomach as though kicked in the solar plexus. His hand shot to his head and clutched his crown, his long fingers squeezing with a pressure normally reserved for stemming the flow of blood. As he fell, he turned to me and said: "What have I done to deserve this?"

I know I was a good and loving wife, had served him well as his life partner. I regret that I could not begin to help ease his pain. Or avert the inevitable.

(ii)

My deepest regret is agreeing to send Lois away. No matter what I attempt to say to explain myself, it is all equivocation.

I can say that I was merely being an obedient wife, following my husband's orders. I can say that I complied with his instructions not believing that he was right, but trusting that in the long run I would see that he was right, and therefore it was the right thing to do. But the truth is, I could have defied him, refused to defer to his wishes. It struck me too late that this was an option. What would be the worst that could happen? He would have had to make those dreadful arrangements himself. Would he have followed through if he had been forced to do so? I wonder. If I had dug in my heels and refused to do his bidding, I doubt very much that he would have thrown me out, for both personal reasons (he loved me too much and he depended on me) and his almighty reputation. Our separation would have brought more public humiliation than any decision he made about Lois.

At the time, I truly thought that Graham was overreacting, but that he would come round. He blamed Lois for being involved in an incident that jeopardized his deeply ingrained pride in the Michelsen family name. A slight to his family's honour was something he could not endure. It was something that endured longer and deeper than his love for his daughter.

The accident also jeopardized his status in the Centrewood community and by extension, to his position at Avro. He felt deeply threatened from the mere prospect of having his name tarnished in any way.

It all makes me want to weep. But what makes me want to weep most was the impact, the crushing blow to every fibre of my being, of sending Lois away. And realizing that despite my best intentions, I was in collusion.

"The road to hell is paved with good intentions"

Yet how could there have been any good intentions behind what we did?

Although Graham would never talk about it, I know he paid a high price. I know that he missed her. He blamed her for his pain, however. He failed to see how he contributed to the pain himself. Surely he must have run his decision over and over in his mind to reassure himself he'd done the right thing. But the way he behaved, it was as though she was dead to him. She had disgraced the family name. It was the worst offence she could commit. There was no forgiveness. No reprieve. That was his position, at least that was his outward stance. He continued to pay for her tuition and expenses. He gave me travel money to visit her during school breaks. But he refused to see her or to allow her to come home. The few times I dared mention her name, he would look at me coldly as if to say: "Lois who?"

I know that I paid a high price. I suddenly found myself alone with no real purpose in a big pretentious house located in an inhospitably superficial suburb in a strange cold country sorely lacking in culture or history, and yet inhabited by a citizenry so proud of itself for virtually nothing. It's true I had my chores: I still had to manage the house (euphemism for cooking, cleaning, shopping—all those traditional housewifely duties) and yes, I still had to prepare Lois's wardrobe from afar. And yes, there was Graham.

I was constantly fighting to put on a brave smile. He wanted me to smile. So I tried. However, it was not easy. I was very angry underneath. I was hurt to the very marrow of my bones. The life I had built for myself since marrying and coming here from England with Graham had been decimated.

Graham was my husband and I loved him.

But Lois was my whole life.

For weeks after Lois left, I kept watching my mind coursing about trying to find something or someone to blame. Was it the event itself in which she became inextricably entangled? How to undo that event? Was it too late?

Was it Graham? Had he been too hasty? Why couldn't he wait to test the waters first? Why did he have to have the 'preemptive strike'? What difference would it have made if he had forestalled any drastic decision?

Was it the political environment that made everything so hard, so impervious, so black and white? What if we brought Lois back? Would anyone notice or care?

I would tell myself: "This too will pass." But what? What will pass?

The pain? The situation? The reality? What reality?

In my heart, I knew that it was pointless waiting for anything to pass because all that might pass would be time, and that was no consolation because every moment, every hour, every day took Lois further and further away from me.

What I wanted was that Lois be returned to me before one more day passed by, before she grew away from me, before she got too much older.

I didn't want to lose her.

If this carried on, I would lose her.

Then the crippling thought:

That day I took her away, I had already lost her.

1959-2
Mitsy in Galt

Ontario Training School for Girls
Galt, Ontario
February 27, 1959
    Mother,
    Thank you for sending me the obituary and the latest dope from the local Centrewood Weekly gossip rag. Yes, I had already heard about the cancellation of the Arrow, it was all over the news. It's shocking that all existing aircraft and remaining parts are to be chopped up and all records of both plans as well as production are to be destroyed! Seems to me that was a terrible waste of taxpayers'

money and Canadian know-how. I'm only a teenager but I'd say the decision was made by a very ignorant man. Perhaps Mr. Diefenbaker should change his name to Butcher and the name of his party to the Regressive Conservatives?

It figures that Mr. Michelsen took it so hard that upon hearing the news, he had a sudden heart attack or a stroke, either of which would be severe enough to kill him. He was the kind of man whose job was the man. The job dies, he expires.

I am considering your request that I express my condolences to Mrs. Michelsen for her loss. I know I should, as she was very good to me. But I doubt she'd be pleased to hear from me. She probably hates my guts now.

One thing for sure: If you expect me to include any glowing remarks about Mr. M., in all sincerity, I cannot. Mr. M. and I did not see eye to eye. He said I lacked respect—as well as manners. But that was because he was so uptight. He ruled the roost like a dictator, had to be the one who was in control in that household—like, when to speak, when not to speak—especially during supper at his sacred Radio News Time. He was so full of himself, he was really hard to take. He was so proud of his elevated position at Avro as chief aeronautical engineer, so pleased as punch with himself, that he had a constant pinched smirk on his face: Look at me, and Who are you, Peon?

Mr. M. was a Perfectionist. He was almost frighteningly impeccably groomed—his neatly clipped barbershop haircut, his ultra-smooth Gillette-shaved face with the glistening aftershave, his scrubbed hands with the pared, rounded nails and white cuticles. He made sure that Mrs. Michelsen prepared his wardrobe with the utmost care so everything was Just So. That included his natty upscale business suits with crisp shirt and tie, and the black highly-polished shoes, his freshly-ironed weekend casual wear with the crease in his shorts and short shirt sleeves and the light brown suede loafers. He had a specific outfit for every occasion, time of the day, day of the week. I can still see him out in his driveway in his khaki bermuda shorts and short-sleeved shirt, his self-designated car-cleaning outfit, buffing and polishing the chrome on his stupid Buick with his chamois like he was caressing pure Aztec silver!

I didn't like him. It didn't help that he disapproved of me. He called me a "little hussy" (yes!!! I heard him!), said that I was "bad news", that he didn't want 'the likes of me' hanging out with his beloved daughter, and I was leading his little darling astray.

If Mrs. M. hadn't come to my defence numerous times, I wouldn't have lasted for more than a week in that household!

I don't know what I disliked about him most, the fact that he was a real wiener or that he was one of the rare grownups I'd ever met who had me pegged. I see now that I didn't do much to change his opinion. Even if I did, he could see right through me.

You also mentioned that I include Lois in my hypothetical sympathy card.

That was an odd suggestion, Mother. She has probably done everything in her power to forget me, as well she should.

As for losing her father, I doubt that she is shedding any tears.

Yes, I heard what he did to her.

That was very cruel.

Mr. Michelsen had only one world view: his own. It wouldn't matter what the issue, it always came around full circle to his own opinion. He thought he knew everything and therefore how matters should be handled. In this regard, he based his decision about Lois on what he thought he knew. He was as right as he was wrong. If he thinks—unlike most others—that she went to that bridge at all, he was right. But if he thinks she went willingly, he was dead wrong.

It's too bad what happened to her. But in a way, she deserved it. It probably did her good in the long run, gave her an electric prod in the backside. What else would wake her up?

Bye for now,

Mitsy

P.S. When I finally get out of here, I have decided that I want to be a war correspondent like Peter Worthington. He travels to many interesting places. Just now he is on assignment in Gaza with the United Nations. His life must be so exciting! It is my firm hope that people in the real world are different from those I've met so far. Being a reporter would help me escape from the pulverizing boredom of contemporary, small-town life and the excruciating dullness of ordinary people! Because of my observations, I might even have something of value to offer! First step would be journalism at Ryerson. If I apply and everything unfolds according to plan, I would start classes one year next September.

Centrewood
March 8, 1959

Mitsy Dear,

I only suggested that you send a sympathy card. I didn't expect you to write a eulogy!

If you have been expecting a letter of reprimand from me for your mean-spirited comments, you are about to be disappointed! You have a right to your own opinions. I appreciate your openness and willingness to share them with me.

I commend you for your perceptive analysis. I must say, you're a chip off the old block.

You have always spoken your truth. This can be your greatest asset as well as your Achilles' heel. By this I mean that your frankness is most likely your saving grace, but its ungroomed persistence may continue to cause you great and needless trouble.

My dear, I'll wear my own Mother's hat, and say it's okay to express your feelings in private with someone trustworthy like myself, but I do trust that you try to practice some tact and diplomacy in real life! The adage about catching more flies with honey than with vinegar is still around because it still works and is good advice, even from what you figure is an old fuddy-duddy like me!!

As for setting your sights beyond the reformatory, there is nothing wrong in having high expectations of life. You have always craved adventure. You have always wanted more than ordinary life can give you. That is why you have always tried to shake things up!

Unfortunately, I'm sure you've already learned that it can be an exercise in futility if you expect to shake some semblance of life from the uptight and the dull. If that is your last and only resort in order to help you feel alive, it will be a failed mission! The world is steeped in stupor! I get that! You have to find other targets to spark your passions and whet your energy!

We all have lessons to learn in this living laboratory called life. Yes, we all do. Even myself. I trust that you are learning in the rigorous routine of your day-to-day life to think before you act. This of course ties in with the lesson you have had to learn since your debacle, which landed you where you find yourself now. By this I mean, that I trust you are honing a sharpened awareness of unpredictable consequences for your actions before ever again running off half-cocked.

Fun is fun. But some fun is neither real fun nor funny.

Am I right?

I think your decision to study journalism and become a reporter is an exciting and worthwhile goal. It will give you the opportunity to hone your descriptive powers of observation and it will give you the excitement and adventure that you crave!

Your very powerful writing skills will stand you in good stead.

Whatever you do, wherever you go, know that you have my full support.

Always,

Mother

P.S. Do you remember Jason Longford?

Galt, Ontario
April 4, 1959

Mother,

Yes, I remember Mr. Jason 'Bud' Longford well!

I was amused to see that he is still "chief newshound and bottle washer" at the Centrewood Weekly. It seems so long ago but really, it has only been two years since I decamped. I guess it makes sense that he is still there. He wasn't that old when I knew him. Does he still have his red-and-white Irish setter Finn? 'Sticky Fingers' here often swung by the pet shop to scoop up some doggie treats for the feller from the loose bin. Hey, who counted the nibbles? Finn was very sweet and intelligent—a prince among dogs, so well-groomed in contrast with his master who was such an unkempt, slovenly slob! Mind you, 'Bud' might have his peccadillos, including his perennial toothpick and the old plaid suit that never saw the cleaners, but he treated me kindly and with respect. He never sniped at me, he accepted me for who I was.

I hung around the newsroom quite a lot and he could rely on me at times for being a fairly reliable source! In fact, he gave me such good tips for hot tip-offs, I can't say I wasn't prone to concocting some of the events myself !! No no Mother, whatever I did was harmless!! I can just see you fretting that I was an arsonist or something! At any rate, it was 'Bud' who encouraged me to record whatever I observed about town and now I come to think of it, he was probably my first entry point into considering a career the world of journalism.

· It's not so bad here. I guess you can get used to anything. The worst is movement being so restricted. 'Rover' here misses the freedom of rambling about unimpeded. All of Centrewood was my domain. Now my only exposure to the outdoors is in the exercise yard. Which is paved. It would be nice if they let more than a few tufts of grass grow in the cracks. You know what? They can restrict my freedom but they will never tame my spirit or reform my expectations of life.

I've been told that my stint in this joint might be over sooner than I thought.

The head honcho called me into her office, commended me for my academic performance and said, if I manage to keep my nose clean and stay out of trouble, I might be released early, on probation. But what's the point? I still have to complete my high school diploma to get into Ryerson. And I have to get good marks! I might as well do that here. Besides, it's free rent, right? I mean, if I get out sooner rather than later, I'll still be a ward of the state, there will still be that restraining order so I won't be able to stay with you. Where would I live? Besides, knowing me, I figure I might just cook up some tomfoolery to ruin my chances. I'd do better if I viewed this place as a dormitory in some private British boarding school, some of which I've heard are even worse than this g.d. training school for "Girls". Girls? Ha! Most of them are wizened-up old witches in teenage clothing. I've sure learned not to mix with most of them. This time the joke is on me. On the outside, I was the Bad Ass. Here, I'm outnumbered.

Your incorrigible daughter,

Mitsy

P.S. All these years and I still do not know how you met my father Kenta. Perhaps you could include those details when and if you ever write your autobiography OR at least, before you kick the bucket!

1959-3
Kenta

Centrewood 1959

I, née Fiona Gardiner, was born in Weston in 1908. My father worked at the CCM plant where it was taken for granted that the market for bicycles would last forever and all jobs were regarded as secure. Even during the Great War, my father's role in management protected him from serving, since bicycles were in high demand all over Great Britain. His job was viewed as essential to the war effort. It certainly made my life easier to have both loving, supportive parents at home who wanted the very best for their children.

I had always wanted to be a doctor, cherished my Doctor Duck doctor's bag as a girl, took all the right academic courses, so I could graduate from Weston High School qualified for entry into med school.

Even though I was a girl, there was no problem in being accepted into medicine at the University of Toronto where I graduated in 1934. By then I knew I did not want to be a general practitioner. And surgery was revulsive to me. I was fascinated by new approaches to mental health care, so I went to Vienna where I obtained my degree in psychiatry even though I became early disaffected with the sexism embedded in Freudian theory. I switched my studies to psychoanalysis under some of the leading minds in both fields.

In 1937, when the second World War broke out, I was obliged to return home to Canada where I joined the Canadian Forces Medical Corps. I was assigned to the Victoria Convalescent Home on Vancouver Island where I used all my skills, both medical and psychiatric to aid injured, traumatized servicemen, navy, army and air force alike. In early 1940, I was transferred to the mainland-Vancouver, where I served as war trauma psychiatrist and medic at the army hospital there.

It was in Vancouver where I met my husband. He was an expert horticulturalist and eminent botanist at the University. I met him while attending workshops where he lectured on his specialty: bonsai.

Japanese Black Pine Bonsai

For various reasons, namely his family's anticipated objections, we were married secretly that same year. Then came the attack on Pearl Harbour on December 7, 1941. It shattered our dreams.

You see, my husband Kenta Hirano was first generation Japanese Canadian. He was born in Vancouver in 1905. His family had done well. He grew up in very refined, elegantly appointed surroundings. His family home was large, gracious and filled with fine art, live music, surrounded by beautifully manicured and sensitively designed gardens complete with the little bridges over ponds filled with koi, the large goldfish that you see in watercolour paintings. His father was assistant director to Mr. Roy Sumi at the world-renowned Nitobi Gardens. Kenta my husband had acquired his advanced degree in botany from UBC where he gave guest lectures and work-shops and at the time, operated his own rooftop greenhouses on a building he had purchased in the city core. He had built an entire commercial venture on his own, marketing bonsai internationally. We lived quietly and inconspicuously—and oh so happily!! in down-town Vancouver.

It all happened so swiftly, with no warning, no chance to prepare or take action. Only weeks after Pearl Harbour, toward the end of December 1941, Kenta was fired from his job at the Nitobi Gardens. Then Kenta's contractual arrangements were cancelled at UBC and he was denied access to his campus greenhouses to tend his plants. His bonsai business upstairs was seized a while later. While its provenance was still in limbo, I succeeded in reaching my brother Ted who was serving in the air force at the time. He arrived with a van, was able to gain access and rescue as many of the bonsai plants from the solarium as he could, took them back to America (with certification of ownership to get them across the border) and promised he would have them tended until after the War.

Either because we had married secretly or because I was not of visible Japanese descent, I resumed using my maiden surname and was able to continue functioning unimpeded in my capacity as a doctor.

In January 1942, Kenta along with his entire family and associ-ates were among those who were rounded up and removed by cattle car to the B.C. interior. Their destination was a deplorable makeshift camp in a place called New Denver.

In 1943, all Japanese Canadian homes and properties were con-fiscated, including the Hirano family home. All their belongings were seized.

Evicted from our apartment below the now defunct bonsai operation, I managed to find a one-bedroom flat in the city core where at my peril I hid and fed other Japanese Canadians who had not yet been culled and who were looking to flee—but where? The same action had been taken by the American government, so there was nowhere for these poor and unjustly persecuted people to go.

As time went by, I became more and more anxious—more precisely 'paranoeic'—and decided it would be best to move. I managed to secure a position at the veterans' hospital in Nanaimo and moved there without telling anyone, not even my closest associates or friends. I felt I could trust no one.

For almost a year, my husband and I lost touch with each other. Mail was monitored. I had no idea where Kenta had been taken. Likewise, he had no inkling what had become of me.

Early 1944, I managed to locate his whereabouts at the New Denver encampment via a tenuous underground grapevine, but permission was denied me to visit him either as doctor or friend. We began to correspond but were never sure that our letters would be delivered. Meanwhile, Kenta had gained the respect of the community at New Denver, and had assumed a leadership role in the camp as a 'Nisei', representative to the authorities, and therefore negotiator on the detainees' behalf. He wrote me that in this capacity he was able to take the train on occasion to Westminster to purchase supplies. The people needed rice, seaweed and other foodstuffs that the army knew nothing of, and wished not to know. He had convinced them that familiar food would prolong lives, and that it would reduce extreme embarrassment when the war ended, should the public discover that all detainees had died from malnutrition.

Late in 1944, I took a leave of absence from the hospital and travelled to Westminster, which at that time was a small whistle-stop town about halfway from Vancouver to the camp. There I booked two small adjacent rooms in our respective names above the local tavern, declaring Kenta as a government agent for New Denver and myself as a medical inspection officer under my maiden name.

Kenta had been green-lighted for Westminster with only a tentative date. I waited on the railway platform every day for him to appear. It was brutally cold. My toes and fingers would freeze while

I stood there. I did not have warm enough apparel for the level of exposure to the wind and ice that blew in maelstroms around the little shed called a station. I worried how those trapped in the camp would ever fare through another winter.

After several days of starving, worrying and fretting, of waving my arms in the air and stamping my feet on the platform to keep from freezing, a train carrying Kenta did indeed, eventually, at long last, pull into town.

When he stepped off, I barely recognized him, he was so thin, his face drawn and gaunt, he had aged so. The spark of our love was still there though. We hugged and cried and whooped with joy. Then I took him back to the tavern. We stayed there round the clock, ostensibly in separate quarters, except when Kenta ventured out to food depots to fulfill his contractual obligations. In order to keep a low profile, I was the one who placed and fetched separate meal orders from the kitchen below. For appearances' sake, I knocked on 'his' door', took his meal to 'his' room.

It broke our hearts to say goodbye. He had to return to camp, or he would be considered AWOL, and I had to return because my leave of absence was about to expire.

After victory was declared over Japan in 1945, and after the initial jubilation among the detainees, many of those who had held out on the premise that once the war ended, they could return home to Vancouver, were faced with the news that their properties had been confiscated. They had a choice of either deportation to Japan or evacuation further east, most likely as farm-labour planting and harvesting turnips on established farms in Manitoba or Saskatchewan.

With those two options at hand, Kenta inveigled his way into staying in the New Denver camp to assist in overseeing its administration to the bitter end of its final dismantlement.

It was the lesser of three options but no mean choice for us. For meanwhile, I was 'expecting'. That's what you said back then, when you were pregnant.

There was no choice for myself but to leave Vancouver and return home to Weston to stay with my Mother. I had told her that I had married, but had not revealed to her that my husband was Japanese Canadian. His family was never exactly ecstatic over the prospect of their beloved son Kenta marrying outside of their tradition and so were never told. I had no idea when we married how my Mother who had been raised in small town Ontario without any contact with other Asian people at all except for the Chinese laundryman and the Chinese restaurant, would handle it and so—to tell the truth—I had never told her.

Back when we married, I figured at some point we would travel to Toronto together to meet her, and then she would find out after the fact and she would have to adjust to the reality. There was already prejudice against Asians in Vancouver. But we married before the hatred for the Japanese began to run rampant, before Pearl Harbour.

What would the townsfolk of Weston say, or do? I admit that I trembled during my pregnancy for fear that the baby would look Japanese—isn't that sad? I had terrible fear of a backlash from the townsfolk that would make it impossible to stay there for very long. I could hear the tongues wagging: Imagine! Did you hear Mrs. Gardiner's daughter went out west and got—you know—by a "Jap" or a "Slant-Eye"? Those were two of the derogatory, terribly hurtful slurs that some people called the Japanese back then.

Meanwhile, the fact that I had continued to use my maiden name left my Mother totally baffled and more than suspicious about my true marital status. I didn't have a marriage certificate either, as the records seemed to have disappeared when I applied.

After the baby was born and I had a chance to recuperate a bit, I found employment as doctor and psychiatrist at Sunnybrook, the soldiers's convalescent home, I left Mother in charge of the baby who truly was a cute little thing!

It was an ordeal for me to commute across the city and back either by bicycle or public transport every day. Eventually, my

Mother let me use my Father's car that just sat in the garage collecting dust. Mother would never dream of getting her driver's licence. It was neither suitable nor fitting for a town matron!

In April 1947 when my little girl was three years old, the blanket deportation order was repealed. Kenta was spared having to leave Canada! Then, in 1949, to my great relief and surprise, it was declared that Japanese Canadians were free to live anywhere in Canada!

Oh, I was overjoyed. I so looked forward to seeing him again. I imagined all the fun we were going to have together—a family at last!!

Shortly after the decree, Kenta came to Ontario. He was run down, emaciated, lacked strength, needed help walking, and had aged terribly. But most devastating, he lacked vitality, had difficulty drumming up any energy at all. It was an effort for him to smile, to enjoy our little girl who was still barely four years old at the time. She loved to climb up on his lap. He loved to hug her and hum to her. He would turn her over across her lap and tickle her back ever so lightly. She loved that and would often fall asleep! A great trick for winding her down for nap time!

Soon after his arrival, my Mother died. I don't know to this day if there was any connection between Kenta's arrival and her death, but I continually fob off the feeling that I did her in somehow. She was astonished when she saw Kenta, that is for sure, and rapidly added things up. As it turned out, my little girl had somewhat flat cheekbones and nose and only slightly angled eyes if you were to look close—and they were the same colour as mine! That she did not look completely Asian was a good thing across the board. I think it had helped toward them bonding. But who knows?

Barely after Mother's rapid demise, Kenta collapsed. I couldn't tend to him and work as well, and there was a problem finding suitable day care for the child. Ironically, I had Kenta moved to Sunnybrook and admitted on compassionate grounds. No one there knew we were husband and wife. We were afraid to tell anyone.

There was still the prejudice. In addition, it might have led to conflict of interest and my dismissal.

Kenta ended up being one of my patients due to his mental state. I saw more of him there than if he were anywhere else. Naturally, I wanted to sit by his bedside as much as possible, but I had to be careful as there were so many distraught and sorely damaged soldiers in that hospital that also required my attention, assessment and treatment.

Kenta became increasingly inconsolable. He told me that he had a suspicion that he warded off despair and depression while at the camp because he would not know how to cope if he buckled. He longed for me, he said, he longed to be free and to go home to me to our apartment that was no more. When it became apparent that he might have to go to Japan or move east to Ontario, he feared when the time came, that he would never be able to overcome his homesickness for his childhood home and former life in Vancouver. He feared he would never see me in Ontario, regardless how much he loved me, wanted to adjust, wanted to be able to change.

Now that he was "free" but not on his terms or expectations, he buckled.

He did not last very long.

My final COD report stated that he died of heart failure. Not far wrong as in truth, he died of heartbreak and culture shock, both of which ultimately led to his suicide. One perfect sunny and warm spring afternoon, after fighting against depression throughout a cold and damp, blustery winter, Kenta left the deck chair on the third floor balcony of the hospital, walked to the rail and after taking a few seconds to catch his breath, he leapt.

My daughter ended up being a 'latch-key kid'. The only way for me to earn a living for us both entailed long work hours, often night shift. Once she had grown too old for daycare, she was left to her own devices in getting to school and back, in joining extra-curricular activities, often having to make her own supper, pack her own lunch.

Needless to say, she found a way to get involved in a lot of monkey business which resulted in a judge's ruling: she was not to consort with the local gang or she would have to be placed in custody, possibly be sent to a foster home.

That was when my daughter turned fourteen and was finished with junior high, Weston had been a wonderful town for raising children. But it was becoming too rough. The small towns were being taken over by a lot of 'roughnecks', the kids called them 'hard rocks', there were too many motorcycle gangs and riff-raff. I had been worrying about her being so vulnerable, out on the streets unsupervised and my fears had come true. It was no place to take care of a teenager who would inevitably be on her own a lot since I was the sole breadwinner and I had to work. I sold Mother's house and moved to Centrewood. I wanted us both to have a new start.

To be honest, even after moving to a safe haven like Centrewood, I continued to worry about leaving her alone so much, as she was an early 'sprouter' so to speak and a bit reckless in nature. I wondered if she could be responsible at that age, to be a reliable 'latch key child' since I worked such long hours and rotating shifts. In retrospect, I saw that I made a mistake. It was one of those classic predicaments when the writing was surely on the wall. After all these years, I I remain confounded as to what else I could have done about the situation. I had to work to support ourselves. If I didn't?

It has never failed to sting when I hear folks joking that the worst behaved children are those of a psychologist or psychiatrist. All I can say as a rejoinder is that I did my best by my daughter and I dare anyone else in my shoes to do better!

●

BIBLIOGRAPHICAL REFERENCES

1) MISSISSAUGA LAND CLAIM: "10 shillings"

AUTHOR'S NOTE: *It was not until 2010 that the Mississauga land claim was settled with the Government of Canada.*

Chief calls land deal 'monumental' [electronic resource (website)]
http:www.mississauga.com/
news-story/3156211-chief-calls-land-deal-monumental-/

Ontario band approves $145M land claim settlement [electronic resource (website)] CTV news staff, June 8, 2010.
http://www.ctvnews.ca/
ontario-band-approves-145m-land-claim-settlement-1.520514

Mississauga First Nation celebrates Toronto land deal [electronic resource (website)]
http://www.canada.com/nationalpost.com/posted-toronto/
mississauga-first-nations-celebrates-toronto-land-deal

2) THE AVRO ARROW

Avro Canada CF-105 Arrow [electronic resource (website)]. Wikipedia, 29 June 2018, https://en.wikipedia.org/wiki/Avro_Canada_CF-105_Arrow

The Avro Arrow [electronic resource (website)] / article by John Kirton. Canadian encyclopedia, 2015, 2016. Illustration: photograph of test pilot Janusz Zurakowski taken after the first flight of the Avro CF-105, Arrow, 25 March 1958 https://www.thecanadianencyclopedia.ca/en/article/avro-arrow/

55 years later : biggest question surrounding Avro Arrow remains 'what if? [electronic resource (website)] by Elton Hobson. Global News, c2018. https://globalnews.ca/news/427985/55-years-later-biggest-question-surrounding-avro-arrow-remains-what-if/

Remembering the death of the Avro Arrow : a tragedy for technology? [electronic resource (website) / Emily Chung. (Technology & science) CBC News, Feb. 23 2009 http://www.cbc.ca/news/technology/remembering-the-death-of-the-avro-arrow-1.788113

Historical drama fuelled by myth, not reality [electronic resource (website)]: the Avro Arrow was a success in the sky, but it was more of a financial burden than the Canada of the late 1950s could afford / by David Bercuson. Financial Post, Jan.18, 1997 http://www.ggower.com/dief/text/fp1.shtml

The AVRO Canada CF-105 Arrow Programme : decisions and determinants. Chapter One [electronic version] / by Russell Steven Paul Isinger, c1997. Thesis — Department of Political Studies, University of Saskatchewan, Saskatoon, Canada.http://scaa.usask.ca/gallery/arrow/thesis/thesis7.htm

The AVRO Canada CF-105 Arrow Programme : decisions and determinants. Chapter Two [electronic version] / by Russell Steven Paul Isinger, c1997. Thesis — Department of Political

Studies, University of Saskatchewan, Saskatoon, Canada.http://
scaa.usask.ca/gallery/arrow/thesis/thesis8.htm
**Cancelling Avro Arrow, a costly nightmare [elec-
tronic resource (website)]** / Ian Robertson.
Toronto Sun, April 15, 2017. https://torontosun.
com/2017/04/15/cancelling-avro-arrow-a-costly-nightmare/
wcm/3ffe32b1-8901-4ca2-af7f-93c7a7052b4c

3) RCMP SPECIAL BRANCH [I.E., PROFUNC]

*In 1957, the undercover unit of the RCMP was named its Special Branch.
After several name changes, it wasn't until 1983 that ProFUNC, its final
name, was uncovered. The then Toronto Liberal Member of Parliament
and Solicitor General of Canada, Bob Kaplan, caused PROFUNC to
become defunct*
—The Author.

**PROFUNC [electronic resource (website) / Wikipedia. 7
September 2017.**
"**PROFUNC**, an acronym for "**PRO**minent **FUNC**tionaries of
the communist party", was a top secret Government of Canada
project to identify and observe suspected Canadian communists
and crypto-communists during the height of the Cold War. In
operation from 1950 to 1983, the goal of the program was to
allow for quick internment of known and suspected communist
sympathizers in the event of war with the Soviet Union (USSR) or
its allies."
"In the 1950s, RCMP Commissioner Stuart Wood had a
"PROFUNC list" of approximately 16,000 suspected communists
and 50,000 suspected communist sympathizers. These lists dictated
who the Special Branch would observe and potentially intern in a

national security state of emergency, such as a Third World War crisis with the Soviet Union and People's Republic of China."

"A separate arrest document, known formally as a C-215 form, was written up for each potential internee and updated regularly with personal information until the 1980s, including but not limited to: age, physical descriptions, photographs, vehicle information. In addition, more obscure information such as potential escape routes from the individual's personal residence were noted. Several prominent Canadians are suspected of being on the PROFUNC list including: Winnipeg alderman Jacob Penner, Roland Penner and the founder of the New Democratic Party of Canada Tommy Douglas.

https://en.wikipedia.org/wiki/PROFUNC

4) JAPANESE-CANADIAN INTERNMENT

It was not until September 1988, that Prime Minister Brian Mulroney signed the agreement to compensate the Japanese-Canadians for the expropriation of their property and their internment during World War II

Japanese Internment: banished and beyond tears [electronic version] / The Canadian encyclopedia.
https://www.thecanadianencyclopedia.ca/en/article/japanese-internment-banished-and-beyond-tears-feature
Japanese Internment Camp, New Denver, B.C., 1943 [electronic resource (website] / Discover Nikkei.
http://www.discovernikkei.org/en/nikkeialbum/items/28/
Illustrations: http://www.whitepinepictures.com/seeds/i/8/sidebar.html

5) HUNGARY, 20th CENTURY HISTORY AND REVOLUTION

ONLINE SOURCES:

http://en.wikipedia.org/wiki/History_of_Hungary

http://en.wikipedia.org/wiki/Siege_of_Budapest

http://en.wikipedia.org/wiki/Operation_Panzerfaust

6) Leave it to Beaver (TV series: 1957-1963)

The author wishes to acknowledge the creators of the television series Leave it to Beaver, whose episodes Season 1, 1-4 aired in real time precisely on the Fridays given in the plots of Part 1 and 2, and whose themes tied in uncannily with the story line. As said in Latin: *beatus accidit*

7) DAYLIGHTING

Daylighting (Streams) [electronic resource (website)] / Wikipedia, 2019.

https://en.wikipedia.org/wiki/Daylighting_(streams)

"In urban design and urban planning, **daylighting** is the redirection of a stream into an above-ground channel. Typically, the rationale behind daylighting is to revert a stream of water to a more natural state, for the purposes of runoff reduction, habitat creation for species in need of it, or for aesthetic purposes. Daylighting is intended to revitalize the riparian environment for a stream which had been previously diverted into a culvert, pipe, or a drainage system. In the UK, the practice is also known as **deculverting**.
Taddle Creek [electronic resource (website)] / Lost Rivers, Toronto Green Community, 2019. http://www.lostrivers.ca/content/taddlekey.html

Lost Rivers Walks [electronic resource (website)] / introduction by Helen Mills …[the driving force in the establishment of Lost Rivers Walks] / Toronto Green Community, 2019. http://www.lostrivers.ca

Rivers rising [electronic resource (website)] / Toronto Green Community, The Toronto Field Naturalists, and community partners including Hike Ontario, 2019. http://www.torontogreen.ca/what-we-do/rivers-rising/

DIGITAL CREDITS

Disclaimer: Every effort has been made to determine the source of all images used in this work and to obtain permission for their use.

TEXT IMAGES

Centrewood Plan. Credit: Concept, The Author; Creation, Keiran Paquette.

Maria Spelterini, tight wirewalker across Niagara Gorge. Credit: George Barker/Hulton Archive

Possé: painting. Credit: artist, Joy Blackburne, Hamilton Parish, Bermuda.

Avro Canada VZ-9 Avrocar. Credit: Wikipedia.

1952 Willys M38A1 Jeep. Credit: militarymuster.ca/vehicles

Eagle hanging mid-air, landing. Credit: Dreamstime.com 18574681

10 shillings. Credit: source unknown.

Avro Canada CF-105 Arrow. Credit: Wikipedia.

'CANCELLED' superimposed across image of Avro Arrow. Credit: neverwasanarrow.blogspot.ca/2010/02

John Diefenbaker portrait Credit: Library and Archives Canada. Photoshopped with moustache added.

Horthy at the Gellert Hotel. Credit: Wikipedia

Black Percherons Credit: 1. Photo source unknown. 2.
Photoshopped: Background features. Gentlemen added. Digitally
enhanced by Keiran Paquette and Joanne Rennie.
Shoes on the Danube Bank. Credit: Wikipedia
Lost Rivers map. Credit: Toronto Green Community. Courtesy of
Helen Mills
Doppler, F. Two flutes & piano, Andante & Rondo. 1874.
Reprod. Andante.
Credit: Creative Commons. Mediawiki. Public domain
Royal Conservatory of Music. Credit: wordpress.com
1950's Blue Prom Dress Credit: etsy.com 109158061
Casa Loma. Credit: Wikipedia.
New Moon. Credit: Dreamstime.com 79800123, c Yuka
Ryabokon. Photoshopped.
Cassiopeia and Perseus in northeast on October evening. Credit:
earthsky.org. Credit: Bruce McClure.
Studebaker Speedster. Credit: Wikipedia. Public domain.
Pumpkin at twilight. [Changed caption in text to Pumpkin at
sundown] Credit: Neil Das. Pinterest.com 22081787957014959
Alma Ladies College, St. Thomas, Ont. Credit: Ghostwalks.com
Ontario Training School for Girls, Galt, Ont. Credit: Canadian
War Museum
Japanese Black Pine Bonsai. Credit: Wikimedia.org, 2011-05-29.
Sage Ross.

DIGITAL CREDITS FOR FRONT COVER

Solar system with eight planets. Credit: Colourbox Vector
#5073031 Artist dagadu. Photoshopped with images of semi-
precious stones added by Friesen Press designer on request of
the author.

Seed of Life. Credit: digitally drawn and embellished with sepia ink by Joanne Rennie, artist.

Red Garnet. Credit: gemselect.com. Permission from Gemselect: Thomas Dahlberg, Derek Lee.

White Opal. Credit: flashopal.com. Permission from Flash opal: Janine Scott.

Amethyst. Credit: gemselect.com. Ibid.

Emerald. Credit: Dreamstime ID37639702

OR 123rf Image ID: 26531402 (L) Copyright:

Rattanapon Muanpimthong

Black Onyx. Credit: 123rf Image ID : 50862006 Copyright: vvoennyy [sic]

Citrine. Credit: gemselect.com. Ibid.

Sapphire. Credit: gemselect.com. Ibid.

Sodalite. Credit: Dreamstime ID 25654079 © Efesan

Malachite. Credit: 123rf Image ID: 21249819 Copyright: wlad 74 [sic]

DIGITAL CREDITS FOR BACK COVER

Blue Prom Dress with Flute. Photoshopped by Keiran Paquette

Blue Dress. Credit: etsy.com. 109158061

Concert flute. Credit: Dreamstime ID 23119612

Alexander Morozov

Blue sodalite pendant. Credit: 'Sue' at Sunny

Crystals, etsy.com.16906079

White opal pendant. Credit: 'Sara' at Gems of London, etsy. com. 266678917

Green malachite ring. Credit: billythetree.com. Photo courtesy of Zohar Ariel.

Pink pebble. Credit: Dreamstime ID 95789787 © Igor Korionov

Coal. Credit: tlaststand.wikia.com/wiki

Sulphur. Credit: commonswikimedia.org
Bloodstone. Credit: mineralguide.org

DIGITAL CREDIT FOR RUNNING TEXT

"New Moon" Original image "Solar Eclipse" Photoshopped by
Keiran Paquette. Dreamstime ID 798900123

Printed in Canada